California Shorts

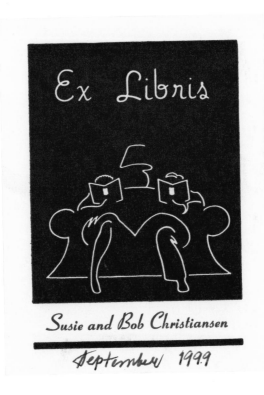

California Shorts

Edited by Steven Gilbar

HEYDAY BOOKS
BERKELEY, CALIFORNIA

© 1999 by Steven Gilbar

Copyright information and permissions for each selection appear on page 337.

Library of Congress Cataloging-in-Publication Data:

California shorts / edited by Steven Gilbar.
p.   cm.
ISBN 1-890771-18-X (pbk.)
1. California—Social life and customs—Fiction. 2. Short stories, American—California. I. Gilbar, Steven.
PS571.C2C247 1999
813'.010832794—dc21

        99-19907
        CIP

Cover Art: "'60 Chevy" by Nicola Wood, courtesy of Sherry Frumkin Gallery, Santa Monica, California
Cover Design: David Bullen Design
Interior Design: Rebecca LeGates
Printing and Binding: Publishers Press, Salt Lake City, Utah

Orders, inquiries, and correspondence should be addressed to:
     Heyday Books
     P. O. Box 9145, Berkeley, CA 94709
     510/549-3564, Fax 510/549-1889
     heyday@heydaybooks.com

Printed in the United States of America

10 9 8 7 6 5 4 3 2 1

Contents

Introduction

THOUGH I HAVE LIVED IN CALIFORNIA for more than half my life, it still remains a source of wonder to me. It sits on the literal edge of the continent, and edgy energy ranges over the land as well. Its wildly disparate scenery is matched only by the astonishing diversity of its 33.5 million people, a population greater than that of all of Canada. It is virtually a separate country, and so fragmented that it is meaningless to speak of it other than as a political entity. It is composed of many Californias.

California is known all over the world; the name has magic, sizzle. It inspires amazement as well as finger-wagging from those who do not live there—and often from those who do. It may be more a state of mind than a state of the union. Of course, much of the popular and media characterization of California is just surface image. For deeper truths about ourselves we must turn to our literature: to Steinbeck's Salinas Valley or Saroyan's Fresno or Austin's Owens River Valley or Chandler's Los Angeles. These truly portray California, at least as it once was—for the California that has emerged since the time of those writers is quite different, although similarities remain.

All of the authors in this anthology are still alive and writing, and all the stories herein were written during the last two decades. They tell us how Californians live today. Some depict the men and women who populate the margins of society, whose California is frenetic and seemingly formless. Others evoke traditional middle-class California life that continues to be lived out amid the alarms and perplexities of change. Together, they portray life in the mountains,

vii

the desert, the small coastal and valley towns, and the big cities. While they may not be specifically about California—place being the slenderest of connections—each is permeated with a particular tint that is distinctive of this state.

I have tried to present more than the usual European-American view of California life. The extraordinary immigrations that have fundamentally changed the state, as well as the powerful voices of its Native American and African American writers, are well represented. The "minority" writers have painted an extraordinary and convincing image of the "new" California that is stubbornly outside the European tradition.

I believe that the short story, more than any other literary form, best captures contemporary California on the wing. It is a form that has reliably inspired brilliant performances by our best writers, in a line unbroken since the gold rush. Though slight in bulk, the short story is as limitless as any other form of literary expression. I agree with R.V. Cassill when he wrote that its "insights are as keen, the display of invention as nimble, and the revelations as profound as the imagination can compass. It abides on the same plateau as poetry, drama, or the novel." It has also been said that short stories are the X-rays of literature. They can pierce the roiling skin of daily life right down to that stratum where all things thrash, break apart, and rejoin in fresh and disturbing arrangements. This elemental force—like that of the earthquakes and fires that plague the state—erupts from each of the stories here. Whether set in a summer cabin in Lake Tahoe where the wealthy are vacationing or a slum apartment in Oakland where a runaway teenager is crashing, the many worlds within California are depicted with complete conviction and startling vivacity.

In this collection, I selected stories rather than authors. I chose stories that in some ways chart the geographical, ethnic, cultural, emotional, and literary range of California. While I agree with William Trevor's description of a Chekhov short story as "the art of the glimpse," I also like stories that seem to have whole novels contained within them. I am also drawn to stories that plummet deep into the psyches of their characters. In the end, I picked what I felt was fine writing. The stories stand, first of all, as good literature, as good as any being written in America today. While it would be impossible to assemble a collection where each story was of equal weight and worth, all of these stories are original and passionately written, and they all will stand the test of repeated readings.

In choosing stories for this collection, I had to read many more; now, looking back at the table of contents, I see that what I have ended up with just touches the surface. There are well-known writers I admire who do not appear here, and there is a wealth of writing by talented newer writers that did not make the final cut because of space. I already envision a sequel. This anthology is no more than a sampling; it is certainly not an attempt at an official canon. Foremost, it is to be read for pleasure, perhaps in some instances for comfort or for courage—or whatever else it is that literature can deliver. It will, I hope, not only portray how life is lived in the final years of twentieth century California, but give the reader—Raymond Carver said it best—"a sense of union maybe, an aesthetic feeling of correctness, nothing less, really, than beauty given form and made visible in the incomparable way only short stories can do."

Steven Gilbar
February 1999

' **Alice Adams**

❀Favors

JULY THAT YEAR IS HOTTER, the air heavier and more sultry than is usual in Northern California, especially up in the Sierras, near Lake Tahoe. Along the Truckee River, which emanates from that lake, mosquitoes flourish in the thick green riverside bushes and grass. Even in the early mornings—most unusual—it is already warm and damp. An absolute stillness, a brooding quiet.

"If this were Maine, there would be a thunderstorm," remarks Maria Tresca, an elderly political activist, just released from jail. By profession she is an architect. A large-boned, heavy woman, with gray-brown hair and huge very dark eyes, she is addressing the much younger couple who are with her on the terrace of her river house. The three of them have just finished a light breakfast in the dining room, inside; they now sit on old canvas deck chairs.

Having spoken, Maria closes her eyes, as though the effort involved in keeping them open were more than she could manage in the breezeless heat, the flat air.

The two young people, the couple, are Danny Michaels, a small, gray-blond young man, rather lined for someone his age, serious, bookish-looking; and thin, bright-red-haired Phoebe Knowles, Danny's very recent wife.

"That would be wonderful, a storm," says Phoebe, who seems a little short of breath.

And Danny: "We sure could use the rain."

1

"Actually, I'd be quite terrified," Maria opens her eyes to tell them. "I always used to be, in Maine. We had the most terrific summer storms." She recloses her eyes.

Danny has known Maria for so long (almost all the thirty-odd years of his life) that nearly all questions seem permitted; also they like and trust each other. However, so far his evident sympathetic interest in her recent experience has been balked. About Pleasanton, where the jail was, Maria has only said, not quite convincingly, "It wasn't too bad. It's minimum security, you know. I felt rather like a Watergate conspirator. The clothes they gave me were terribly uncomfortable, though. Just not fitting, and stiff."

Only Maria's posture suggests discouragement, or even age. On the old rattan sofa she slumps down in a tired way among the cushions, her large hands clasped together on the knees of old corduroys.

And goes on about Maine. "The chipmunks there were much bigger than the ones out here," she tells Phoebe and Dan. "Or maybe they only seemed bigger because I was very small. I haven't been back there since I was a child, you know."

Phoebe and Dan are in the odd position of being both Maria's hosts and her guests: it is her house—in fact, very much her house, designed by Maria for her own use. But it was lent to Danny and Phoebe by Ralph Tresca, Maria's son and a great friend of Danny's. This was to be their wedding present, two weeks alone in this extraordinary, very private house. For which they had both arranged, with some trouble, to take off from their jobs. Phoebe and her best friend, Anna, run a small restaurant on Potrero Hill; Danny works in a bookstore, also on Potrero, of which he is part owner.

Danny and Ralph have been friends since kindergarten, and thus Danny has known Maria for all that time. He and Phoebe have known each other for less than four months; theirs was a passionate, somewhat hasty marriage, indeed precipitated by Ralph's offer of the house. Danny called Ralph in Los Angeles, where Ralph is a sometime screenwriter, to say that he had met a girl about whom he was really serious. "I think we might get married." To which Ralph responded, "Well, if you do it this summer you can have the house for two weeks at the end of July. It's rented for most of the rest."

Not the reason, surely, but an impetus. Danny has always loved the beautiful, not entirely practical house, at which he has often been a guest. A wonderfully auspicious beginning to their marriage, Danny believed those weeks would be.

But after the first week of their time at the house had passed, there was suddenly the phone call from Ralph, asking if it would be all right for Maria to come up and stay with them; Maria was about to be released, after fourteen days in jail. Danny had known about Maria's sentencing; he and Phoebe had talked about it, early on—so severe for an antinuclear protest, and for a woman of Maria's age. But they had not been entirely clear as to when Maria started to serve, nor when she was to get out. And it had certainly not occurred to Danny that Maria might want to come from jail to her house on the Truckee River. However: *Of course,* he told Ralph.

Hanging up the phone, which is in the kitchen, and walking across the long living room toward their bedroom, where he and Phoebe had been taking a semi-nap, Danny considered how he would put it to Phoebe, this quite unforeseen interruption to their time. Danny knows that he is crazy about Phoebe, but also acknowledges (to himself) some slight fear; he suspects that she is perceptibly stronger than he is. Also, it was he who insisted on marriage and finally talked her into it, mentioning their ages ("we're not exactly kids") plus the bribe of the house. But the real truth was that Danny feared losing her—he had indecisively lost a couple of other really nice women; now he wanted to settle down. In any case, although he feels himself loved by Phoebe, feels glad of their marriage, he worries perhaps unduly about her reactions.

"You see, it was such a great favor that I couldn't not do it" was one of the things he decided to say to Phoebe, approaching their room. "All that time in jail, a much longer sentence than anyone thought she would get. I think her old protest history worked against her. I know it was supposed to be our house for these two weeks, Ralph kept saying that. He really felt bad, asking me to do this," Danny meant to add.

What he did not mean to say to Phoebe, in part because he did not know quite how to phrase it, was his own sense that if Maria were to come up to them, Ralph should come too. Ralph's presence would make a better balance. Also, Ralph's frenetic nervous energy, his offbeat wit—both qualities that made Danny smile, just to think about—would have lightened the atmosphere, which so far has been more than a little heavy, what with the weather and Maria's silences, her clearly sagging spirits.

However, Dan had barely mentioned to Phoebe that Maria was getting out of jail on July 19 when Phoebe broke in, "Oh, then she must come right up. Do you think we should leave, or stay on and sort of take care of her? I could cook a lot, prison food has to be horrible. Tell Ralph not to worry, it'll be fine."

All of which led Danny to think that he does not know Phoebe well at all.

Phoebe herself has had certain odd new problems on this trip: trouble eating, for one thing; she who generally eats more than her envious friends can believe, scrawny Phoebe of the miraculous metabolism now barely manages a scant first helping of the good cold rice salads, the various special dishes she planned and made for this first leisurely time alone with Dan. And she is sometimes short of breath. Also, despite long happy nights of love, she has trouble sleeping. All these problems clearly have to do with the altitude, six thousand feet, Phoebe knows that perfectly well; still, does it possibly have something to do with being married—married in haste, as the old phrase used to go?

By far her worst problem, though, is sheer discomfort from the heat, so much heavy sun all day. Like many redheads, Phoebe does not do well in very warm weather, the affliction being an inability to perspire. Instead, out in the sun her skin seems to wither and burn, both within and without. Very likely, she thinks, if it cooled off even a little, all her troubles would disappear; she could eat and sleep again, and enjoy being married to Dan.

However, she reminds herself, there would still be the house. Danny talked about it often; he tried to describe Maria's house, and

Phoebe gathered that it was beautiful—impressive, even. Still, she was unprepared for what seems to her somewhat stark: such bare structural bones, exposed textures of pine and fir, such very high, vaulted ceilings. Phoebe has never been in a house with so definite a tone, a stamp. In fact, both the house's unfamiliarity and the strength of its character have been more than a little intimidating. (Phoebe is from a small town in New Hampshire of entirely conventional, rather small-scale architecture.)

Even the bookcases have yielded up to Phoebe few clues of a personal nature, containing as they do a large, clearly much used collection of various field guides, to birds, wildflowers, trees, and rocks; some yellowed, thumbed-through Grade-B detective fiction; and a large, highly eclectic shelf of poetry—Rilke, Auden, Yeats, plus a great many small volumes of women poets. Marianne Moore, Elizabeth Bishop, Louise Bogan. Katha Pollitt, Amy Clampitt. Clues, but to Ralph or to Maria? Ralph's father, Maria's husband, died young, Dan has said; he has spoken admiringly of Maria's uncompromising professionalism, her courage—never a shopping center or a sleazy tract. The poetry, then, might belong to them both? There are no inscriptions.

Thus, occupying the house of two very strong, individualistic people, neither of whom she has met, fills Phoebe with some unease, even a sort of loneliness.

The site of the house, though, is so very beautiful—magical, even: that very private stretch of clear brown river, rushing over its smoothly rounded, wonderfully tinted rocks. And the surrounding woods of pine and fir and shimmering gray-green aspens, and the lovely sky, and clouds. The very air smells of summer, and earth, and trees. In such a place, Phoebe thinks, how can she not feel perfectly well, not be absolutely happy?

Indeed (she has admitted this to herself, though not to Dan), she welcomed Maria at least in part as a diversion.

Though since her arrival Maria has seemed neither especially diverting, as Phoebe had hoped, nor heroic—as they both had believed.

"It would be a lot better if Ralph were here too, I know that," Dan tells Phoebe, later that morning, as, barefoot, they pick their way back across the meadow to the house; they have been swimming in the river—or, rather, wading and ducking down into the water, which is disappointingly shallow, slow-moving, not the icy rush that Danny remembers from previous visits.

Phoebe, though, seems to feel considerably better; she walks along surefootedly, a little ahead of Dan, and her tone is reassuring as she says, "It's all right. I think Maria's just really tired. I'm doing a vitello tonnato for lunch, though. Remember, from the restaurant? Maybe she'll like that. God, I just wish I could eat!"

Avoiding sharp pinecones and sticks and skirting jagged rocks requires attention, and so they are quiet for a while as they walk along. But then, although he is in fact looking where he is going, Dan's foot hits something terrible and sharp, and he cries out, "Damn!"

"What's wrong?"

"My foot, I think a stone."

"Oh dear." Phoebe has stopped and turned to ask, "Shall I look?"

"No, it's okay, nothing," Dan mutters, striding on past her.

But he is thinking, Well, really, how like Ralph to saddle me with his mother on my honeymoon. And with Maria just out of jail, for God's sake. So politically correct that I couldn't possibly object. Damn Ralph, anyway.

Never having met Ralph, who has been in Los Angeles for all the time that Dan and Phoebe have known each other (the long, not long four months), Phoebe has no clear view of him, although Dan talks about him often. What has mostly come across to Phoebe is the strength of the two men's affection for each other; so rare, in her experience, such open fondness between men. She has even briefly wondered if they could have been lovers, ever, and concluded that they were not. They are simply close, as she and her friend-partner, Anna, are close. Danny would do almost anything for Ralph, including taking in his mother at a not entirely convenient time.

In fact, his strong, evident affections are among the qualities Phoebe values in Dan—and perhaps Ralph is more or less like that? His closeness to his mother has had that effect? Although so far Maria herself has not come across as an especially warm or "giving" person.

Early common ground, discovered by Dan and Phoebe on first meeting, was a firm belief in political protest. They had both taken part in demonstrations against the Nicaraguan embargo, against South African racism; both felt that there was, generally, a mood of protest in their city, San Francisco, that spring. By which they were encouraged.

And they had had serious talks about going to jail. Taking part in demonstrations is not the same as being locked up, they are agreed.

"It's hard to figure out just how much good it does. Jail."

"Especially if you're not famous. Just a person. Ellsberg going to jail is something else."

"Do famous people get lighter sentences?"

"I'd imagine. In fact, I'd bet."

"So hard to figure. Is it better to go to jail, or to stay out and do whatever your work is and send money to your cause?"

Impossible to decide, has been their conclusion.

However, someone probably has to go to jail; they think that too. So why not them?

Working in the kitchen, making lunch, Phoebe feels better than she has for several days. Good effects of the dip into the river seem to last, a lively sense of water lingers on her skin. Carefully, thinly slicing the firm moist white turkey (she is good at this, a good carver), Phoebe feels more in control of her life than she has in days just past, no longer entirely at the mercy of weather and altitude. She even feels more at peace with the house. Here in the kitchen, its bareness and extreme simplicity seem functional; the oversized butcher-block table with its long rack for knives is a great working space.

She is happily breaking an egg into the blender, reaching for oil, when she hears the sound of slow footsteps approaching the kitchen. It must be Maria, and the distress that Phoebe then experiences is both general and particular: she likes best to cook alone; in fact, she loves the solitary single-mindedness of cooking. Also, none of her conversations with Maria have been very successful, so far.

Hesitantly, distractedly, Maria comes to stand outside the kitchen doorway. Vaguely she says, "I'm sure I can't help you." She is not quite looking at Phoebe but rather out the window, to the river. "But I did wonder—you're finding everything you need?"

"Oh yes, it's a wonderful kitchen." Working there, it has become clear to Phoebe that Maria herself must be a very good cook; this is the working space of a dedicated person. "I feel bad displacing you this way," she says to Maria.

This earns the most direct and also the most humorous look from Maria yet seen. "You're good to say that. But actually I could use a little displacement, probably."

Phoebe ventures, "Do you have trouble letting people help you, the way I do?"

A wide, if fleeting, grin. "Oh, indeed I do. I seem to believe myself quite indispensable, in certain areas."

They smile, acknowledging some kinship.

"Well, I won't keep you." Maria begins to leave; then, from whatever inner depths of thought, she remarks, "I do wish Ralph were here too. It would be nice for you to meet him here."

"It would have been," agrees Phoebe. "But sometime."

Lunch, though, is no better than breakfast, conversationally, and in Phoebe's judgment even the food is not entirely successful.

They are gathered again on the terrace above the river, joined at the too large round table—scattered around it.

However, partly because he knows that Phoebe is genuinely curious, as he is himself, Danny persists in asking about Maria's time in jail. (Also, he is convinced that talking about it will help Maria.) "What does Pleasanton look like?" he asks her. "I can't even imagine it."

"Oh—" At first Maria's vague, unfocused glance goes out to the river, as though for help, but then she seems to make an effort—

for her guests. "It's quite country-club-looking," she tells them. "Very clean and bland." In a tantalizing way, she adds, "It's rather like the White House."

"Really? How?" This has been a chorus, from Dan and Phoebe.

Maria sighs, and continues to try. "Well, externally it's so clean, and behind the scenes there's total corruption." Having gone so far, though, she leans back into her chair and closes her eyes.

Dan looks at Phoebe. On her face he sees both blighted curiosity and genuine if momentary helplessness. He sees too her discomfort from the increasing heat. Her skin is so bright, dry, pink. The sultry air has curled her hair so tightly that it looks uncomfortable. At that moment Danny believes that he *feels* all Phoebe's unvoiced, unspoken sensations; her feelings are his. And he further thinks, I am married to Phoebe permanently, for good.

And, looking at his wife, and at Maria, whom he has always known, Danny thinks how incredibly complex women are. How *interesting* they are.

"In Maine the air never felt exactly like this air," Maria tells them, as though Maine had been under discussion—again. "A little like it, fresh and clean, but not exactly. It's interesting. The difference, I mean. Though hard to describe," she trails off.

"I know what you mean, though," comments Phoebe. "In the same way that all the colors are different, but you can't exactly say how."

"Phoebe grew up in New Hampshire," Danny tells Maria, wondering why this fact had not emerged earlier, or did it?

"Oh, did you really." But Maria has returned to her own privacy, her thoughts. New Hampshire could be across the continent from Maine, for all of her.

The heat has gathered and intensified. Phoebe feels that she will burst, her skin rent apart, the way a tomato's skin will split in heat. What she also feels is a kind of rage, though she tries to tell herself that she is simply hot, that she feels so ill-tempered only because of the weather, the temperature. And, knowing herself, certain bad tendencies, she determines that she will not *say* how angry she is, and especially she will not take it out on Danny.

I love Dan. The weather is not his fault—nor, really, is absent Ralph. Gross, inconsiderate, totally selfish Ralph. Some friend, thinks Phoebe.

She and Dan are lying across their bed, ostensibly napping, although the turgid air seems entirely to forbid real sleep. Naked, they still do not touch, although earlier Dan has asked, "Can I douse you with some cold water, or maybe an alcohol rub?"

"No thanks, but really, thanks." (It was at that moment that Phoebe determined not to vent her ire on Dan, who is genuinely kind, well-meaning.)

They have both been whispering, although no one could conceivably hear them, the rooms being so spread apart; Maria's is several rooms away. "Maria simply clutches that prison experience to herself, doesn't she?" now whispers Phoebe. "Not that she much wants to talk about anything else either."

"Except Maine." Danny tries a small laugh. "Lots of Maine."

"And the way she eats," complains Phoebe bitterly. "Just bolting down a few bites and then a dead stop. It's not exactly flattering. Not that I really care, I mean. Did she always eat like that?"

"I sort of can't remember. Maybe not. I didn't notice, really."

"I have to say, though," announces Phoebe, "I really think this is a very selfish move on Ralph's part."

Dan very lightly sighs, just shifting in bed. "I'm afraid I agree. But people change, I think. Maybe he's pure L.A. these days. More selfish than he used to be. He's been seeing some shrink down there for years."

"That whole culture's so selfish. Crass."

"Oh, *right.*"

Feeling a little better, Phoebe reaches her fingers just to graze the top of Danny's hand. They look at each other; they smile.

Dinner that night, which again is out on the terrace, is in many ways a repeat of lunch, except of course for the menu; provident

Phoebe has made a nice cold pasta, with garlicky brandied prawns. But Maria again eats very little, and that most rapidly.

And again she talks about Maine. "The soil was so rocky around our house it was hard to grow flowers," she says. "I've never even tried to plant anything out here."

The night is densely dark, pitch black; in an absolute and final way it is still. And heavy; the air seems weighted. Oppressive, stultifying.

"I do wish Ralph could have been here." It is Dan who has said this, not having at all intended to. It simply slipped out, like a sigh, and now he feels tactless. "But it's great that he has so much work down there," he feebly amends.

"I suppose so." Unhelpful Maria puts her fork down and stares out into the black.

Going about the house, as every night he has—checking door locks, turning off lights—for the first time on this visit Danny has a sad sense of spuriousness: this is not his house, he is much more guest than host. And he recalls now that this place has always been somewhat daunting; its proportions make him feel even less tall than in fact he is. And very possibly Phoebe's deepest reactions have been similar? She too has been made uncomfortable by the house, in addition to the appalling heat, her enemy? None of these facts augur poorly for their marriage, though, Danny believes. Once they are back in San Francisco, in the cool foggy summer weather, in their own newly painted rooms, then they will be fine.

He admits to himself, however, some real disappointment over what he feels as the failure of connection between Maria and Phoebe. When Ralph called about Maria's coming up, just out of jail, along with disappointment at the curtailment of their privacy, Danny experienced a small surge of happy expectation. Maria and Phoebe, despite obvious differences of age, career, could become great friends, a complement to his own friendship with Ralph. And now that this rapport seems entirely unlikely, Danny recognizes the strength of his hope—his conviction, even—that it might have taken place.

Before starting his tour of the house, Dan urged Phoebe to go and take a long cool bath. "Do you a world of good," he told her. And that presumably is where Phoebe is now, in the bathroom down the hall. (The distance between bathrooms and bedrooms in this house seems an almost deliberate inconvenience.)

As Dan gets into bed, he hears nothing, no sound from anywhere. Outside the window the air is motionless, still; the river is soundless, slow. And although he knows that in a few minutes Phoebe will be there with him, Danny experiences a solitude that seems entire, and final.

And then, around midnight, everything breaks. Brilliant flashes of lightning split open the sky, thunder roars—a sound of huge rocks falling down a mountainside. Slits of light, crashing noise.

Entirely awake, and a little scared, Phoebe abruptly remembers Maria this morning as she talked about thunderstorms in Maine. "Actually, I'd be quite terrified, I always used to be" is what Maria said.

To Dan, who is much less fully awake (he seemed to have trouble going to sleep at all), Phoebe whispers, "I'm just going down to see if Maria's all right."

Slipping into her sandals, pulling on her light cotton robe—in the new blessed cool!—Phoebe begins to feel her way down the narrow, pine-smelling hall to Maria's room at the end, the room nearest the river.

Seeing no light beneath the door, she hesitates, but then very gently she knocks, at the same time saying firmly and loudly enough to be heard across the thunder crashes, "It's Phoebe."

For a moment there is no response at all; then some faint sound comes from Maria that Phoebe chooses to interpret as assent.

Entering, she sees Maria upright in bed, sitting erect but pressed back, braced against the headboard. "Oh" is all she says to Phoebe.

Coming over to stand beside her, Phoebe asks, "Should I turn the light on?" and she reaches toward the bedside lamp, on its table.

Maria stops her, crying, "Electricity—don't!"

Recognizing true panic, Phoebe quietly tells her, "I'll just stay here for a minute, if you don't mind."

In the strange half-light between crashes, Maria reaches for her hand. She says, "Thank you," and can just be seen to smile before quickly releasing Phoebe.

Outside, a heavy pounding rain has now begun, but the thunderstorm seems suddenly to be over; there is only the hard drumbeat of rain on the shingled roof, the thud of water on windowpanes.

Phoebe pulls the small bentwood chair from Maria's desk over to the bed, and sits down.

Maria says, "It was good of you to remember."

"I was a little scared," admits Phoebe.

"The thing about prison," Maria takes this up as though prison had just then been under discussion, "is that they do everything to wreck your mind. 'Mind-fuck,' some of the younger women called it." A faint, tight smile. "But they do. Rushing you all the time. Starting you in to do something, and then right away it's over. Even eating, even that horrible food I never got to finish. And they mix up everyone's mail so you think it must be on purpose. And the noise. Radios. And people smoking."

"Jesus" is all Phoebe can manage to say.

Maria is leaning forward now, her eyes luminous, deep, immense. "At my age," she says. "I mean, I often wonder where my mind is going anyway, without all that."

"That's frightful. Terrible."

"Well, it was terrible. I didn't want to admit it to myself. I got just so plain scared. The truth is I'm still scared."

"Well, of course. Anyone is scared of jail. I'm not even sure I could do it."

Maria's gaze in the semi-dark seems to take all of Phoebe in. "I think you would if you had to, or thought you had to," she says.

"I hope so."

"But I'm worried about going back there," Maria tells her. "If for some reason I had to. Again."

At that moment, however, a new sound has begun, just audible through the steady, heavy rain. And lights can be seen to approach the house, very slowly.

Lights from a car, now visible to them both. Unnecessarily, Phoebe announces, "Someone's coming. A small sports car. Whoever—?"

"It must be Ralph," says Maria, smiling. And she exclaims, "Oh! I do think things will be better now. It's even got cool, do you feel it?" But in an anxious way her face still searches Phoebe's. "Do you want to turn on the light?"

Phoebe reaches to touch Maria's hand, very quickly, lightly— before she pushes the switch.

Standing up, then, in the sudden brightness, smiling, as Phoebe moves toward the door she turns back to Maria; she tells her, "I'll get Danny. We'll go make sandwiches—some tea? Poor Ralph, all that driving. We'll celebrate!"

Gina Berriault

Wilderness Fire

A WILDERNESS FIRE WAS RAGING in the mountains east of Los Angeles, and a great brown cloud of smoke, tinged copper by the sunrise, lay over the desert and the small towns she passed through on her way to her mother. The first few miles she was alarmed under the cloud. Only in a nightmare could the sky be like this. Or was it this bad only because she wanted to turn back and the smoke gave her a good enough reason? If she wasn't going to be forced over to the side of the road by the highway patrol and interrogated as to why she was driving so fast in this smoke, she just might pull over on her own, under that long row of eucalyptus up ahead, under those towering, dry, lonely, gray trees, and bend her head to the steering wheel and sleep. Sleep, to put off the moment when she would embrace her mother, bringing her news from the world outside the pink stucco bungalow on the desert's edge.

She went past the eucalyptus row and past the acres of fields planted with something she'd never remember the name for even if she were told twelve times; past shacks far away at the end of dirt roads; past a huge, dusty fig tree branching out over the highway; past a black dog ambling along in a ditch. On the seat beside her—the novel, untouchable, ominous, like an object stolen from a tomb. It slipped closer when she took a curve, and she hit it away with the side of her hand.

The folded letter slipped out from the book and fell to the floor, and it, too, slipped sideways. It was slipping close to the pedals and in another minute she could put her foot on it and grind it

15

down. *All those who practice this profession betray. No, not all. Not the great ones. But maybe they betrayed, too. Just because everybody said "See how far they can see into the human heart," that didn't exonerate them in their own eyes. I have betrayed you, your confidences, your soul, and I will regret it for the rest of my life.*

She went faster past the entrance to a trailer park. Above the hedge the trailer homes swept by with their green awnings of rippled plastic. Oh, thank God her mother didn't live in a trailer park. She almost wept, imagining it. The heat of this desert edge was enough, and to have to live in a trailer with all its dinky built-in things, with plastic flowers planted in tanbark by the doorstep—that was the end. She had always wanted to be rich, not just for herself but for her mother, too. And she had never got rich and never would, not the so-so actress that she was, and married, not now but not long ago, to a man just as poor, though he was going to be less so, now, because his novel might elevate him into all kinds of upper brackets.

The scorched air, the dark cloud were almost left behind. The tall, tall date palms, acres of them, she was passing had always seemed from some far reaches of the earth, brought to a desert from deep swamps, and grotesquely lonely, out of place. She had told only her mother about how they looked to her. Who else would see they wanted swamps? And her mother had agreed they did look like prehistoric swamp plants, out of their element, enduring.

On the outskirts of the town where her mother lived, she slowed down past clapboard houses and stucco bungalows, low to the ground, some in weeds, some in squares of very green grass, one with the same silver porpoise-shape trailer out in back, one with the lemon tree; past the small, stucco school. And now the pink stucco house, small, too, boxlike, but showy in this place because it had two stories. Before it, a squat palm tree that never gave dates, just tiny, yellow, waxy droppings, and a midget fig tree; and, in the back, towering way above the house, one lone palm. All around the yard, a scalloped-wire fence, a foot high, protecting the house and the short dry grass and the three trees from nothing. *Oh, Mother, I had wanted an airy glass house for you by a blue, blue sea, say the*

Caribbean, lush plants all around with large, deep green leaves, always with drops of clear water on their surface. And birds, birds of miraculous plumage. She parked in the gravel driveway, stuck the letter into the book and the book into her purse, and, swinging along, very erect in high heels, purse slung over her shoulder, she went up the paved walk to the front door.

For the moments of their embrace and the moments after, her mother couldn't speak, and then she went on ahead, leading the way into the kitchen, tossing her head from side to side with delight, like a child. Her mother was bare-legged and clopping along artfully on backless wedge sandals. Her flowered cotton dress had once been her daughter's in an awful movie, but it had been expensive and was kept neater now than its original owner had ever kept it. Her mother's short hair was tinted a pink-blond, like a faint reflection indoors of the exterior of the house. In the four months since the daughter's last visit, the mother seemed to have got quite a bit older. Or maybe it was the heat of the desert summer that shrinks the thin ones and expands the fat ones. And, coming along behind her mother, she said, *Mother, Mother, Mother,* just to herself. *If there was anything I did that made you get old, forgive me for that.*

"Penny, dear shiny bright Penny," her mother said, and here in the dim kitchen, the striped curtains closed against the heat swarming at the windows, here where her mother turned to clasp her again, the daughter felt again how much she was thought about in this house. Her mother's face in the shade of the room told her again how brief was the time of their knowing each other, only twenty-five years so far, and told her again of the unknowable limits of the time left.

"There's a fire in the mountains, if I smell of smoke," she said.

"You've brought me Chris's book," her mother said, hands palm to palm under her chin, like a child praying at bedtime. Bless everybody, amen.

"Oh, yes, that's right," the daughter said, tantalizingly wagging her finger under her mother's nose. "Patience, patience."

"You left so early," her mother said. "Shall I make you some breakfast?"

"Never hungry till two," she said. "Same as always. Let's just drink a toast. Some mineral water will do fine."

"Is he happy?" her mother asked. She had been an actress and had even got her name up on the screen—in much smaller letters than the leads. She had always played innocents, girls from small towns, from farms, and now, when she was called upon to express happiness, it came across like that of a girl who didn't know yet that happiness wasn't that simple. Her mother was a smart woman, but seeing her smile like that, you couldn't guess how smart she really was.

"Oh, he's happy, of course," she said, smiling at her mother the same sort of smile from the backwoods. "A novel with his name on it, what else can he be but happy? He's living with a friend of his— I guess it's a woman, he just says *friend*—at her or his apartment in New York. He's happy."

"He says that?"

"He says what?"

"That he's happy?"

"If he says so it must be so," she said, coming out smiling from behind her hands, as if she had spread them over her face only to rub away the soot or the dust or whatever that cloud of smoke had left. "He says he's going to write to you. You and he always had such wonderful discussions. Just about everything from quasars to cucumbers. He says he's going to mail you an autographed copy with something like 'Love to Melody, whom I thank for giving birth to Penelope.'"

"That's nice, but you're making it up."

The daughter was wandering around the kitchen, restlessly, as if she'd come to the wrong house and was going to have to leave at once. She came to the other end of the long kitchen, where there was a couch and a television and a sewing machine, and where, on a table, there were magazines and a row of African violets in little painted Mexican pots that had been hers when she was a little girl—a collection of sorts, and her mother brought over the misted glass to her, there.

"I made it up and it's not nice," she said. "He admires you for just being you and he loves you. It's easy, you know, to love you.

He'll just write, 'To Melody, dear friend, all my love.' Let's drink to that. If he gets to be famous, your copy will be worth a small fortune." But how little love, none at all, he had shown in his novel for her mother; she wasn't mentioned, but what he had written about the daughter was to wound the mother beyond amends.

They raised their glasses.

"Chris has a good heart," her mother said.

"Chris has a great heart," she said. "Everybody's going to know that soon, not just you and me." But she couldn't drink, because the ice cubes were making such a racket she had to set her glass down.

"Sit down now," her mother said, sharply.

"Mother, it isn't me," she said. "The girl in his novel isn't me. He got it wrong. There's no resemblance whatsoever. I never gave him all that trouble and I was never loved like the girl in there was loved. Everybody will think it's me and it isn't me."

"Where is it?" her mother asked, afraid.

"Mother, he was always fascinated by women made of words. If you want to know their names I'll try to remember. Emma Bovary and Molly Bloom and Brett, and that girl who was mad over Heathcliff. Oh, and women in the flesh, too. Of course. But when he put me into words he got me wrong. It's not me, Mother."

"Sit down," her mother said, and the daughter sat down. "It's all made up," her mother said soothingly, sitting, facing her daughter. "Everybody knows that. That's what novels are all about."

"If I gave him trouble, Mother," she said, "it was because he gave me trouble."

"That's usually the way it goes," her mother said, stroking her daughter's arms, down and down again along the long silk sleeves. "And nobody ever knows who started the trouble."

"Mother, nobody can ever know what life feels like in another person. You only think you know. I never could know him, his desires for his life, his life in here," taking her hands away from her mother's to spread them over her chest, "and he could never know me. It's unknown territory. It's unknown in here, Mother. I don't know myself. All I hear is the uproar."

"Give me your hands," her mother said, reaching for her daughter's hands again and holding them down.

The daughter had been avoiding the mother's face. She had been looking everywhere, sideways and down, anywhere but at her mother, and now she looked at her mother's face, at the slack cheeks, at the waiting fear in the eyes. And the ears through the pink curls seemed comically large, waiting.

"Once I tried to kill myself," she said, and began to sob. She pulled her hands away and held them up, palms toward her mother, and the long sleeves slipped away from the wrists, exposing on each wrist the thin, pale line of an old scar.

They stood up at the same time and came together, clasping each other. She had betrayed this woman who had given her birth, betrayed this woman's hopes for her daughter to endure, endure against all the unsolvable puzzles life comes up with. She was taller than her mother—her mother, over the past few years, was getting smaller, and the daughter was wearing high heels—and her mother's face was pressed against her breasts, her tears wetting the blouse and the nipples under the cloth. Long ago, her mother had told her that when she was newborn and began to cry, the milk seeped out at once from her mother's breasts, wetting her dress. At once, though mother and child were rooms apart.

"Mama, I didn't die," she pleaded. "You see I didn't die. I'm alive. I'm alive." But her mother would not let go and would not raise her head.

With her arm about her mother, she walked her out into the yard, because the broad desert light might force them to calm down and to endure. Even the tall palm they stood beside might force them to endure. Way far to the west, the smoke was like evening at the wrong time of day.

T. Coraghessan Boyle

Sitting on Top of the World

PEOPLE WOULD ASK HER what it was like. She'd watch them from her tower as they weaved along the trail in their baseball caps and day packs, their shorts, hiking boots and sneakers. The brave ones would mount the hundred and fifty wooden steps hammered into the face of the mountain to stand at the high-flown railing of the little glass-walled shack she called home for seven months a year. Sweating, sucking at canteens and bota bags, heaving for breath in the undernourished air, they would ask her what it was like. "Beautiful," she would say. "Peaceful."

But that didn't begin to express it. It was like floating untethered, drifting with the clouds, like being cupped in the hands of God. Nine thousand feet up, she could see the distant hazy rim of the world, she could see Mount Whitney rising up above the crenellations of the Sierra, she could see stars that haven't been discovered yet. In the morning, she was the first to watch the sun emerge from the hills to the east, and in the evening, when it was dark beneath her, the valleys and ridges gripped by the insinuating fingers of the night, she was the last to see it set. There was the wind in the trees, the murmur of the infinite needles soughing in the uncountable branches of the pines, sequoias and cedars that stretched out below her like a carpet. There was daybreak. There was the stillness of 3:00 a.m. She couldn't explain it. She was sitting on top of the world.

Don't you get lonely up here? they'd ask. Don't you get a lit-tle stir-crazy?

And how to explain that? Yes, she did, of course she did, but it didn't matter. Todd was up here with her in the summer, one week on, one week off, and then the question was meaningless. But in September he went back to the valley, to his father, to school, and the world began to drag round its tired old axis. The hikers stopped coming then too. At the height of summer, on a weekend, she'd see as many as thirty or forty in the course of a day, but now, with the fall coming on, they left her to herself—sometimes she'd go for days without seeing a soul.

But that was the point, wasn't it?

She was making breakfast—a real breakfast for a change, ham and eggs from the propane refrigerator, fresh-dripped coffee and toast— when she spotted him working his way along one of the switch-backs below. She was immediately annoyed. It wasn't even seven yet and the sign at the trailhead quite plainly stated that visitors were welcome at the lookout between the hours of ten and five *only*. What was wrong with this guy—did he think he was exempt or something? She calmed herself: maybe he was only crossing the trail. Deer season had opened—she'd been hearing the distant muted pop of gunfire all week—and maybe he was only a hunter tracking a deer.

No such luck. When she glanced down again, flipping her eggs, peering across the face of the granite peak and the steep snaking trail that clung to it, she saw that he was coming up to the tower. Damn, she thought, and then the kettle began to hoot and her stomach clenched. Breakfast was ruined. Now there'd be some stranger gawking over her shoulder and making the usual banal comments as she ate. To them it might have been like Disneyland or something up here, but this was her home, she lived here. How would they like it if she showed up on their doorstep at seven o'clock in the morning?

She was eating, her back to the glass door, hoping he'd go away, slip over the lip of the precipice and disappear, vanish in a puff of smoke, when she felt his footfall on the trembling catwalk that ran round the outside of the tower. Still, she didn't turn or look up. She was reading—she went through a truckload of books in the course of a season—and she never lifted her eyes from the page. He could gawk round the catwalk, peer through the telescope and hustle himself back on down the steps for all she cared. She wasn't a tour guide. Her job was to watch for smoke, twenty-four hours a day, and to be cordial—if she was in the mood and had the time—to the hikers who made the sweaty panting trek in from the trailhead to join her for a brief moment atop the world. There was no law that said she had to let them in the shack or show them the radio and her plotting equipment and deliver the standard lecture on how it all worked. Especially at seven in the morning. To hell with him, she thought, and she forked up egg and tried to concentrate on her book.

The problem was, she'd trained herself to look up from what she was doing and scan the horizon every thirty seconds or so, day or night, except when she was asleep, and it had become a reflex. She glanced up, and there he was. It gave her a shock. He'd gone round the catwalk to the far side and he was standing right in front of her, grinning and holding something up to the window. Flowers, wildflowers, she registered that, but then his face came into focus and she felt something go slack in her: she knew him. He'd been here before.

"Lainie," he said, tapping the glass and brandishing the flowers, "I brought you something."

Her name. He knew her name.

She tried a smile and her face froze around it. The book on the table before her upset the salt-shaker and flipped itself shut with a tiny expiring hiss. Should she thank him? Should she get up and latch the door? Should she put out an emergency call on the radio and snatch up the kitchen knife?

"Sorry to disturb you over breakfast—I didn't know the time," he said, and something happened to his grin, though his eyes—a hard metallic blue—held on to hers like pincers. He raised his voice to penetrate the glass: "I've been camping down on Long

Meadow Creek and when I crossed the trail this morning I just thought you might be lonely and I'd surprise you"—he hesitated— "I mean, with some flowers."

Her whole body was frozen now. She'd had crazies up here before—it was an occupational hazard—but there was something unnerving about this one; this one she remembered. "It's too early," she said finally, miming it with her hands, as if the glass were impervious to sound, and then she got up from her untouched ham and half-eaten eggs and deliberately went to the radio. The radio was just under the window where he was standing, and when she picked up the mike and depressed the talk button she was two feet from him, the thin wall of glass all that separated them.

"Needles Lookout," she said, "this is Elaine. Zack, you there? Over."

Zack's voice came right back at her. He was a college student working on a degree in forestry, and he was her relief two days a week when she hiked out and went down the mountain to spend a day with her son, do her shopping and maybe hit a bar or movie with her best friend and soul mate, Cynthia Furman. "Elaine," he said, above the crackle of static, "what's up? See anything funny out there? Over."

She forced herself to look up then and locate the stranger's eyes—he was still grinning, but the grin was slack and unsteady and there was no joy in the deeps of those hard blue eyes—and she held the black plastic mike to her lips a moment longer than she had to before answering. "Nothing, Zack," she said, "just checking in."

His voice was tinny. "Okay," he said. "Talk to you. Over and out."

"Over and out," she said.

And now what? The guy wore a hunting knife strapped to his thigh. His cheeks were caved in as if he were sucking candy, and an old-fashioned mustache, thick and reddish, hid his upper lip. Instead of a baseball cap he wore a wide-brimmed felt hat. Wyatt Earp, she thought, and she was about to turn away from the window, prepared to ignore him till he took the hint, till he counted off the hundred and fifty wooden steps and vanished down the path and

out of her life, when he rapped again on the glass and said, "You got
something to put these in—the flowers, I mean?"

She didn't want his flowers. She didn't want him on her platform. She didn't want him in her thirteen-by-thirteen-foot sanctuary, touching her things, poking around, asking stupid questions,
making small talk. "Look," she said finally, talking to the glass but
looking through him, beyond him, scanning the infinite as she'd
trained herself to do, no matter what the problem, "I've got a job to
do up here and the fact is no one's allowed on the platform
between the hours of five in the afternoon and ten in the morning"—now she came back to him and saw that his smile had col-
lapsed—"you ought to know that. It says so in plain English right
down there at the trailhead." She looked away; it was over, she was
done with him.

She went back to her breakfast, forcing herself to stare at the
page before her, though her heart was going and the words meant
nothing. Todd had been with her the first time the man had come.
Todd was fourteen, tall like his father, blond-headed and rangy. He
was a good kid, her last and final hope, and he seemed to relish the
time he spent with her up here. It was a Saturday, the middle of
the afternoon, and they'd had a steady stream of visitors since the
morning. Todd was in the storage room below, reading comics (in
its wisdom, the Forestry Service had provided this second room,
twenty-five steps down, not simply for storage but for respite too—
it was a box, a womb, with only a single dull high-placed window
to light it, antithesis and antidote to the naked glass box above).
Elaine was at her post, chopping vegetables for soup and scanning
the horizon.

She hadn't noticed him coming—there'd been so many visitors she wasn't attuned to them in the way she was in the quiet
times. She was feeling hospitable, lighthearted, the hostess of an
ongoing party. There'd been a professor up earlier, an ornithologist,
and they'd had a long talk about the golden eagle and the red-tailed
hawk. And then there was the young girl from Merced—she couldn't
have been more than seventeen—with her baby strapped to her
back, and two heavyset women in their sixties who'd proudly made

the two-and-a-half-mile trek in from the trailhead and were giddy
with the thin air and the thrill of their own accomplishment. Elaine
had offered them each a cup of tea, not wanting to spoil their fun
and point out that it was still two and a half miles back out.

She'd felt his weight on the platform and turned to give him
a smile. He was tall and powerful across the chest and shoulders and
he'd tipped his hat to her and poked his head in the open door.
"Enjoying the view?" he said.

There was something in his eyes that should have warned her
off, but she was feeling sociable and buoyant and she saw the gen-
erosity in his shoulders and hands. "It's nothing compared to the
Ventura Freeway," she deadpanned.

He laughed out loud at that, and he was leaning in the door
now, both hands on the frame. "I see the monastic life hasn't hurt
your sense of humor any—" and then he paused, as if he'd gone too
far. "Or that's not the word I want, 'monastic'—is there a feminine
version of that?"

Pretty presumptuous. Flirtatious, too. But she was in the
mood, she didn't know what it was—maybe having Todd with her,
maybe just the sheer bubbling joy of living on the crest of the sky—
and at least he wasn't dragging her through the same old tired conversation about loneliness and beauty and smoke on the horizon
she had to endure about a hundred times a week. "Come in," she
said. "Take a load off your feet."

He sat on the edge of the bed and removed his hat. He wore
his hair in a modified punk style—hard irregular spikes—and that
surprised her: somehow it just didn't go with the cowboy hat. His
jeans were stiff and new and his tooled boots looked as if they'd just
been polished. He was studying her—she was wearing khaki shorts
and a T-shirt, she'd washed her hair that morning in anticipation of
the crowd, and her legs were good—she knew it—tanned and
shaped by her treks up and down the trail. She felt something she
hadn't felt in a long time, an ice age, and she knew her cheeks were
flushed. "You probably had a whole slew of visitors today, huh?" he
said, and there was something incongruous in the enforced folksi-

ness of the phrase, something that didn't go with his accent, just as the haircut didn't go with the hat.

"I've counted twenty-six since this morning." She diced a carrot and tossed it into the pan to simmer with the onions and zucchini she'd chopped a moment earlier.

He was gazing out the window, working his hands on the brim of his hat. "Hope you don't mind my saying this, but you're the best thing about this view as far as I can see. You're pretty. Really pretty."

This one she'd heard before. About a thousand times. Probably seventy percent of the day-trippers who made the hike out to the lookout were male, and if they were alone or with other males, about ninety percent of those tried to hit on her in some way. She resented it, but she couldn't blame them really. There was probably something irresistible in the formula: young woman with blond hair and good legs in a glass tower in the middle of nowhere—and all alone. Rapunzel, let down your hair. Usually she deflected the compliment—or the moves—by turning officious, standing on her authority as Forestry Service employee, government servant and the chief, queen and despot of the Needles Lookout. This time she said nothing. Just lifted her head for a quick scan of the horizon and then looked back down at the knife and the cutting board and began chopping green onion and cilantro.

He was still watching her. The bed was big, a double, one of the few creature comforts the Forestry Service provided up here. There was no headboard, of course—just a big flat hard slab of mattress attached to the wall at window level, so you could be lying in bed and still do your job. Presumably, it was designed for couples. When he spoke again, she knew what he was going to say before the words were out of his mouth. "Nice bed," he said.

What did she expect? He was no different from the rest—why would he be? All of a sudden he'd begun to get on her nerves, and when she turned her face to him her voice was cold. "Have you seen the telescope," she said, indicating the Bushnell Televar mounted on the rail of the catwalk—beyond the window and out the door.

He ignored her. He rose to his feet. Thirteen by thirteen: two's a crowd. "You must get awfully lonely up here," he said, and his voice was different now too, no attempt at folksiness or jocularity, "a pretty woman like you. A beautiful woman. You've got sexy legs, you know that?"

She flushed—he could see that, she was sure of it—and the flush made her angry. She was about to tell him off, to tell him to get the hell out of her house and stay out, when Todd came rumbling up the steps, wild-eyed and excited. "Mom!" he shouted, and he was out of breath, his voice high-pitched and hoarse, "there's water leaking all over the place out there!"

Water. It took a moment to register. The water was precious up here, irreplaceable. Once a month two bearded men with Forestry Service patches on their sleeves brought her six twenty-gallon containers of it—in the old way, on the backs of mules. She husbanded that water as if she were in the middle of the Negev, every drop of it, rarely allowing herself the luxury of a quick shampoo and rinse, as she had that morning. In the next instant she was out the door and jolting down the steps behind her son. Down below, outside the storage room where the cartons were lined up in a straight standing row, she saw that the rock face was slick with a finely spread sheen of water. She bent to the near carton. It was leaking from a thin milky stress fracture in the plastic, an inch from the bottom. "Take hold of it, Todd," she said. "We've got to turn it over so the leak's on top."

Full, the carton weighed better than a hundred and sixty pounds, and this one was nearly full. She put her weight behind it, the power of her honed and muscular legs, but the best she could do, even with Todd's help, was to push the thing over on its side. She was breathing hard, sweating, she'd scraped her knee and there was a stipple of blood on the skin over the kneecap. It was then that she became aware of the stranger standing there behind her. She looked up at him framed against the vastness of the sky, the sun in his face, his big hands on his hips. "Need a hand there?" he asked.

Looking back on it, she didn't know why she'd refused—maybe it was the way Todd gaped at him in awe, maybe it was the old pretty-woman/lonely-up-here routine or the helpless-female syndrome—but before she could think she was saying "I don't need your help: I can do it myself."

And then his hands fell from his hips and he backed away a step, and suddenly he was apologetic, he was smooth and funny and winning and he was sorry for bothering her and he just wanted to help and he knew she was capable, he wasn't implying anything—and just as suddenly he caught himself, dropped his shoulders and slunk off down the steps without another word.

For a long moment she watched him receding down the trail, and then she turned back to the water container. By the time she and Todd got it upended it was half empty.

Yes. And now he was here when he had no right to be, now he was intruding and he knew it, now he was a crazy defining new levels of the affliction. She'd call in an emergency in a second—she wouldn't hesitate—and they'd have a helicopter here in less than five minutes, that's how quick these firefighters were, she'd seen them in action. Five minutes. She wouldn't hesitate. She kept her head down. She cut and chewed each piece of meat with slow deliberation and she read and reread the same paragraph until it lost all sense. When she looked up, he was gone.

After that, the day dragged on as if it would never end. He couldn't have been there more than ten minutes, slouching around with his mercenary grin and his pathetic flowers, but he'd managed to ruin her day. He'd upset her equilibrium and she found that she couldn't read, couldn't sketch or work on the sweater she was knitting for Todd. She caught herself staring at a fixed point on the horizon, drifting, her mind a blank. She ate too much. Lunch was a ceremony, dinner a ritual. There were no visitors, though for once she longed for them. Dusk lingered in the western sky and when night fell she didn't bother with her propane lantern but merely sat there on the corner of the bed, caught up in the wheeling immensity of the constellations and the dream of the Milky Way.

And then she couldn't sleep. She kept thinking of him, the stranger with the big hands and secretive eyes, kept scanning the catwalk for the sudden black shadow of him. If he came at seven in the morning, why not at three? What was to prevent him? There was no sound, nothing—the wind had died down and the night was clear and moonless. For the first time since she'd been here, for the first time in three long seasons, she felt naked and vulnerable, exposed in her glass house like a fish in a tank. The night was everything and it held her in its grip.

She thought about Mike then, about the house they'd had when he'd finished his degree and started as an assistant professor at a little state school out in the lost lush hills of Oregon. The house was an A-frame, a cabin with a loft, set down amidst the trees like a cottage in a fairy tale. It was all windows and everywhere you looked the trees bowed down and stepped into the house. The previous owner, an old widower with watery eyes and yellow hair climbing out of his ears, hadn't bothered with blinds or curtains, and Mike didn't like that—he was always after her to measure the windows and order blinds or buy the material for drapes. She'd balked. The openness, the light, the sense of connection and belonging: these were the things that had attracted her in the first place. They made love in the dark—Mike insisted on it—as if it were something to be ashamed of. After a while, it was.

Then she was thinking of a time before that, a time before Todd and graduate school, when Mike sat with her in the dormitory lounge, books spread out on the coffee table before them, the heat and murmur of a dozen other couples locking their mouths and bodies together. A study date. For hours she clung to him, the sofa like a boat pitching in a heavy sea, the tease of it, the fumbling innocence, the interminable foreplay that left her wet and itching while the wind screamed beyond the iced-over windows. That was something. The R.A. would flash the lights and it was quarter of one and they would fling themselves at each other, each step to the door drenched in hormones, sticky with them, desperate, until finally he was gone and she felt the loss like a war bride. Until the next night.

Finally—and it must have been two, three in the morning, the Big Dipper tugged down below the horizon, Orion looming overhead—she thought of the stranger who'd spoiled her breakfast.

He'd sat there on the corner of the bed; he'd stood beyond the window with his sad bundle of flowers, devouring the sky. As she thought of him, in that very moment, there was a dull light thump on the steps, a faint rustle, movement, and she couldn't breathe, couldn't move. The seconds pounded in her head and the rustling—it was like the sweep of a broom—was gone, something in the night, a pack rat, the fleeting touch of an owl's wing. She thought of those hands, the eyes, the square of those shoulders, and she felt herself being drawn down into the night in relief, and finally, in gratitude.

She woke late, the sun slanting across the floor to touch her lips and mask her eyes. Zachary was on the radio with the news that Oakland had clinched the pennant and a hurricane was tearing up the East Coast. "You sound awful," he said. "I didn't wake you, did I?"

"I couldn't sleep."

"Stargazing again, huh?"

She tried out a laugh for him. "I guess," she said. There was a silence. "Jesus, you just relieved me. I've got four more days to put in before I come back down to the ground."

"Just don't get mystical on me. And leave me some granola this time, will you? And if you run out, call me. That's my breakfast we're talking about. And lunch. And sometimes, if I don't feel like cooking—"

She cut him off: "Dinner. I know. I will." She yawned. "Talk to you."

"Yeah. Over and out."

"Over and out."

When she set the kettle on the grill there was gas, but when she turned her back to dig the butter out of the refrigerator, the flame was gone. She tried another match, but there was nothing. That meant she had to switch propane tanks, a minor nuisance. The tanks, which were flown in once a year by helicopter, were located at the base of the stairway, one hundred and fifty steps down. There was a flat spot there, a gap cut into the teeth of the outcrop and overhung on one side by a sloping twenty-foot-high wall of rock. On the other side, the first step was a thousand feet down.

She shrugged into her shorts, and because it was cold despite the sun—she'd seen snow as early as the fifth of September, and the month was almost gone now—she pulled on an oversized sweater that had once belonged to Mike. After she'd moved out she'd found it in a pillowcase she'd stuffed full of clothes. He hadn't wanted it back. It was windy, and a blast knifed into her when she threw open the door and started down the steps. Big pristine tufts of cumulus hurried across the sky, swelling and attenuating and changing shape, but she didn't see anything dark enough—or big enough—to portend a storm. Still, you could never tell. The breeze was from the north and the radio had reported a storm front moving in off the Pacific—it really wouldn't surprise her to see snow on the ground by this time tomorrow. A good snowfall and the fire season would be over and she could go home. Early.

She thought about that—about the four walls of the little efficiency she rented on a dead street in a dead town to be near Todd during the winter—and hoped it wouldn't snow. Not now. Not yet. In a dry year—and this had been the third dry year in a row—she could stay through mid-November. She reached the bottom of the steps and crouched over the propane tanks, two three-hundred-gallon jobs painted Forestry Service green, feeling depressed over the thought of those four dull walls and the cold in the air and the storm that might or might not develop. There was gooseflesh on her legs and her breath crowded the air round her. She watched a ground squirrel, its shoulders bulky with patches of bright gray fur, dart up over the face of the overhang, and then she unfastened the coupling on the empty tank and switched the hose to the full one.

"Gas problems?"

The voice came from above and behind her and she jumped as if she'd been stung. Even before she whirled round she knew whose voice it was.

"Hey, hey: didn't mean to startle you. Whoa. Sorry." There he was, the happy camper, knife lashed to his thigh, standing right behind her, two steps up. This time his eyes were hidden behind a pair of reflecting sunglasses. The brim of the Stetson was pulled down low and he wore a sheepskin coat, the fleecy collar turned up in back.

She couldn't answer. Couldn't smile. Couldn't humor him. He'd caught her out of her sanctuary, caught her out in the open, one hundred and fifty steep and unforgiving steps from the radio, the kitchen knife, the hard flat soaring bed. She was crouching. He towered above her, his shoulders cut out of the sky. Todd was in school. Mike—she didn't want to think about Mike. She was all alone.

He stood there, the mustache the only thing alive in his face. It lifted from his teeth in a grin. "Those things can be a pain," he said, the folksy tone creeping into his voice, "those tanks, I mean. Dangerous. I use electricity myself."

She lifted herself cautiously from her crouch, the hard muscles swelling in her legs. She would have risked a dash up the stairs, all hundred and fifty of them, would have put her confidence in her legs, but he was blocking the stairway—almost as if he'd anticipated her. She hadn't said a word yet. She looked scared, she knew it. "Still camping?" she said, fighting to open up her face and give him his smile back, insisting on banality, normalcy, the meaningless drift of meaningless conversation.

He looked away from her, light flashing from the slick convexity of the sunglasses, and kicked at the edge of the step with the silvertipped toe of his boot. After a moment he turned back to her and removed the sunglasses. "Yeah," he said, shrugging. "I guess."

It wasn't an answer she expected. He guessed? What was that supposed to mean? He hadn't moved a muscle and he was watching her with that look in his eyes—she knew that look, knew that stance, that mustache and hat, but she didn't know his name. He knew hers but she didn't know his, not even his first name. "I'm sorry," she said, and when she put a hand up to her eyes to shade them from the sun, it was trembling, "but what was your name again? I mean, I remember you, of course, not just from yesterday but from that time a month or so ago, but..." She trailed off.

He didn't seem to have heard her. The wind sang in the trees. She just stood there, squinting into the sun—there was nothing else she could do. "I wasn't camping, not really," he said. "Not that I don't love the wilderness—and I do camp, backpack and all that—but I just—I thought that's what you'd want to hear."

What she'd want to hear? What was he talking about? She stole a glance at the tower, sun flashing the windows, clouds pricked on the peak of the roof, and it seemed as distant as the stars at night. If only she were up there she'd put out an emergency, she would, she'd have them here in five minutes....

"Actually," and he looked away now, his shoulders slumping in that same hangdog way they had when she'd refused his help with the water carton, "actually I've got a cabin up on Cedar Slope. I just, I just thought you'd want to hear I was camping." He'd been staring down at the toe of his boots, but suddenly he looked up at her and grinned till his back fillings glinted in the light. "I think Elaine's a pretty name, did I tell you that?"

"Thank you," she said, almost against her will, and softly, so softly she could barely hear it herself. He could rape her here, he could kill her, anything. Was that what he wanted? Was that it? "Listen," she said, pushing it, she couldn't help herself, "listen, I've got to get back to work—"

"I know, I know," he said, holding up the big slab of his hand, "back to the nest, huh? I know I must be a pain in the—in the butt for you, and I'll bet I'm not the first one to say it, but you're just too good-looking a woman to be wasted out here on the squirrels and coyotes." He stepped down, stepped toward her, and she thought in that instant of trying to dart past him, a wild thought, instinctual and desperate, a thought that clawed its way into her brain and froze there before she could move. "Jesus," he said, and his voice was harsh with conviction, "don't you get lonely?"

And then she saw it, below and to the right, movement, two bobbing pink hunter's caps, coming up the trail. It was over. Just like that. She could walk away from him, mount the stairs, lock herself in the tower. But why was her heart still going, why did she feel as if it hadn't even begun? "Damn," she said, directing her gaze, "more visitors. Now I really have to get back."

He followed her eyes and looked down to where the hunters sank out of view and then bobbed back up again, working their way up the path. She could see their faces now—two men, middle-aged, wispy hair sticking out from beneath the fluorescent caps. No guns. Cameras. He studied them a moment and then looked into her eyes, looked deep, as if he'd lost something. Then he shrugged, turned his back and started down the path toward them.

She was in good shape, the best shape of her life. She'd been up the steps a thousand times, two thousand, but she'd never climbed them quicker than she did now. She flew up the stairs like something blown by the wind and she felt a kind of panic beating against her ribs and she smelled the storm coming and felt the cold to the marrow of her bones. And then she reached the door and slammed it shut behind her, fumbling for the latch. It was then, only then, that she noticed the flowers. They were in the center of the table, in a cut-glass vase, lupine, groundsel, forget-me-not.

It snowed in the night, monstrous swirling oversized flakes that clawed at the windows and filled her with despair. The lights would only have made her feel vulnerable and exposed, and for the second night running she did without them, sitting there in the dark, cradling the kitchen knife and listening for his footfall on the steps while the sky fell to pieces around her. But he wouldn't come, not in this weather, not at night—she was being foolish, childish, there was nothing to worry about. Except the snow. It meant that her season was over. And if her season was over, she had to go back down the mountain and into the real world, real time, into the smog and roar and clutter.

She thought of the four walls that awaited her, the hopeless job—waitressing or fast food or some such slow crucifixion of the spirit—and she thought of Mike before she left him, saw him there in the black glass of the window, sexless, pale, the little butterfly-wing bifocals perched on the tip of his nose, pecking at the typewriter, pecking, pecking, in love with Dryden, Swift, Pope, in love with dead poets, in love with death itself. She'd met a man at a party a month after she'd left him and he was just like Mike, only he was in love with arthropods. Arthropods. And then she came up to the tower.

She woke late again and the first thing she felt was relief. The sun was out and the snow—it was only a dusting, nothing really— had already begun to recede from the naked high crown of the rock. She put on the kettle and went to the radio. "Zack," she called, "Needle Rock. Do you copy?"

He was there, right at her fingertips. "Copy. Over."

"We had some snow up here—nothing much, just a dusting really. It's clear now."

"You're a little late—Lewis already checked in from Mule Peak with that information. Oversleep again?"

"Yeah, I guess so." She was watching the distant treetops shake off the patina of snow. A hawk sailed across the window. She held the microphone so close to her lips it could have been a part of her. "Zack—" She wanted to tell him about the crazy, about the man in the Stetson, about his hands, wanted to alert him just in case, but she hesitated. Her voice was tiny, detached, lost in the electronic crackle of time and space.

"Lainie?"

"Yes. Yes, I'm here."

"There's a cold front coming through, another storm behind it. They're saying it could drop some snow. The season's still on— Reichert says it will be until we get appreciable precipitation—but this one could be it. It's up to you. You want to come out or wait and see?"

Reichert was the boss, fifty, bald, soft as a clam. The mountains were parched—six inches of powdery duff covered the forest floor and half the creeks had run dry. The season could last till November. "Wait and see," she said.

"Okay, it's your choice. Lewis is staying too, if it makes you feel better. I'll keep in touch if anything develops on this end."

"Yeah. Thanks."

"Over and out."

"Over and out."

It clouded up late in the afternoon and the sky closed in on her again. The temperature began to drop. It looked bad. It was early for snow yet, but they could get snow any time of the year at this altitude. The average was twenty-five feet annually, and she'd seen storms drop four and five feet at a time. She talked to Zack at four and he told her it looked pretty grim—they were calling for a seventy-percent chance of snow, with the snow level dropping to three thousand feet. "I'll take my chances," she told him. There was a pair of snowshoes in the storage room if it came to that.

The snow started an hour later. She was cooking dinner—brown rice and vegetables—and she'd opened the bottle of wine she'd brought up to commemorate the last day of the season. The flakes were tiny, pellets that sifted down with a hiss, the sort of configuration that meant serious snow. The season was over. She could drink her wine and then think about packing up and cleaning the stove and refrigerator. She put another log on the woodstove and buttoned up her jacket.

The wine was half gone and she'd sat down to eat when she noticed the smoke. At first she thought it must be a trick of the wind, the smoke from her own stove twisting back on her. But no. Below her, no more than five hundred feet, just about where the trail would be, she could see the flames. The wind blew a screen of snow across the window. There hadn't been any lightning—but there was a fire down there, she was sure of it. She got up from the table, snatched her binoculars from the hook by the door and went out on the catwalk to investigate.

The wind took her breath away. All the universe had gone pale, white above and white beneath: she was perched on the clouds, living in them, diaphanous and ghostly. She could smell the smoke on the wind now. She lifted the binoculars to her eyes and the snow screened them; she tried again and her hair beat at the lenses. It took her a moment, but there, there it was: a fire leaping up out of the swirling grip of the snow. A campfire. But no, this was bigger, fallen trees stacked up in a pyramid—this was a bonfire, deliberate, this was a sign. The snow took it away from her. Her fingers were numb. When the fire came into focus again she saw movement there, a shadow leaping round the flames, feeding them, reveling in them, and she caught her breath. And then she saw the black stabbing peak of the Stetson and she understood.

He was camping.

Camping. He could die out there—he *was* crazy, he *was*—this thing could turn into a blizzard, it could snow for days. But he was camping. And then the thought came to her: he was camping for her.

Later, when the tower floated out over the storm and the coals glowed in the stove and the darkness settled in around her like a blanket, she disconnected the radio and put the knife away in the drawer where it belonged. Then she propped herself in the corner of the bed, way out over the edge of the abyss, and watched his fire raging in the cold heart of the night. He would be back, she knew that now, and she would be ready for him.

Michelle Cliff

Apache Tears

APACHE TEARS IS A SMALL community thirty miles east-northeast of downtown Los Angeles. Unlike most of the communities that impinge on the city, Apache Tears is discrete, the secret of a canyon as the desert begins, set out by a railwayman who longed for his hometown and worshipped the orderliness of a grid.

Apache Tears is the kind of place where, at the end of the twentieth century, milk is delivered to the front door, placed on porches in wooden boxes stamped in red APACHE TEARS DAIRY, contained in glass bottles with cardboard stoppers stamped in black HOMOGENIZED.

Not a silhouette of a missing child in sight. No "Have you seen me?" (And what would you do if you had?) next to a lost face. Rather the bottles are etched with a herd of Jersey cows standing on the deck of a clipper ship heading around the Horn in the nineteenth century. Brave cows, lashed to the mast in a gale.

Cream, eggs, orange juice, and butter are also available, and a milkman with the teeth of a puppy and a black plastic bow tie leaves a pad and pencil for the lady of the house to communicate her wishes.

He visits in the dark, ending his tour of Apache Tears just as the sun begins its rise. Few have seen him, but many lying between dreamtime and waking have heard the gentle rattle of milk bottles being exchanged. This lends them comfort and allows them another few moments of rest.

WELCOME TO APACHE TEARS, the sign says at the edge of town, IF YOU'RE QUIET, YOU'LL NEVER HAVE TO LEAVE. Some believe this motto had its origin when Alfred Hitchcock scouted the town as a location for *Shadow of a Doubt* only to settle on Santa Rosa up north. Others have their doubts.

The town of Apache Tears is entirely self-contained. Along with the dairy, there's the Apache Tears Agricultural Project, the Apache Tears *Clarion,* Apache Tears College, the Apache Tears Bach Society, the Apache Tears Medical Center, and what some consider the crown jewel, the Apache Tears Museum, presided over by the town raptor.

The Museum is at first glance unassuming, kept in a residence on one of the many tree-lined streets. Apparently just another Victorian, one of many on streets past clean, fronted by lawns so green, cut so close, they might have been painted (as Santa Barbarans were forced to do in the years of drought). Water tells the story of much of the West and Apache Tears owes its well-being to an underground river, diverted by means of dynamite and careful planning. This is the edge of the desert after all. Desert scrub, creosote mountains blacken the horizon. Joshua trees stark as a lynched hombre, rattlers that go straight for the nervous system, chasing the victim into unconsciousness.

None see past the danger of the desert into its tender nature. It blooms at its heart.

It surrounds them.

Small black stones mark the town's perimeter.

Perfectly folded newspapers lie each at the same angle on the flagstone walks, while lines of porch swings move gently in the clear morning air. Doors are opened, greetings exchanged, the day has begun.

The town raptor is a woman, a natural-born collector. She has been drawn to collecting since childhood. Of course many children collect, have collected. The usual things: baseball cards, seashells, rocks, bottle caps, dolls from around the world. The raptor stands apart from the usual. Her speciality since childhood has been the possessions of the dead.

And she's a natural.

There is very little gossip in Apache Tears so it's hard to tell where the raptor got her enthusiasm for death, and back issues of the *Clarion* shed no light.

In the depths of her walk-in closets upstairs is an extraordinary array. Clothes of every age, type, but also accouterments, medicaments, passports, cigarette lighters, diaries, tie clasps, canned goods, bridgework, handkerchiefs, watches, eyelash curlers, moisturizers, corkscrews, car keys, bracelets, lockets, stacks and stacks of ticket stubs, bowling shoes, golf balls, catgut rackets.

From the expanse of those closets to the public rooms on the first floor, the heart and soul of the museum, the raptor has proved herself the best at what she does. But who's to compare?

She dresses herself from the upstairs closets and descends to greet visitors at the front door. She is in a way the first exhibit, a taste of what is to come.

One day she may sport the leather jacket of a dead lover, lean on the shooting stick of a departed Jesuit, wear the eyeglasses of a cleaning woman stricken on the job, drape her neck with a locket containing the hair of an infant found in the trash behind the Apache Tears Motel (the *Clarion* reported an outbreak of measles), paint her nails with the savage choice of a long gone (but not forgotten) actress.

She will tell visitors to the museum about the dead she wears that day after a fashion. They expect from her the unexpected, the strange, never knowing who will greet them, interrupting their dailiness. This is prologue.

She will lead them into the public rooms and tell them again how she circumvented everyone, from local police to U.S. Customs, transporting bits and pieces from the burial places of Sumeria and Crete, the graves of Hittites and Etruscans, the inner chambers of Egyptians, and, closer to home, with only reservation cops between her find and her station wagon, the leavings of Hopi and Acoma, bones that sing.

From one wall, in what would be the dining room were this an ordinary place, the feathered burial robe of a Hawai'ian elder threatens flight. Illusion.

In her guide to the collection, the raptor goes into great detail about the process of acquisition. The guide covers everything from the beginning of the raptor's passion, excising childhood. The raptor, whose face is not reflected in the hall mirror, quicksilver worn away in a nun's cell, explains that her mentor was her first and only husband, a necrologist who led her by the hand from her freshman year at Apache Tears College into the days of the dead of the rest of the world.

She left him behind once she was expert, she says, and when she found him pissing into the embalmed mouth of a Javanese princess, which remains unsaid.

The artifacts are confused. Restless.

A Sumerian beanpot intended for the next world is lost in southern California on a shelf at the edge of the desert in a place with its back to the desert, encircled by small black stones.

>   pots   shards   rattles   gourds   urns
>   words   pictograph
>   petroglyph   message
>   code   allusion   poetry   quip   devotion
>   gods they know   gods who make love
>   to them
>   who make fun
>   of them
>   outlines of the ghost-dance on a buckskin shirt
>   dance them into the sea
>   dance them off
>   when grasses are high
>   into the Great Silence.

on a beach thousands of miles away a female is tossed up
slashes across her breast   lines etched by iron
        trace of a braid   face
the sea was not responsible for this   for you
        some someone was   sweetheart
echoes collide in this silence
unheard by the raptor, who looks at these things, strokes
them, relies on their company, but cannot imagine their
awful noise.

Loneliness.

Like the aboriginal child waking at twenty-five to no memory. Is she not fortunate?

Their properties may drift. Cut from their gods as they are, their dreamtime. They may become corrupt. Then what? What may be summoned?

This place is not the toy shop after dark (Toyland, Toyland, wonderful girl-and-boy-land Follow the bouncing ball!), after the Gepetto has gone home and the marionettes and tin soldiers and porcelain ballerinas make merry.

Things linger.

In the back room under lock and key, in the chamber where the raptor works, in what would be the butler's pantry were this an ordinary place, something bobs in a jar of spirits. The liquid turns blood-red as the sun drops.

Outside the town limits, in the desert proper, beyond the stone circle is a settlement known to outsiders as Cactusville.

Cactusville consists of a few motels, a gas station, a taquéria, a convenience store that once had a million-dollar winner. Like the infant found in the Dumpster behind the Apache Tears Motel, a million-dollar winner seemed an anomaly in a dried-up place like Cactusville.

The motels are from the forties, fifties, miniature Mission revival, small adobe rooms facing a central courtyard. The residents of those rooms come from across the border, down Mexico way, and travel to the fields in school buses with portable toilets strapped to the back of the bus.

At the border, behind the streams leading from the *maquilladoras,* there is an outbreak of anencephalic children.

The lottery winner left behind a snapshot, which the convenience store manager displays over the lottery ticket dispenser. He has drawn a jagged outline around her, fixed false roses at each corner, and cut a crescent moon from cardboard that he has placed at her feet. A line of red glasses with white candles stands in front of her, on top of the lottery ticket dispenser, and *milagros* hang like earrings around this apparition of Nuestra Señora de la Lotéria.

Outside the convenience store, out back in the arroyo once coursing with water from underground, where wild grapevines coiled around telegraph poles, a Mojave rattler draws circles in the dust, knowing his protective coloring cannot save him.

Chitra Divakaruni

Clothes

THE WATER OF THE women's lake laps against my breasts, cool, calming. I can feel it beginning to wash the hot nervousness away from my body. The little waves tickle my armpits, make my sari float up around me, wet and yellow, like a sunflower after rain. I close my eyes and smell the sweet brown odor of the *ritha* pulp my friends Deepali and Radha are working into my hair so it will glisten with little lights this evening. They scrub with more vigor than usual and wash it out more carefully, because today is a special day. It is the day of my bride-viewing.

"Ei, Sumita! Mita! Are you deaf?" Radha says. "This is the third time I've asked you the same question."

"Look at her, already dreaming about her husband, and she hasn't even seen him yet!" Deepali jokes. Then she adds, the envy in her voice only half hidden, "Who cares about friends from a little Indian village when you're about to go live in America?"

I want to deny it, to say that I will always love them and all the things we did together through my growing-up years—visiting the *charak* fair where we always ate too many sweets, raiding the neighbor's guava tree summer afternoons while the grown-ups slept, telling fairy tales while we braided each other's hair in elaborate patterns we'd invented. *And she married the handsome prince who took her to his kingdom beyond the seven seas.* But already the activities of our girlhood seem to be far in my past, the colors leached out of them, like old sepia photographs.

45

His name is Somesh Sen, the man who is coming to our house with his parents today and who will be my husband "if I'm lucky enough to be chosen," as my aunt says. He is coming all the way from California. Father showed it to me yesterday, on the metal globe that sits on his desk, a chunky pink wedge on the side of a multicolored slab marked *Untd. Sts. of America.* I touched it and felt the excitement leap all the way up my arm like an electric shock. Then it died away, leaving only a beaten-metal coldness against my fingertips.

For the first time it occurred to me that if things worked out the way everyone was hoping, I'd be going halfway around the world to live with a man I hadn't even met. Would I ever see my parents again? *Don't send me so far away,* I wanted to cry, but of course I didn't. It would be ungrateful. Father had worked so hard to find this match for me. Besides, wasn't it every woman's destiny, as Mother was always telling me, to leave the known for the unknown? She had done it, and her mother before her. *A married woman belongs to her husband, her in-laws.* Hot seeds of tears pricked my eyelids at the unfairness of it.

"Mita Moni, little jewel," Father said, calling me by my childhood name. He put out his hand as though he wanted to touch my face, then let it fall to his side. "He's a good man. Comes from a fine family. He will be kind to you." He was silent for a while. Finally he said, "Come, let me show you the special sari I bought in Calcutta for you to wear at the bride-viewing."

"Are you nervous?" Radha asks as she wraps my hair in a soft cotton towel. Her parents are also trying to arrange a marriage for her. So far three families have come to see her, but no one has chosen her because her skin-color is considered too dark. "Isn't it terrible, not knowing what's going to happen?"

I nod because I don't want to disagree, don't want to make her feel bad by saying that sometimes it's worse when you know what's coming, like I do. I knew it as soon as Father unlocked his mahogany *almirah* and took out the sari.

It was the most expensive sari I had ever seen, and surely the most beautiful. Its body was a pale pink, like the dawn sky over the women's lake. The color of transition. Embroidered all over it were tiny stars made out of real gold *zari* thread.

"Here, hold it," said Father.

The sari was unexpectedly heavy in my hands, silk-slippery, a sari to walk carefully in. A sari that could change one's life. I stood there holding it, wanting to weep. I knew that when I wore it, it would hang in perfect pleats to my feet and shimmer in the light of the evening lamps. It would dazzle Somesh and his parents and they would choose me to be his bride.

When the plane takes off, I try to stay calm, to take deep, slow breaths like Father does when he practices yoga. But my hands clench themselves on to the folds of my sari and when I force them open, after the *fasten seat belt* and *no smoking* signs have blinked off, I see they have left damp blotches on the delicate crushed fabric.

We had some arguments about this sari. I wanted a blue one for the journey, because blue is the color of possibility, the color of the sky through which I would be traveling. But Mother said there must be red in it because red is the color of luck for married women. Finally, Father found one to satisfy us both: midnight-blue with a thin red border the same color as the marriage mark I'm wearing on my forehead.

It is hard for me to think of myself as a married woman. I whisper my new name to myself, Mrs. Sumita Sen, but the syllables rustle uneasily in my mouth like a stiff satin that's never been worn.

Somesh had to leave for America just a week after the wedding. He had to get back to the store, he explained to me. He had promised his partner. The store. It seems more real to me than Somesh—perhaps because I know more about it. It was what we had mostly talked about the night after the wedding, the first night we were together alone. It stayed open twenty-four hours, yes, all night, every night, not like the Indian stores which closed at dinnertime and sometimes in the hottest part of the afternoon. That's why his partner needed him back.

The store was called *7-Eleven*. I thought it a strange name, exotic, risky. All the stores I knew were piously named after gods and goddesses—*Ganesh Sweet House, Lakshmi Vastralaya for fine Saris*—to bring the owners luck.

The store sold all kinds of amazing things—apple juice in cardboard cartons that never leaked; American bread that came in cellophane packages, already cut up; canisters of potato chips, each large grainy flake curved exactly like the next. The large refrigerator with see-through glass doors held beer and wine, which Somesh said were the most popular items.

"That's where the money comes from, especially in the neighborhood where our store is," said Somesh, smiling at the shocked look on my face. (The only places I knew of that sold alcohol were the village toddy shops, "dark, stinking dens of vice," Father called them.) "A lot of Americans drink, you know. It's a part of their culture, not considered immoral, like it is here. And really, there's nothing wrong with it." He touched my lips lightly with his finger. "When you come to California, I'll get you some sweet white wine and you'll see how good it makes you feel...." Now his fingers were stroking my cheeks, my throat, moving downward. I closed my eyes and tried not to jerk away because after all it was my wifely duty.

"It helps if you can think about something else," my friend Madhavi had said when she warned me about what most husbands demanded on the very first night. Two years married, she already had one child and was pregnant with a second one.

I tried to think of the women's lake, the dark cloudy green of the *shapla* leaves that float on the water, but his lips were hot against my skin, his fingers fumbling with buttons, pulling at the cotton night-sari I wore. I couldn't breathe.

"Bite hard on your tongue," Madhavi had advised. "The pain will keep your mind off what's going on down there."

But when I bit down, it hurt so much that I cried out. I couldn't help it although I was ashamed. Somesh lifted his head. I don't know what he saw on my face, but he stopped right away. "Shhh," he said, although I had made myself silent already. "It's OK, we'll wait until you feel like it." I tried to apologize but he smiled it away and started telling me some more about the store.

And that's how it was the rest of the week until he left. We would lie side by side on the big white bridal pillow I had embroidered with a pair of doves for married harmony, and Somesh would describe how the store's front windows were decorated with a flashing neon Dewar's sign and a lighted Budweiser waterfall *this big*. I would watch his hands moving excitedly through the dim air of the bedroom and think that Father had been right, he was a good man, my husband, a kind, patient man. And so handsome, too, I would add, stealing a quick look at the strong curve of his jaw, feeling luckier than I had any right to be.

The night before he left, Somesh confessed that the store wasn't making much money yet. "I'm not worried, I'm sure it soon will," he added, his fingers pleating the edge of my sari. "But I just don't want to give you the wrong impression, don't want you to be disappointed."

In the half dark I could see he had turned toward me. His face, with two vertical lines between the brows, looked young, apprehensive, in need of protection. I'd never seen that on a man's face before. Something rose in me like a wave.

"It's all right," I said, as though to a child, and pulled his head down to my breast. His hair smelled faintly of the American cigarettes he smoked. "I won't be disappointed. I'll help you." And a sudden happiness filled me.

That night I dreamed I was at the store. Soft American music floated in the background as I moved between shelves stocked high with brightly colored cans and elegant-necked bottles, turning their labels carefully to the front, polishing them until they shone.

Now, sitting inside this metal shell that is hurtling through emptiness, I try to remember other things about my husband: how gentle his hands had been, and his lips, surprisingly soft, like a woman's. How I've longed for them through those drawn-out nights while I waited for my visa to arrive. He will be standing at the customs gate, and when I reach him, he will lower his face to mine. We will kiss in front of everyone, not caring, like Americans, then pull back, look each other in the eye, and smile.

But suddenly, as I am thinking this, I realize I cannot recall Somesh's face. I try and try until my head hurts, but I can only visualize the black air swirling outside the plane, too thin for breathing. My own breath grows ragged with panic as I think of it and my mouth fills with sour fluid the way it does just before I throw up.

I grope for something to hold on to, something beautiful and talismanic from my old life. And then I remember. Somewhere down under me, low in the belly of the plane, inside my new brown case which is stacked in the dark with a hundred others, are my saris. Thick Kanjeepuram silks in solid purples and golden yellows, the thin hand-woven cottons of the Bengal countryside, green as a young banana plant, gray as the women's lake on a monsoon morning. Already I can feel my shoulders loosening up, my breath steadying. My wedding Benarasi, flame-orange, with a wide *palloo* of gold-embroidered dancing peacocks. Fold upon fold of Dhakais so fine they can be pulled through a ring. Into each fold my mother has tucked a small sachet of sandalwood powder to protect the saris from the unknown insects of America. Little silk sachets, made from *her* old saris—I can smell their calm fragrance as I watch the American air hostess wheeling the dinner cart toward my seat. It is the smell of my mother's hands.

I know then that everything will be all right. And when the air hostess bends her curly golden head to ask me what I would like to eat, I understand every word in spite of her strange accent and answer her without stumbling even once over the unfamiliar English phrases.

Late at night I stand in front of our bedroom mirror trying on the clothes Somesh has bought for me and smuggled in past his parents. I model each one for him, walking back and forth, clasping my hands behind my head, lips pouted, left hip thrust out just like the models on TV, while he whispers applause. I'm breathless with suppressed laughter (Father and Mother Sen must not hear us) and my cheeks are hot with the delicious excitement of conspiracy. We've stuffed a towel at the bottom of the door so no light will shine through.

I'm wearing a pair of jeans now, marveling at the curves of my hips and thighs, which have always been hidden under the flowing lines of my saris. I love the color, the same pale blue as the *nayantara* flowers that grow in my parents' garden. The solid comforting weight. The jeans come with a close-fitting T-shirt which outlines my breasts.

I scold Somesh to hide my embarrassed pleasure. He shouldn't have been so extravagant. We can't afford it. He just smiles.

The T-shirt is sunrise-orange—the color, I decide, of joy, of my new American life. Across its middle, in large black letters, is written *Great America*. I was sure the letters referred to the country, but Somesh told me it is the name of an amusement park, a place where people go to have fun. I think it a wonderful concept, novel. Above the letters is the picture of a train. Only it's not a train, Somesh tells me, it's a roller coaster. He tries to explain how it moves, the insane speed, the dizzy ground falling away, then gives up. "I'll take you there, Mita sweetheart," he says, "as soon as we move into our own place."

That's our dream (mine more than his, I suspect)—moving out of this two-room apartment where it seems to me if we all breathed in at once, there would be no air left. Where I must cover my head with the edge of my Japan nylon sari (my expensive Indian ones are to be saved for special occasions—trips to the temple, Bengali New Year) and serve tea to the old women that come to visit Mother Sen, where like a good Indian wife I must never address my husband by his name. Where even in our bed we kiss guiltily, uneasily, listening for the giveaway creak of springs. Sometimes I laugh to myself, thinking how ironic it is that after all my fears about America, my life has turned out to be no different from Deepali's or Radha's. But at other times I feel caught in a world where everything is frozen in place, like a scene inside a glass paperweight. It is a world so small that if I were to stretch out my arms, I would touch its cold unyielding edges. I stand inside this glass world, watching helplessly as America rushes by, wanting to scream. Then I'm ashamed. Mita, I tell myself, you're growing westernized. Back home you'd never have felt this way.

We must be patient. I know that. Tactful, loving children. That is the Indian way. "I'm their life," Somesh tells me as we lie beside each other, lazy from lovemaking. He's not boasting, merely stating a fact. "They've always been there when I needed them. I could never abandon them at some old people's home." For a moment I feel rage. You're constantly thinking of them, I want to scream. But what about me? Then I remember my own parents, Mother's hands cool on my sweat-drenched body through nights of fever, Father teaching me to read, his finger moving along the crisp black angles of the alphabet, transforming them magically into things I knew, water, dog, mango tree. I beat back my unreasonable desire and nod agreement.

Somesh has bought me a cream blouse with a long brown skirt. They match beautifully, like the inside and outside of an almond. "For when you begin working," he says. But first he wants me to start college. Get a degree, perhaps in teaching. I picture myself in front of a classroom of girls with blond pigtails and blue uniforms, like a scene out of an English movie I saw long ago in Calcutta. They raise their hands respectfully when I ask a question. "Do you really think I can?" I ask. "Of course," he replies.

I am gratified he has such confidence in me. But I have another plan, a secret that I will divulge to him once we move. What I really want is to work in the store. I want to stand behind the counter in the cream-and-brown skirt set (color of earth, color of seeds) and ring up purchases. The register drawer will glide open. Confident, I will count out green dollars and silver quarters. Gleaming copper pennies. I will dust the jars of gilt-wrapped chocolates on the counter. Will straighten, on the far wall, posters of smiling young men raising their beer mugs to toast scantily clad redheads with huge spiky eyelashes. (I have never visited the store— my in-laws don't consider it proper for a wife—but of course I know exactly what it looks like.) I will charm the customers with my smile, so that they will return again and again just to hear me telling them to have a nice day.

Meanwhile, I will the store to make money for us. Quickly. Because when we move, we'll be paying for two households. But so far it hasn't worked. They're running at a loss, Somesh tells me. They had to let the hired help go. This means most nights Somesh has to take the graveyard shift (that horrible word, like a cold hand up my spine) because his partner refuses to.

"The bastard!" Somesh spat out once. "Just because he put in more money he thinks he can order me around. I'll show him!" I was frightened by the vicious twist of his mouth. Somehow I'd never imagined that he could be angry.

Often Somesh leaves as soon as he has dinner and doesn't get back till after I've made morning tea for Father and Mother Sen. I lie mostly awake those nights, picturing masked intruders crouching in the shadowed back of the store, like I've seen on the police shows that Father Sen sometimes watches. But Somesh insists there's nothing to worry about, they have bars on the windows and a burglar alarm. "And remember," he says, "the extra cash will help us move out that much quicker."

I'm wearing a nightie now, my very first one. It's black and lacy, with a bit of a shine to it, and it glides over my hips to stop outrageously at mid-thigh. My mouth is an O of surprise in the mirror, my legs long and pale and sleek from the hair remover I asked Somesh to buy me last week. The legs of a movie star. Somesh laughs at the look on my face, then says, "You're beautiful." His voice starts a flutter low in my belly.

"Do you really think so," I ask, mostly because I want to hear him say it again. No one has called me beautiful before. My father would have thought it inappropriate, my mother that it would make me vain.

Somesh draws me close. "Very beautiful," he whispers. "The most beautiful woman in the whole world." His eyes are not joking as they usually are. I want to turn off the light, but "Please," he says, "I want to keep seeing your face." His fingers are taking the pins from my hair, undoing my braids. The escaped strands fall on his face like dark rain. We have already decided where we will hide my new American clothes—the jeans and T-shirt camouflaged on a hanger among Somesh's pants, the skirt set and nightie at the bottom of my suitcase, a sandalwood sachet tucked between them, waiting.

I stand in the middle of our empty bedroom, my hair still wet from the purification bath, my back to the stripped bed I can't bear to look at. I hold in my hands the plain white sari I'm supposed to wear. I must hurry. Any minute now there'll be a knock at the door. They are afraid to leave me alone too long, afraid I might do something to myself.

The sari, a thick voile that will bunch around the waist when worn, is borrowed. White. Widow's color, color of endings. I try to tuck it into the top of the petticoat, but my fingers are numb, disobedient. It spills through them and there are waves and waves of white around my feet. I kick out in sudden rage, but the sari is too soft, it gives too easily. I grab up an edge, clamp down with my teeth and pull, feeling a fierce, bitter satisfaction when I hear it rip.

There's a cut, still stinging, on the side of my right arm, halfway to the elbow. It is from the bangle-breaking ceremony. Old Mrs. Ghosh performed the ritual, since she's a widow, too. She took my hands in hers and brought them down hard on the bedpost, so that the glass bangles I was wearing shattered and multicolored shards flew out in every direction. Some landed on the body that was on the bed, covered with a sheet. I can't call it Somesh. He was gone already. She took an edge of the sheet and rubbed the red marriage mark off my forehead. She was crying. All the women in the room were crying except me. I watched them as though from the far end of a tunnel. Their flared nostrils, their red-veined eyes, the runnels of tears, salt-corrosive, down their cheeks.

It happened last night. He was at the store. "It isn't too bad," he would tell me on the days when he was in a good mood. "Not too many customers. I can put up my feet and watch MTV all night. I can sing along with Michael Jackson as loud as I want." He had a good voice, Somesh. Sometimes he would sing softly at night, lying in bed, holding me. Hindi songs of love, *Mere Sapnon Ki Rani,* queen of my dreams. (He would not sing American songs at home out of respect for his parents, who thought they were decadent.) I would feel his warm breath on my hair as I fell asleep.

Someone came into the store last night. He took all the money, even the little rolls of pennies I had helped Somesh make up. Before he left he emptied the bullets from his gun into my husband's chest.

"Only thing is," Somesh would say about the night shifts, "I really miss you. I sit there and think of you asleep in bed. Do you know that when you sleep you make your hands into fists, like a baby? When we move out, will you come along some nights to keep me company?"

My in-laws are good people, kind. They made sure the body was covered before they let me into the room. When someone asked if my hair should be cut off, as they sometimes do with widows back home, they said no. They said I could stay at the apartment with Mrs. Ghosh if I didn't want to go to the crematorium. They asked Dr. Das to give me something to calm me down when I couldn't stop shivering. They didn't say, even once, as people would surely have in the village, that it was my bad luck that brought death to their son so soon after his marriage.

They will probably go back to India now. There's nothing here for them anymore. They will want me to go with them. You're like our daughter, they will say. Your home is with us, for as long as you want. For the rest of your life. *The rest of my life.* I can't think about that yet. It makes me dizzy. Fragments are flying about my head, multicolored and piercing sharp like bits of bangle glass.

I want you to go to college. Choose a career. I stand in front of a classroom of smiling children who love me in my cream-and-brown American dress. A faceless parade straggles across my eyelids: all those customers at the store that I will never meet. The lace nightie, fragrant with sandalwood, waiting in its blackness inside my suitcase. The savings book where we have $3605.33. *Four thousand and we can move out, maybe next month.* The name of the panty hose I'd asked him to buy me for my birthday: sheer golden-beige. His lips, unexpectedly soft, woman-smooth. Elegant-necked wine bottles swept off shelves, shattering on the floor.

I know Somesh would not have tried to stop the gunman. I can picture his silhouette against the lighted Dewar's sign, hands raised. He is trying to find the right expression to put on his face, calm, reassuring, reasonable. *OK, take the money. No, I won't call the police.* His hands tremble just a little. His eyes darken with disbelief as his fingers touch his chest and come away wet.

I yanked away the cover. I had to see. *Great America, a place where people go to have fun.* My breath roller-coasting through my body, my unlived life gathering itself into a scream. I'd expected blood, a lot of blood, the deep red-black of it crusting his chest. But they must have cleaned him up at the hospital. He was dressed in his silk wedding *kurta.* Against its warm ivory his face appeared remote, stern. The musky aroma of his aftershave lotion that someone must have sprinkled on the body. It didn't quite hide that other smell, thin, sour, metallic. The smell of death. The floor shifted under me, tilting like a wave.

I'm lying on the floor now, on the spilled white sari. I feel sleepy. Or perhaps it is some other feeling I don't have a word for. The sari is seductive-soft, drawing me into its folds.

Sometimes, bathing at the lake, I would move away from my friends, their endless chatter. I'd swim toward the middle of the water with a lazy backstroke, gazing at the sky, its enormous blueness drawing me up until I felt weightless and dizzy. Once in a while there would be a plane, a small silver needle drawn through the clouds, in and out, until it disappeared. Sometimes the thought came to me, as I floated in the middle of the lake with the sun beating down on my closed eyelids, that it would be so easy to let go, to drop into the dim brown world of mud, of water weeds fine as hair.

Once I almost did it. I curled my body inward, tight as a fist, and felt it start to sink. The sun grew pale and shapeless; the water, suddenly cold, licked at the insides of my ears in welcome. But in the end I couldn't.

They are knocking on the door now, calling my name. I push myself off the floor, my body almost too heavy to lift up, as when one climbs out after a long swim. I'm surprised at how vividly it comes to me, this memory I haven't called up in years: the desperate flailing of arms and legs as I fought my way upward; the press of the water on me, heavy as terror; the wild animal trapped inside my chest, clawing at my lungs. The day returning to me as searing air, the way I drew it in, in, in, as though I would never have enough of it.

That's when I know I cannot go back. I don't know yet how I'll manage, here in this new, dangerous land. I only know I must. Because all over India, at this very moment, widows in white saris are bowing their veiled heads, serving tea to in-laws. Doves with cut-off wings.

I am standing in front of the mirror now, gathering up the sari. I tuck in the ripped end so it lies next to my skin, my secret. I make myself think of the store, although it hurts. Inside the refrigerated unit, blue milk cartons neatly lined up by Somesh's hands. The exotic smell of Hills Brothers coffee brewed black and strong, the glisten of sugar-glazed donuts nestled in tissue. The neon Budweiser emblem winking on and off like a risky invitation.

I straighten my shoulders and stand taller, take a deep breath. Air fills me—the same air that traveled through Somesh's lungs a little while ago. The thought is like an unexpected, intimate gift. I tilt my chin, readying myself for the arguments of the coming weeks, the remonstrations. In the mirror a woman holds my gaze, her eyes apprehensive yet steady. She wears a blouse and skirt the color of almonds.

Judith Freeman

The Rake People

NEAR MY HOUSE THERE'S an empty lot where, twice a year, according to city ordinance, the weeds are cut by a crew of Mexican men who work without interruption from the time the sun rises until it sets. The earth always looks damaged to me when they're finished. The green lot becomes brown and bare. It's too bad everything has to go like that, the wild poppies and morning glories and other plants whose names I don't know. They just come and chop things down and pass armfuls of vines and branches to each other. One man stands by a truck and throws the cuttings onto the bed. Another man stands in the truck and jumps up and down on the pile to pack it down and make room for more. These men don't work too fast, but they have a lazy, constant way of moving. They swing machetes, bend and lift, rake up cuttings into piles, moving slowly as if all their lives they've worked hard in the sun, pacing themselves throughout the day, in order to reserve energy for their other, better lives, which begin in the evening.

When I woke up this morning and looked outside and saw the men working, once again it reminded me of another time when we lived on a narrow street in a canyon on the outskirts of Beverly Hills, in a neighborhood where everyone had a gardener. On Tuesdays and Fridays, the days which, for whatever reasons, the gardeners preferred to work, the sound of their rakes carried from yard to yard. Worse, those portable machines that blow leaves and dirt from patios started up early in the morning and sounded like chain saws.

There were so many gardeners working at the same time that their noises mingled all day, and it sometimes seemed like they were the only people you saw walking around outside. Everyone else stayed in their air-conditioned houses, or else got into their cars and immediately drove away.

We, too, had a gardener, since neither my wife nor I had time to take care of the place ourselves. His name was Lupe Batista, and he came with the house when we bought it. In other words, he had worked for the former owner and, out of convenience, we chose to keep him on. He arrived and left while I was at work, on Tuesdays and Fridays, so I never had much contact with him, or reason to think one way or another of him, until something happened one spring and we had to let him go. Or maybe he let us go, since the circumstances are somewhat complicated.

It began on a morning in April. My wife, Pat, stood at the sink looking out the window at Lupe working in the garden. Our dog, Elmo, had his nose pressed against the screen door. He was also watching Lupe, and barking with a grim persistence.

"Why do you think Elmo dislikes Lupe so much?" Pat said. "He doesn't dislike anybody and suddenly he's got this thing about Lupe. I don't understand it."

It did seem mysterious, the way the dog had turned against the gardener. I'd noticed it, too. Even the sound of a rake in another part of the neighborhood was enough to cause him to jump up and rush to the door barking.

"It's gotten so he goes crazy every time he hears a rake," Pat said. "Maybe Lupe hit him once, or poked him with his rake."

In truth, I found it sort of amusing. Elmo was a rather sedentary old Labrador retriever. His new quirk animated him.

"What is it, Elmo?" I said, looking into his large, knowing eyes. "Is it the rake people, huh? An attack of the rake people?" Elmo, his hair standing up along his back in a fluffy ridge, cocked his head and pressed his ears forward. Sometimes he gave me such intelligent looks I expected him to speak. I liked Elmo, though he wasn't my dog, he was Pat's. She had had him when I met her eight years earlier. People were always surprised to learn Elmo was twelve years old. He didn't look it, because he'd had a good life. We had a large fenced-in yard, and there was a hole in the fence that gave him access to the hills. At night, when coyotes howled, Elmo listened with an intense and distant look on his face. Deer came down regularly to eat the roses, and raccoons traversed a path that cut across the corner of our garden. All this was fine with Elmo. He sensed in this urban world a distinct trace of the natural order that preceded the more recent residents, who drove Mercedes and lived in houses on stilts, cantilevered over the chaparral. Each night, when the coyotes howled, he traveled a road back to the beginning, and sent up his own primordial cries.

But the barking, the hostility toward the gardener, was something recent and quite inexplicable. Armies of the rake people seemed to trouble him in some way that nothing else did.

I confess, I liked egging him on. "You're doing a splendid, absolutely splendid job, Elmo," I said. "Those rake people have been warned. They'd be fools to come closer."

Elmo barked even louder.

"Don't aggravate him, Russ," Pat said, trying to pull him away from the door. Elmo didn't wear a collar because Pat thought they were too restrictive, so it was difficult at times to get him to move.

"Alarm! Alarm! Elmo sounds the alarm!"

"I wish you'd cut it out, Russ," she said. We both looked out at Lupe to see if he'd noticed the racket, but he raked around the lemon tree, seemingly unconcerned, moving with that purposeful slowness that was characteristic of him.

"Honey," Pat said suddenly, "I didn't tell you this, but Lupe tried to kiss me last week."

"What do you mean he tried to kiss you?"

"Don't talk so loud, Russ, he'll hear us." She closed the door and sat down across the table from me. She told me that on Tuesday, while Lupe was working on the patio, she went out to ask him to cut the camellias back. His children were with him, the twin boys who sometimes came along when he worked. She asked him why the kids weren't in school. He said they were too young, but Pat knew they were beyond school age. She told him they really ought to be in school, but he just smiled at her and shrugged.

"In truth, I don't even know whether they let children like that go to school," she said. "I mean children of illegals."

"I don't know either," I said, wishing she'd get on with her story.

The day was warm, she said, and she felt like getting some sun, so she changed into a bathing suit and went outside. She offered Lupe a beer and gave the kids colas. They helped her clean out the fish pond, catching the goldfish with a kitchen strainer and transferring them to a pan while she hosed down the cement basin and refilled it with water. All the time they were cleaning the pond, the kids seemed happy, and Lupe worked nearby. She said she felt him watching her but she didn't think anything about it. Then she went inside to get him a check. When she came out, he was rolling up the hose. She handed him the check, and he reached out and took her hand. She regarded it as a gesture of gratitude, and squeezed it and said, "Yes, you're welcome." It happened at that moment. He reached up and put his hand on the back of her neck and pulled her face toward him. It was so sudden, and she didn't know how to react, but before he could put his lips on hers, she pulled back and said, "No."

"What happened then?"

"Nothing happened. I went inside."

"You didn't say anything to him?"

"No. I was so surprised. What could I say? I just went inside."

Weeks went by. I didn't know what to think of Pat's story about Lupe trying to kiss her, but in time, we began to treat it as a joke. Actually, I was increasingly troubled by it. Could this have happened, I wondered, the way Pat said it did? Pat told the story to a few people. Everyone agreed it was pretty ridiculous, the gardener making a pass at her. At dinner one night, someone said, "It's just like Constance and the gamekeeper," and everyone laughed.

At least I thought I understood Elmo's animosity now. It seemed clear he was defending Pat. Through a system of signals and sympathies long established between them, they had an emotional connection. Obviously, Elmo had picked up on the situation.

Some mornings now, on Tuesdays and Fridays when Lupe was due for work, I delayed leaving the house in order to study him. I looked at him quite differently. I saw that he was about my age, maybe thirty-five—perhaps forty—but he was in much better shape. He always turned up in jeans and wore a clean, white T-shirt, tucked in. In fact, I realized he was quite handsome, though small in build. I was aware of his trim middle because that's where I'd recently put on weight and the first place I looked whenever I glanced into a mirror. Whenever I spoke to him, it wasn't clear how much English he really understood, but it seemed pretty limited. His manner was polite, but our few exchanges were vague and artificial. He seemed to prefer not to look at me when we spoke. He was mysterious to me. I didn't feel I could know him. As time went on, I wondered more and more what his life was like.

I began paying more attention to news reports that contained information on illegal aliens. In one month forty thousand Mexicans were arrested at the border and sent back. The border patrol wore helmets and masks with infrared lenses that made them look like creatures from space. A sweatshop was raided in East Los Angeles and the women, herded against a wall, were shown with their hands on top of their heads. In another report, it was disclosed that a motel in the Valley called The Snooty Fox was being used by the Immigration and Naturalization Service as a temporary detention center for illegals who were awaiting hearings. The detainees were shown on the nightly news sitting around the swimming pool, looking sullen and detached from their surroundings. The Snooty Fox had been enclosed by a chain-link fence.

Another evening, on the six o'clock news, I learned that more business licenses were issued to gardeners in Beverly Hills than to anyone else. There could be as many as ten thousand gardeners in the city, but the number was uncertain, since many gardeners were illegals who didn't bother applying for licenses. The average pay per household was sixty dollars a month, a rate that ensured that nearly everyone could afford a gardener, and thus could be said to have at least one servant. However, police had recently become suspicious that burglars were posing as gardeners, cruising the streets of Beverly Hills in trucks laden with rakes and lawn mowers, staking out houses to rob. As a result, spot checks were being initiated. Deportations were certain to result. During the following weeks, while driving home from work I several times saw police who had pulled a truck over and were questioning the driver, who was always Mexican or Central American.

Lupe's truck broke down one morning. He used the phone to call his cousin, but couldn't reach anyone. "Don't you have triple A?" Pat asked. I hooked jumper cables to the Mercedes and tried to get his truck started, but no luck. In the end, I gave him a ride to his apartment, and he came back later to get his truck. He lived in a pretty rough-looking neighborhood over near Sunset and Echo Park, in a building that was very run-down.

Pat's friend Marilyn took to calling and when I answered, would say to me, "Hi, darling, is Constance there?" It was going too far, but I really didn't know how to stop it. I felt maybe I ought to fire Lupe, but I couldn't bring myself to do it. I suppose I had to admit that I still wasn't sure he was the one at fault, or what had really happened.

Then something interesting happened. Elmo had a change of heart. He suddenly took a liking to Lupe and began following him around while he worked, begging him to play with the ball he carried in his mouth. What's more, it was clear Lupe liked the dog. I felt it as an alienation of affection.

One day when I was home alone, down with the flu, I watched Lupe and Elmo from a place where I couldn't be seen. They had become absolutely buddy-buddy. Whenever Lupe stopped work for a moment, he scratched Elmo's head or threw his ball for him. In response, Elmo licked his hands enthusiastically. Since I was certain Elmo's feelings were a barometer of Pat's, I began to wonder, what did this mean?

I grew increasingly certain that Pat had been unfaithful to me, not necessarily with Lupe, but with someone, perhaps the house painter, a Greek with whom she had developed a friendship that lasted until he moved back to Ithaca. There was no evidence, only the fact that he'd called her frequently at night. Was my wife really true to me? In the past, we had talked about fidelity, but only in general terms. We had talked about it as if we were in a position to make policies for others, instead of holding the policies ourselves. A terrible jealousy began building in me. Sometimes I sat and thought, What's happening here?

"Do you want to pick up a lemon tree and plant it this week?" Pat asked Lupe. They stood just outside the door to my study, near the camellias. On that day, I suppose you could have said I was eavesdropping. Once again I had stayed home from work. This time it was an ear complaint.

"OK," said Lupe.

"All right then," she said. "Do you want the money now?"

"OK," he said again.

"Bring me a receipt," she said, "and I'll reimburse you."

Looking at his face, it was clear to me he didn't understand words like receipt and reimburse, but Pat didn't notice this.

"By the way," she said, touching his arm as he turned to go, "the roses look great. You've done a wonderful job with them. They've never bloomed like this before."

Later, Lupe's twin boys ran past the window while we were eating lunch and looked in at us. Pat waved at them.

"Do you know the boys' names?" I asked her.

"Hmmm," she said, thoughtful for a moment. "One of them is Manny, I think."

That night Elmo, who must have gotten out sometime during the afternoon, didn't come home. The next morning we noticed his absence and began looking for him. By night, he still hadn't returned, and Pat was in a terrible state.

"That damned dog," she said when we were in bed. Then she began to cry.

"He's never gone this long."

"Maybe after twelve years he deserves a night out."

"I can't joke, Russ. If anything happened to him, I don't know what I'd do."

The next morning, Sissy, who lived across from us, heard us calling around the neighborhood for Elmo and stopped us in the street. She said she thought she had seen Elmo in the back of our gardener's truck the day before yesterday. She couldn't be certain, she said, because he was driving pretty fast. But she thought it was Elmo she saw in Lupe's truck.

We didn't have a telephone number for Lupe, but of course I knew where he lived since I'd driven him home that time.

"What can we do but go over there?" Pat said.

I thought Sissy was mistaken. I didn't think Lupe had Elmo, and I told her that.

"But what can it hurt to just go over there and talk to him?" Pat asked.

The door to Lupe's apartment was covered with little paste-on stickers, goofy cartoon characters, Penzoil labels, trading stamps, even Chiquita banana logos. A girl of about twenty answered the door. "No here," she said when I asked for Lupe and she started to close the door, but Pat stopped her.

"Could you tell us where to find him, or when he'll be back?"

"No speak English."

"Does anybody speak English?"

The girl shook her head. Another woman, older, perhaps Lupe's mother (certainly not his wife?), came to the door and spoke rapidly to the girl. Then they just looked at us, silent and unsmiling.

"What about the twins?" Pat said to me. "Wait, don't let them close the door, let me get the twins." The twins, whom we had seen playing in a vacant lot next to the apartment when we first drove up, did speak some English, and Pat was certain they could help us.

"Just a minute," I said to the older woman, who regarded me impassively, but I felt her calm looks concealed an edgy traffic between fear and contempt. I tried to introduce myself and said that Lupe worked for us.

"No comprendo," she said.

Pat returned with the boys. "Is this your mother?" she asked.

"She my aunt."

"Tell her we need to find your daddy."

"He's in Mexico," one of the boys said.

"Where in Mexico?"

Before he could answer, the older woman spoke to the boys rapidly, as if scolding them, and they answered at length.

"Where in Mexico?" Pat said again. She took a few bills from her purse. "Where?" she said, showing them the money. "We owe him money," she said. "We're going down there on a vacation, we want to see him." Pat smiled. Pat laughed. Pat made it seem we wanted suggestions for tours of the old country. I couldn't believe it. I couldn't get over how effective, and determined, she was.

By the time we left, Pat, who had become persistent to the point of obnoxiousness, had bullied the woman into telling her the name of a café in Ensenada where we might find Lupe.

"Oh, God," she said, once we were in the car again, "I don't know what's going on. I don't know why Lupe would do this. We've got to go to Ensenada, Russ."

"We don't even know if he has Elmo. You didn't even ask them that."

"I couldn't ask them. They'd have never told us anything if they thought we suspected him."

"It's too convoluted," I said. "This is crazy."

"Revenge. Maybe he took him to get back at me for rejecting him. But it's so cruel. He wouldn't be that cruel, would he? What did we ever do to him except give him a job?"

"Yes, we're exemplary employers, cream of the crop."

"We've got to go to Ensenada, Russ."

"Look," I said wearily, "give it one more day. If Elmo isn't back by tomorrow night, we'll think about going to Mexico."

"We won't think about it, Russ. We'll just do it."

Elmo didn't show up, and two days later, Pat started packing. We were going to Mexico.

I didn't really want to go. When it came right down to it, I was a big chicken. I had no faith in the theory that Lupe had taken Elmo, but if he had, I didn't believe we would ever find him, and if we did find him with Lupe, I envisioned trouble, which is how it all came down to me being a chicken. I realized this. Little Russell Grover, the perpetual chicken, the fraidy-cat, no-dukes Grover, who, as he grew up, gave anybody anything he wanted as long as he agreed not to harm him. I didn't want to go to Mexico to get into a fight with somebody over a dog I didn't think he'd taken. But Pat had crawled right up to the brink of hysteria and was peering over the edge and the only way I could see getting her to back away was to make this last ditch effort to locate what was ours. We would fling ourselves over the border, drop some cash in the corrupted economy created by tourist-gringos, and fetch back some cheap tequila or tin trinkets to remind ourselves that we had tried, by God we'd tried, to find what we loved.

"Did you leave Sissy a key?" Pat asked while we were loading the car. I assured her I had. Sissy was to put Elmo in the house if he returned while we were gone.

"Keep the cooler out in case we want a beer," she said. Even in these tumultuous times, she thought of comfort, providing sandwiches and beer, magazines and tanning lotion, protective hats and sunglasses, and a dozen different tapes for the car stereo. We took off amid this panoply of middle-class props as if setting out on vacation, except our moods were subdued instead of festive.

The freeway from Los Angeles to San Diego is remarkable for its passage through industrial pallor, a gray, unspeakably fouled landscape at the edge of the City of Angels, which dissolves, the farther south you go, into the sublime green of golf courses and meticulously planned dream communities, homogeneous boxes creeping over hill and dale. I drove. Pat slept in the seat beside me. Just before Laguna, I took an exit, remembering a road that cut through the low green hills and dropped down toward the coastline.

With the green hills as a backdrop, the drive seemed suddenly much nicer. I began to feel better just looking at trees and rocks and the sky. We came out onto the highway that ran along the ocean, where it was possible to appreciate just how beautiful California really can be. Later, in trying to cut back to the freeway, I somehow took a wrong road, which came to a dead end in a college parking lot. Pat woke up.

"Where are we?"

"I got off the freeway for a while. Frankly, we're lost. I took a wrong turn."

"I need to get out and stretch my legs anyway," she said.

Just beyond the parking lot lay the college's experimental agricultural station. Above a ribbon of stream, a large barn sat atop a hill, surrounded by corrals filled with animals. As we walked toward the stream Pat commented on how funny it felt to be taking a walk without Elmo there with us. We'd always taken walks because of him, it was true. Without either of us mentioning it, we realized at that moment how much of a triumvirate we were, a fact made clear by his absence. You can't understand loss until something's gone and then there's the mortifying realization that you might never see it again. You don't know the truth of this until you've lived with someone, even an animal, for so long that his daily sounds have infiltrated your thinking to the point that a precise presence, thick and rich, is created out of the absence of those sounds. So it was with Elmo, who could announce himself in so many ways: a door creaking, the clanging of a metal tag against a metal dish, lapping at the toilet, the muffled gathering of a throw rug into a nest, or a clack—distant yet growing—of toenails approaching across the wooden floor.

Pat picked up a stick and threw it into the stream cutting through the bottom of the ravine. The sheep, who were grazing in a pen opposite us, looked up, startled, and held their breathless pose.

As if reading my mind, she said, "When I go into a room, I expect to find him there. Even though he isn't, it's almost as if he is there."

Trees, their buds formed into perfect conical shapes, gave off a pleasantly pungent smell. We walked down into the ravine, stepped on stones to cross the stream, and climbed up the other side. Elmo, had he been there, would have been up the hill before us. I believed he was dead. I didn't know what had happened, but I thought, he is gone. Suddenly I felt this weariness and I just wanted to tell Pat about it. It wasn't Elmo I was thinking about then, but fidelity. Somehow I made that switch from one thing to another, so smoothly. I was sick of living in the clutter of our age. Just because we lived in the 1980s didn't mean we had to act like it. What I really wanted to talk to her about was love.

We walked up to the corrals and Pat put out her hand and flattened it, trying to get the attention of a big brown horse.

"I feel like we might just get lucky and find Elmo," she said. When I didn't respond, she looked up at me. "You don't think we're going to find him with Lupe, do you?"

"I don't know."

"I don't think I did anything to make Lupe think I'd want him to kiss me."

"No?"

"Maybe I handled it wrong, though. Someone else might have reacted differently."

"It's no use imagining how Katharine Hepburn would have handled the situation," I said.

"But there's a point you're missing," I added, "and that is, Lupe may be our gardener but he's also just another guy."

"What do you mean, he's just another guy?"

"All this stuff is going back and forth between men and women all the time. Men make passes or women flirt, or the other way around. There's this big area of activity, you know, where people test things. The real question is, Are you settled, or are you looking? I thought we should try being monogamous but I don't think you're finding it too easy."

"You're so moral, Russ, you know where it all begins and ends. You know where chaos stops and order begins. You know at which point something that isn't possible becomes possible."

"What's not possible? What are you talking about? It's not so difficult, Pat. All I'm wondering about now is whether we're faithful to each other, whether we have been and if we can be from now on. Do you think it's important we're faithful to each other?"

There was a long pause, and then she said, "Do you believe me about Lupe?" I told her I thought I did. "Then why bring this up now?"

"Because it matters to me, the fidelity. I'm very corny about it. I want you, that's the point. Nobody else. Nobody gets you either. Isn't that crazy? You look at me like I'm crazy, but that's what I want."

A truck came down the road and the driver slowed down to look at us. When he'd gone, I continued.

"You just resist me on this," I said. "You won't give in."

Pat frowned. "What makes you think I haven't already given in?"

"Have you?"

"You want me to say it your way, spell it out for you, take away all your uncertainties. You don't have to ask for this kind of reassurance all the time."

"Just tell me."

"An old schoolteacher of mine," Pat said, "a woman who was in her eighties the last time I saw her, had one of the best marriages I'd ever seen. She loved her husband so much it wasn't funny, right up to the day he died. When she spoke about him, it was all still there, all that love and passion. And devotion. But she once said to me, 'I felt conquered by my husband. I told him once, "How does it feel to be the victor?"'"

What was I supposed to think of this? There was a long silence while I tried to figure out what Pat meant by telling this story.

"We should go," she said, and turned and strode away.

Walking back to the car, I realized I hadn't said everything I wanted to, but the moment had passed. I wanted to tell her that in the whole terrifying length of a life—terrifying because of its shortness—I sensed that the only true available solace came through sincere devotion to another human being. Did this imply conquest? I thought not. Rather, within a transitory arrangement of elements, a fixed harmonious union was the means through which chaos became order. It was the point at which you found a location.

In Tijuana, we stopped briefly to buy *galletitas* at a bakery, then drove on through the dusk, as the light faltering over the ocean and land gave way broadly across the surface of things, until we found a motel on the coast, a few miles north of Ensenada. In the morning, after a breakfast on the terrace, we drove into town. It took us most of the morning to locate the restaurant where the twins had told us we might find Lupe. It was not in the main part of town that appealed to the tourists, but on one of the dirt roads that radiated out from the paved streets, where buildings were thrown together out of patchwork lumber, and a thick layer of dust covered every-thing. The restaurant had a piece of billboard for a door. Inside, a ceiling fan turned but barely stirred the air. In the corner, on an overturned wooden crate, stood a big jar filled with milky liquid. The place smelled of chili, roasted meat, and steaming beans. No one was in the restaurant except the cook, a boy who looked no older than twenty. Pat asked him if he knew Lupe Batista. He did-n't readily understand her, but Pat repeated his name, then wrote it out for him, persistent, until the cook, now definite in his manner, shook his head and went back to work. He gave her an uninter-ested look when she tried to talk to him again, but Pat was unfazed. However, finally she turned away.

"It's still early," she said to me. "Let's try later."

We drove back into town and sat for a while on the steps of a wide, sun-filled plaza, then walked to the pier, where, at the edge of the water, in a shed that served as a fish market, men were cleaning their catch. The rough, fish-bloodied men looked Pat up and down as we walked the length of the shed. Coming out into the sunlight, I took her hand, and walking along, with our hands clasped and held high as though we were dancing, I felt something ceremonial in our atti-tude, and I finally remembered what it reminded me of—a scene in a Yugoslavian film I once saw, where the bride and groom, their hands clasped in just this way, came slowly toward a wedding altar.

"What are you doing?" she said.

"What?"

"You've got hold of my hand like you were presenting me at auction."

"Actually, I was thinking of a film where a couple are walking toward an altar."

"Well, there you have it," she said.

I looked down, saddened.

She touched my face. "Russ," she said. "Lighten up," and she jiggled my arm, and lifted our hands a little higher.

We returned to the restaurant, and the first thing we saw as we came around the comer was Elmo, lying on his back, all four feet up, warming his stomach just in front of the door.

"My God," Pat said, and jumped out of the car as soon as I'd stopped. Elmo greeted us in a faltering manner, as if he were having déjà vu and trying to recall where he'd seen us before. The door to the restaurant was open, and I saw Lupe, sitting at a table with three other men. Pat, who was bent over Elmo, patting his muzzle and kissing his head, didn't see Lupe. "Let's go," I said. But at that moment, she stood up and saw Lupe in the restaurant and walked right in before I could stop her.

She said, "Why did you take him? We trusted you." Lupe said nothing. He didn't look at either one of us. The fan overhead turned uselessly. I ought to be helpful, I thought, I should set something straight here. But I felt afraid to say anything.

Elmo had followed us into the restaurant and gone over to Lupe. Lupe picked up a scrap of meat, ignoring Pat, who stood very close to him, and gave it to Elmo. The thing about Elmo was, he made friends very easily where there were prospects of a meal. One of the men at the table said, "Hey, Alamo," and dropped a tortilla on the floor for him.

Alamo? Did they really think his name was Alamo instead of Elmo, or was this their way of making a little joke? Lupe still didn't look at us, but tipped a full glass of the milky liquid up to his lips and swallowed it all down. It was a strangely obscene gesture to me. Then he put his plate on the floor for Elmo to lick.

The guy across from Lupe said, *"Qué quieren?"*

"Quieren su perro viejo."

"Se lo llevaron?"

"No, no me lo lleve."

The same guy turned to Pat and said, "Nice dog, lady."

I don't know why it happened then, but I felt I really had to say something. I said to Lupe, "You know, only a real jerk would steal a dog." He looked up at me.

"I mean, why did you do it? It's totally crazy to take some-body's dog like that."

He stared at me and shrugged his shoulders, his lips curling into a grin of dismissal, as if he couldn't care less that he'd caused us some little inconvenience.

"Take your damned dog," he said to me, and then looked at his companions and jerked his head toward the door. He looked at me again. I stared at him. I can't say what passed between us at that moment, but I knew it was only between us, that he had cut Pat out of everything, that he'd managed to avoid even acknowledging her presence and that he would continue to do so, dealing only with me. In truth, I felt calm for the first time in a while. I'd spo-ken up and nothing terrible had happened.

"Don't come around again," Pat told Lupe. "Not ever. I'll land your ass in jail if I ever see you in our neighborhood." Her voice was hard and firm. He still did not look at her. I didn't know whether she got this or not, how completely she was being ignored.

We tried to leave then, but Elmo, who seemed caught up in divided loyalties, wouldn't follow us when we called to him, and he even resisted, as he had always done, any attempt to force him to move. Lupe stood up. He gave Elmo a pat on his haunches on the way out. Each of the men, as he filed past us, said, "Adios, Alamo," and once outside, we heard them laughing as they walked down the street.

At the border, we were stopped because we didn't have the proper papers for Elmo. We needed something certifying that he'd had a rabies vaccination. Over and over again, to one official after another, Pat tried to explain the situation. Our dog was stolen by an illegal alien. We'd come down to get it back. We hadn't thought about papers. Couldn't they understand this? The officials peered into the car. They looked at Elmo, who placidly gazed back at them. They looked me over. They studied Pat. They seemed to think there was something we were hiding, some truth we hadn't told. At one point, we had to open the trunk so they could search inside. They turned their flashlights onto the backseat and they looked in the glove compartment. Pat, who became more and more outraged by their behavior, scolded them for not showing us more sympathy. Finally, perhaps convinced of our innocence, or perhaps because they'd exhausted their authority or just grown tired of us, they let us cross over the border, and, under a moonless sky, with music filling the car and Elmo nestled on the seat between us, we drove toward home, a triumvirate, somehow miraculously restored.

Dagoberto Gilb

Photographs Near a Rolls Royce

AT NIGHT, STANDING IN THE middle of the street in front of the building I call home, I can see into another apartment, through its smearless picture window, a chandelier sparkling above a grand piano and men with crystal goblets stirring with white wine. If I turn around and look into the apartments facing that one, I see, between the louvers of another kind of glass, other men playing poker under a bare kitchen light, drinking Bud in the can, listening to Radio Trece-La Mejicana. From where I stand, the calm blend of Pedro Infante and Mozart is strange, though it still remains true that the Mercedes and Cadillacs are the ones parked in the garages, while the Chevys and Fords of the sixties and early seventies squeeze into the open spaces on the street.

We live on the east side of our complex, which seems right since the tenant next to us is a nervous type involved with the business, which is to say the film industry, and his apartment, a mirror ditto of ours without the furnishings, is westside luxurious. We're decorated by the working class, though I've been unemployed for quite some time, a state of today's economy which I try to make the best of since it does offer its pleasures—every morning I pour some extra water through our Mr. Coffee for another cup to read the sports section with. I go over every word of it now, every detail about the Lakers, struggling this year after their championship last season, about the Dodgers' possible trades and the new kids from

75

Albuquerque and San Antonio and Garvey's new team and Cey's bitterness, Fernando's million-dollar screwball. I don't care much about the new spring-to-summer football league, about who thinks Larry Bird might be better than Magic Johnson (no way), but unemployment means I have time to read about the Angels, who I didn't care much about before. I also go through the "Style" section, which is about movies and movie stars and television, and I tell Gloria if the TV critic says there's going to be something good on that night. I read the rock critic too, since I like to know what music to hate and why, and so that even if we don't ever go out, which we don't, I feel like I'm still hip to the L.A. music scene.

After the paper and the coffee I invariably look out the window and into Ralph's window across the way. Ralph is my oldest son David's friend. David's almost five, Ralph's eight, nine or ten—we don't know which because he's given each as his true age. He and his older brother and his mother live in an apartment situated on the hill like us, though in a newer building with stucco and sheetrock, not the hard, textured plaster, inside and out, that was common in the less prefab days of construction that designed our building. Each apartment has one exceptionally large window in the dining area which face each other, and both large curtains are usually open to the daylight, and because of that we've come to know of each other from the distance as we share meals at our separate tables. Ralph and his brother like to wave, and David waves back. Sometimes, from the decks in front of the windows, they yell at each other across the lot that divides us—an ivy-covered piece of the hill that makes the decks, both old, not the safest place for kids to play since the fall is a good fifteen to twenty feet. There's an ugly little building at the bottom of the hill where the ivy ends, and we both can see a corner of its green tarpapered roof, and from our windows we view each other's lives through the right triangle of smoggy air that butts into that ivied soil, and then through those glass windows. It's more than enough distance to keep adults from knowing each other through words and conversation.

Yet Ralph and David became friends, despite the difference in ages. We don't know why, and we stopped asking. Ralph is a well-mannered boy and he likes to play with David. David also has plenty of toys, and Ralph doesn't. We aren't rich, even when I'm employed, and have never been, but Ralph is poor. His mother takes a bus to her fulltime job at the downtown Burger King, and his father is still in Nicaragua. His older brother is fourteen, likes the Dodgers and has talked to Pedro Guerrero twice when he came across him in the neighborhood streets, where he spends most of his out-of-school time. Ralph is alone a lot, a circumstance that resembled my own so much that when he started coming around everyday after school, or earlier if he didn't go, which he often doesn't, we opened the door and the boys would play until an hour after sunset, or later if the lights in his apartment were still not on, usually until his brother came for him.

Ralph and my son played so well together that Ralph started to feel like family, so we fed him and took him on little trips—making sure he called his mother and got permission—to the zoo, to Hollywood Boulevard, to Olvera Street for a sentimental festival, to Griffith Park. He's run errands for us, and when Gloria's gone to the store he's walked back carrying a grocery bag. For Christmas we decided to buy him one of those small footballs with an L.A. Raiders decal on it. It cost two dollars for one and three for two. We gave the other one to David. We think it might have been the only present Ralph got besides the very small plastic replica of E.T. his mother gave him. He wasn't only surprised when we gave him the package from under our Christmas tree, he was utterly grateful, with expressions that Hallmark makes its living on. I'd been thinking about taking him to see the movie *E.T.* since he hadn't seen it yet, but we had all seen it, and that money buys some food. I wanted to take him though, and I promised myself I would.

We always talk about going out, though neither of us waxes nostalgic about all the times we went out before marriage and children, when we were a mere couple who often did nightclubs, which is where we met. We hit it off so well because we both liked the same rock'n'roll, restaurants, and movies. Later, both of us agreed that we'd traveled here to meet each other, that Los Angeles had been cold and fake until it became the L.A. of lights and dance and sun-shine. We made love, but we weren't from here—eventually David was born and we were married.

David was two when we moved back out here. We wanted to stay in New Mexico, where Gloria's parents live, but the money just wasn't there, and I was doing okay when we lived here before. I thought, we thought, that this would be the best place for us.

Like I said, we haven't gone out since we've been here. Not alone, only the two of us. It's hard for us to find a babysitter. We've moved three times and we don't know many people, especially ones that are married with children. A girl down the street has babysat after school, when Gloria had to go to the doctor, but she can't at night. We hate to ask the neighbors because we don't know them that well. And now our youngest is only six months, and that's a hard age for someone who's not family to take care of, even for a few hours.

But we made an attempt after this one morning. I'd read the rock section in the paper, and the critic was raving about Saturday night at the Club Lingerie when the best bands from East L.A. would be doing a two-set performance. The East Side Review, he said, would feature the hottest music in L.A. at the moment, like Los Lobos, and from the past, like Cannibal and the Headhunters. I wanted to go, and so did Gloria. We ran over as many options as we could—like asking that teenage girl's mother, or the neighbor who just got back from Mexico, with much immigration difficulty, who might need a few extra dollars. When we thought of Ralph's moth-er, it was only a question of how many hours.

It should be said that Gloria wasn't as confident as I was that she'd agree to it. Ralph's mother was obviously not simple. She liked to drink and dance, and we've seen her a few times moving inside her apartment to loud rumbas and later outside on her deck with a boyfriend. She's a big, tall woman, hefty, strong looking, and dark, very dark, like Ralph. Her hair is tinted red, for what looks like fun. But she's also timid, and the two times she came near our door for Ralph, she never got next to it or knocked when it was closed. She only called his name, and not too loudly, definitely not with anger, just meekly matter-of-fact. The time Gloria went with her and Ralph and David for a Christmas show in school—Ralph was in it, and asked several times that we all go, please. I said no thanks, while Gloria thought the invitation was too cute to be turned down—she told me that they barely talked and that Ralph's mother seemed to want to stay secretive about herself and even her country. The little they did say to one another, which came out strained and brief, was about Gloria's New Mexico, how each of them liked it in Los Angeles, and how well Rafael—it was Ralph who wanted to be known as Ralph—was doing and how fast he was learning English, whereas she didn't think she ever would. We thought that that had been the reason she was shy, that we speak English in our home, unlike our parents, but after Gloria was with her that night she came away thinking it was something else, though she had no idea what it might be. Through Ralph, we gave her pictures Gloria took at the Christmas show. Later, when Ralph let it be known that the pictures weren't, in his words, bright enough, we decided that this is what made the world go round.

Still she was the clear first choice for babysitter, though we both wanted her to agree to it only if she really didn't mind, and really did not. Gloria went over to ask, not plead, and to allow her any easy way out. If she accepted, then she was to understand that we would pay. It would be her decision where.

I wasn't surprised that she said yes, but I wanted to celebrate. That she might be a little later than seven—we decided that from then to the Cinderella hour would be the best we could get, and enough—was nothing important. And Gloria said the woman seemed honestly willing, not the least bothered. She even said that it was the best Saturday for her because she wasn't going out dancing. And she would stay at our place, with Ralph, which meant David would be happy. So we were out the door—Where would we eat? What kind of food? God, a night *out*—and parking our Chevy Nova on Sunset Boulevard, between the Berwin Music Complex and Maxim, where a red carpet exits the entrance of the restaurant and crosses the sidewalk and ends at a curb where patrons get out and let valets do the parking. We were getting out of our car to buy advance tickets for the show. I even brought my camera—the day felt eventful—and I told Gloria to stand in front of the ivory Rolls Royce we parked right ahead of. David sat on a bumper, and Gloria held the baby and I shot two angles hurriedly, stealthily, afraid someone would suspect me of stealing something from the car. I was glad we posed so fast too because not a moment after I took the second picture a beautiful woman in a pink and white cashmere outfit rushed from the building and into the Rolls like she was afraid fans would torment her if she didn't. Stevie Nicks? Kim Carnes? We were excited and the first to buy tickets, and I took a photograph inside of the bar of the empty Club Lingerie like I was a photo artist.

The next day I told Gloria that she could buy some new rags if she wanted, that we should go for broke and have a night of it. I somehow felt like it might be our last of this kind, I don't know why. She said no and I didn't argue. We made plans so that it would work out just right. Gloria taught herself to express milk from her breasts with one of those pumps and she worked at it hours to get a large bottle full. She bathed the baby and David and went to the laundromat and washed clothes. She ironed her best pants and blouse and polished some stylish boots. She washed her hair and set it while I cleaned the house, vacuumed, emptied trash, washed dishes, and put all the children's toys away. It even seemed like fun.

I worried about how much to pay Ralph's mother. The going rate would have been about seven or eight dollars for five hours; ten would be good. But three an hour was below minimum wage to my mind. Would she think we were insulting her if we paid the rate, patronizing if we paid too much? She would be in our home, which has furniture. Gloria told me they had very little. What would she think of these pochos going to dinner and a nightclub while she, who's older than us and works with teenagers for the same money, watches the kids with all the toys she can't afford to give her children? I asked Gloria, but I decided, despite her reasoning, to give Ralph's mother fifteen bucks before we left because I'd feel better if she thought I was a big spender, however right or stupid it might seem.

When I went to the store to buy beer and some soda and potato chips so everybody could party while we were, I ran into Roberto, who I worked with at a job about a year previously. Roberto is from Salvador, is ten years older than me, is very religious, and enjoys drinking beer, so I bought an extra six-pack of Bud. He'd been working on his car, already drinking some, and we sat on the curb by his car and near his place and started talking about the times. He wasn't working either, but he wasn't collecting any unemployment. He was in a mood that I wasn't. From the street I could hear a 76ers–Celtics basketball game on someone's nearby television and I was with it until I cracked my third beer when I realized how much he'd been talking and I hadn't. I guess they aren't the best of times, I told him, not good at these things. He was still going on, telling me about how he got here and how hard it was for him to leave his country and that they'd killed his brother and his brother's family and they were after him. The mierdas were everywhere, both sides are filled with mierdas, he said, shits who will kill for all the good and bad reasons in the world. There is no meat without blood, he said, but why the blood of children?

Well I'd heard this before from him and gotten mad along with him, but this time it hurt. I felt bad for having listened to the game, for sitting on the curb unemployed, drinking beer. I've worked for a living, when I could, when it was there. I don't like being unemployed, and I didn't decide where I was born. So I told him we were going out tonight, Gloria and I. I felt American about it. I made myself sound sincere and deserving, determined to live the life I understood.

Though I'd changed my mood some when I got home, Gloria's peaceful happiness made me hold back. She was writing out a list of things to tell Ralph's mother—where the diapers were, the baby's milk and water, the food for them, the toys, the names and phone numbers of the places we'd be, to let David go to bed whenever he wanted. I went to our bedroom and looked around. I wanted to put things away since I knew Ralph's mother would take a tour. Anybody would. I hid some cash that I had in a top dresser drawer in a bottom one, under clothes, not because I didn't trust her, only because I don't trust anybody. I don't know. I took down our miniature El Salvador Libre flag—we went to this demonstration in MacArthur Park right after I met Roberto—and I slipped it under the clothes and on top of the money. I didn't want to wage an ideological war in my home with someone I don't know or haven't talked to, and one time Ralph told me his father was in prison back in Nicaragua, that he was a bodyguard in Managua for the president. Ralph has told us many things that conflict with one another, and for a while he told us that his father lived right there with him. If his mother's husband had been with Somoza, though we knew she had her boyfriends here, I believed the least I could do was not possibly antagonize the woman who was going to care for our children that night.

We were ready at six-thirty. Everybody was dressed and David was satisfied with Ralph coming over. I counted the dollars in my jeans and made sure the tickets were in my pocket and said what I said, that the show started at eight-thirty. We figured to be home by eleven-thirty. I turned on the television to kill time, and I had the curtains open at seven so I could watch over at Ralph's for the lights. I asked Gloria several times whether or not Ralph's mother said she got off work at seven or got home around seven. We watched the national news, which not inappropriately had a feature about the Central American countries in turmoil and how all this might affect the United States.

At seven-thirty I decided to go out and bring back some food. The important thing was to get to hear the music and have a couple of drinks, for Gloria to get away from the baby for a few hours. I could see Gloria wasn't taking it too well and I insisted that she not give the baby milk from the bottle to see how he liked it that way. I drove over to this new restaurant across the street from the grocery store. I drank a beer while I waited and ate the warmed chips the owner offered me. I was trying to figure out if I should go to the show by myself. I was mad that we were so dependent on a stranger, that we didn't have a string of friends and acquaintances like on TV shows, or family like at home. I started thinking about being unemployed.

I could see from my car driving back that the lights at Ralph's apartment still weren't on. It was eight o'clock. Gloria suggested at the dinner table that I go sell the tickets. I said we should all go. She said she wanted to wait. I waited too.

I think it was pretty stupid and impractical of me not to sell those tickets. Money is money. Anyway, somehow, I figure we had a good time preparing for our night out. It made some average days more interesting, and I got two decent photographs of Gloria and my boys next to a Rolls Royce. The other one didn't come out.

That night, at about ten, Ralph had dropped by looking for his mother and seemed surprised that she wasn't with us. We didn't understand what that was all about either and chose to wait and let the explanation come without questioning. It didn't and hasn't yet, already months later.

There were some changes for a while. Ralph didn't come around and for weeks the curtains stayed closed at his place. We talked about whether or not we were mad at Ralph's mother. We really weren't—we don't even know her—although Gloria still thinks she should have known better. I guess for the first week I expected her to apologize or at least send Ralph over to. I did get angry at Ralph one day when we passed him playing in the street with some friends. He was ignoring us, so I asked him if he didn't know how to say hello or what. The next day he came by. At first we had mixed feelings about his visiting again. But we fought it off. Ralph and David are little kids.

Ralph doesn't drop over quite as often as he used to though, and sometimes when he does it's at late hours and we send him home, wondering if he thinks we're getting back at his mother through him because he acts so hurt. We're not. It's just that nobody ever comes to take him home like before.

I put that flag back. From now on I leave it where it is until I don't want it there at all. You can never be sure what people think and I've learned that there's no point in hiding what you believe to be true. I also start a job tomorrow and I hope it lasts. Today I brewed more coffee and then melted some chocolate in it. My feeling is that the Lakers are better than the 76ers, that the Dodgers are going to do fine without Garvey or Cey. I'd rather think about these things when I look through that wedge of L.A. air that distances us from Ralph and his mother's apartment.

Gerald Haslam

Condor Dreams

STANDING WITH HIS NEARLY empty coffee cup in one hand, Dan gazed into tule fog dense as oatmeal. It obscured the boundary between sky and earth, between breath and wind, and he was momentarily uncertain where or what he was. He could see nothing. He could not be seen. This must be what nothingness is, he thought, what extinction is…like what's happened to the condors. Then he chuckled at himself: Don't lose it, pal. Don't lose it. Stress will do that to you.

He rubbed his chest where it was again tightening. This field is real and those critters are gone, as defunct as family farmers soon will be. As I'll be, Dan thought. His chuckle turned grim.

Nearly fifty years before, on a morning as sunny and clear as this one was foggy and obscure, he had stood next to his father in this same field and seen for the first time a wonder soaring high above—a vast black shape like death itself. Frightened, he moved closer to his father. Then he noticed the bird's bare head and its vast wings. Those dark sails were cored with white, their farthest feathers spread like fingers grasping sky. It appeared to belong to another, sterner time.

"Look, Daniel," his father said, "that's a California condor. See, its wings, they never move. It rides the wind."

"It rides the wind? How, Papa?"

"Ahhh…it is just a wind rider, I guess."

"Can I be one?"

"Only in your dreams, Daniel."

"Where did he come from, Papa?" Dan asked.

His father pointed southeast, where the Tehachapi Mountains loomed, where mysterious canyons slashed into them. "There," he explained. "They live where men can't. Years ago, when I come here from the old country, those condors they'd fly out here over the valley every spring to eat winter kills. Sometimes fifty or sixty of 'em. Sometimes maybe a hundred. You could hear their beaks clicking. Now, only four or five ever come."

"Why, Papa?"

"Why?" His father had migrated here from the Azores and worked for other people until he could buy a patch of worn-out range, which he'd then turned into this farm. "I don't know," he finally replied. "Things they changed, eh? Maybe some ranchers they shoot 'em 'cause they think those condors take calves...or for the fun of it. Maybe there's not so much for 'em to eat no more. All I ever seen 'em eat is winter kills. I don't know..." His voice trailed off, and he seemed genuinely puzzled. A few years later, the boy's father had been a winter kill, drowned by a freak flood pouring from one of those mountain canyons.

Just a few days before his father's death, the two of them had stood on the edge of this very field and spied a dot high against the mountains. They leaned on their shovels and watched it grow larger, closer, since by then appearances of condors over the valley had become rare indeed. A young heifer had died and, as was his habit, his father had left the carcass next to the reservoir, and a cluster of buzzards busied themselves cleaning it up.

Neither man said anything and they stood waiting. Perhaps the great condor might strip this heifer's bones. As though tantalizing them, it approached slowly, so slowly, its white-splotched wings tipping, never pumping, as it sailed far above, then began to swing lower, its great shadow sliding over these acres. Finally, the antique flier swooped down from the wind, and the smaller, squabbling birds quickly bounced away and scrambled into the sky. As the condor began to feed, father and son turned and smiled at one another; they were gazing at a California older than memory.

Dan stood now on the land his family had reclaimed, and he could not see the sky because of the fog that had risen, as it so often did following rains, obscuring nearly everything. If the condors were out there anymore, they were as hidden as other people's dreams. If they were there. Crazy thoughts.

He walked up one long row, grapevines staked on both sides of him, their bare branches trained on wires. Normally the campesinos would be pruning them now, but not this year. Not any year, perhaps. Dan had grown up working these fields that his father and uncle had originally cleared and plowed, that his brothers and sisters and he had irrigated and cultivated and reaped. Now a bank would take it all, the land and the memories. It was grinding to accept. One part of him wanted to weep, another wanted vengeance. He wandered the field now because he could not bring himself to tell Mary everything he had heard the day before at the bank. It was the first significant thing he had ever withheld from her, and that too compounded his tension. Thank God the kids were grown.

He stopped, far from house or road, surrounded by the gray-velvet haze, and listened closely. He had heard a voice. Then he realized it was his own, arguing with himself. That's what this was doing to him, driving him nuts. It would take nearly $300,000 to convert his fields to profitable crops now that table grapes with seeds no longer sold well, but five consecutive losing years had so eroded his credit that he could not raise that kind of backing. His note was due and the once friendly banker demanded payment.

Dan tilted his face skyward and stared into the colorless miasma surrounding him, wanting to scream like a dying animal. Were there condors left up there? Would they come clean his bones? He trudged back toward the house to give his wife the bad news.

The next morning, they sat at the dinette table sipping coffee and gazing out the window at fog as soft as kittens' fur. "Another cold one," he sighed, meaningless talk to fill the silence.

"Why don't you start the pruning?" his wife asked. "It's not like you to give up."

"What's the point?" His voice edged toward anger, for he'd sensed reproach even before she spoke. She didn't understand. This land was his body, and now it would be torn from him. Her way was to stay busy; when her mother'd died, Mary had cooked for three days. But you can't stay busy when your land, your flesh, is being devoured like so much carrion. She didn't understand that.

No, Dan simply wanted revenge. But on whom? The banker who had urged him to expand and had staked him for so many years? The public that ate only Thompson seedless grapes and Perlettes? The county agriculture agent who hadn't warned him about changing tastes? Who?

There was the sharp sound of a car door slamming, then a light knock at the kitchen door. It was 6:45 a.m., and the two glanced at each other across the table before Dan stood and strode to the door.

"Buenos días, Señor Silva," said the old man who stood there, battered five-gallon hat in hand. *"Estoy aquí para trabajar."* His chin was not quite half shaven, and his faded jeans were only partly buttoned.

"Come on in, Don Felipe," Dan smiled. "You want coffee?"

"Sí, por favor."

"Como? Americano o Mexicano?" It was an old joke between them.

"Solo Mexicano, por favor." The grin was nearly toothless.

Despite the gentle humor, here was one more problem. Felipe Ramirez had been working on this land as long as Dan could remember. His father had originally employed the old man years before. Despite his name and fluent Spanish, he was more than half Yokuts—local Indian. In his prime he had been a vaquero in those far away condor mountains. Dan had always liked him, with his strange but amusing yarns, his unabashed belief in the supernatural—which he said *was* natural.

The old man now lived with a niece in Bakersfield, and Dan annually hired him to help prune grapevines, then kept him on over the summer as a general helper. He was a link to the past, to Dan's own father. Don Felipe remained a strong worker, but his peculiar tales—amusing during good times—would be a burden now.

At the table, Don Felipe bowed to Mary, who smiled and greeted him. He seated himself and accepted a steaming mug of coffee into which he spooned a great mound of sugar. Their conversation was, as always, conducted in two languages, a comfortable weaving of Spanish and English. "Where are the others?" asked the old man.

Dan was suddenly embarrassed. "We haven't begun pruning yet."

"It is too wet?"

"No."

There was a long silence, for the old man would not ask why. It was not his way to probe. "It will be a fine growing year," he finally observed, "all this rain. In my dream, the great green gods were touching you."

"It could be a good year," Dan responded.

"Tell him," said Mary. Her husband briefly glared at her. This was difficult enough without being rushed. She had never understood how men speak to one another...or don't speak to one another about some things.

Again there was silence. The old man did not appear anxious. "Would you like some tobacco?" he asked, extending his pouch of Bull Durham.

"No thanks."

Don Felipe knew Mary did not smoke, so no tobacco was offered her. Instead, he rolled a drooping cigarette, carefully twisting both ends. "Do you no longer wish to employ me, Daniel?" He pronounced the name "Don-yale."

"We are losing our ranch, Don Felipe. A bank will take it. But I want you to work with me because there are still some things to be done."

"I am your servant."

"Just take it easy today. Tomorrow I'll have a list of jobs."

"As you wish, Daniel."

Two hours later, a brisk wind broke from the mountains and cleared the fog. Dan emerged from the barn when he heard its swift whine, and walked into cold sunlight, then noted on what they called the old section a lone figure among the vines. What the hell? He strode to the place where Don Felipe pruned grapes.

"Why are you doing this?" he asked, almost demanded, for this land would soon no longer be his, and to work it was suddenly a personal offense. He had not even told Mary that it was rumored the bank would subdivide ranchettes here, a prospect too painful for words.

"It must be done."

"Don't you understand, I won't own this land much longer. I won't harvest grapes this year."

"Daniel," the old man said in a tone Dan had heard before, "no one owns the land. The earth must be nurtured, never owned. Your father knew that and you, deep within, you know that too. It is like a woman, to be loved but never owned. It is not an empty thing but full of life. And these vines are our children."

"Tell the bank that," Dan spat.

"They will build no houses here."

"Houses? Who won't?"

"The bank will build no houses here."

"Of course not. Who said they would?" How had the old man guessed that?

A smile lit the leathery face and the eyes rolled skyward. "Your father started here with only eighty acres, true?"

"Yes."

"How many do you plant now?"

"About thirteen hundred. Why?"

"I am pruning the old eighty acres. You must save them. No houses here, Daniel."

This conversation was crazy. He didn't need it; he had problems enough. "I'm saving all of it or none of it," he snapped. His chest began tightening as he fought rage. Why didn't the old man sense the trouble he was causing? Dan was tempted to call Don Felipe's niece and have her come back for him.

Wind was picking up, blowing north from the distant mountains, and dust was beginning to pepper them. The old man removed a thong from one pocket, wrapped it over his sombrero, and tied it under his chin. "It is the dust of the condors," he said, squinting toward the peaks and canyons to the south. "They will protect this land."

"The condors are dead."

The old man's eyes seemed to crackle for a second, then he smiled. "No, not all of them."

"I'll need some condors, or buzzards maybe, when the bank is through with me."

"The condors, my son, are not mere carrion birds. They bring life from death. They renew, that is why their dust is a good sign. It will be a good year."

"For the bank," Dan said, and he turned toward the house.

That night he could not relax. In the cusp between sleep and wakefulness near dawn, he saw the earth rupture and a gray flatus ooze out, then a great inky bird seemed to swim from it while he struggled to find light...find light. He awoke, his breast tight, and immediately stared out the window: Heavy fog pressed against the glass, the world rendered low-contrast and colorless. He couldn't even see the land he was about to lose, and the compression in his chest and jaw were edging toward pain.

He rose quietly, but Mary stirred. "Getting up?" she asked drowsily.

"Yeah." He headed for the bathroom, where he gulped two antacid tablets, then pulled on his jeans and boots, shrugged on a shirt, and finally washed up. In the kitchen, he started coffee, one hand holding his aching breast, then put on his hat and walked out the back door to smell the morning fog.

As he stood in that near-darkness, he heard—or thought he heard—an irregular clicking. Condors? Condors' beaks? For a moment he was puzzled, rubbing his chest, then realized what it had to be: someone was pruning grapes.

On the old field, he confronted Don Felipe. "Why are you doing this? I'm going to lose the ranch, don't you understand?"

The leathery face smiled, and the old man, still bent with pruning shears in one hand, replied, "When I was a young man, I worked with an old Indian named Castro on the Tejon Ranch in those mountains. He was what you call it? a...a wizard, maybe, or a...a medicine man. He could do many strange things. He could turn a snake by looking at it. One time I saw him touch a wolf that had killed some sheep and the wolf understood; it never came back. No horse ever bucked him.

"That guy, one time he told me that this life we think is real isn't real at all. He said we live only in the dreams of condors. He said that us Indians were condors' good dreams, and you pale people were their nightmares." The old man smiled, then he continued, "He said we can live only if those birds dream of us."

Dan didn't need this nonsense. "Condors are extinct," he pointed out. He was sure he'd read that in the newspaper.

The old man only grinned. "Then how are we talking? We are still here, Daniel, so the condors cannot be gone. You are still here." The old man paused, then added, "I think that guy he *was* a condor."

Too much, this was just too damned much. He would have to call Don Felipe's niece as soon as he returned to the house. He just didn't need this mumbo jumbo on top of the distress he was already suffering. "Why do you think that?" the younger man snapped.

"Because one day he flew away up a canyon into the heart of the mountains, and we never saw him again. He said that if the condors disappeared, so would their dreams. That's what that old Indian told me."

"Right," said the despondent farmer, turning away. Why couldn't this old man understand? Why couldn't he deal with reality? Dan was becoming agitated enough to fire Don Felipe on the spot.

Before he could speak, though, the pain surged from his chest into his arm and jaw. "Listen...," he began, but did not finish, for breath left him. "Listen...," he croaked just before he swayed to the damp soil.

"Daniel!" Don Felipe cried. He knelt, and his hard old hands, like talons, touched the fallen man's face. Dan was straining to speak when he sensed the fog beginning to swirl and vaguely saw the old man's body begin to deepen and darken and oscillate. A shadowy shape suddenly surged and a liquid wing swelled beneath Dan, lofting him from his pain.

A startled moment later, he hovered above a great gray organism that sent misty tendrils into nearby canyons and arroyos, that moved within itself and stretched as far north into the great valley as his vision could reach. It was...all...so...beautiful, and his anxiety drained as he skimmed wind far above the fog, far beyond it, as he rode his own returning breath, and below the mist began clearing. His fields focused as the earth-cloud thinned. The land too was breathing, he suddenly realized, its colors as iridescent as sunlight on the wings of condors. It was all so alluring that he stretched a hand to touch...touch...it.

"Dan," Mary's voice startled him, "are you all right?" She cradled his head in her hands and her own face was tight with fear.

It was like waking from his deepest dream but, after a second of confusion, he managed a smile. "I'm okay." An edge of breathlessness remained, that and pain's shadow, so he hesitated before, with her help, climbing to his feet. Past his wife's shoulder he saw the old man, whose dark eyes merged momentarily with his. "I just let tension get to me," he explained. Rising, he brushed wet earth from his jeans. "I'll drive into town and see the doc just in case."

The easy tone of his voice seemed to reassure his wife. "Let's go have our coffee," she urged.

"Sure," he replied, putting an arm around her waist, his relief at being able to touch her as tangible as breath itself, then turning toward the old man. "Don Felipe, are you coming in?"

"I must finish the field."

"Okay," Dan replied, "I'll bring something out, and I'll give you a hand when I get back from the doctor's." This place, even eighty acres of it, was worth saving. There had to be a way.

"I will be grateful," the old man nodded.

After Dan and Mary turned, they could hear Don Felipe's shears clicking like a condor's beak. Arm in arm, they walked toward home. The fog had dissipated enough so that their house shone sharp and white across the field of dormant vines. Behind it, bordering the hazy valley, those mountains, the Tehachapis, bulked like the land's surging muscles: creased and burnished and darkened with bursts of oaks and pines, flexing into silent summits and deep canyons where valley winds were born, into the hidden heart of the range where Dan now knew a secret condor still dreamed.

Mark Helprin

The Pacific

THIS WAS PROBABLY THE last place in the world for a factory. There were pine-covered hills and windy bluffs stopped still in a wavelike roll down to the Pacific, groves of fragrant trees with clay-red trunks and soft greenery that made a white sound in the wind, and a chain of boiling, fuming coves and bays in which the water— when it was not rocketing foam—was a miracle of glassy curves in cold blue or opalescent turquoise, depending upon the season, and depending upon the light.

A dirt road went through the town and followed the sea from point to point as if it had been made for the naturalists who had come before the war to watch the seals, sea otters, and fleets of whales passing offshore. It took three or four opportunities to travel into the hills and run through long valleys onto a series of flat mesas as large as battlefields, which for a hundred years had been a perfect place for raising horses. And horses still pressed up against the fences or stood in family groupings in golden pastures as if there were no such thing as time, and as if many of the boys who had ridden them had never grown up and had never left. At least a dozen fishing boats had once bobbed at the pier and ridden the horizon, but they had been turned into minesweepers and sent to Pearl Harbor, San Diego, and the Aleutians.

The factory itself, a long low building in which more than five hundred women and several hundred men made aircraft instruments, had been built in two months, along with a forty-mile railroad spur that had been laid down to connect it to the Union Pacific main line. In this part of the state the railroad had been used heavily only during the harvests and was usually rusty for the rest of the year. Now even the spur was gleaming and weedless, and small steam engines pulling several freight cars shuttled back and forth, their hammerlike exhalations silencing the cicadas, breaking up perfect afternoons, and shattering perfect nights.

The main halls and outbuildings were only a mile from the sea but were placed in such a way, taking up almost all of the level ground on the floor of a wide ravine, that they were out of the line of fire of naval guns. And because they were situated in a narrow trench between hills, they were protected from bombing.

"But what about landings?" a woman had asked an Army officer who had been brought very early one morning to urge the night shift to maintain the blackout and keep silent about their work. Just after dawn the entire shift had finished up and gathered on the railroad siding.

"Who's speaking, please?" the officer had asked, unable to see in the dim light who was putting the question.

"Do you want my name?" she asked back in surprise. She had not intended to say anything, and now everyone was listening to her.

Nor had the officer intended to ask her name. "Sure," he answered. "You're from the South."

"That's right," she said. "South Carolina. My name is Paulette Ferry."

"What do you do?"

"I'm a precision welder."

That she should have the word *precision* in her title seemed just. She was neat, handsome, and delicate. Every gesture seemed well considered. Her hands were small—hardly welder's hands, even those of a precision welder.

"You don't have to worry about troop landings," the officer said. "It's too far for the Japanese to come in a ship small enough to slip through our seaward defenses, and it's too far for airplanes, too."

He put his hands up to shield his eyes. The sun was rising, and as its rays found bright paths between the firs, he was blinded. "The only danger here is sabotage. Three or four men could hike in with a few satchels of explosive and do a lot of damage. But the sea is clear. Japanese submarines just don't have the range, and the Navy's out there, though you seldom see it. If you lived in San Francisco or San Diego, believe me, you'd see it. The harbors are choked with warships."

Then the meeting dissolved, because the officer was eager to move on. He had to drive to Bakersfield and speak at two more factories, both of which were more vulnerable and more important than this one. And this place was so out of the way and so beautiful that it seemed to have nothing to do with the war.

Before her husband left for the South Pacific, he and Paulette had found a place for her to live, a small house above the ocean, on a cliff, looking out, where it seemed that nothing would be between them but the air over the water.

Though warships were not visible off the coast, she could see from her windows the freighters that moved silently within the naval cordon. Sometimes one of these ships would defy the blackout and become a castle of lights that glided on the horizon like a skater with a torch.

"Paulette," he had said, when he was still in training at Parris Island, "after the war's over, everything's going to be different. When I get back—if I get back," he added, because he knew that not all Marine lieutenants were going to make it home—"I want to go to California. The light there is supposed to be extraordinary. I've heard that because of the light, living there is like living in a dream. I want to be in a place like that—not so much as a reward for seeing it through, but because we will already have been so disconnected from everything we know. Do you understand?"

She had understood, and she had come quickly to a passionate agreement about California, swept into it not only by the logic and the hope but by the way he had looked at her when he had said "—if I get back." For he thought truly nothing was as beautiful as Paulette in a storm, riding above it smoothly, just about to break, quivering, but never breaking.

When he was shifted from South Carolina to the Marine base at Twentynine Palms, they had their chance to go to California, and she rode out with him on the train. Rather than have them suffer the whole trip in a Pullman with stiff green curtains, her parents had paid for a compartment. Ever since Lee had been inducted, both sets of parents had fallen into a steady devotion. It seemed as if they would not be satisfied until they had given all their attention and everything they had to their children. Packages arrived almost daily for Paulette. War bonds accumulated for the baby that did not yet exist. Paulette's father, a schoolteacher, was a good carpenter, and he had vowed that when Lee got back, if they wanted him to, he would come out to California to help with his own hands in building them a house. Their parents were getting old. They moved and talked slowly now, but they were ferociously determined to protect their children, and though they could do little more than book railway compartments and buy war bonds, they did whatever they could, hoping that it would somehow keep Lee alive and prevent Paulette from becoming a widow at the age of twenty-six.

For three nearly speechless days in early September, the Marine lieutenant and his young wife stared out the open window of their compartment as they crossed the country in perfect weather and north light. Magnificent thunderstorms would close on the train like Indian riders and then withdraw in favor of the clear. Oceans of wheat, the deserts, and the sky were gold, white, and infinitely blue, blue. And at night, as the train charged across the empty prairie, its spotlight flashing against the tracks that lay far ahead of it straight and true, the stars hung close and bright. Stunned by the beauty of all this, Paulette and Lee were intent upon remembering, because they wanted what they saw to give them strength, and because they knew that should things not turn out the way they wanted, this would have to have been enough.

Distant whirlwinds and dust storms, mountain rivers leaping coolly against the sides of their courses, four-hundred-mile straightaways, fifty-mile bends, massive canyons and defiles, still forests, and glowing lakes calmed them and set them up for their first view of

with manage their books.

Optimization: realistic in world of alpha extraction
market input — biggest hurdle.
multiple forecasts ⇒ target? Market signals so large
Input ⇒ large Tilt? Yes but most in large
India: regn — w/ their books   for high conviction
Final Scale — computer — divisi (Optimized)   high Req.

_____

Works w/ managers + lots of $\underline{data\ sets}$
Don't think of earnings as part of
Dynamic mix; earnings, events, P

_____

Implicit price target
detection work on a timescale.   Commits to regret
                        ⎰ positive
                        ⎱ press

_____

Very process driven — cleaner data can
do more w/ quant.

the Pacific's easy waves rolling onto the deserted beaches south of Los Angeles.

Paulette lived in a small white cottage that was next to an orange grove, and worked for six months on instrumentation for P-38s. The factory was a mile away, and to get to it, she had to go through the ranks of trees. Lee thought that this might be dangerous, until one morning he accompanied her and was amazed to see several thousand women walking silently through the orange grove on their way to and from factories that worked around the clock.

Though Lee had more leave than he would have had as an enlisted man, he didn't have much, and the occasional weekends, odd days, and one or two weeks when he came home during the half year at Twentynine Palms were as tightly packed as stage plays. At the beginning of each furlough the many hours ahead (they always broke the time into hours) seemed like great riches. But as the hours passed and only a few remained, Lee no less than Paulette would feel that they would soon be parting as if never to be reunited. He was stationed only a few hours away and they knew that he would try to be back in two weeks, but they knew as well that someday he would leave for the Pacific.

When his orders finally came, he had ten days before he went overseas, and when Paulette came home from work the evening of the first day and saw him sitting on the porch, she was able to tell just by looking at him that he was going. She cried for half an hour, but then he was able to comfort her by saying that though it did not seem right or natural that they should be put to this kind of test in their middle twenties, everyone in the world had to face death and separation sometime, and it was finally what they would have to endure anyway.

On his last leave they took the train north and then hitchhiked forty miles to the coast to look at a town and at a new factory to which Lockheed was shifting employees from its plants in Los Angeles. At first Paulette had refused to move there, despite an offer of more money and a housing allowance, because it was too far from Twentynine Palms. But now that Lee was on his way overseas, it seemed perfect. Here she would wait, she would dream of his return, and she would work so hard that, indirectly, she might help to bring him back.

This town, isolated at the foot of hills that fronted the sea, this out-of-the-way group of houses with its factory that would vanish when the war was over, seemed like the proper place for her to hold her ground in full view of the abyss. After he had been gone for two or three weeks, she packed her belongings and moved up there, and though she was sad to give up her twice-daily walks through the orange groves with the thousands of other women, who appeared among the trees as if by magic, she wanted to be in the little house that overlooked the Pacific, so that nothing would be between them but the air over the water.

To withstand gravitational forces as fighter planes rose, banked, and dived, and to remain intact over the vibrations of 2,000-horsepower engines, buffeting crosswinds, rapid-fire cannon, and rough landings, aircraft instruments had spot welds wherever possible rather than screws or rivets. Each instrument might require as many as several hundred welds, and the factory was in full production of a dozen different mechanisms: altimeters, air-speed indicators, fuel gauges, attitude indicators, counters, timers, compasses, gyroscopes— all those things that would measure and confine objective forces and put them, like weapons, in the hands of the fighter pilots who attacked fortified islands and fought high over empty seas.

On fifteen production lines, depending upon the instrument in manufacture, the course of construction was interspersed with anywhere from twenty to forty welders. Amidst the welders were machine-tool operators, inspectors, assemblers, and supervisors. Because each man or woman had to have a lot of room in which to keep parts, tools, and the work itself as it came down the line, and because the ravine and, therefore, the building were narrow, the lines stretched for a quarter of a mile.

Welders' light is almost pure. Despite the spectral differences between the various techniques, the flash of any one of them gives rise to illusions of depth and dimension. No gaudy showers of dancing sparks fall as with a cutting torch, and no beams break through the darkness to carry the eye on a wave of blue. One sees only points of light so faithful and pure that they seem to race into themselves. The silvery whiteness is like the imagined birth of stars or souls. Though each flash is beautiful and stretches out time, it seldom lasts long. For despite the magnetizing brightness, or perhaps because of it, the flash is born to fade. Still, the sharp burst of light is a brave and wonderful thing that makes observers count the seconds and cheer it on.

From her station on the altimeter line, Paulette could see over gray steel tables down the length of the shed. Of the four hundred electric arc or gas-welding torches in operation, the number lighted varied at any one time from twenty or thirty to almost all of them. As each welder pulled down her mask, bent over as if in a dive, and squeezed the lever on her torch, the pattern of the lights emerged, and it was never the same twice. Through the dark glass of the face plate the flames in the distance were like a spectacular convocation of fireflies on a hot, moonless night. With the mask up, the plane of the work table looked like the floor of the universe, the smoky place where stars were born. All the lights, even those that were distant, commanded attention and assaulted the senses—by the score, by the hundreds.

Directly across from Paulette was a woman whose job was to make oxyacetylene welds on the outer cases of the altimeters. The cases were finished, and then carried by trolley to the end of the line, where they would be hooded over the instruments themselves. Paulette, who worked with an electric arc, never tired of watching this woman adjust her torch. When she lit it, the flame was white inside but surrounded by a yellow envelope that sent up twisting columns of smoke. Then she changed the mixture and a plug of intense white appeared at the end of the torch, in the center of a small orange flare. When finally she got her neutral flame—with a tighter white plug, a colorless core, and a sapphire-blue casing—she lowered her mask and bent over the work.

Paulette had many things to do on one altimeter. She had to attach all the brass, copper, and aluminum alloy parts to the steel superstructure of the instrument. She had to use several kinds of flux; she had to assemble and brace the components; and she had to jump from one operation to the other in just the right order, because if she did not, pieces due for insertion would be blocked or bent.

She had such a complicated routine only because she was doing the work of two. The woman who had been next to her got sick one day, and Paulette had taken on her tasks. Everyone assumed that the line would slow down. But Paulette doubled her speed and kept up the pace.

"I don't know how you do it, Paulette," her supervisor had said, as she worked with seemingly effortless intensity.

"I'm going twice as fast, Mr. Hannon," she replied.

"Can you keep it up?"

"I sure can," she answered. "In fact, when Lindy comes back, you can put her down the line and give her work to me." Whereas Lindy always talked about clothes and shoes, Paulette preferred to concentrate on the instrument that she was fashioning. She was granted her wish. Among other things, Hannon and just about everyone else on the line wanted to see how long she could continue the pace before she broke. But she knew this, and she didn't break. She got better, and she got faster.

When Paulette got home in the morning, the sea was illuminated as the sun came up behind her. The open and fluid light of the Pacific was as entrancing as the light of the Carolinas in springtime. At times the sea looked just like the wind-blue mottled waters of the Albemarle, and the enormous clouds that rose in huge columns far out over the ocean were like the aromatic pine smoke that ascended undisturbed from a farmer's clearing fire toward a flawless blue sky.

She was elated in the morning. Joy and relief came not only from the light on the waves but also from having passed the great test of the day, which was to open the mailbox and check the area near the front door. The mailman, who served as the telegraph messenger, thought that he was obliged to wedge telegrams tightly in the doorway. One of the women, a lathe operator who had had to go back to her family in Chicago, had found her telegram actually nailed down. The mailman had feared that it might blow into the sea, and that then she would find out in some shocking, incidental manner that her husband had been killed. At the factory were fifty women whose husbands, like Lee, had passed through Twentynine Palms into the Second Marine Division. They had been deeply distressed when their men were thrown into the fighting on Guadalcanal, but, miraculously, of the fifty Marines whose wives were gathered in this one place only a few had been wounded and none had been killed.

When her work was done, knowing that she had made the best part of thirty altimeters that would go into thirty fighters, and that each of these fighters would do a great deal to protect the ships on which the Marines sailed, and pummel the beaches on which they had to fight, Paulette felt deserving of sleep. She would change into a nightgown, turn down the covers, and then sit in a chair next to the bed, staring at the Pacific as the light got stronger, trying to master the fatigue and stay awake. Sometimes she would listen to the wind for an hour, nod asleep, and force herself to open her eyes, until she fell into bed and slept until two in the afternoon.

Lee had returned from his training at Parris Island with little respect for what he once had thought were human limitations. His company had marched for three days, day and night, without stopping. Some recruits, young men, had died of heart attacks.

"How can you walk for three whole days without stopping?" she had asked. "It seems impossible."

"We had forty-pound packs, rifles, and ammunition," he answered. "We had to carry mortars, bazookas, stretchers, and other equipment, some of it very heavy, that was passed from shoulder to shoulder."

"For three days?"

"For three days. And when we finally stopped, I was picked as a sentinel. I had to stand guard for two hours while everyone else slept. And you know what happens if you fall asleep, God help you, on sentry duty?"

She shook her head, but did know.

"Article eighty-six of the Articles of War: 'Misbehavior of a sentinel.'" He recited it from memory. "'Any sentinel who is found drunk or sleeping upon his post, or leaves it before he is regularly relieved, shall, if the offense is committed in time of war, suffer death or such other punishment as a court-martial may direct.'

"I was so tired...My eyelids weighed ten thousand pounds apiece. But I stayed up, even though the only enemies we had were officers and mosquitoes. They were always coming around to check."

"Who?" she asked. "Mosquitoes?"

"Yeah," Lee replied. "And as you know, officers are hatched in stagnant pools."

So when Paulette returned from her ten-hour shifts, she sat in a chair and tried not to sleep, staring over the Pacific like a sentinel.

She had the privilege of awakening at two in the afternoon, when the day was strongest, and not having to be ashamed of having slept through the morning. In the six hours before the shift began, she would rise, bathe, eat lunch, and gather her garden tools. Then she walked a few miles down the winding coast road—the rake, hoe, and shovel resting painfully upon her shoulders—to her garden. No shed was anywhere near it, and had one been there she probably would have carried the tools anyway.

Because she shared the garden with an old man who came in the morning and two factory women who were on the second day shift, she was almost always alone there. Usually she worked in the strong sun until five-thirty. To allow herself this much hard labor she did her shopping and eating at a brisk pace. The hours in the garden made her strong and fit. She was perpetually sunburned, and her hair became lighter. She had never been so beautiful, and when people looked at her, they kept on looking. Seeing her speed through the various and difficult chores of cultivation, no one ever would have guessed that she might shoulder her tools, walk home as fast as she could, and then set off for ten hours on a production line.

"Don't write about the garden anymore," he had written from a place undisclosed. "Don't write about the goddamned altimeters.

Don't write about what we're going to do when the war is over. Just tell me about you. They have altimeters here, they even have gardens. Tell me what you're thinking. Describe yourself as if we had never met. Tell me in detail exactly how you take your bath. Do you sing to yourself? What do the sheets on the bed look like—I mean do they have a pattern or are they a color? I never saw them. Take pictures, and send them. Send me your barrette. (I don't want to wear it myself, I want to keep it in my pocket.) I care so much about you, Paulette. I love you. And I'm doing my best to stay alive. You should see me when it gets tight. I don't throw myself up front, but I don't hold my breath either. I run around like hell, alert and listening every second. My aim is sure and I don't let off shots when I don't have to. You'd never know me, Paulette, and I don't know if there's anything left of me. But I'm going to come home."

Although she didn't write about the garden anymore, she tilled it deep. The rows were straight, and not a single weed was to be seen, and when she walked home with the tools on her shoulders, she welcomed their weight.

They exchanged postscripts for two months in letters that were late in coming and always crossed. "P.S. What do you eat?" he wrote.

"P.S. What do you mean, what do I eat? Why do you want to know? What do you eat?"

"P.S. I want to know because I'm hungry. I eat crud. It all comes from a can, it's very salty, and it has a lot of what seems to be pork fat. Some local vegetables haven't been bombed, or crushed by heavy vehicles, but if you eat them you can wave good-bye to your intestines. Sometimes we have cakes that are baked in pans four feet by five feet. The bottom is cinder and the top is raw dough. What happened to steak? No one has it here, and I haven't seen one in a year. Where are they keeping it? Is there going to be a big barbecue after the war?"

"P.S. You're right, we have no beef around here and practically no sugar or butter, either. I thought maybe you were getting it. I eat a lot of fresh vegetables, rice, fish that I get in exchange for the stuff in my garden, and chicken now and then. I've lost some weight but I look real good. I drink my tea black, and I mean black, because at the plant they have a huge samovar thing where it boils for hours. What with your pay mounting up in one account, my pay mounting up in another, and what the parents have been sending us lately, when the war is over we're going to have a lot of money. We have almost four thousand dollars now. We'll have the biggest barbecue you've ever seen."

As long as she did her work and as long as he stayed alive, she sensed some sort of justice and equilibrium. She enjoyed the feminine triumph in the factory, where the women, doing men's work, sometimes broke into song that was as tentative and beautiful as only women's voices can be. They did not sing often. The beauty and the power embarrassed them, for they had their independence only because their men were at risk and the world was at war. But sometimes they couldn't help it, and a song would rise above the production lines, lighter than the ascending smoke, more luminous than the blue and white arcs.

The Pacific and California's golden hills caught the clear sunshine but made it seem like a dream in which sight was confused and the dreamer giddy. The sea, with its cold colors and foaming cauldrons in which seals were cradle-rocked, was the northern part of the same ocean that held ten thousand tropical islands. All these things, these reversals, paradoxes, and contradictions, were burned in day by day until they seemed to make sense, until it appeared as if some great thing were being accomplished, greater than perhaps they knew. For they felt tremendous velocity in the way they worked, the way they lived, and even in the way they sang.

On the twentieth of November, 1943, five thousand men of the Second Marine Division landed on the beaches of Tarawa. The action of war, the noise, smoke, and intense labor of battle, seemed frozen when it reached home, especially for those whose husbands or sons were engaged in the fighting. A battle from afar is only a thing of silence, of souls ascending as if drawn up in slow motion by malevolent angels floating above the fray. Tarawa, a battle afar, seemed no more real than a painting. Paulette and the others had no chance to act. They were forced to listen fitfully to the silence and stare faithfully into the dark.

Now, when the line broke into song, the women did not sing the energetic popular music that could stoke production until it glowed. Nor did they sing the graceful ballads that had kept them on the line when they would otherwise have faltered. Now the songs were from the hymnal, and they were sung not in a spirit of patriotism or of production but in prayer.

As the battle was fought on Tarawa, two women fell from the line. One had been called from her position and summoned to what they knew as the office, which was a maze of wavy-glass partitions beyond which other people did the paperwork, and she, like the lathe operator from Chicago, simply dropped away. Another had been given a telegram as she worked; no one really knew how to tell anyone such a thing. But with so many women working, the absence of two did not slow their industry. Two had been beaten. Five hundred were not, and the lights still flickered down the line.

Paulette had known from the first that Lee was on the beach. She wondered which was more difficult, being aware that he might be in any battle, or knowing for sure that he was in one. The first thing she did when she got the newspaper was to scan the casualty lists, dropping immediately to the Fs. It did not matter that they sent telegrams, telegrams sometimes blew into the sea. Next she raced through reports of the fighting, tracing if she could the progress of his unit and looking for any mention of him. Only then would she read the narrative so as to judge the progress of the offensive and the chances of victory, though she cared not so much for victory as for what it meant to the men in the field who were still alive.

The line was hypnotic and it swallowed up time. If she wanted to do good work, she couldn't think about anything except what was directly in front of her, especially since she was doing the work of two. But when she was free she now dreamed almost continually of her young husband, as if the landings in Tarawa, across the Pacific, had been designed to make her imagine him.

During these days the garden needed little attention, so she did whatever she could and then went down to a sheltered cove by the sea, where she lay on the sand, in the sun, half asleep. For as long as her eyes were closed and the sea seemed to pound everything but dreams into meaningless foam and air, she lay with him, tightly, a slight smile on her face, listening to him breathe. She would awake from this half sleep to find that she was holding her hands and arms in such a way that had he been there she would have been embracing him.

She often spoke to him under her breath, informing him, as if he could hear her, of everything she thought and did—of the fact that she was turning off the flame under the kettle, of the sunrise and its golden-red light flooding against the pines, of how the ocean looked when it was joyously misbehaving.

These were the things she could do, the powers to which she was limited, in the town on the Pacific that was probably the last place in the world for a factory or the working of transcendent miracles too difficult to explain or name. But she felt that somehow her devotion and her sharp attention would have repercussions, that, just as in a concert hall, where music could only truly rise within the hearts of its listeners, she could forge a connection over the thin air. When a good wave rolled against the rocks of the cove, it sent up rockets of foam that hung in the sun, motionlessly and—if one could look at them hard enough to make them stand still—forever. To make them a target, to sight them with concentration as absolute as a burning weld, to draw a bead, to hold them in place with the eye, was to change the world.

The factory was her place for this, for precision, devotion, and concentration. Here the repercussions might begin. Here, in the darkness, the light that was so white it was almost blue—sapphire-colored—flashed continually, like muzzle bursts, and steel was set to steel as if swords were being made. Here she could push herself, drive herself, and work until she could hardly stand—all for him.

As the battle of Tarawa became more and more difficult, and men fell, Paulette doubled and redoubled her efforts. Every weld was true. She built the instruments with the disciplined ferocity that comes only from love. For the rhythm of the work seemed to signify something far greater than the work itself. The timing of her welds, the blinking of the arc, the light touch that held two parts together and was then withdrawn, the patience and the quickness, the generation of blinding flares and small pencil-shots of smoke—these acts, qualities, and their progress, like the repetitions in the hymns that the women sang on the line, made a kind of quiet thunder that rolled through all things, and that, in Paulette's deepest wishes, shot across the Pacific in performance of a miracle she dared not even name—though that miracle was not to be hers.

James D. Houston

Faith

MAYBE IT HAPPENED as the first long earth-wave rolled through our town. Maybe it was later. We had aftershocks all night. Faith, my wife, wouldn't sleep inside. No one would but me. Everyone spent the night in the driveways on cots, or on the lawns in sleeping bags, as if this were a neighborhood slumber party. I think I had to prove to myself that if all else failed I could still believe in my own house. If that first shaker had not torn it to pieces, I reasoned, why should I be pushed around and bullied by these aftershocks rated so much lower on the Richter scale?

When the second big one hit us, just before dawn, I was alone and sleeping fitfully, pinned to my bed, dozing like a corporal in the combat zone waiting for the next burst of mortar fire. I sat up and listened to rafters groaning, calling out for mercy. I heard dishes leap and rattle in the kitchen. I listened to the seismic roar that comes rushing toward you like a mighty wind. I should have run for the doorjamb. I couldn't. I could not move, gripped by the cold truth of my own helplessness.

I sat there with the quilt thrown back and rode the tremor until the house settled down. Outside I heard voices. They rose in a long murmur of anxiety laced with relief, as children called to their parents, as neighbor talked to neighbor from lawn to lawn, from driveway to driveway. Eventually the voices subsided, and I was aware for the first time of a hollow place within, a small place I could almost put my finger on. Describing it now, I can say it felt as if a narrow hole had been scooped out, or drilled, right behind my sternum, toward the lower end of it, where the lowermost ribs come together.

At the time I had no words for this, nor did I try to find any. From the rising of the sun we had to take things one hour at a time. We were out of water. Sewage lines had burst, contaminating the mains. Phone lines were down. Power was out all over the county, and many roads were cut off. Long sections of roadbed had split. In the central shopping district, several older buildings, made of brick and never retrofitted, were in ruins. They'd been built on flood plain. As the tremor passed through it, the subsoil liquified. Faith and I live in a part of town built on solider stuff. No one's house jumped the foundation. But indoors, everything loose had landed on the floor—dishes, pictures, mirrors, lamps. Half our chimney fell into the yard. Every other house had a square hole in the roof or a chimney-shaped outline up one wall where the bricks once stood.

The next day I was working side by side with neighbors I had not talked with for weeks, in some cases, months. As we swapped stories and considered the losses, the costs, the federal help that might be coming in, I would often see in their eyes a startled and questioning fear that would send me inward to the place where whatever was now missing had once resided. I found myself wondering whether it was something new, or an old emptiness that had gone unnoticed for who knows how long. I'm still not sure.

By the third morning we had electricity again. We could boil water without building a campfire outside or cranking up the Coleman. I sat down at the kitchen table with a cup of coffee and I guess I just forgot to drink it. Faith sat down across from me and said, "What's the matter, Harry?"

"Nothing."

"Are you all right?"

"No, I'm not all right. Are you?"

"You've been sitting here for an hour."

"I don't know what to do. I can't figure out what to do next."

"Let's sell this place. Let's get out of here while we're still alive."

She looked like I felt. Along with everything else we were getting three or four aftershocks a day. It kept you on the ragged edge.

I said, "Where can we go?"

"Inland. Nevada. Arizona. I don't care."

"You said you could never live in Arizona."

"That was last year."

"The desert would drive you bananas, you said."

Halfway through that sentence, my voice broke. My eyes had filled with water. It would have been the easiest thing in the world to break into heaving sobs right there at the table.

"It's too hard," she said, "trying to clean up this mess and never know when another one's going to hit us. Who can live this way?"

"What does it feel like to have a nervous breakdown?" I said.

"Maybe all we need is a trip. I don't care where. Let's give ourselves a week, Harry, while we talk things over."

"That's not it."

"What's not it?"

I didn't answer. She waited and asked again, her voice on the rise, "What's not it? What's the matter, Harry? What's happening to us?"

Her eyes were blazing. Her mouth was stretched wide in a way I have learned to be wary of. It was not a smile. Faith has a kind of chiseled beauty. As the years go by, her nose, her cheeks, her black brows get sharper, especially when she's pushed. We were both ready to start shouting. Thirty more seconds we would be saying things we didn't mean. I didn't need a shouting match just then. Somehow she always prevails. Her background happens to be Irish and Mexican, a formidable combination when it's time to sling the words around.

Thankfully the phone rang. We hadn't heard it for so long, the jangle shocked us both. It was her mother, who had been trying to get through. Once they knew the houses were standing and no one had been injured, they talked on for half an hour or so, the mother mostly, repeating all the stories she'd been hearing, among them the story of a cousin with some acreage here in the county, where he grows lettuce and other row crops. Some men on the cousin's crew had recently come up from central Mexico on labor contracts, and one of them had asked for a morning off to take his wife to a local healer. During the quake the wife's soul had left her body, or so she feared, and this healer had ways to bring a soul back. Faith's mother reminded her that after the big one in Mexico City back in 1987, numerous stories had drifted north, stories of people who found themselves alive and walking around among the ruins, while inside something had disappeared.

I still have to wonder why the mother called when she did. Whether it was by chance or by design, I still can't say. Probably a little of both. She claims to have rare intuitive powers. This healer, the *curandera,* happened to be a woman she knew by name and had been visiting for a year or so, ever since her husband had passed away. Faith had been visiting her, too. Her skills, they said, remedied much more than ailments of the flesh.

As soon as her mother hung up, Faith repeated the story of the field worker's wife. It came with an odd sort of pressure, as if she were testing my ability to grasp its importance. I don't know. I'm still piecing that day together. Maybe Faith, too, was feeling some form of inexpressible loss, and maybe she, too, was groping for a way to voice it.

"This healer," I said, "what does she do?"

"It's hard to explain."

"Is it some kind of Catholic thing? The devil creeping in to steal your soul away?"

She shook her head. "I don't think it's like good spirits and evil spirits or anything along those lines."

"What is it, then?"

"Maybe it's like the door of your life springs open for a second."

"Why do you say that?"

"Maybe your soul flies out and the door slams shut again."

"You think that can happen?"

"I'm just thinking out loud."

"It's a hell of a thing to say."

"Don't look at me that way."

"Just tell me if you believe something like that could happen."

"You hear people talk about it."

"When are you going down there again?"

"Sometime soon, I hope. It would be a good time for a treatment."

"Is that what they call it?"

"You can call it whatever you want."

"A treatment? That sounds like..."

"Like what?"

"Some kind of medical deal."

"Please, Harry. If you're going to get defensive, I don't want to talk about it."

"I'm not defensive."

"Your guard goes up."

"Gimme a goddamn break, Faith!"

"I can feel it, Harry! You know I can!"

My guard goes up. What guard, I was thinking. I had no guards left. That was the problem. Everything I had ever used to defend myself or support myself was gone. I was skidding. That's how I felt. Supportless. I had to get out of there. I had to think. Or perhaps I had to get out of there and not-think.

I took off for the hardware store, to pick up some new brackets for the bookshelves. I switched on one of the talk shows out of San Francisco. The guest was a trauma counselor. The theme was, "Living With the Fault Line." Someone had just called in a question about betrayal.

"Can you give me an example?" the counselor said.

"Maybe that isn't the right word," the caller said.

"You feel like something has been taken away from you." It wasn't a question.

"It's almost like my body opened up and something escaped."

A long chill prickled my arms, my neck. I had just reached the hardware store. I pulled into the parking lot, switched off the engine, and turned up the sound.

"That's big," the talk show host said. "That's major."

"Hey," said the counselor, "let's think about it together for a minute."

"Think about what?" the host said. "Betrayal?"

"The earth. Think about the umbilical tie. From your mother, to your grandmother, and on down the line. On back through the generations to whatever life forms preceded ours. Sooner or later we all have to trace our ancestry to this nurturing earth, and meanwhile we have laid out these roads and trails and highways and conduit pipes and bridges and so forth in full faith that she is stable and can be relied upon. You follow me? Then when she all of a sudden gives way, splits open, lets off this destructive power without even the little advance notice you get for a hurricane or a killer blizzard, why, it's like your ground wire disconnects. It's so random...you realize how we're all just hanging out here in empty space. Believe me, folks, you're not alone. I've been feeling this way myself for days..."

He had a low, compelling voice that sent buzzes through me. I was tingling almost to the point of nausea. The tears I had not been able to release in the kitchen now began to flow. I sat in the hardware store parking lot weeping the way a young child lost on a city street might weep for the missing parents.

When my tears subsided, I tried to call the house. The line was busy. I started driving south, sticking to roads I knew were open, more or less following a route I'd followed once before, on a day when Faith's car was in the shop and she needed a ride. It only takes twenty minutes, but you enter another world. Down at that end of the county it's still mostly fertile delta land. From the highway you look for a Burger King and a Stop-N-Go. Past a tract of duplexes you enter an older neighborhood of bungalows and windblown frame houses from the 1920s and earlier. The street leading to her cottage was semi-paved. Beyond the yard, row crops went for a mile across broad, flat bottomland—lettuce, chard, broccoli, onions. The grass in the yard was pale and dry. Low cactus had been planted next to the porch.

The fellow who answered my knock said he was her son, Arnoldo, lean and swarthy and watchful. He wore jeans and dusty boots, as if he might have just walked in by another door. When I mentioned my wife's name he did not seem impressed. Anglos never came to see this woman. In his eyes I could have been an infiltrator from County Health, or from Immigration, or someone shaking them down for a license. When I mentioned my mother-in-law's family name, he softened a little. Dredging up some high school Spanish, I tried to describe my symptoms. Arnoldo spoke a little English, but not much. I touched my chest.

"*Mi alma,*" I said. "*Después del temblor, tengo mucho miedo. Es posible que mi alma...*"

"*Ha volado?*" he said. Has flown away?

"*Sí. Comprende?*"

He looked at me for quite a while, making up his mind. He looked beyond me toward the curb, checking out the car. At last he stepped aside and admitted me into a small living room where a young mother and her son were sitting on a well-worn sofa. There was a TV set, a low table with some Spanish-language magazines, a sideboard with three or four generations of family photos framed. In one corner, votive candles flickered in front of an image of the blue-robed, brown-faced Virgin of Guadalupe. Between this room and a kitchen there was a short hallway where a door now opened. A moment later a pregnant woman appeared, followed by an older woman, short and round and very dark. She stopped and looked at me while Arnoldo explained the family tie. The names seemed to light her face with a tiny smile of recognition. I heard him mutter, "*Susto.*" A scare. She nodded and said to me, "*Bienvenidos.*" Welcome. Please make yourself at home.

She beckoned to the woman on the sofa and the son, who limped as he started down the hallway. The rear door closed, and Arnoldo offered me a chair. I couldn't sit. I was shivering. I made him nervous. I was sure he regretted letting me inside. He pointed to a long, jagged lightning streak of a crack across the sheetrock wall behind the TV set. "*El temblor,*" he said. The earthquake.

Again, I pointed at my chest. "*El temblor.*"

We both laughed quiet, courteous laughs and looked away. I sat down then, though I could not bear the thought of waiting. This was crazy. I was out of control. What was I doing? What did I think would happen? I remembered the day I'd driven over there with Faith and parked at the curb. I remembered the glow on her face and how I had extinguished the glow. She had wanted me to come inside with her. "What for?" I said. "There's nothing wrong with me." The idea filled me with resentment. "It's not a lot of money, Harry," she had said. "She doesn't charge. You just leave something on the table, whatever you feel like leaving."

It wasn't the money. It was the strangeness of being there with her. Faith has these dramatic, mixed-blood looks that have kept people guessing, and have kept me guessing, too, I suppose. Greek? they ask. Portuguese? Italian? Black Irish? Mexico has always been somewhere on that list, but when we first started dating she would never have emphasized it. Her Spanish was no better than mine. Faith McCarthy was her maiden name. Suddenly I did not know this woman. Mexican on her mother's side, that was one thing. Going into the barrio to visit healers, that was something else. I wasn't ready for that. When did it start? Where would it lead? I remembered the rush of dread that day in the car as I realized I was looking at a complete stranger who was inviting me to some place I had never been.

Sitting there with Arnoldo I felt it again, the dread of strangeness. Who was he, after all, with his boots and his lidded eyes? Her son? He could be anyone. What if this was the wrong house?

I heard voices from the hallway. Then the young mother and the limping boy passed through the living room, out the front door, and the healer was beckoning to me. I, too, was limping, crippled with doubt. I had no will. I followed her to another room, with a backyard view across the fields, once a bedroom, now furnished with a chest of drawers, a couple of chairs, a long couch with a raised headrest. She didn't speak for quite some time. She just looked at me. She was no more than five feet tall, her hair silver, pulled back in a short braid. I guessed she was in her sixties, her body thick and sturdy, covered by a plain dress with short sleeves that left her arms free. Her face was neutral, neither smiling nor frowning. Her eyes seemed to enter me, black eyes, the kind that go back in time, channels of memory. She knew my fear. She knew everything about me.

She asked me to take off my shoes and my shirt, nodding toward a chair before she turned away, as if occupied with some small preparation on top of the chest. My panic welled up. It was mad to be doing this, stripping down at the edge of a broccoli field, inside the house of people I'd never seen before. I imagined the old woman asking me to swallow something terrible. Above the chest a shelf was lined with jars and small pouches. Who knew what they contained? My panic turned to fury. I could have taken the old woman by the throat. I wanted to. She knew too much. Maybe I began to understand hysteria just then, how a person can start to spin around and fly to pieces. Why didn't I spin? Why didn't I run? I stood there swearing that if she tried to give me something, I would not swallow it. That was the little contract I made with myself as I lay down on the long couch.

She covered me to my neck with a sheet. From a pouch tied around her waist she withdrew a clump of leafy fragrant stems and waved it up and down the length of my body. Her lips moved but made no sound. She leaned in close, pushing her thumbs across my forehead, digging into the furrows there, digging in close to my eyes. She began to speak, a soft murmur of words that were not Spanish. Later on, Faith's mother would tell me these may have been Yaqui words, a Yaqui incantation. There is something to be said for not knowing the literal meaning of words. If you trust the speaker to be using them in the proper way, it makes it easier to surrender. You can surrender to the sound. Is that what was happening? Did I trust the sound of the *curandera's* voice? Let's say I wanted to. Let's say my need to trust her outweighed my fear. Who else could I have turned to? In her hands I began to drift. I would not say she put me to sleep. I was not asleep. I did not feel asleep. I just wasn't entirely awake. My eyes weren't open. But I was still aware of being in the room. I was outside the room, yet in it, too, listening to her gentle voice.

While her hands worked on my forehead, my temples, my eyes, my nose and cheeks, her voice became the voice of wings, large and black and wide as the couch, as wide as the room, as wide as the house, sheets of darkness moving toward me, undulating, until I saw that these were the wings of an enormous bird, a dark eagle or a condor hovering. It finally settled on my chest, its feet on my skin so I could feel the talons. They held me as if in the grip of two great hands. They dug in. They were on my chest and inside my chest. From the talon grip I understood some things about this bird. I knew its solitary drifting on the high thermal currents, soaring, waiting. I knew its hunger. I knew the power of the beak. When the flapping of the wings increased, I wasn't surprised. They made a flapping thunder that sent a quiver through me, then a long shudder, then a shaking as sudden and as terrifying as the shaking of the earth, with a sound somewhere inside it, the slap of a ship's sails exploding in a gale. I was held by the chest and shaken by this huge bird until my body went slack, exhausted by the effort to resist. In that same moment the wings relaxed. The hold upon my chest relaxed. I watched the bird lift without any motion of the wings, as if riding an updraft. It hovered a while, and I had never felt so calm. A way had been cleared at last, that's how it felt. Everything had been rattled loose again and somehow shaken into place. A rim of light edged the silhouette of dusky feathers. I saw the fierce beak open as if about to speak. Its piercing cry almost stopped my heart.

My eyes sprang wide. The woman's dark brown face was very close. The heel of her hand had just landed on my forehead with a whack. Her black eyes were fixed on mine. What did I see there? Who did I see?

When I got back home Faith met me at the door. She, too, had been crying. I'd been gone maybe three hours. She stood close and put her arms around me. We didn't speak. We looked at each other. In her face I recognized something I would not, until that afternoon, have been able to identify. Her eyes were like the old woman's eyes, that same fierce and penetrating tenderness. It swept me away. We kissed as if we had not seen each other in weeks, as if we had had the fight that nearly happened and we were finally making up. It was a great kiss, the best in years. It sent us lunging for the bedroom, where we made love for the first time in many days.

In our haste we forgot to pull the curtains. Afternoon light was pouring through the windows. At first she was bathed in light, though as we thrashed and rolled she seemed to be moving in and out of shadow. Then she was above me and so close she blocked the light. As she rose and fell and rose and fell I could only see her outline. When she abruptly reared back, her arms were wings spread wide against the brightness, while she called out words I could scarcely hear. A roaring had filled my ears. A thousand creatures were swarming towards the house, or a storm-driven wind. Maybe it was another aftershock. Maybe it was the pounding of my own blood.

"Oh! Oh! Harry!" Her voice came through the roar. "Harry! Harry!" as if I were heading out the door again. Had I been able to speak I would have called to her. Maybe I did call. I know I heard my voice. "I'm here!" I cried. "I'm here! I'm here!"

Catherine Ryan Hyde

Castration Humor

COWBOY ASKS IF SHE'S afraid of snakes. He's six bales up in the hay barn, a roofed structure with open sides, and he has one in his hand. It's green, not all that big but big enough, two or three feet long and the width of Cowboy's thumb, which is to say twice the width of her own.

"'Fraid of snakes?" Cowboy asks because he's looking to hand it off. He's using twin hay hooks to pull bales off the top of the stack in order to see if they are "moldery"; he doesn't want to crush the snake.

She *is* afraid of snakes. But she takes it from him. She expects it to be slimy, but it's not. Just dry and cool and strong, a long muscle. It whips both its halves around her wrist and hand, frightened.

This is the moment she knows. How it will be with them, how far it will, by necessity, go. She wants to be wrong, but that won't help. Someday soon he will stand before her with only himself to hand off, and use the same tack. What's the matter, girl? Scared? And she will take that bait too.

Cowboys are like that. They test you all the time. If you fail, it's funny to them. That's the sense of humor they've got.

She sets the snake down on the loose alfalfa and packed dirt, and it slithers away. Cowboy pulls a bale off the top of the stack and lets gravity bring it down. It lands with a muffled thump, dusting the retreating snake with greenish-gold hay flakes. A dozen mice scurry from their now exposed cover, and Bob the barn cat goes

121

crazy trying to chase them all at once. Splits his personality, fragments his little cat self and has a temporary breakdown as they scatter.

"Git 'em, Bob," Cowboy says. But Bob ends up with none.

Cowboy doesn't feed Bob. So mousing is a vocation, Bob's livelihood. Not a hobby by any means. So he takes his mousing seriously. He twitches, waiting for Cowboy to tumble another bale. Diane briefly wonders at the fact that snakes should be saved and mice eaten. But in spite of her wanting it not to, it makes a degree of sense.

"Gonna ride today?" Cowboy asks. She knows it's another test, but not what the correct answer should be. She should write these things on her sleeve before leaving the house.

"He's being snarky today. I'd have to lunge him for an hour to get the snark out of him, and I don't have that much time. I might just bottle-feed the orphans and go home."

Cowboy says, "Fletch is snarky every day."

Diane realizes she adopted that word from Cowboy, and feels ashamed. She has done that sponge thing again, taking up bits of the people around her. It's one thing with Gil, one thing to absorb the man she lives with, but another thing with Cowboy. She doesn't even like Cowboy. "I thought horses were supposed to mellow with age."

"Depends on where they started off, I guess."

Another bale comes down. Only three mice scurry this time, and Bob learns from his mistake, targets one, and takes it. As he slinks around the side of the barn with his warm breakfast, Diane notices a baseball-sized swelling on his side. Too sudden to be a growth. It wasn't there two days ago. Abscess, maybe.

"You should have a vet look at that," she says.

Cowboy laughs. "Bob don't need all that."

"Fine. I'll take him."

"They take care of themselves. And if they don't, they don't belong on a ranch."

Great, she thinks. If they belong, they work their whole lives to survive, and if they don't belong, they have to die to prove it. Hell of a thing.

Just before she leaves the hay barn, Cowboy asks if she's heard about the bleeding-heart idiots who are out trying to make a game of messing up the state mountain-lion lottery.

"I didn't hear that," she says, and her face feels numb. She thinks she'll sell the damn horse, or give him away. Then she won't have to work off his board anymore. Then she'll never have to come back here and get caught in that lie, or in any of the other messes she now sees as inevitable.

Diane sets the three warm bottles in the dirt at her feet. Plastic quart-sized bottles with gigantic rubber nipples, filled with formula made of hot tap water and powdered milk replacer. The three orphan calves run to the fronts of their respective pens and do that cow dance. Swinging back and forth, voicing their strange impatient complaint.

She doesn't go in to feed them anymore, because they're too big. Because they step on her feet and butt her thighs when the nipple clogs. And because last night's rain has mixed with the mud and manure, and they've stomped it all into a homogenized toxic muck that she doesn't care to experience firsthand. Their tails and flanks are caked with the horrible loose greenish stool of a nursing calf. They're not cute anymore.

When they first came in from pasture, when their mamas died, they broke her heart with their cuteness. Lanky and fragile and doe-eyed, no bigger than a good-sized dog. Especially this one with the black eye patch. She vaguely remembers thinking, How can people eat them, although she has never been a vegetarian. Two months later they'd grown so brutish and awkward and stupid that she actually heard herself ask Cowboy, "Feel like a hamburger?" But maybe she only said that because it was Cowboy, because she had to say something.

She pushes the nipple through the welded wire, letting the cross-hatched fencing prevent the little monster from pulling it off the bottle, which he tends to do. The sides of the nipple suck in, and she has to pull it away to allow air; he butts the fence hard in protest three times before she can offer it back. A foamy white drool dribbles from his mouth as he sucks.

She hears Cowboy's flatbed truck pull up. Come to check on that baby Barby as he calls it, a Barbary sheep orphan. One of his new imports. He's been trying to pair it with the nursing mother who lost one of her twins to a lion. Maybe. Fish and Game investigated and denied Cowboy a lion permit, judging it a coyote kill. But try convincing Cowboy. He's tied part of the dead baby's skin on the orphan to get the mom to nurse it. Good thing for everybody the undetermined predators are so goddamned brazen around here they don't even bother to drag the kill away.

"How's it working?" she asks, to have something to say.

"Too soon to tell." He glances over at the singing, dancing calves. "Roundup's coming."

It strikes Diane as a misnomer in the case of the orphans. How can you round up an animal already trapped in a six-by-six pen? But she knows what Cowboy is telling her. These three, along with all those pasturing free, will be vaccinated, castrated, tagged. Horns will be cut. The bellowing will be a nightmare, even from home. She's been warned not to eat the prairie oysters at a roundup barbecue. She prefers not to go.

Before he vaults back in the truck he says, "Remind 'em to enjoy their balls while they can."

It rankles Diane, because castration isn't funny. Necessary, okay, but not funny. But the calf knocks her out of that thought, literally, because the bottle won't draw.

She decides she will not try to ride her snarky gelding today. Just finish up as fast as she can and get home to Gil.

On her way out she does one more thing, something she hadn't planned. She kidnaps the ailing Bob.

Gil says, "That's an interesting-looking cat."

"He's one-quarter bobcat. I saw his daddy."

She had, in fact, been the only one on the ranch to see him. Coming around a corner of the hay barn when Bob's mom, barely more than a kitten herself, first came into heat. The tom froze and looked at Diane, and Diane froze and looked at the tom. And wondered what exactly she was seeing. It was a wild cat, but no, it wasn't. But it was the size of a house cat. No, bigger. But not big enough to be a wild cat. But it had the face of a big cat, with tufted ears, and a stump for a tail. Only later did she learn that bobcats and house cats have been known to mate.

"Of all the kittens, he looks most like his daddy." He is also the only one who has thus far survived. "But his nature is one hundred percent house cat."

Gil scratches Bob behind the ears, and he purrs.

They stand in their studio apartment above the sprawling home of the old woman Gil works for, cares for, shops for, gardens for. Until he met the old woman, until they fled their last home, Diane had thought Gil to be increasingly unemployable.

Gil says, "There are twelve of us now. We're all converging on the same hunter safety course on Saturday. So we can get our licenses. We'll need licenses."

Diane says, "I'm taking Bob to the vet. I know there's some money involved...."

Gil says, "Did you hear what I said? We have twelve now."

"Yeah. That's good. Can we afford it if I take him?"

"I think you should." His shoulders are sloped, belying his immense height, and his downturned head gives her a perfect view of his widening bald spot. Just once, if he would argue with her, make her life difficult. She would feel so much less guilty. So much more justified. But Gil never does anything to give her cause. Gil never does anything.

The straw bedding scratches her bare skin, but it's not altogether unpleasant. It's completely dark in this clean stall in the night, which is good. She is the first to speak. "I've just been thinking that my life would be simpler without him."

Cowboy is quiet for a beat or two, but she can hear his breath. He still has his Wranglers half on, bunched around his thighs. She can feel that, where her leg drapes against his. Finally he says, "That's a decision only you and Gil can make."

Diane laughs out loud. Spits laughter like a mouthful of something she meant to swallow. Even in the pitch dark she knows she has wounded his pride in a manner impossible to quantify. "Not Gil. I was talking about Fletch." It was a continuation of a conversation they'd abandoned earlier. She can't believe he thought she meant Gil. Wishful thinking, maybe.

"Oh. Fletch. Now why on earth would you go and give up on a good horse?"

"We're not talking about a good horse. We're talking about Fletch. Fletch is an idiot."

An uncomfortable silence radiates. Then, like spare ammunition drawn from a back pocket, he says, "Know what I heard in town today?"

"If it's about the goddamn lion lottery, I don't want to know. It's not something I want to talk about."

Cowboy stands and rattles around briefly in the darkened stall, as if in search of lost clothing. "Fine," he says. "Just so you know a thing is true whether you talk about it or not." Then he rolls back the big heavy stall door and disappears.

She thinks it an unpleasant thing for him to have said. She's spent so much of her life trying to unknow that very thing.

The old woman has two fat, ancient horses in her two-and-a-half acre backyard. One of the reasons Gil took this job, one of the reasons they moved here, was in the hope that Fletch could come to stay. But the woman is concerned about an extra horse wearing down her tree roots, and she is zoned for only one per acre; old as they are, neither one of them ever seems likely to pass away.

As Diane throws two big flakes of hay over the fence for their morning feeding she hears a beefy truck engine. She turns to see Cowboy pull up in front of the house. A surprise, because he never did before. He has hay lashed on the back of the flatbed, about ten bales. He sticks his head out the window.

"Want some free hay?"

What she wants is for him to call before he invades her home space, but she doesn't say that. "Since when do you give anything away?"

"It'll go to waste. Started to mold a little, but if you pick through it. Don't feed the outsides of the bales. It'll be okay. Not that I wouldn't feed it to my horses. I got twenty more bales just like 'em at home and I plan to. But there's only just so much I can use before it goes bad." He climbs down from the truck and begins to undo the canvas lashings.

Gil comes out and stands on the upstairs patio, looking down to see who has arrived. His chest seems a bit sunken in that shirt, a poor choice of shirt, really.

"Gil, this is Derek, the guy who boards Fletch; Derek, Gil."

Cowboy tips his cowboy hat, an absurdly stereotypical gesture. "Heard a lot about you," he calls up in a voice that sounds weighted, not entirely pleasant. Gil seems to catch that; in fact, he seems to have been expecting it.

"Thanks for the hay," Gil says, but he doesn't sound grateful. Just then Bob the cat saunters through the open patio door to see what gives. Gil wisely scoops him up, and they both disappear inside. Diane is not sure if Cowboy saw.

"That's Gil?" he says, rolling the straps around one hand.

"Meaning what?"

"I dunno. Just seems like he's maybe..."

"What?" But she knows what.

"A little old for you?"

"And this is your business because...."

"It's not. Sorry." He throws both hands up in a gesture of surrender, dropping the coiled straps in the dirt.

"Why in God's name does everybody feel so goddamned free to comment on a thing like that?"

"Sorry to offend," Cowboy says, picks up the straps, and jumps back in his truck. He hits the gas hard, spilling the bales off into the old woman's front yard as he drives away.

Good, she thinks. He's afraid of me. That's good.

Not ten minutes later, Gil is out on the back acre plinking cans off the fence. The scary part is that he's getting good. And she still can't feature it on him because he hates guns, hates violence, hates for anything to be killed. Gil is practicing for his class in hunter safety so he can get a hunting license. So he can join the lion lottery in hopes of winning one of the twenty sought-after permits. So he can not use it.

She wonders if the timing is significant. That Gil got a look at Cowboy and then wanted to shoot something.

That night in bed she thinks Gil is asleep until he speaks. He says, "You think I'm right. Right?"

"About what?"

"You know damn well about what."

"And you know I think you're right."

"I might have known, at one time. Now I'm not sure. Maybe your new friend has been putting ideas in your head."

"I'm capable of having my own ideas. And he's not my friend. He just boards Fletch."

Bob jumps up on the bed with them in the dark. Lies between them, purring, and Diane rubs him behind the ears.

Gil says, "I made an appointment with the vet for tomorrow. While he's got Bob under, checking that thing out, I told him to go ahead and neuter him."

"I don't know if—"

"I don't care. It doesn't matter what Derek wants. Because we're not giving Bob back."

Diane leads Fletch into the biggest ring. Closes the welded pipe gate. She has to lift the gate to get it latched. Everything on the ranch is old and sags a little. Except Cowboy.

She unclips Fletch's lead rope. A shot startles them both. Fletch throws his head high and takes off, spraying her with sand and gravel mixture. He streaks for the far rail so fast that he fails to make the turn. He falls onto one haunch, sliding and struggling. Then he swings to his feet and gallops on.

Behind him, Diane looks halfway across the cattle pasture and sees Cowboy with his .22 rifle, picking off ground squirrels.

Fletch gallops the fence with his tail raised like a flag, his neck stiff and high. He sweeps around in a big wild circle, flashes between her and Cowboy again. Diane feels drawn to watch them both. Fletch is a stunning horse, Polish Arabian with long legs, a classic dish face, a mane that touches the ground when he grazes. Diane stands in the center of the ring, turning around and around to watch him, dizzied by the blur of background, which seems to rush by the horse, rather than vice versa.

She knows now that she bought Fletch because he's so handsome. She halfway knew it at the time, only not out loud. She fell in love with the image of him, never stopped to consider practical matters. Could she handle him. Would she like him. Was he the right horse to buy.

She sees Cowboy leaning on the rail, watching. She halts her spinning abruptly, and a wave of vertigo comes and then gradually goes again.

Cowboy says, "Just tell me this one thing." He has his rifle up across one shoulder. Fletch comes down to a flashy, extended trot. "Do you agree with Gil? After everything you've seen out here? The Barbary sheep I've lost, and those calves got brought down? You still think I got no right to shoot one?"

Fletch stops short and stands with his head down, blowing through wide nostrils; she turns her attention away from him. As soon as she does he pokes his head through the pipe railings and nibbles at the grass outside.

"You raise the calves to eat. Why can't you understand if somebody else wants to eat them?"

"They're my calves."

"We all belong to anything fast enough to bring us down."

"So you agree with him."

"Yeah."

"Figures." He has one hip cocked; his jeans are tight, his short sleeves rolled to expose tanned muscles. It irks her when men are frustrating and attractive at the same time. It's tiring being drawn to men she doesn't like or trust. It drains her. "The way I hear it, you stand by that guy no matter what fool stunt he pulls. And you're not even married to him. I figure if you were sure about him, you'd've gotten married after all these years."

She doesn't want to do this, and he can't make her. She crosses the arena, pushing hard into the resistance of deep sand, clips the lead rope back on Fletch, and leads him to the gate.

Cowboy says, "I hear he talks a better game than he plays. I hear he shoots his mouth off about this cruelty-to-animals thing a lot. I hear he started a fight in the city over some shit like this and then chickened out and moved."

"No. The other guy chickened out."

"That's not what I hear."

Truth is, both men chickened out. Diane was set to go along for backup, for protection. To wait in the car, run for help in case it wasn't a fair fight. In case Gil's opponent brought backup of his own. Terrifyingly against her nature, but out of loyalty to Gil she volunteered to do it. And intended to. But the whole mess fell down around everyone, and she was the only one left standing, left to face the truth: only she had the guts to follow through. And it wasn't even her fight.

She opens the gate.

As she heads back to the barn, she hears Cowboy call after her, "And another thing. I want my damn cat back."

She stops, turns. "You don't care about that cat."

"Hell I don't. I like that cat. He's the only one of his litter left alive. Bad enough I got to worry about lions and coyotes getting my cats, now I got you to contend with."

"You'll have to take it up with Gil." The words sting a little on their way out, like a rope that snaps back and whips her as she tries to swing it away. Because she's always liked to think of this rivalry between Gil and Cowboy as an unfortunate accident, something she never intended to promote.

When she leads Fletch into the barn, Cowboy's already there. He must have run all the way and come in through the back. His mood has changed. He's smiling.

"Just in a bad mood over the damned squirrels," he says. "Overrun with 'em. Undermine the whole landscape. Dangerous having all those holes around horses. Anyway. I'm sorry."

She puts her horse away.

He comes up behind and circles her waist with his arms. She sinks back into him just as she wills herself not to.

"Come 'ere," he says. "Something in the tack room I want to show you."

"I'll bet." But against her will she is smiling. She knows what he's doing. He tried to win her allegiance one way and failed; now he's going with a more tested method. She sees this, but her body has already begun to react to him, so she goes.

Later, as she's putting her jeans back on, Cowboy says, "I really do miss that cat."

She looks into his eyes, but it's a mistake. Because she learns that Cowboy really does miss that cat.

On the eve of the lion lottery Diane arrives home from her fourth transgression with Cowboy to find Gil sitting at the kitchen table. His shotgun lies on the table beside him; his head is sprawled across one arm, his eyes open. Staring, blank. His hair has grown out just to the borderline of seedy. In this brief moment she sees both aspects of Gil, both sides. That charming boyish thing that made it easy to love him in the first place, and all the changes that make it hard.

Before she can even ask he says, "I never meant to hurt him. Last thing I ever wanted was to shoot anybody." Diane sits at the table beside him, not to be near him so much because her legs have gone cold and trembly. "I was out back plinking cans. He jumped up on the fence just as I was squeezing off a shot. Just out of nowhere, he was there. I buried him in the garden."

"Who, Gil? Who jumped up on the fence?"

"Bob." He says it roughly, as if he blames her for making him spell it out. "I shot Bob."

Diane draws breath briefly, wondering when she last breathed. First she feels relief that it was just Bob. Then a pang of loss, because it was Bob. "It was just an accident."

"Yeah. One of those accidents that only happen when people start playing with guns."

It hits her then. "Gil, the lottery is tomorrow. You have your license already. Why were you still practicing?"

He folds his arms on the table. Before he lays his face in that cradle he says, "Just blowing off steam, I guess."

She decides to bathe and retire without saying more. She knows to leave him alone with this thing. She can't help him. Even if he would let her, she couldn't.

She hears his voice follow her into the bathroom. "He trusted me. That's the worst part. His mistake. Humans can't be trusted. Cats can be trusted."

Unless you're a mouse, she thinks. But she doesn't say it.

Now it's her fifth time with Cowboy, and Diane respects the addictive nature of a fifth time. This time her body knows what it needs, knows on the first touch, jumps from zero to a hundred percent without permission. She likens a fifth time, with a man she shouldn't have had once, to a double lungful of nicotine-laden smoke when you quit quitting after two or three days. Or you can wait four days for the same sensation, but if you're going to give in, why? What does waiting accomplish?

They have gone to the trouble of removing all of their clothing, and they are already done, sprawled on three or four scattered saddle blankets on the concrete tack-room floor. Cowboy's fingers are entwined with hers, moving. Playing, almost. A game in the air above their spent bodies. It smacks of something like affection, something that was never scheduled.

The thoughts that have distracted her all day return, and she needs to ruin this moment by asking. Or maybe she just needs to ruin this moment. "I know I said I didn't want to talk about it. But tell me. Did you get one?"

"A permit? No. Did Gil?"

"No."

"Any of his lion-loving buddies?"

"No. So that's that, then. We lose twenty lions, but you don't get to take one out by hand. You can live with that, right?" After all, his calves were just as safe.

"Actually, no. I can't. But it turns out I can buy one off a guy whose name got drawn. Seven hundred dollars."

"For seven hundred dollars you could replace every animal ever killed on your ranch."

"It's the principle of the thing by now."

They dress in silence, and she goes off to feed the orphans.

The three calves are standing at the far corners of their pens when she arrives. She shows them the bottles. "Come on, guys, go into your dance." They eye her with heads down.

The air has gone warm and strange, charged. The clouds have darkened, their fat black bellies close to the ground. For a moment she thinks the calves are reacting to the electric forecast of this change in weather.

Then she sees. Tags in each left ear, cauterized-looking circles at the base of what might have been horns someday soon. The two males stand with legs slightly apart, traces of blood on their rear hocks and hooves.

"Okay, guys," she says, covering, for their benefit, the fact that she is slightly shaken too. "It's only me. You know me. I don't cut little calves. I just feed them. Come on, guys."

But the guys do not come. Today they choose hunger.

She hears Cowboy's voice behind her. "What'sa matter, kids; was I mean to you?" Then, more to Diane, "I told 'em to enjoy them while they could."

Diane turns, wanting him not to look the same as he did a moment ago on the tack-room floor. It works. He looks ungentle, unappealing. A man who would never weave his fingers through hers and play games with them in the air; nor would she want him to. She throws the big plastic bottles down on the dirt; one bounces, loses its nipple. Formula splashes onto Cowboy's battered boots. He looks up at her with darkening surprise.

"It's not so damn funny," she says.

She walks away before he can answer. She wants to look back, to see him standing under heavy clouds, watching her go, his face a blank canvas unable to paint itself with comprehension of her outburst. But she doesn't look back. She has crossed a line that needed crossing. She has seen Cowboy as undesirable. And she knows those lines can be uncrossed just as easily, so she never wants to see him again.

She walks back to the barn and saddles Fletch for a ride. She doesn't want to stay here but she doesn't want to go home. And she hasn't ridden Fletch in weeks. And she wants Cowboy to see that she's not afraid. She wants everybody, including herself, to see that she has the guts to ride this beast. Even if she has to find the guts and paste them on.

Fletch jitters and dances his way up the hill. She squeezes tightly with her legs to stay with him, but he reacts to that, absorbing her edginess. Or maybe it's the painted, buzzing air, the webs of lightning crackling at the horizon. Or maybe he just hasn't been ridden enough. She steers him kitty-corner across the pasture to the uphill trail, worried about squirrel holes in the blowing rattlesnake grass. Knowing he may bolt at some point, wanting him to at least do it on the packed trail.

He does not bolt. Just skitters up the hill trail toward the ridge road. Diane holds the reins too tightly with one hand, the saddle horn with the other. She looks over her shoulder into the valley and sees Cowboy walking down the paved road toward his double-wide trailer home. He is too far away to look ugly or appealing, callous or kind.

She allows Fletch to break into a long, extended trot and turns him onto the ridge road, into pine and scrub oak, causing the image of Cowboy to disappear. She relaxes into the horse's gait. It feels strangely smooth for a trot, easy to sit.

Then Fletch stops so sharply that she falls forward against his neck. She corrects just in time. Fletch's head tosses suddenly and violently; it would have broken her nose or split her lip if she hadn't pulled back when she did. His muscles feel like concrete between her legs, and his head is so high she can see the panicky flare of his nostrils. He rears, drawing high onto his hindquarters, and almost in the same motion he leaps.

The ground smacks up to meet her. She lies on her back on the dirt road for a second or two, disoriented and possibly injured, hearing and feeling the pounding of Fletch's hooves as he runs off and leaves her. The sky over her head is black; the rain will let go soon. Fletch will run all the way back to the barn. Maybe Cowboy will see him run back riderless. Maybe he'll come out to rescue her from a long and wet and painful walk back.

She shouts after the horse, though he's long out of earshot. "Goddamn you, Fletch. What was it this time?"

She rolls to her left side to rise, and she sees.

He is the color of wheat, the color of the grass in which he crouches. A near perfect camouflage. Except grass doesn't have gold eyes with vertical black pupils, a broad, almost Roman nose, stiff, alert ears. Not tufted ears, but smooth and short and rounded. Not a bobcat but a full-grown mountain lion. She is staring into his eyes. He is staring into hers. His sharp shoulder blades rise up to frame his back. He is crouched, watching. She knows there is a right and wrong thing to do; she has been told. But her mind spins and the information won't come around. Only her own words: We all belong to anything fast enough to bring us down. Easy words, quickly thrown. Then she remembers: Stand up. Look strong and big. No sudden moves.

She tries to stand, but she's wrenched muscles in her lower back. Her left leg feels weak, doesn't seem to hold. So she rolls right to stand. Which means she must turn her back on him. In that instant she sees him pounce in her mind, feels him behind her, winces at the perceived moment of impact. But then she is standing, facing him. He hasn't moved. She stands tall, her hands raised. His ears flatten. She knows this fear in herself. It's the one you have to move into to survive. She shouts, a big noise like a karate yell, and takes one step toward him. The cat bends upon himself and slinks away, viscous liquid inside fur and skin. She watches him leave, consciously holds her bladder, feels her knees go watery and loose. Breathes survival.

Begins the long walk home.

Every step with her left leg is short, wincing. She cuts straight down the hill, looking over her shoulder every third step. A quarter mile into the miserable hike the rain lets go, soaking her through, melding one kind of shiver with the next.

Cowboy is herding goats and Barbary sheep in the pouring rain. Herding them into covered pens, on foot, by hand, because they get sick sometimes if they get drenched. His head is down; he doesn't see her hobble up. Rain pours in sheets off the brim of his hat. He runs and shouts, looking almost naked in his wet clothes. He looks up and sees her.

"Where's Fletch?" she says, glad now, when she's safely back, that she didn't need him to come save her. "He ran home."

"I closed up the barn when it started to rain. He wasn't here then, and he's not here now."

"You don't suppose he got lost."

"Shit, no. You could let that beast off in Miami, Florida, and he'd find the barn. You okay?"

"Hey, Derek. Can a mountain lion bring down a grown horse?"

"You saw one? Where did you see one?"

Now she has to answer, or not. Maybe sign the lion's death warrant. Maybe choose a side. "Up on the ridge road, about a mile this side of the spring."

"Going which way?"

"Northeast."

Cowboy starts for the barn at a run. Diane stands in the sheeting rain and watches him go. Then she corrals the last of the goats and latches their gate.

A moment later Cowboy rides out of the barn on his big chestnut quarterhorse, his rifle across his thighs. He nudges the horse into a lope and heads through the downpour up the hill. Diane watches, feeling a strange satisfaction. He has gone off to avenge her for what almost happened, what could have happened. Either that or he just wants to shoot one, and this one will do.

She arrives home needing empathy from Gil. Well, from someone. Instead she gets this: "Your asshole friend went and bought one of those permits."

"He's not my friend. And I heard he was going to, not that he already did."

"You heard wrong. He got it this morning."

"Well, I guess that explains why he's out hunting."

"In the middle of a storm he went out hunting?"

"I saw one," she says. "Up on the ridge road by the spring. He went off after it."

She waits, dripping onto the carpet, for him to say things. Things like, Are you okay? You're limping. Were you scared?

When she grows tired of waiting, she limps into the bathroom and draws a hot bath.

She soaks until the shivering stops, until her stiff back and hip loosen slightly. When she closes her eyes she sees the face of the lion, staring at her, and wonders if she wants Cowboy to find him or not. If she wants him to miss or not.

When she dries off and comes out of the bathroom, feeling somewhat better, Gil is gone. She looks in the closet for his shotgun. That's gone too.

By the time she arrives back at the ranch, Gil's car is parked by the barn. Diane steps into the barn, out of the rain. Looks for Fletch, and calls for him, but he's still gone.

She saddles the most docile of Cowboy's horses, the big roan he bought for his six-year-old son to ride during his court-ordered visitations. Her left leg won't reach the stirrup; it hurts too much, so she leads him over to a hay bale to mount. They ride off together into the rain.

On their way up the hill she sees Gil a half mile up, on foot. She tries to kick the roan into a gallop, but only her right leg gives pressure, and he steps crabwise to the left. She uses the ends of the long reins to slap him first on one flank, then the other. They break into an uncomfortable trot.

Gil disappears onto the ridge road; then she hears the shot.

When Diane rides into the wet scene, she notices first that both men are alive. Lost in a confrontation, which involves being alive. Then she sees Fletch, but he is not alive. He's sprawled on his side not far from where he threw her, his eye open to the rain, free of the tack he wore. It's nearly dusk, and the lightning and thunder have moved close. Neither man seems to notice as she rides up. Cowboy has dismounted; his horse is grazing at the side of the road; he's pushing Gil back with a hand on his chest. Both have their guns in hand, but neither is raised.

She hears Gil say, "You had no right. No right to touch that horse. Any more than you had to touch *her.*"

Cowboy's arms fly out to his sides, rifle and all, a wet gesture of inculpability in the pouring rain. "Hey. I don't put my hands where they're not welcome."

Gil drops his shotgun, and Diane knows he's going to jump Cowboy. Even though she doesn't want this fight, part of her is glad to know he really would this time.

"Hey!" They both look up, startled, and the roan twitches. She wants to dismount, to go to Fletch. She wants to know what happened. He doesn't look like he crossed paths with a lion. He looks untouched. But she knows she'd never be able to remount.

Gil says, "He shot your horse, Diane."

Cowboy says, "His leg was broke. Stuck his foot in a squirrel hole running home. Clean broke, Diane. I just put him out of his misery is all."

Before she can answer Gil says, "You had no right."

"Yeah, well, what would you have done?"

"Get the vet out here."

"Vet can't save a horse with a broken leg."

"That's for the vet to decide."

"Wait!" she shouts. The horse twitches again; the men go silent. Cowboy's balled-up fist slackens. "Do I get to say something about this?" Diane sits her horse a second or two, watching the trees rain, tired of feeling soaked and cold. "Derek is right." Silence. "Why make him lie in the rain with a broken leg until the vet comes?"

She looks down at Gil, wanting to see his eyes, but it's too dim. Then he turns and walks away, toward the barn and his car.

Cowboy calls after him, "Forgot your shotgun." No reply. "I still want my damn cat back." Gil keeps walking. Cowboy looks up at Diane. "I still want my damn cat back." He looks more innocent somehow, soaked, like a dog freshly bathed. Not worthy of all the power she's vested in him.

"Bob passed away."

"From that thing on his side?"

So it's that easy. All she has to say is yes. Then it's Cowboy's fault, a closed subject. "No, the vet pulled him through that. There was an accident."

"Oh, great. You stole him so he'd be safe. Now he's dead. He'd've been better off with me."

"Maybe."

"Shit. I liked that cat."

"I know you did. I'm sorry."

After a moment Cowboy shrugs. Walks back to his horse, mounts up, and heads northeast, away from home.

Diane cups her hands around her mouth and calls after him. "Derek." He turns and rides back. "Are you insane? It's almost dark. That lion is two hours gone. The lightning is coming closer. My God, Derek. Give it up."

His horse shifts underneath him as he looks into her eyes. A flash of lightning illuminates them; thunder follows without a beat. He says, "I hung your tack on that tree." Then he heads for home.

Diane rides over to Fletch. Looks down at him, then down toward the valley. Lightning flashes, and she sees Gil on the hill trail, walking down. She looks back at Fletch. When it flashes again she sees the small, neat bullet hole between his eyes, the impossibly angled leg. It should be a relief. Because he was a mistake. She didn't want him. But he was her horse, anyway, and it hurts to lose something even if it was something you didn't entirely want.

She rides back leaving the shotgun in the mud. Leaving the saddle to hang on the tree in the rain. If Cowboy wants it, he can have it. She isn't going to get another horse.

When she arrives home, Gil is not only there, he has half her clothes packed.

"Where am I supposed to go?" she says.

"Should have thought of that before you did it. Why would you do that to me, Diane? With anyone. Especially with him. How could you even *like* a man like that?"

She sits down on the bed, soaking a spot on the blankets. "I mostly *don't* like him."

"Why would you sleep with a man you don't even like?"

She thinks, Maybe to get away from the ones I do. Which is partly true. But she says, "I don't know." Which is also partly true. "I'd rather leave tomorrow if it's all the same."

"Fine, whatever," he says, but he doesn't stop packing.

Diane's car crests the mountain and enters the pass. She pulls off to the side of the highway, parks in the dirt. Limps onto the rise to see what she can see. She always knew you could see the mountain pass from the valley but never thought to turn it around. Maybe because she wasn't likely to be up here again.

She thinks she can see the ridge road, but it's hard to be sure. She goes back for her binoculars, which are in the car somewhere. Everything she owns is in there somewhere. She finds them in a duffle bag in the trunk.

It's nearly dusk again by now, and twenty or more vultures circle the ridge road above the dark shape of her horse.

After sunset a few coyotes come out, but that's not what she was waiting for. She was hoping against odds to see the lion again, still in the neighborhood, looking for an easy meal. But soon it's too dark to see, and he hasn't shown himself.

He's probably moved on to the safety of fresh ground.

They probably both have.

Laura Kalpakian

Veteran's Day

1

THIS IS A SMALL TOWN, or maybe it just seems small because I been living here nearly thirty years, the only thirty years I've lived at all. It's a beach town, but most our tourists are overnighters, people on their way somewheres else. Everyone in my high school always swore they was going somewheres else too, San Francisco or Los Angeles, but almost nobody went nowhere, except maybe to the Army or the pen. My brother went to both.

My brother Walter put Esperanza Point on the map. When Walter turned himself in we had TV cameras and reporters and law-men crawling all over this town, snooping, sniffing like dogs at the grease can. They come into the DeLite Bakery to have a look at the mother of this criminal and certified loony and they hung out at Phil's Mobil where my dad works and they lined up at Lillian's Salon of Beauty to talk to me. They interviewed everyone who ever knew, or thought they knew, or might have known Walter Sutton. Yes, they just should have let school out in Esperanza Point the day Walter give himself up. It was a regular holiday.

I was sorry to see him give himself up. Walter's smart and he could have gone on a long time besting the sniffers and snoopers.

They was all after Walter: police in a half dozen cities, sheriffs in four counties and the FBI besides. Walter stole more cars than they could count. He set off two small bombs in Orange County, one at the Bank of America and one at the courthouse and one small bomb in Los Angeles at a Bank of America there. The bombs didn't hurt no one, just blacked up the place and made a mess. Then he set fire to some oil storage tanks down the coast that belonged to one of them big oil companies. They caught him for the fires and then they figured out about the bombs. At first they said he was a political terrorist and then they said he was just a disturbed Vietnam veteran, but when Walter told them he was proud of setting them fires and bombs, they changed their minds and declared he was insane and committed him to the State Loony Bin. Walter didn't seem so insane to me. Those bombs wasn't meant to kill anyone and they didn't. The fires was real cleverly set too. The man that can do that is pretty smart if you ask me.

But when they drug Walter out of the courtroom, he looked crazy. He was kicking and screaming and cursing, calling the judge and jury pigs and sheep and sonsofbitches with a lot other stuff thrown in, mostly about how they was tools and stooges in the government's plan to make us all sick, destroy our brains, and when we was all reduced to tapioca pudding, the government and the oil companies and the banks would lead us all to destruction because there wouldn't be one thinking person left to stop them. Robots, meat-hooks and hot dogs, that's all that would be left of human beings. "They're killing you with Radio Carbons in the air you breathe!" Walter screamed while they drug him out of the courtroom, "They're killing you with Killer Enzymes in the food you eat!"

So maybe he did sound kind of crazy. But you'd be crazy too if you hadn't ate for days. And maybe he did look kind of crazy because he kept his gas mask on the whole trial. I don't think the jury liked looking at that mask with its goggles and long nozzle of a face. Anyway, they never would have caught him for setting fire to those tanks in the first place, but Walter already had a record and a man with a record is as good as deeded, stamped, and delivered up to the police. A man with a record can't go nowhere the computers don't snarl and snap at his heels.

About a year before the bombs and the oil tanks, Walter got caught child-stealing, but it was his own child, Tommy, that he stole and he didn't do Tommy no harm, just kept him out of school and tooting around the state for about three weeks. They got Walter for that and for speeding (which is how they happened to get him at all), speeding and evading an officer because Walter had to run out of gas before that cop could catch him. All that and Grand Theft Auto because Walter took Tommy around the state in stolen cars. Walter wouldn't steal a car that wouldn't do 90.

There never was a car Walter Sutton couldn't steal. In high school he used to brag he could start a car just by looking at it right, tuning his electric vibes to the car's. I never saw him do that, but I watched him steal a Mustang once to show off for Shelly Smith. The Mustang belonged to the math teacher. It took Walter about five minutes to have that Mustang unlocked and humming. Shelly Smith was so excited she was popping sweat all over. The girls just loved Walter. They always have. But Walter and the law's never gotten on too well. The judge sent him to the reformatory for the Mustang, and then again for stealing a firebird, and on the third time the Judge sent him into the Army because he said that Walter was getting real close to being an adult and if he kept up the way he was going, he'd be in the pen before he was old enough to drink. Walter's social worker claimed he was just high spirited with a bit more mischief in him than most boys. The judge said even if that was so, the Army would still make a man of him.

My dad said the judge was right. My dad said the Army would shape Walter up and root him down. My dad's been rooted his whole life. He went to the same high school we did and he's worked at Phil's Mobil since before it was Phil's. My mom has worked in the DeLite Bakery for twenty years. I worked there myself when I was in high school, but I couldn't see living with my arms and hair and lungs caked with flour, so I went to beauty school, and I haven't done too bad. I've had a regular station at

Lillian's Salon of Beauty for eight years and regular customers too and it's a good thing because my ex ain't any too regular with the child support. Me and my two kids though, we never once been hungry, but as I say, my mother works at the bakery.

I got two younger sisters too, Ginna and Val, but in our family, I always stuck with Walter because Walter was the smart one, and between them Ginna and Val don't have the sense of polliwogs. They was both pregnant when they got married. Ginna was showing. So me, I always sided with Walter because he's no dummy.

He proved it too. He escaped from the State Loony Bin about six months after that arson trial. The papers and the news only said that Walter escaped from two orderlies who was taking him from the Bin to Veterans' Hospital to be tested for Agent Orange. That's all they said, but Walter told me how it happened and I can just picture how he done it.

Walter's got real charm. He's tall and has thick sandy hair and clear blue eyes and skin that's smooth as cake paper except for the creases at his eyes and mouth. He's got a wide smile that no one can resist. When he's not smiling he looks a lot older than thirty-three, but when he smiles, why he's just a boy and no one can make you laugh the way Walter can. I can see him, smiling, joking with those orderlies on the drive down to Veterans' Hospital. Walter don't say a word about Killer Enzymes and Radio Carbons, just joked about the nurses' behinds probably.

When they're waiting in the hospital lobby, Walter asks the orderlies to unshackle him because how could a man pee with his hands in bracelets? "I gotta be able to hold my dick," Walter says, "or else I'll pee all over myself and people will think I'm crazy." The orderlies laugh and unlock the cuffs and Walter did go to the bathroom, but then he just walked out and stole the first car he saw.

Walter and me had a good laugh over that because one night about two months after his escape, Walter come up and visited me. He wasn't only smart, Walter was brave.

I knew it was Walter. I could tell from the sound of the car that pulled into the trailer park lot. No one around here drives a car like that, growling and rumbly, hungry for speed and the road. It was

9:30 at night, my kids was in bed, and I looked out and saw a low sleek gray car with a kind of muzzle over the front to keep it from biting you. "Hi Betty!" says Walter. "How you been?"

"You better get inside," I said. "Ray Stoddard's been by twice this week already." But that was all I said, didn't ooh and ahh and squeal. I knew Walter'd be by sooner or later, and Ray Stoddard knew it too. He's a cop here in Esperanza Point (we got ten, one for each Commandment). Ray and me dated pretty serious in high school. Now we're both divorced with kids, but Ray keeps up his support payments and my ex don't. Ray told me he would be watching for my brother. He said he was going to capture Walter Sutton and get his picture on the evening news.

I told Walter this while he ate. He hadn't ate in days, but still he wouldn't have anything but eggs or oranges or bananas or melons. He said he couldn't eat anything touched by human hands because the government was putting Killer Enzymes in our food to turn us into robots and hot dogs. Pretty soon they would be able to do anything they wanted to us and we'd all obey because by then our brains would be nothing but compost. But I did talk Walter into having some bread and cake from the DeLite. He wouldn't touch the margarine though.

Walter finishes eating and leans back. "Well Betty," he says, "Ray Stoddard could put you in jail too for harboring a fugitive."

"Is that what they call it nowadays when you give your own brother a bite to eat?" I picked up Walter's dishes and put them in the sink. "Ray Stoddard ain't putting me nowhere."

"Not even to bed these days?" Walter grins.

"How did you hear about that?" I feel the blush roll up my face.

"Bad news travels fast."

"I went out with Ray a few times, but you can't do nothing in this town. Next thing I know, my clients are coming up to me and asking if Ray and me are taking up where we left off in high school. I couldn't hack it."

"Mom wrote me about you and Ray while I was in the Bin. She was real happy you two were dating."

"She acted like I broke it off just to spite her."

"Mom takes things personally."

"You going to go by and see them?"

"No. Mom would just cry. I can't stand to watch her cry. It tears me up inside. And Dad, well, he don't want to see me anyway."

"Dad's strange."

"It's the Killer Enzymes and Radio Carbons. Wished I'd known about them when I was in high school. Dad and me might have gotten on better if I'd known it was the Killer Enzymes making him take the strap to me so often."

"Dad's strange," I said again, not knowing what else to say. Dad had taken the strap to me a few times too.

"Anyway, Betty, you tell Ray Stoddard it's going to take a lot more than him to catch Walter Sutton. Why, the FBI's sent their best men after me and I'm too smart for them. The government wants me real bad, Betty."

"They think you're crazy."

"No, that ain't it. They know I'm not crazy. They know I'm onto them. I been onto them since Nam. And they know they can't buy me off, so they got to shut me up. If they don't, I'll tell everyone what the government's doing to them. They know I know." He tapped his forehead and nodded. "That's why they sent me to the Bin."

"What was it like in the Bin, Walter?"

"That Bin is nothing but a meat grinder. They just force your flesh through the place and you come out in little strings. Even if you was sane when you went in, you'd be crazy when you got out. Those doctors are nothing but paid assassins. They don't give a shit about the crazies. It's the sane ones—the ones like me—they got to grind down and out."

"Well I'm glad you're out. I couldn't sleep nights while you was in the Bin."

Walter pats my hand. "We always was a team, Betty."

"That's right and you just tell me if you need any help from me. What are you going to do now?"

"I'm going to tell the whole country what the government's doing to them! I'm going to tell the whole world what I figured out in Vietnam." Walter leans over toward me and whispers. "It started over there, Betty. You don't think they cared about those little gooks or their little gook country, do you? Hell no. They got us into Vietnam so the banks could make more money and so folks at home would have something besides their own bad luck and hard times to think about. You notice how much worse everything's gotten since we been out of Vietnam, don't you? Well, things have always been bad, but while we had Vietnam to watch on the news and read about, we didn't notice what they was doing to us over here. But that ain't the worse of it." Walter quit whispering and his nice blue eyes lit like flints. "The worst of it is, they had the Vietnam War so's they could have a bunch of civilians trained to kill on command. To be like dogs. They turned us into dogs over there. 'Bark!'" He shouted so loud I thought he'd wake my kids. "'Bite!' 'Kill on command!' And we did. They did it to us with chemicals. How else could they take all those thousands of men and turn them into animals if it wasn't with Killer Enzymes and Radio Carbons? Chemicals, Betty. They got chemicals in the air and everything we eat and our water. They didn't get out of Vietnam till they was sure they could do to the whole United States what they done to the soldiers." Walter sounded sad. "They got what they wanted out of that war even if they lost it. Every veteran, Betty, every one of them is a walking bomb. Every soldier got his triggers primed in Nam, but they don't know it and they won't until the government sends out a radio signal that will activate their Killer Enzymes, and then those vets will take up their guns and shoot their neighbors and friends. They'll kill anyone who doesn't hear that radio signal. Anyone who hasn't breathed in enough Radio Carbons or eaten enough Killer Enzymes, they'll be shot by guys like Ray Stoddard and Jerry Burns."

Jerry Burns and Ray Stoddard was in Nam just a little after Walter. People said Jerry's brains was zapped in Nam, but he never was real smart to begin with. Now Jerry calls everyone "Hot Rod" because he can't remember names, even if he is our mailman. I could believe what Walter said about Jerry Burns and it made me scared, but I wasn't going to show it. Walter and me's always gotten on because we was never scared of anything. We're not like Ginna and Val who are scared of everything and always have been.

Walter sipped his tea. He'd drink the tea because I boiled the water ten minutes and the tea was from China. "Maybe I'll steal Ray Stoddard's car on my way out of town," Walter said.

"You wouldn't want it. He's still got that old Dodge."

"Not that car," says Walter, his eyes twinkling behind the tea-steam. "His police car. I bet that police car will do 150. Why Betty, that little 28OZ I got out front will do 110 in a quarter mile. There's nothing that puts you in control like speed! I love speed. I love all that machinery packed around me, doing what I tell it to do. Cams and pistons and shafts turning and pushing and working and all that oil pumping and gas igniting! Speed is control, Betty. Control! It's the only control I've ever had in my whole life."

Walter's hands clenched at a make-believe wheel and he slouched down and pressed on the make-believe gas. His knuckles and face went white. "Speed and Control! Go!" He seemed to shoot right out of his chair, swerved and screeched like he could see the end of the world in front of him, and for a minute I was with him and I screamed too.

Walter laughed. "Gotcha, didn't I?" He got up and turned on the TV. "Let's watch the 11 o'clock news. I like to hear Tammy Takahara tell me to have a nice night and a good day tomorrow. She's real pretty, isn't she? Sort of reminds you of a little flower. Besides, maybe she'll have some news about me."

Me and Walter moved to the couch and settled in. "I'm like Paul Revere, Betty," he says to me at the commercial. "They got to catch me before I tell the whole country what they're doing to our brains with Killer Enzymes and Radio Carbons."

Walter fell asleep before the news was over, but I stayed up and listened to all of it. There was nothing about Walter. Tammy Takahara told me to have a nice night and a good day tomorrow and then I turned the TV off and covered Walter with a blanket and went to bed. I knew he wouldn't be there in the morning.

About a week later he calls me. His voice sounds scratchy and far away and the coins rattle as he puts them in the box. He wanted me to make Shelly let Tommy come over and play with my two kids on Saturday afternoon so he could see Tommy. Shelly and Walter got married on Walter's first leave from Vietnam, and they got divorced right after he come back. He never had too much time with Tommy, but he loved that boy. He was crazy about that boy.

I said I'd try. Shelly Smith and me was good friends in high school (mostly because she was in love with my brother, I think), and even after the divorce, I still did her hair once a week and our kids played together. Shelly and me got on all right as long as we didn't talk about Walter.

When Walter come on Saturday afternoon he was driving an old Chevy with bent fenders and a rusted-out paint job like you might have seen anywhere in this trailer park. He was wearing a disguise too, a wooly-looking wig and a hat and a pea jacket. But Tommy knew who it was the minute Walter walked into that trailer. Tommy flew into his arms. I nearly cried to see Walter on his knees with his arms around that little boy. I left and took my kids to the beach and I told them: the first one to open his yap about Uncle Walter gets a wallop in the chops. They knew I'd do it too.

When we come back from the beach, Walter had gone, but he left four gas masks, one for each of us. Tommy said his dad showed him how to use it and told Tommy to wear his whenever his mother wasn't looking. Tommy said we could save ourselves from the Radio Carbons if we wore the gas masks enough.

The next I heard about Walter was from Tammy Takahara. On the news she says the Customs people caught a boatload of marijuana in a port just south of us and they said they were told that Walter Sutton was hiding on that boat. But they couldn't find him. I chuckled. Walter must have squeezed himself into a little ball of dust and blown right past them Customs men.

I read about Walter in the San Angelo County *Gazette* (Esperanza Point's too small to have its own paper) and in the big-city Sunday papers too. They said he'd been seen in San Francisco and Lake Tahoe and as far north as Oregon and as far south as San Diego. They said he was armed and dangerous, which was just a crock. Walter swore he'd never carry another gun after Vietnam, and he never has. So if he was armed, it was only with his brains; and if he was right about the government, then brains was probably the same thing as a gun. Maybe worse.

Me and Mom talk about Walter when my dad's not in the house. He won't have Walter's name spoke. He says he can't stand to be the father of a jailbird. Sometimes, though, it's hard to talk to Mom because she cries so much. Her whole face is puffed up like yeast dough. My two sisters say: That lunatic Walter has ruined us in this town—our husbands are so ashamed of the Suttons, they're sorry they even married us. I say: Your husbands didn't have no choice about marrying you, did they?

Sometimes my clients ask me about Walter and I say—Oh, Walter just stopped by last Saturday and took me and the kids out for ice cream and the movies. But it wasn't so funny after Shelly found the gas mask under Tommy's bed and shook out of him where he'd got it. Shelly stormed into Lillian's Salon of Beauty and threw the gas mask at me (nearly hit me too, right while I was in the middle of a henna) and she started screaming so the whole world could hear I was no better than my crazy, criminal brother and she'd kill me if I ever came close to Tommy again.

I began to think Walter was right about the Killer Enzymes and Radio Carbons because I'd never seen anyone froth about the mouth like Shelly did. I was lucky Lillian didn't sack me on the spot. I don't relish the thought of unemployment.

Ray Stoddard come by my trailer late one night not too long after this. (I figured Shelley screamed at him too. She was a real screamer, that girl, though you never would have guessed it in high school. In high school she was just a little flower.) Ray rapped at the door like he was using his boot instead of his knuckles. He said it was the police, but I knew it was only Ray. I said "Wait a minute" and I went in the bathroom and took the Nitey-Net off my hair and gave it a quick spray and put on a dab of lipstick and mascara.

"I got a message for your lunatic brother, Betty," Ray says when I come to the door. His black uniform was buttoned and badged with silver and his white helmet glowed in the night and he was resting his hands on a leather holster. He looked like a shiny beetle. "You tell Walter I'm watching this trailer like a hawk. You tell him if he sets foot in Esperanza Point again, I'm going to nail his balls to the station door."

"Tell him yourself, Ray. I'm no errand boy." I started to slam the door, but he stuck his boot in.

"Next time I come, I'll have a warrant."

"Next time you'll need it. Now bug off."

Ray bugged, but I was pretty shaken-up. I turned on the news, but I couldn't stand to hear Tammy Takahara tell me to have a nice night, so I switched it to the old re-runs of *Love American Style* instead and watched that till I fell asleep sitting up.

2

When I was in high school, it seemed like every week one of my brother's friends was joining the Army or being drafted. A few of them went to San Angelo Community College down the coast and a couple, like Jerry Burns' older sister, went to colleges far away. I'd come home from school and watch the news and see college kids— kids I might have known—in San Francisco and Washington D.C. having what looked like peace picnics, protesting the war and singing "Give Peace a Chance" and calling for a halt to the sense- less slaughter. I'd watch them being clubbed and gassed and lying limp while they was drug off to jail. Then there'd be a commercial for Anacin or Ex-Lax and then I'd see boys in Vietnam—boys I might have known—getting gassed and shot at and scrambling up dirty hills and lying limp and dying in the mud.

People I'd known all my life suddenly stopped talking to each other. Ray Stoddard's mother, for instance, she quit talking to my mother and Jerry Burns' mother. Jerry Burns' mom would come into the DeLite Bakery and she and my mom would go into the back room and have a cry together. Ray Stoddard's mom, she would come into the DeLite and have a look around to make sure every- one was watching and then she'd say in a loud voice: "My boy is

over there protecting the free world from Communism. We only
have to bomb the hell out of those little gooks to have the war over
and done with and all the boys can come home."

Most of the boys came home. There was a few military funerals that left something like soot and ash over Esperanza Point for
days and over whole families for years. Ernie Little's mother was
never the same after they buried him. She wrote a note to Richard
Nixon saying she was going to kill him and the Secret Service came
out and investigated the Littles. Jerry Burns' older sister come back
from college at Christmas and said she'd been gassed and in jail and
she was proud of it.

"At least she ought to have the sense to keep her mouth shut
about it," my dad said. We were sitting in the office at Phil's Mobil.
The office always smelled like Dad—oil and metal and disinfectant
and carbon paper. "I wouldn't brag about going to jail."

"Well Dad, maybe they're right," I said, "maybe we shouldn't be
over there fighting the gooks' war for them. Maybe our boys should-
n't be dying over there for nothing. What if something happened to
Walter? I wouldn't trade Walter for their whole gook country."

My dad threw down his cigarette and stomped it out. "That's
what we have to do to Communism," he said, "Stomp it out. No
matter what it takes."

It took plenty. Plenty out of the Suttons. Walter didn't come
home when he was supposed to because he was in a military jail in
Nam for going AWOL and then he was in a military hospital for
hepatitis and then, before they'd send him home, they had to court-
martial him. When the Army was all through with Walter Sutton,
they gave him a dishonorable discharge and spit him back at us like
he was a slug we'd tried to slip in the juke box.

But at least he came back. My mom took a few days off from
the DeLite and did nothing but cook. Me and Ginna and Val stayed
home to help with the cleaning and getting everything ready. Shelly
(who'd been living with her folks all this time, her and baby Tommy),
she moved into our house and started getting Walter's old room all
ready for the two of them. My dad took some of Walter's old clothes
and drove all the way down to Fort MacArthur to bring him back.

But when Walter walked in, no one moved and no one spoke. All we could hear was Mom's groan. She sounded like a beast.

Walter's old clothes hung all over him. Even his skin hung all over him. He was so baggy and gray and colorless, he looked like a toad. He didn't fit into nothing. Not his clothes. Not the house. Not the family. He wouldn't talk so we had to sit at dinner and chat about ourselves, just as if we was giving him a refresher course on the Suttons and Esperanza Point. It was terrible. Bad enough, Walter wouldn't talk, but he was clutching a sandal. He was clutching it when he come in the door and he clutched it all during dinner. We couldn't see it, but we knew it was there, in his lap and no one could bring themselves to ask. Finally Big-Mouth Ginna says, "Why won't you let go of that smelly old sandal, Walter?"

Walter's lips peeled back. His teeth and gums and tongue was yellow. "I killed the man who wore this sandal," he said, "I took it off him after I killed him. I made a promise when I killed him and I'm keeping this sandal so I won't forget even though I can't remember exactly what it was I promised."

Mom had to run to the bathroom to barf and I thought when she was done, I'd go too. Ginna and Val and Shelly, their faces looked like vacuum bags with eyes. Shelly left the table and took Tommy out of his highchair; he was goo-gooing the whole time. What did he care?

My dad put down his fork. My dad says: "You're lucky you weren't wounded, Walter. You came through without a scratch."

When he'd been home about a week, Walter put the sandal down and Mom rooted through his room till she found it. She put it in a bakery box and took it to the DeLite and put it in the dumpster there. She found other things in Walter's room she wouldn't talk about. She wrote the Pentagon a terrible nasty letter about Walter's rotten discharge, calling them a bunch of ungrateful sonsofbitches. I thought sure we'd have the Secret Service on our doorstep too, but they never came. The Pentagon never even wrote back.

So the sandal was gone, but then Walter went out and bought a gas mask. He wore it all the time except when he was playing with baby Tommy. He always was crazy about that child. But the gas mask was too much for Shelly and she moved home within the week and started to divorce him.

For the next few years Walter had about three dozen jobs. Sometimes he'd quit. Sometimes they fired him. Sometimes he lived at home and sometimes he lived with this woman or that woman and sometimes we didn't know where he lived. We'd just notice we hadn't seen him around town in a while. He never did stay away too long though because of Tommy. He never missed too many visitation days. He just loved to be with Tommy, push him in his stroller down to Esperanza Point Park and fly kites or feed the gulls from the top of the cliffs.

Walter said he was writing a book about Killer Enzymes and Radio Carbons and the last time he left town (he stole a car so he couldn't come back after that) he give me this book in a box tied up with rope. He said I was to keep it no matter what happened to him. I promised I would, but I couldn't keep my promise because later, when my husband and me was splitting up, we had some killer fights. We had one nearly every night of the week just before the end. One night I come home from the Beauty Salon and I see smoke pouring out the kitchen window. I ran in and got my kids who were huddling in their room and I yanked them out and sent them next door and then I went into the kitchen. My husband had started a bonfire in the sink, burning up Walter's book.

I guess I would have shot him if I could. Without bullets there was nothing I wanted to say. Anyway, I already called him every name there was to call and I'd hit him as much as I could. So I went next door and got my kids and got back in the car and spent the night at my mom and dad's. The very next day I rented this trailer and I been here ever since. I didn't bother to pack nothing when I left my husband. But I'm like Walter, I'm no dummy. I took the checkbook and the first thing next morning I went down to the bank and cleaned that bastard out. I wrapped the money up and put it in the freezer and got me a smart lawyer and my old man never saw a penny of it.

3

Jerry Burns brought me Walter's letter one Saturday morning. There was no return on it, but I knew Walter's writing and I was glad old Jerry didn't know tit from tat. I took Ray Stoddard at his word though—I mean about watching the trailer—so I took my letter into the bathroom and locked the door and sat on the can and read it.

It wasn't a crazy man's letter. Walter said at last he had a plan. He knew how he could let everyone know about Killer Enzymes and Radio Carbons. (For a minute I was afraid he was going to ask for his book back. I never could tell him what my husband done.) But Walter didn't mention the book. He had a new plan.

He wanted me to call up Tammy Takahara at the news and tell her Walter Sutton was willing to give himself up to her and no one else. Walter would turn himself in to Miss Takahara as long as there was cameras rolling and he could read his speech (which he said he was already writing) to the whole world. He said he wanted Tommy by his side when he read this speech on TV, but after that, they could do whatever they wanted with him, though he hoped they'd put him in the San Angelo County Jail and not the Los Angeles one. He said this plan was the only way, even though it was a sacrifice. He said if he didn't do it, no one would ever know about what the government was doing to them.

Well, Walter's letter sounded simple enough, but I had a devil of a time. When I called Tammy Takahara first I told the secretary I was Betty Lusky and it was personal. Two days go by. Then I called and I said I was Betty Sutton Lusky and it was personal. Three more days. Finally I called up and I told the secretary I was Betty Sutton Lusky, sister of Walter Sutton who wanted to give himself up to Tammy Takahara at 10 a.m. on Thursday, the 25th of May at Esperanza Point.

The girl said: Miss Takahara don't accept invitations over the phone.

"Take the gum out of your ears, spitwad! This isn't an invite! I'm talking about Walter Sutton—the man who bombed out the

Bank of America! Walter Sutton wants to turn himself in! He wants Miss Takahara and the news crew there when he does it!" I slammed down the phone.

About half an hour later the phone rings. "Good evening, Mrs. Lusky. This is Tammy Takahara." She sounded just like she did on TV, but it's hard to talk to someone who seems like they've just glugged down a whole can of 30-weight.

It was easier to talk to her in person. She come up to Esperanza Point to see the letter from Walter and make sure all this was on the level. (She wanted me to mail it, but I said nothing doing.) She said they'd do everything Walter wanted and she would take care of contacting the police and the FBI. She said the news would like to interview me too and she'd like my kids beside me on the couch, but I drew the line and said no. Then she said, how about little Tommy? I said, ask Shelly. (I knew what Shelly'd say.) Then she wanted Mom and Dad, but I knew Mom was too weepy for television and Dad wouldn't have nothing to do with this. I told Miss Takahara: "It's me and me alone or no one." She said okay.

I cleaned up the trailer for them, but no one seemed to notice. Miss Takahara and her camera crew got dirt all over my rug, filled up my trailer with cameras and cords and nearly blinded me with the lights. I had to sit on the couch and chat, like they'd just popped in for a cup of tea and caught me in the middle of a manicure.

Miss Takahara explained to me what they'd do while the camera crew was getting ready. She was real pretty and little, but when I was talking to her, I felt like I was littler than her, even though two of her would fit in my clothes. She wore a cute navy blue suit with brass buttons and a red satin lining. I wondered who did her hair.

Once the cameras was rolling, I had to explain all over again how I got this letter from my brother. Then Miss Takahara explained to the camera all about Walter Sutton, as if the whole world hadn't heard about him. Then she turned back to me and said: "What does Walter Sutton want out of all this?" Just as if she didn't know.

"He wants to tell everyone," I said, and then I coughed and started again. I wanted to be a credit to Walter. "My brother is like

Paul Revere. He is trying to warn people that they're in terrible danger. Our minds are being poisoned by Killer Enzymes in the food we eat and Radio Carbons in the air we breathe. The government is putting chemicals everywhere so they can putrefy our brains and we'll obey them and not have a single thought of our own. They're controlling us just like they controlled all those boys who went to Vietnam. They turned those boys into killer dogs and primed their triggers so that when they hear the radio signal the government's going to send out one day, they'll turn and shoot their neighbors and friends."

"Yes, Mrs. Lusky, thank you very much."

"They'll kill anyone who hasn't already been got by the Killer Enzymes and Radio Carbons. We're being sickened and drugged so that the banks and the oil companies and the—"

"This is Tammy Takahara for the News."

The lights went out even though I was still talking and when the lights died, I was invisible. In my own house I was invisible. I was still talking but the camera crew banged and clanked their way out of the trailer and Miss Takahara shook my hand and thanked me like I'd just given her a back rub.

There was an Esperanza Point before there ever was a town. It's a high cliff overlooking the ocean that slopes back down to the highway. The city has put in a little park up there with privies and picnic tables. There's grass and pine trees and old junipers, but most of the time it's too windy up there for picnics. Even the trees have been bent almost horizontal with the wind that comes up off the ocean. Lots of hang-gliders jump off Esperanza Point and a few suicides too. This was the place where Walter wanted to give himself up at 10 a.m. on the 25th of May.

By the 24th, every motel room in town was three deep with people from the newspapers and TV and law enforcement types and state doctors and nurses. Our town crawled with squad cars and ambulances and camera vans and reporters interviewing everything that walked on two legs. All these visitors wore little badges and tags—law or press or medical—so they'd know who each other was.

By 8 a.m. on the 25th Esperanza Point (the park, not the town) was roped off and all the people with badges was checking out everyone without badges. They probably asked for ID from the gulls overhead. By 9 a.m. everyone in town was there. Bar none. Except my dad who said he had to work and my two kids. My kids hated me for it, but I made them go to school. I didn't want them to see something so horrible they wouldn't be able to forget because on the morning of the 25th I woke up with worms churning my guts. Fear dried up my tongue and made it thick.

I rode with Ginna and Val and Mom to Esperanza Point about nine. Ray Stoddard strutted around the Point like he owned it, shooing school children and kicking out on-lookers. He tried to shoo me too and I told him to bug off. Ray patted his club. "I can make you move."

"You and who else, turdbrain?" I said. I had the feeling I had maybe said the same thing to him years ago, when we was still kids in high school. But now I hated his everlasting guts and I knew I always would.

Just then Miss Takahara comes up and brushes Ray Stoddard aside like he is bellybutton lint. She nods at my mother and sisters and takes my arm. "We need you," she says and she marches me over to the picnic table where everything's set up and the cameras are in position. Little Tommy was there too. I had a new respect for Tammy Takahara if she could talk Shelly into letting Tommy be there. We all sat down and I put my arm around Tommy's shoulders and we waited.

Miss Takahara looked just lovely. She had nice black patent leather pumps and a gray suit with a short jacket and a lavender blouse. The makeup people fussed over her while we waited. She had a simple enough hair-do, but they fussed just the same and touched up the lilac on her lips and the lilac and gray shadows under her eyebrows. They gave her a nice blush across the checks.

Then they came after me with their tubes and pots and brushes. "I am a beautician myself," I said, "and no one puts on my makeup but me. Besides," I turned to Miss Takahara, "I thought we was here for serious business. I didn't think it was the goddamned school play." Miss Takahara's little black eyes squinched up and glared at me.

We waited some more. The camera crews lit up cigarettes and people in the crowd left for the little coffee and coke stands the Chamber of Commerce had set up at the bottom of the hill. The police and law types got restless; you could see them snorting and stamping like horses. The nurses put on pastel sweaters and chatted about the fog coming up off the ocean and the chill it brought with it. We waited.

At 10:40 Miss Takahara says to me, "I'm going to have your ass if he doesn't come, Mrs. Lusky."

"I hope he doesn't!" I said back, "I hope to God he never comes! Walter's so smart he could go on for months—for years! Just stealing cars and bombing out banks. Walter don't have to turn himself in. He's doing this so people will know, but I don't care if they never know! I hope he doesn't show! I hope—"

But even as the words was tumbling off my thick tongue, I could hear it somewhere, far away. I could hear it even if no one else could. Pistons pumping and shafts swirling and gears grunting and gas igniting. Speed and Control. *It's the only control I've ever had in my whole life.*

"Go back, Walter! Don't do it! There's no control here, Walter! Go back!" I bolted and ran hollering toward the sound of Walter's car, but a cameraman tackles me and they drag me back to the picnic bench and Miss Takahara gives me a hard shake and a swift kick in the ankle.

"Shut up! Sit down and shut up! You'll ruin everything. Stop blubbering. Get over here and fix this up, will you?" she says to the makeup people who mop me up and give me a Kleenex to hold and make me sit back down by Tommy. I shake and cry and try to hold Tommy's hand, but he won't have none of it. He looks at me like he don't even know me. His eyes are big and clear and eager because by now everyone can hear the car roar *(don't do it Walter, no, no, no)* and the motor snarl and the brakes squeal there at the foot of Esperanza Point. And then Walter kills the engine and gets out.

The crowd makes way for him slowly. Don't no one speak to Walter and he don't speak to them. He comes toward us and the picnic tables. He's carrying his speech in one hand and he's wearing his gas mask. He looks strange to everyone but me. And Tommy. Tommy knows who it is. Tommy springs up from the table, I reach out to catch him, but he's gone, he's past anyone who could stop him and he runs straight into Walter's arms. Walter gets down on his knees and holds Tommy and for one moment, quiet smothers us all. No ocean. No wind. No voices. All you can hear are the ants inching up the trees and the grass straightening itself up and Tommy crying into Walter's shoulder and Walter crying into his gas mask.

"STOP HIM! DO SOMETHING! HE'S CRAZY!" Shelly screams, ripping through the fog and the quiet. "He's crazy! Stop him!"

And they did. The doctors and the police and the three-piece-suit law types jumped Walter and fell into a pool of bodies and thumps and crunches and strangles and thuds. Someone dug Tommy out of the pile, but Shelly never quits screaming and crying out Tommy's name and I could hear my mother somewhere in the crowd crying out Walter's name. Miss Takahara was up like a shot and threw herself on the lawmen and doctors, but she got a belt in the mouth and fell backward and nobody helped her up because they was all too busy getting Walter Sutton into a strait-jacket and his feet in chains.

When they was done with him, Walter didn't even look human anymore, not between the gas mask, the chains and the strait-jacket. He hadn't a human thing except his voice screaming inside the mask and his kicking twisting and thrashing while they carried him off to the ambulance. The pages of Walter's speech blew away, high over the trees and the heads of the crowd. They flew like tiny tail-less kites out of control.

"You lousy lying shitheads!" Miss Takahara chased after Walter and the lawmen. "Walter Sutton is mine! Mine!" She kicked a cop and started beating on his chest. "I told you you could have him after I got my story! You promised, you shitheads! You promised!"

"He's dangerous, Miss Takahara," the cop said, taking her fists off his chest and handing them back to her. "He might have been armed. We can't take chances with a dangerous lunatic."

They shoved Walter in an ambulance and car doors slammed like a hundred rifles going off at once and sirens screeched and red and blue lights flashed as the ambulances and police cars started their engines roaring, all trying to get off the bluff at the same time. Their exhaust blackened up the fog at Esperanza Point.

Miss Takahara turned around and come back at me. I was still sitting on the picnic bench like I had sprouted roots from my bottom. "You bitch," she barked at me. Her lilac lipstick had smeared across her mouth like an ugly bruise and one of her false eyelashes hung off. "You bitch! You set me up for this."

I opened my mouth and it stayed open, but by now my tongue had got so thick, it filled up my mouth and I couldn't speak. My nose was running and I could not lift my hand to wipe it. I was crying without no sound. I had turned into a tree. I stayed a tree while Miss Takahara yelled and swore at me and even when she quit and went back to the makeup van. I stayed a tree while the sirens wailed and the cars fought to get off the bluff and while the people broke down the ropes and spilled all over the park. I stayed a tree while my sisters carried my mother away because she couldn't walk by herself.

I stayed a tree for a long time, it seemed, until I see Ray Stoddard pushing back the crowds, flinging his club around—not hitting anyone, just using that club to prod and push people into what he wanted them to do, and then I quit being a tree and I become a rocket launched at Ray Stoddard. I hit him so hard he falls over and drops his club and I jump on top of him before he can reach for it. I rip off his sunglasses and gouge at his eyes and bite him on the cheek and kick him in the balls and then people are all over me too, pulling me off Ray, holding my arms and trying to catch my feet while Ray scurries away on all fours.

"Get off her! Leave her alone! Put her down!" someone cries, and people quit pulling at my hair and legs and arms and I fall to the ground.

"She's as crazy as her brother," Ray sputtered through the blood coming out of his nose.

"She's the only sane one here. Come on, Hot Rod. Get up. It's okay now." Jerry Burns picked me up and gave me something to hold against my bloody lips and kept his arm around me all the way back to the mail truck. He wouldn't let no one touch me or come close.

I sat on the floor of the mail truck and bawled. "Go ahead and cry all you want, Hot Rod." Jerry patted my head all the time when he didn't have to shift. "You just cry all you want. Cry all over the mail if you want. Drown it all. It's nothing but a bunch of bills from the banks and oil companies anyway. Drown it."

It took Esperanza Point about a week to clean up after Veteran's Day and about a month to simmer down. And about a year to forget.

Shelly moved away and took Tommy, but not before she found a judge to certify that Walter was so insane she didn't have to let Tommy visit his father. My mom and dad split up. Never divorced. My mom still goes over there and cooks supper for him now and then and she makes sure he gets his favorite cookies at the DeLite. But Mom lives with me and the kids in the trailer now and she don't cry as much because I won't let her do it in front of the kids and that cuts down on her crying time.

About twice a month Mom and me go to the high-security Loony Bin to visit Walter. This Bin is closer to Esperanza Point so we see more of him than when he was first committed. He still won't eat nothing but eggs and oranges and bananas and melons, that and bread from the DeLite which we bring him. He's got that baggy look again, like his bones are shrinking inside his skin. His teeth are going bad, but he talks clear as he ever did, and now and then he gives us his old smile. He don't wear the gas mask anymore because he says he don't care if he lives or not. That's what he says, but I know Walter Sutton. I know he's just saying that for their benefit—the meatgrinders at that hospital. Walter's so smart one day he'll turn himself into a kite and fly right out of there, hot-wire a hot car and be gone. He'll outsmart them all. He's not crazy. He never was.

Mom has to be to work at five so she goes to bed real early. I sit up by myself and watch the 11 o'clock news. I swear at Tammy Takahara. Sometimes I reach under the couch and I get out the gas mask Walter give me and hold it. I feel better when I hold it, like Walter must of felt when he held that dead man's sandal. I feel like I'm holding onto the promise I made Walter, but I don't exactly remember what it was. Can't imagine what I promised him, but it must of been something important, otherwise why should I hold that gas mask in my arms when I watch the news?

Sometimes I put the gas mask on. Tammy Takahara swims in front of my goggles. It's real quiet inside that gas mask. I can hear myself breathe and I know if I wear it enough, they'll never get me.

Steve Lattimore

Separate States

DAD USED TO DRIVE UP and spend his nights at Shadow's apartment, but he had to stop because I was giving his stuff away. If he stayed gone a full night, I'd drive around the next day with items he particularly cherished—a handful of Snap-On wrenches, the ugly black Stetson he wore to bars—and give them to someone who looked like he might want them. No one ever turned me down. After a month or so of that, Dad sold my car. I came appropriately unglued, and he stayed home every night for a week. Then he spent a night at Shadow's. Fine. When he came home the next day nothing was gone, I didn't say a word. Then he spent two nights away. I put a sign on the bulletin board at the True Value: "Free—Brand New Stay-Rite pool pump and man's Citizen watch at…" The pool was clouding up nicely by the time Dad got home. He grounded me, but my generous nature grounded him right back.

So he took to the phone. You could bet that if he wasn't at work, he was lying in bed, fiber optically connected to his hideous scag mistress. Not being a veteran of the phone, though, he wasn't prepared for the bill that came—$1,200 for a single month. Shadow lives up in Fresno, not far, but still a long-distance call. "A phone ain't worth $1,200," Dad said, and let the bill go unpaid. He's no cheapskate by any means, in fact if anything he's the opposite—a sucker for a brand name, whatever the cost. But he wants a show for his dollar—maximum horsepower, a glossy finish, the most gadgetry and lines of resolution per inch. He likes the look on people's faces as they reconsider him in the flattering light of his purchases.

I love Dad and try to be patient with him, but when I picked up the phone and heard no tone, I went homicidal. "Does she have a 900 number?" I screamed. "Can't you find a woman in this whole area code?"

"What was I supposed to do?" he whined.

"Make *her* pay it."

"But she ain't got a pot to piss in," he said, "and I'm union." Then he blindly hit the rawest possible nerve. "No one ever calls you anyway."

I lined up his shot glasses from different states and crushed them one by one with the blender base as he watched. "If you ever speak to me again," I told him, "I'll sue you."

"Gonna be pretty quiet around here, I guess."

Rather than reconnect phone service, Dad decided to bring Shadow down to Hanford to live with us. I felt bad about giving his things away, breaking his jiggers—he *does* work hard—so I tried to be positive. "The phone savings can go toward my next car," I said.

Then I met Shadow. She was pale and sickly, gaunt and skinny as a switch. I didn't know what the word "ragamuffin" meant exactly but I'd heard it, and when I saw Shadow I understood. Holding on to the back pockets of her jeans were two tangly looking seaweed creatures, girls, silent and unsmiling. Nobody had said anything about kids.

"This is a real nice place," Shadow said to me. "You're a real lucky girl."

Pointing to Shadow's girls, I told Dad flatly, "They are *not* to use my bathroom."

"They won't," he said. "Now hush up."

Shadow inspected her new quarters, clearly pleased. Given Dad's personality, she probably expected something made of tin that ran just fine on leaded gas. "Welcome home," Dad said. He pulled

Shadow full against him, beaming. She gave him a little squeeze around the pot and he about gacked his pants with pride. The thing I've never been able to abide in Dad is how grateful he is for so little affection. It's endearing for about a nanosecond, then you want to vomit.

"Don't expect me to entertain these waifs while you two are doing it," I said.

"What's with the mouth?" Shadow asked, whether of me or Dad I wasn't sure, but oooh, I had that bitch in my cross hairs. Then the bruises on her arms caught my eye, the needle marks, and for the first time in my life I was struck dumb. My brain was already packing a suitcase, picking out this top and those pants.

"Shadow," I said. "How are your T cells these days?"

Dad had had enough. "Why don't you haul your damn smart mouth to your room until you can act like a person."

"What's that supposed to mean?" Shadow asked. "My cells?"

Dad wilted visibly, meek and pathetic, terrified that I was going to wreck his grotesque abomination of a romance. Which I definitely was. "Erin," he begged. "C'mon."

"I just meant your health," I said then to Shadow. "You look tired."

Apropos of nothing in the known universe, Shadow said, "I fell down stairs last month and had some internal bleeding. I've got a tilted uterus."

I would have thrown up right there if I was my normal self. But as Shadow said "tilted uterus," something inside *me* shifted as well. I can't trace it for you and say, *That made me think of this, which reminded me of that, which clued me in on this other.* It doesn't work that way. Shadow just said those two words and I looked at Dad and saw a man who raised me from a baby and loved me and put up with all my shit, but who had no genetic claim on me, no blood connection at all. I realized then that my real father lived somewhere else. I saw the shape of his state in my mind, its lean finger pointing skyward, but I couldn't name it. Then, like a time snap, I heard Mom's voice: "Thank God I screwed around." It was a sideways crack she'd made when I was little, but the words didn't find me until the very day I'm describing. If you think it doesn't work that way, you're wrong.

Dad suddenly looked scared. "What's the matter?" he asked. "What's wrong with you?" My chest was tight, my breath coming shallow. He left Shadow's side and put his arm around me. I suppose I was crying by then. "You had a naked Norman," he said.

I nodded. "I saw my father's state," I said. "It's not our state. He's not you."

Dad pulled back from me a little and looked into my eyes, something he never did. He hugged me tight. "I love you, girlie," he said. He looked scared.

"Is something going on?" Shadow asked. "Should I leave?"

This is embarrassing to admit, but just then I left my father's—this man's—arms, and steered Shadow by the shoulders into them. "Stay," I said. Like she was a dog.

When I was in kindergarten I up and left the playground one day without a word and walked home alone. The school called Dad at work and he rushed home in a panic to find me on the living room floor, asleep. "I slapped your face," he later told me, "but you were zonked." In my sleep, or maybe at school, I saw my Uncle Norman lying naked on his bathroom floor, unmoving. I woke up screaming, then I sobbed and sobbed, telling Daddy what I'd seen. He took me to my uncle's to show me that it was just my imagination—my overmation, he called it—that Norman was okay. He wasn't, though; he was dead. Naked on the bathroom floor. He'd had a fit and swallowed his tongue. More than once I'd seen him nearly die this way, seen Dad's fingers in his mouth, Uncle Norman's teeth clamped hard onto them, drawing blood.

After that day, Daddy was almost openly afraid of me. And I was afraid of myself.

I left Dad and Shadow like that, went to my room, and fell fast to sleep. It was night when I woke, the darkness chilling me inside and out. I didn't know quite where I was. A tingle, a fright ran through me. Then I lifted the handset of the phone and heard silence. I was home.

I slipped on some jeans and a sweater and walked down to the Beacon station to call my mother. She and Dad had always been separated, always.

"You whore!" I said when she answered. "You cheated on him. How could you?"

Mom yawned. "If you were married to Dodd, you'd know how easy it was."

My mother had a talent for the truth. She used it to quiet me, to cheat me out of my anger. It was a trick I'm sure Dad wished he knew.

Mom told me my real father's name. She told me what he looked like, what she sees of him in me. "Fire and wind and rain all at once," she said. "A walking natural disaster, just like you." Then she was quiet a minute. "But with him," she said, "it was just armor for a broken heart. I worry that your armor is really you."

She didn't apologize for that, she just went on, which is what Mom always did. "Your father didn't lay a finger on me," she told me. "All he cared about was our friendship, the way we were together, talking and laughing and telling the truth because I was married so friends was all we could be." She gave him plenty of chances, she said, but where other men would see opportunity, my father saw only her, and that she was hurting. "Things weren't very pretty with Dodd," she said. I asked how she got knocked up with me if this guy wouldn't touch her. "Because I'm a woman," she said. "That's how. Any woman can screw any man if she really wants to. I loved that your father didn't take advantage, but God, it also turned me on."

"You're disgusting," I said. "If you ever talk to me again..." Nothing more came out.

"It was the only time I've ever been in love," Mom said. "I still love him."

"Still?"

"Still."

"I know where he lives," I said. "I saw it in my head."

"He lives somewhere in Idaho, I think."

"Idaho."

"He'd love to meet you, Erin. It's the way he is." She didn't know what to say after that, and neither did I. So we said goodbye.

School was like a nightmare the next day. I woke up late and missed my first two classes, and in fourth period home ec, Brenda Arnsparger held up a picture drawn in her notebook of a huge dick with a face impaled on it, my name beneath the face. I didn't kick her ass at lunch. I was too tired, too something. A couple of weeks earlier she'd flashed me a dirty look from the pizza line, so I hit her in the face with a plate of stir fry. She was a nobody, a hopeless, bug-eyed loner who had no right to look at me like that. After our fight, she made friends with Avis and Mavis Davis, two white-trash sisters the size of Porta Potties who pretended to be Mexican, for what reason even God, I'm sure, is wondering. The Davises were mean. No one in the history of Kings County has ever stood up to them, not even guys. Now Brenda dressed like them, long plaid shirts buttoned at the neck and baggy chinos. She smoked and called people *ese* and *pinche* and spray-glued her bangs straight up. She looked like a peacock's ass.

In fifth period, Understanding Our World, Mr. Unzueta talked about Pangaea, this humongous landmass that long ago contained all seven of today's continents. He put diagrams on the overhead that showed how the shapes of the continents all fit together, like pieces of a puzzle. And it was true, they did—one big chunk of land surrounded by all this water. Then, over a long time, this big super-continent broke into two pieces, Laurasia and Gondwanaland. Unzueta started to say something about continental drift but there was a fight outside and he went out to break it up. The land kept going on like that, I guess, pieces breaking off and drifting apart. When Unzueta came back, we watched a movie about geodesic domes and I started crying. I got up and left for the nurse's office, told her I had a migraine and only a dark room would help. She called Dad to come get me.

But Shadow came instead of Dad. She was driving his Bronco, which even I wasn't allowed to drive.

"Does Dad know you're a junkie?" I asked her.

"I don't do junk," Shadow said.

"Don't even *try* the diabetic thing."

"I used to shoot a little," she said, "but I don't anymore."

"Oh my God! What a maggot! Where did my father meet you?"

"Look," Shadow said. She pulled the truck over. "Your dad and I like each other and we want to hang out. Are me and you gonna have to throw blows before we can get some peace?"

I slumped down in my seat. "Not if you keep out of my way," I said.

Shadow put the truck in gear. "Why are you such a bitch, anyway?"

"I have issues."

"Yeah?" Shadow looked puzzled. "Well...I have two left feet."

A strange silence followed, then Shadow cracked up laughing, and then I did.

"Willis Dodd isn't my dad," I said.

"So I hear. That was quite a moment you two had."

"It was something you said that made me see it. About your uterus being tilted. Which, by the way, grossed me *completely* out."

Laugh lines forked at the corners of her eyes. "Then you'll like this," she said. "I have to make adjustments when I have sex, because of the tilt. The normal angles don't work."

"I'm just going to turn my imagination right off."

"You're a virgin, huh?"

"That's none of your business."

"I guess not," Shadow said. "But you shouldn't take it out on everyone else."

"Just drop me off right here," I said. But Shadow drove on.

Dad was sitting at the table drinking whiskey when we got home. He looked morose and unfed. When he saw me he said, "Migraine, huh. Since when?"

"Why are you drinking in the middle of the day?" I asked.

"I guess it's still my house," he said. "I guess I can drink in it if I want to." He took his jackknife out of his pocket, opened the blade and set it on the table in front of him. He unbuttoned his sleeve and rolled it to the elbow. "Turn out the light," he said. "Leave me alone."

"You're making an ass of yourself," I said. Shadow looked at me hard.

"You're gonna try and find him, ain't you?" Dad asked. "Your biological fuckface."

I said nothing. What would be the point?

"Go on then," Dad said. He put the knife to his wrist. "Leave me alone. Both of you." I left Shadow to deal with him. What a piece of theater.

I don't have a lot of friends. I have no friends. The day I picked up the phone and found it dead I was about to call that public service number that rings you right back. People hate me. They started hating me early and I grew up as the girl people hated. So I did the only thing I could: I hated them back. Maybe this is sick, but when I figured out about my real dad, when I saw Idaho silhouetted in my head, the first thing I thought was: Would people hate me there too? There are so many people in California, it's such a big state to be hated in.

I took out the encyclopedia and lay with it on my bed. Idaho is between Ictinus and Idalium. Only a million people live there. It's almost all mountains. It has the deepest gorge in the country, nearly 8,000 feet beneath the peaks. The chief industry used to be mining, but now it's agriculture. It's a Republican state but they elect Democrats for governor. It has four electoral votes. It's just this side of the Continental Divide.

When I got home from school the next day, Dad, Shadow, and the fright wig twins were in the family room watching *Star Wars* on the biggest television screen I'd ever seen. X-wing fighters screeched into the picture from every direction. Wall-mounted speakers hissed with laser fire. Dad grinned like a schoolboy. "Greetings, Princess Erin."

"Greetings, Darth. What's all this shit?"

"It's new," Shadow said.

"Duh."

"Listen to that sound," Dad said. "And look at that." He pointed to the new VCR. "We taped *All My Children* for you."

"We figured you wouldn't want to watch it with us," Shadow said, "so we put the old TV and VCR in your room."

"You figured right," I said. But then I dropped onto the couch at Shadow's feet and watched the big screen with everyone else. The picture was crisp, the sound cutting, like razors through brain. It was amazing.

Dad shut everything off with the remote control and Shadow said, "Girls, go outside. Grownups have to talk." The girls got up without a word and left. Scary.

Dad said, "About this other deal, um…"

"Dodd's going to help you find your biological father," Shadow said.

"I hope you'll still think of me as your father too," Dad said.

"There's this private investigator," Shadow said. "He's real good. Can I tell her the story?"

Dad grimaced. "I don't want to hear that again."

"Nothing happened," Shadow said. "We didn't do anything, just hung out a couple of times." Dad mumbled something and Shadow went ahead. She said she'd worked for an insurance company, in claims. She figured out how to file phony claims and have the checks sent to her friends. She got away with it only twice before she got caught. The company hired a private eye who got her on videotape—receiving the envelopes, cashing the checks, the whole enchilada. "He had videotape of me inside my own apartment," she said. "I was blown away." Shadow was fired but for some reason not prosecuted. Then, a few days later, the PI showed up at her door and asked her out. "Is that balls or what?" she said. Dad bristled at this, so she skipped forward. "I'm sure he could find your father for you," she said. "That's an easy job for them guys."

I said I'd think about it, which Dad didn't like. "Offer ain't open till doomsday." He remote-controlled *Star Wars* back into reeling, screeching Technicolor, and at hearing the movie, Shadow's girls came back in. I left them to themselves. Luke Skywalker is such a fag.

Over the next couple of weeks, Dad went crazy buying stuff for the house: a Stairmaster, a mountain climber, a Soloflex, and a treadmill. The screened-in patio became a home gym. Dad patted the minuscule ledge of Shadow's ass. "If there's a muscle in there," he said, "we'll find it." She rubbed the bowl of his paunch. "No problem finding this." It was sort of cute. Dad looked happy. I pretended to be disgusted by it all, but at night when everyone was asleep I snuck out and used the Stairmaster, dreaming, as I climbed and climbed, of showing up in Idaho a new person, skinny and without armor.

After working out just two times, Dad was stiff as a cyborg. His eyes filled with tears when he lowered himself onto the couch. We all laughed watching him, and he laughed too. "It hurts," he said. So he bought a spa. The salesman guaranteed that the whirlpool setting would turn Dad's muscles to jelly. About every ten minutes Dad assured us that it did. "Feels good," he said.

After my late-night workouts, I'd fold the spa cover back and slip in. Ten minutes of that heavenly churning water and I slept like an Egyptian.

One night while lying back in the spa, the water pounding beneath me, I opened my eyes to find Dad standing there, smiling proudly. He had a towel in his hand. "I didn't know you was out here," he said.

"I was just trying it out," I said. "I'm done." I started to climb out but Dad stopped me.

"No," he said. "Stay. I don't have to use it."

"It's okay," I said.

"Really," he said. "Stay there. Sit." He stood with hands on hips, fairly beaming. "Feels good, don't it?"

"Yeah," I said. "It's nice."

"See. I'm not such an idiot."

"I didn't say you were an idiot."

"Well." He shifted from foot to foot. "It seats eight people. I guess we could both use it."

"I guess."

Dad hung his towel on a hook and started to get in.

"Actually," I said, "I'm getting kind of hot. I think I'll get something to drink. You want anything?" He shook his head. "I'll bring it to you," I said.

"Don't bother."

I got out and wrapped myself quickly in a towel. "Okay," I said. "Well, good night." I went inside and watched from the glass door as Dad covered the spa and took a seat on the redwood steps beside it. For a long time he sat with his hands on his knobby knees, looking toward the house.

After that I kept my distance. I was waiting—I knew that—but for what I wasn't sure. I listened to the goings-on outside my bedroom door, the movies they all watched on the big screen and the songs Dad and Shadow drank and even danced to. Dad extended his credit for an old-fashioned Wurlitzer jukebox with bubbles and electric lights and stocked it with sad, chin-in-your-beer country songs for him and lava lamp acid-flashback stuff for Shadow, Janis Joplin and other dead junkies. For the first time ever, the house had a pulse.

The next time I used the spa, Shadow slipped out of the house stark naked and joined me. "That's not how you do it," she said, snapping the strap of my swimsuit top. She climbed into the tub and sprawled out like a spider, one leg bobbing gently in my lap. "Let it hit you everywhere," she said. She moaned then like some kind of barn animal and I scooted away from her. She lay back, eyes closed, taking in water and spitting it out. "No one likes you," she said. "You don't go out, there are never any guys around. What's wrong with you?" I turned the air bubbles on, the blower *whirring* loudly now. Shadow hollered above the noise. "You're not ugly."

"That makes one of us," I said, mostly to myself.

She reached past me and shut the whole thing off. The swirling water slowed. "Face it," she said, "you're socially retarded."

"What should I do?" I asked.

"My opinion? I'd pick out some guy at school, someone you like a little but not a lot, and make it your job to fuck his brains out. You're the terminator: Don't stop until he's totally in love with you. And trust me—at that age he will be. Then ditch him. Word will get out, and you'll have more friends and dates than you'll know what to do with."

"Are you, like, some fuck monster or something?"

"No," Shadow said. "But yours is an extreme case. I'd lay someone. Only don't fall in love. Then your ass is his, he owns you. A virgin in love? I wouldn't wish that on anyone."

"There's no one here I could fall in love with anyway," I said. "People are scummy here."

Shadow got out of the tub and stood rubbing herself with the towel until she shone pink in the moonlight. "No they're not."

Ricky Machado wasn't a complete jerk. He was in my home ec class. He whisked egg whites into soft peaks with some style, flexing his jaw because he knew it looked cool. Until he got hit by a car while he was riding his skateboard, he was medium popular. Then he got a thigh-high cast on his leg and suddenly everyone liked him. The cast was marked with cartoons and colorful signatures like you'd expect. By Shadow's reasoning, he'd be a good choice; I couldn't *really* fall for someone who greeted people with the Vulcan peace sign.

We were supposed to be making V-neck shirts in class, but I think Ricky was making a kite. I stopped at his table and he looked up at me with pins in his mouth, eyes wide like he'd been busted. His material was skulls and crossbones on a black field. I asked if I could sign his cast.

He looked puzzled. "What are you going to write?"

"I don't know. My phone number maybe." I remembered then that I no longer had a phone, but I kept my wits. "I'll think of something."

"Yeah," he smiled. "Okay." From his backpack he took a pouch of felt-tip pens. "Pick a color," he said. I took red. Ricky scooted his leg out from under the table and I kneeled down. The only white space left was on the inside of his thigh, so I had to scooch down some. As I steadied the cast with my free hand, Brenda Arnsparger shouted, "Look out, it's a blowjob!" Ricky grabbed the back of my head and pulled me toward him. I broke loose and fell backward into the aisle. The bell rang for lunch then, and people poured by me.

Dad and Shadow drove up to Fresno the following day to see Shadow's private eye. The house was dark when they got back, the only light coming from the big screen. The girls were sprawled on the floor as usual, and I was lying like a corpse on the new couch. Shadow ignored me and dropped to the floor with her girls, who intertwined their arms and legs with Shadow's until they looked like a giant bird's nest. It was nice how they all fit to each other, how the girls went right to Shadow without a thought, how she accepted them and let them be as they would, all of a body. For his part, Dad went to his room without a word. Through the noise of the TV, I heard his door click shut at the far end of the dark hall.

The next few days creaked by. I didn't take a step toward school, and Dad said not a word. He started working double shifts, whether to keep away from me or to pay for his spending spree I didn't know. Shadow and the girls had the run of the house, blasting the TV and the jukebox, using the spa like a splash pool. I stayed in my room.

Idaho was granted statehood in 1890, the forty-third state. Its nickname was the Gem State, its bird the mountain bluebird, its flower the syringa, whatever that is. Its tree, I learned, was the Western white pine. The state song: "Here We Have Idaho."

The Nez Perce was the big Indian tribe in Idaho. They were renowned for large herds of appaloosa horses. Their leader was Chief Joseph. A cunning fighter, he defeated huge federal troops with a small band of warriors. The government kept finding stuff they wanted on Nez Perce land, though, and moved the tribe farther and farther into the desert southern regions of the state. A few young warriors rebelled by killing some settlers, and the army went after the whole tribe. Chief Joseph took all his people and fled toward Canada to escape the soldiers. They eluded the troops for nearly fifteen hundred miles, but finally they were caught, just thirty miles from the border and freedom. "I will fight no more forever," Chief Joseph said. The Nez Perce were banished to a barren, hopeless reservation, but he kept his promise.

When the letter from Shadow's PI came, Dad turned a shade of crimson as he read it. "What does it say?" I asked. Dad said nothing, so I grabbed it away from him.

> Mr. Dodd,
> Your check bounced. I hate working for the general public. Anyway, I have all the stuff you want but you're going to have to bring a cashier's check to my office to get it. It was an easy job and, as you can see by the enclosed invoice, didn't cost much. Which makes all this a pain in the ass. Why don't you get a phone?

"Do you have the money?" I asked.

Dad shook his head. "I get paid next week," he said.

"Idaho has a population of one million," I said. "It's called the Gem State. The state bird is the turkey buzzard."

"I could take a cash advance on my credit card," Dad said.

"They test nuclear weapons on the Indians there. And diseases too. Bubonic plague, black death. And they hunt them for sport. But the Indians keep smiling. They're a proud people."

"I'm sorry I've been such a terrible father."

"You haven't been terrible," I said. "I just hate my life."

"Okay," Dad said, his eyes glassy now with tears. "I'll go."

I went to my room. A few minutes later, Shadow knocked, then came in. "You should go with him," she said. "You really should."

"Will you come too?" I asked her.

She climbed onto the bed and gathered my hair at the back, took a scrunchie from her pocket and doubled it over and over until I had the taut ponytail of a little girl. "You should probably go just the two of you," she said. "Don't you think?"

"Yeah." Then I said, "He really is a good man."

"He's a prince," Shadow said. She laughed dryly, her smile hanging a beat too long in her cheeks.

"Do you love him?" I asked.

"Sister," she said, "he knows all my angles."

It turned out that Dad didn't know Shadow's angles at all, though. When we got home from Fresno, me gripping the bright white envelope of my real father's life, the house had been cleaned out and Shadow and the girls were gone. Dad and I walked silently from room to room, pausing at the dents like fresh scars in the carpet. Everything was gone. Everything. All the rooms were empty except for clothes strewn here and there. How big our little house looked.

I sat on the family room floor where the big screen had been and cried. Dad walked the rooms again, looking, I knew, for a note. When he didn't find it, he sat back against the wall beside me. "I guess that's that," he said.

"We should call the police."

He nodded, cupped his hands to his mouth. "Police!" he called. "Hey you dumb sonsabitches!" He sat quiet for a while, his fingers absently tracing furniture outlines in the carpet. "I'm just not meant to hold on to things," he said.

"I'm going to miss her," I said.

Dad laughed. "One crazy bitch after the other. I guess that's my lot in life."

"Does that include me?" I asked.

Dad pressed the keys to the Bronco into my hand and squeezed it shut. His last possession. "It does today," he said. "About tomorrow I couldn't even guess."

I drove to the Beacon station and dropped a handful of change into the phone, punched the numbers to my father's house in Sand Point, Idaho, the area code exotic to the touch. Immediately it was answered.

Have you ever heard yourself on tape, the voice that is but isn't you? This was the voice I heard. It was almost me, but not quite. The girl laughed into the phone. "Hello?" Band music shimmied in the background, party chatter reaching me as a happy din.

"Hello," I said. "I'm calling for—"

"Hello?"

"Hello. I'm calling—"

"Daddy," the girl shouted above the noise. "The phone's doing it again." Something made of glass broke in the distance. A peal of laughter echoed. "Are you there?" the girl asked. "If you are, I can't hear you."

"I think I might be your sister," I said.

"Whoever this is, I guess you'll have to come over now. Don't worry, we'll be going late."

"Maybe someday we'll meet."

"Don't bring anything, we have plenty."

"I have to go now," I said. "Goodbye."

"Sorry, I can't hear you. If this is Tim, where are you?" She hung up.

I dropped my last quarter into the phone and tapped out my number. It too was strange, nearly forgotten. Then the recording came on. *You've reached a number that has been disconnected.* For better or worse, I knew this time I was calling home.

John L'Heureux

The Comedian

CORINNE HASN'T PLANNED to have a baby. She is thirty-eight and happy and she wants to get on with it. She is a stand-up comedian with a husband, her second, and with no thought of a child, and what she wants out of life now is a lot of laughs. To give them, and especially to get them. And here she is, by accident, pregnant.

The doctor sees her chagrin and is surprised, because he thinks of her as a competent and sturdy woman. But that's how things are these days and so he suggests an abortion. Corinne says she'll let him know; she has to do some thinking. A baby.

"That's great," Russ says. "If you want it, I mean. I want it. I mean, I want it if you do. It's up to you, though. You know what I mean?"

And so they decide that, of course, they will have the baby, of course they want the baby, the baby is just exactly what they need.

In the bathroom mirror that night, Russ looks through his eyes into his cranium for a long time. Finally he sees his mind. As he watches, it knots like a fist. And he continues to watch, glad, as that fist beats the new baby flat and thin, a dead slick silverfish.

Mother. Mother and baby. A little baby. A big baby. Bouncing babies. At once Corinne sees twenty babies, twenty pink basketball babies, bouncing down the court and then up into the air and—whoosh—they swish neatly through the net. Babies.

Baby is its own excuse for being. Or is it? Well, Corinne was a Catholic right up until the end of her first marriage, so she thinks

180

maybe it is. One thing is sure: the only subject you can't make a good joke about is abortion.

Yes, they will have the baby. Yes, she will be the mother. Yes.

But the next morning, while Russ is at work, Corinne turns off the television and sits on the edge of the couch. She squeezes her thighs together, tight; she contracts her stomach; she arches her back. This is no joke. This is the real thing. By an act of will, she is going to expel this baby, this invader, this insidious little murderer. She pushes and pushes and nothing happens. She pushes again, hard. And once more she pushes. Finally she gives up and lies back against the sofa, resting.

After a while she puts her hand on her belly, and as she does so, she is astonished to hear singing.

It is the baby. It has a soft reedy voice and it sings slightly off-key. Corinne listens to the words: "Some of these days, you'll miss me, honey...."

Corinne faints then, and it is quite some time before she wakes up.

When she wakes, she opens her eyes only a slit and looks carefully from left to right. She sits on the couch, vigilant, listening, but she hears nothing. After a while she says three Hail Marys and an Act of Contrition, and then, confused and a little embarrassed, she does the laundry.

She does not tell Russ about this.

Well, it's a time of strain, Corinne tells herself, even though in California there isn't supposed to be any strain. Just surfing and tans and divorce and a lot of interfacing. No strain and no babies.

Corinne thinks for a second about interfacing babies, but forces the thought from her mind and goes back to thinking about her act. Sometimes she does a very funny set on interfacing, but only if the audience is middle-aged. The younger ones don't seem to know that interfacing is laughable. Come to think of it, *nobody* laughs much in California. Everybody smiles, but who laughs?

Laughs: that's something she can use. She does Garbo's laugh: "I am so hap-py." What was that movie? "I am so hap-py." She does the Garbo laugh again. Not bad. Who else laughs? Joe E. Brown. The Wicked Witch of the West. Who was she? Somebody Hamilton. Will anybody remember these people? Ruth Buzzi? Goldie Hawn? Yes, that great giggle. Of course, the best giggle is Burt Reynolds's. High and fey. Why does he do that? Is he sending up his own image?

Corinne is thinking of images, Burt Reynolds's and Tom Selleck's, when she hears singing: "Cal-i-for-nia, here I come, Right back where I started from…." Corinne stops pacing and stands in the doorway to the kitchen—as if I'm waiting for the earthquake, she thinks. But there is no earthquake; there is only the thin sweet voice, singing.

Corinne leans against the doorframe and listens. She closes her eyes. At once it is Easter, and she is a child again at Sacred Heart Grammar School, and the thirty-five members of the children's choir, earnest and angelic, look out at her from where they stand, massed about the altar. They wear red cassocks and white surplices, starched, and they seem to have descended from heaven for this one occasion. Their voices are pure, high, untouched by adolescence or by pain; and, with a conviction born of absolute innocence, they sing to God and to Corinne, "Cal-i-for-nia, here I come."

Corinne leans against the doorframe and listens truly now. Imagination aside, drama aside—she listens. It is a single voice she hears, thin and reedy. So, she did not imagine it the first time. It is true. The baby sings.

That night, when Russ comes home, he takes his shower, and they settle in with their first martini and everything is cozy.

Corinne asks him about his day, and he tells her. It was a lousy day. Russ started his own construction company a year ago just as the bottom fell out of the building business, and now there are no jobs to speak of. Just renovation stuff. Cleanup after fires. Some-times Victorian restorations down in the gay district. But that's about it. So whatever comes his way is bound to be lousy. This is Russ's second marriage, though, so he knows not to go too far with a lousy day. Who needs it?

"But I've got you, babe," he says, and pulls her toward him, and kisses her.

"We've got each other," Corinne says, and kisses him back. "And the baby," she says.

He holds her close then, so that she can't see his face. She makes big eyes like an actor in a bad comedy—she doesn't know why; she just always sees the absurd in everything. After a while they pull away, smiling, secret, and sip their martinis.

"Do you know something?" she says. "Can I tell you something?"

"What?" he says. "Tell me."

"You won't laugh?"

"No," he says, laughing. "I'm sorry. No, I won't laugh."

"Okay," she says. "Here goes."

There is a long silence, and then he says, "Well?"

"It sings."

"It sings?"

"The baby. The fetus. It sings."

Russ is stalled, but only for a second. Then he says, "Rock and roll? Or plainchant?" He begins to laugh, and he laughs so hard that he chokes and sloshes martini onto the couch. "You're wonderful," he says. "You're really a funny, funny girl. Woman." He laughs some more. "Is that for your act? I love it."

"I'm serious," she says. "I mean it."

"Well, it's great," he says. "They'll love it."

Corinne puts her hand on her stomach and thinks she has never been so alone in her life. She looks at Russ, with his big square jaw and all those white teeth and his green eyes so trusting and innocent, and she realizes for one second how corrupt she is, how lost, how deserving of a baby who sings; and then she pulls herself together because real life has to go on.

"Let's eat out," she says. "Spaghetti. It's cheap." She kisses him gently on his left eyelid, on his right. She gazes into his eyes and smiles, so that he will not guess she is thinking: Who is this man? Who am I?

Corinne has a job, Fridays and Saturdays for the next three weeks, at the Ironworks. It's not The Comedy Shop, but it's a legitimate gig, and the money is good. Moreover, it will give her something to think about besides whether or not she should go through with the abortion. She and Russ have put that on hold.

She is well into her third month, but she isn't showing yet, so she figures she can handle the three weekends easily. She wishes, in a way, that she were showing. As it is, she only looks....She searches for the word, but not for long. The word is *fat*. She looks fat.

She could do fat-girl jokes, but she hates jokes that put down women. And she hates jokes that are blue. Jokes that ridicule husbands. Jokes that ridicule the joker's looks. Jokes about nationalities. Jokes that play into audience prejudice. Jokes about the terrible small town you came from. Jokes about how poor you were, how ugly, how unpopular. Phyllis Diller jokes. Joan Rivers jokes. Jokes about small boobs, wrinkles, sexual inadequacy. Why is she in this business? she wonders. She hates jokes.

She thinks she hears herself praying: Please, please.

What should she do at the Ironworks? What should she do about the baby? What should she do?

The baby is the only one who's decided what to do. The baby sings.

Its voice is filling out nicely and it has enlarged its repertoire considerably. It sings a lot of classical melodies Corinne thinks she remembers from somewhere, churchy stuff, but it also favors golden oldies from the forties and fifties, with a few real old-timers thrown in when they seem appropriate. Once, right at the beginning, for instance, after Corinne and Russ had quarreled, Corinne locked herself in the bathroom to sulk and after a while was surprised, and then grateful, to hear the baby crooning, "Oh, my man, I love him so." It struck Corinne a day or so later that this could be a baby that would sell out for *any* one-liner...if indeed she decided to have the baby...and so she was relieved when the baby turned to more classical pieces.

The baby sings only now and then, and it sings better at some times than at others, but Corinne is convinced it sings best on weekend evenings when she is preparing for her gig. Before she leaves home, Corinne always has a long hot soak in the tub. She lies in the suds with her little orange bath pillow at her head and, as she runs through the night's possibilities, preparing ad-libs, heckler put-downs, segues, the baby sings to her.

There is some connection, she is sure, between her work and the baby's singing, but she can't guess what it is. It doesn't matter. She loves this: just she and the baby, together, in song.

Thank you, thank you, she prays.

The Ironworks gig goes extremely well. It is a young crowd, mostly, and so Corinne sticks to her young jokes: life in California, diets, dating, school. The audience laughs, and Russ says she is better than ever, but at the end of the three weeks the manager tells her, "You got it, honey. You got all the moves. You really make them laugh, you know? But they laugh from here only"—he taps his head—"not from the gut. You gotta get gut. You know? Like feeling."

So now the gig is over and Corinne lies in her tub trying to think of gut. She's gotta get gut, she's gotta get feeling. Has she ever *felt?* Well, she feels for Russ; she loves him. She felt for Alan, that bastard; well, maybe he wasn't so bad; maybe he just wasn't ready for marriage, any more than she was. Maybe it's California; maybe nobody *can* feel in California.

Enough about feeling, already. Deliberately, she puts feeling out of her mind, and calls up babies instead. A happy baby, she thinks, and at once the bathroom is crowded with laughing babies, each one roaring and carrying on like Ed McMahon. A fat baby, and she sees a Shelley Winters baby, an Elizabeth Taylor baby, an Orson Welles baby. An active baby: a mile of trampolines and babies doing quadruple somersaults, back flips, high dives. A healthy baby: babies lifting weights, swimming the Channel. Babies.

But abortion is the issue, not babies. Should she have it, or not?

At once she sees a bloody mess, a crushed-looking thing, half animal, half human. Its hands open and close. She gasps. "No," she says aloud, and shakes her head to get rid of the awful picture. "No," and covers her face.

Gradually she realizes that she has been listening to humming, and now the humming turns to song—"It ain't necessarily so," sung in a good clear mezzo.

Her eyes hurt and she has a headache. In fact, her eyes hurt all the time.

Corinne has finally convinced Russ that she hears the baby singing. Actually, he is convinced that Corinne is halfway around the bend with worry, and he is surprised, when he thinks about it, to find that he loves her anyway, crazy or not. He tells her that as much as he hates the idea, maybe she ought to think about having an abortion.

"I've actually gotten to like the singing," she says.

"Corinne," he says.

"It's the things I see that scare me to death."

"What things? What do you see?"

At once she sees a little crimson baby. It has been squashed into a mason jar. The tiny eyes almost disappear into the puffed cheeks, the cheeks into the neck, the neck into the torso. It is a pickled baby, ancient, preserved.

"Tell me," he says.

"Nothing," she says. "It's just that my eyes hurt."

It's getting late for an abortion, the doctor says, but she can still have one safely.

He's known her for twenty years, all through the first marriage and now through this one, and he's puzzled that a funny and sensible girl like Corinne should be having such a tough time with pregnancy. He had recommended abortion right from the start, because she didn't seem to want the baby and because she was almost forty, but he hadn't really expected her to take him up on it. Looking at her now, though, it is clear to him that she'll never make it. She'll be wacko—if not during the pregnancy, then sure as hell afterward.

So what does she think? What does Russ think?

Well, first, she explains in her new, sort of wandering way, there's something else she wants to ask about; not really important, she supposes, but just something, well, kind of different she probably should mention. It's the old problem of the baby…well, um, singing.

"Singing?" he asks.

"Singing?" he asks again.

"And humming," Corinne says.

They sit in silence for a minute, the doctor trying to decide whether or not this is a joke. She's got this great poker face. She really is a good comic. So after a while he laughs, and then when she laughs, he knows he's done the right thing. But what a crazy sense of humor!

"You're terrific," he says. "Anything else? How's Russ? How was the Ironworks job?"

"My eyes hurt," she says. "I have headaches."

And so they discuss her vision for a while, and stand-up comedy, and she makes him laugh. And that's that.

At the door he says to her, "Have an abortion, Corinne. Now, before it's too late."

They have just made love and now Russ puts off the light and they lie together in the dark, his hand on her belly.

"Listen," he says. "I want to say something. I've been thinking about what the doctor said, about an abortion. I hate it, I hate the whole idea, but you know, we've got to think of you. And I think this baby is too much for you, I think maybe that's why you've been having those headaches and stuff. Don't you think?"

Corinne puts her hand on his hand and says nothing. After a long while Russ speaks again, into the darkness.

"I've been a lousy father. Two sons I never see. I never see them. The stepfather's good to them, though; he's a good father. I thought maybe I'd have another chance at it, do it right this time, like the marriage. Besides, the business isn't always going to be this bad, you know; I'll get jobs; I'll get money. We could afford it, you know? A son. A daughter. It would be nice. But what I mean is, we've got to take other things into consideration, we've got to consider your health. You're not strong enough, I guess. I always think of you as strong, because you do those gigs and you're funny and all, but, I mean, you're almost forty, and the doctor thinks that maybe an abortion is the way to go, and what do I know. I don't know. The singing. The headaches. I don't know."

Russ looks into the dark, seeing nothing.

"I worry about you, you want to know the truth? I do. Corinne?"

Corinne lies beside him, listening to him, refusing to listen to the baby, who all this time has been singing. Russ is as alone as she is, even more alone. She is dumbfounded. She is speechless with love. If he were a whirlpool, she thinks, she would fling herself into it. If he were...but he is who he is, and she loves only him, and she makes her decision.

"You think I'm losing my mind," she says.

Silence.

"Yes."

More silence.

"Well, I'm not. Headaches are a normal part of lots of pregnancies, the doctor told me, and the singing doesn't mean anything at all. He explained what was really going on, why I thought I heard it sing. You see," Corinne says, improvising freely now, making it all up, for him, her gift to him, "you see, when you get somebody as high-strung as me and you add pregnancy right at the time I'm about to make it big as a stand-up, then the pressures get to be so much that sometimes the imagination can take over, the doctor said, and when you tune in to the normal sounds of your body, you hear them really loud, as if they were amplified by a three-thou-sand-watt PA system, and it can sound like singing. See?"

Russ says nothing.

"So you see, it all makes sense, really. You don't have to worry about me."

"Come on," Russ says. "Do you mean to tell me you never heard the baby singing?"

"Well, I heard it, sort of. You know? It was really all in my mind. I mean, the *sound* was in my body physiologically, but my hearing it as *singing* was just...."

"Just your imagination."

Corinne does not answer.

"Well?"

"Right," she says, making the total gift. "It was just my imagination."

And the baby—who has not stopped singing all this time, love songs mostly—stops singing now, and does not sing again until the day scheduled for the abortion.

The baby has not sung in three weeks. It is Corinne's fifth month now, and at last they have been able to do an amniocentesis. The news is bad. One of the baby's chromosomes does not match up to anything in hers, anything in Russ's. What this means, they tell her, is that the baby is not normal. It will be deformed in some way; in what way, they have no idea.

Corinne and Russ decide on abortion.

They talk very little about their decision now that they have made it. In fact, they talk very little about anything. Corinne's face grows daily more haggard, and Corinne avoids Russ's eyes. She is silent much of the time, thinking. The baby is silent all the time.

The abortion will be by hypertonic saline injection, a simple procedure, complicated only by the fact that Corinne has waited so long. She has been given a booklet to read and she has listened to a tape, and so she knows about the injection of the saline solution, she knows about the contractions that will begin slowly and then get more and more frequent, and she knows about the dangers of infection and excessive bleeding.

She knows moreover that it will be a formed fetus she will expel.

Russ has come with her to the hospital and is outside in the waiting room. Corinne thinks of him, of how she loves him, of how their lives will be better, safer, without this baby who sings. This deformed baby. Who sings. If only she could hear the singing once more, just once.

Corinne lies on the table with her legs in the thigh rests, and one of the nurses drapes the examining sheet over and around her.

The other nurse, or someone—Corinne is getting confused; her eyesight seems fuzzy—takes her pulse and her blood pressure. She feels someone washing her, the careful hands, the warm fluid. So, it is beginning.

Corinne closes her eyes and tries to make her mind a blank. Dark, she thinks. Dark. She squeezes her eyes tight against the light, she wants to remain in this cool darkness forever, she wants to cease being. And then, amazingly, the dark does close in on her. Though she opens her eyes, she sees nothing. She can remain this way forever if she wills it. The dark is cool to the touch, and it is comforting somehow; it invites her in. She can lean into it, give herself up to it, and be safe, alone, forever.

She tries to sit up. She will enter this dark. She will do it. Please, please, she hears herself say. And then all at once she thinks of Russ and the baby, and instead of surrendering to the dark, she pushes it away.

With one sweep of her hand she pushes the sheet from her and flings it to the floor. She pulls her legs from the thigh rests and manages to sit up, blinded still, but fighting.

"Here now," a nurse says, caught off guard, unsure what to do. "Hold on now. It's all right. It's fine."

"Easy now. Easy," the doctor says, thinking, Yes, here it is, what else is new.

Together the nurses and the doctor make an effort to stop her, but they are too late, because by this time Corinne has fought free of any restraints. She is off the examining couch and, naked, huddles in the corner of the small room.

"No," she shouts. "I want the baby. I want the baby." And later, when she has stopped shouting, when she has stopped crying, still she clutches her knees to her chest and whispers over and over, "I want the baby."

So there is no abortion after all.

By the time she is discharged, Corinne's vision has returned, dimly. Moreover, though she tells nobody, she has heard humming, and once or twice a whole line of music. The baby has begun to sing again.

Corinne has more offers than she wants: The Hungry I, The Purple Onion, The Comedy Shop. Suddenly everybody decides it's time to take a look at her, but she is in no shape to be looked at, so she signs for two weeks at My Uncle's Bureau and lets it go at that.

She is only marginally pretty now, she is six months pregnant, and she is carrying a deformed child. Furthermore, she can see very little, and what she does see, she often sees double.

Her humor, therefore, is spare and grim, but audiences love it. She begins slow: "When I was a girl, I always wanted to look like Elizabeth Taylor," she says, and glances down at her swollen belly. Two beats. "And now I do." They laugh with her, and applaud. Now she can quicken the pace, sharpen the humor. They follow her; they are completely captivated.

She has found some new way of holding her body—tipping her head, thrusting out her belly—and instead of putting off her audience, or embarrassing them, it charms them. The laughter is *with* her, the applause *for* her. She could do anything out there and get away with it. And she knows it. They simply love her.

In her dressing room after the show she tells herself that somehow, magically, she's learned to work from the heart instead of just from the head. She's got gut. She's got feeling. But she knows it's something more than that.

By the end of the two weeks she is convinced that the successful new element in her act is the baby. This deformed baby, the abnormal baby she has tried to get rid of. And what interests her most is that she no longer cares about success as a stand-up.

Corinne falls asleep that night to the sound of the baby's crooning. She is trying to pray, Please, please, but with Russ's snoring and the baby's lullaby, they all get mixed up together in her mind—God, Russ, the baby—and she forgets to whom she is praying or why. She sleeps.

The baby sings all the time now. It starts first thing in the morning with a nice soft piece by Telemann or Brahms; there are assorted lullabies at bedtime; and throughout the day it is bop, opera, ragtime, blues, a little rock and roll, big-band stuff—the baby never tires.

Corinne tells no one about this, not even Russ.

She and Russ talk about almost everything now: their love for each other, their hopes for the baby, their plans. They have lots of plans. Russ has assured Corinne that whatever happens, he's ready for it. Corinne is his whole life, and no matter how badly the baby is deformed, they'll manage. They'll do the right thing. They'll survive.

They talk about almost everything, but they do not talk about the baby's singing.

For Corinne the singing is secret, mysterious. It contains some revelation, of course, but she does not want to know what that revelation might be.

The singing is somehow tied up with her work; but more than that, with her life. It is part of her fate. It is inescapable. And she is perfectly content to wait.

Corinne has been in labor for three hours, and the baby has been singing the whole time. The doctor has administered a mild anesthetic and a nurse remains at bedside, but the birth does not seem imminent, and so for Corinne it is a period of pain and waiting. And for the baby, singing.

"These lights are so strong," Corinne says, or thinks she says. "The lights are blinding."

The nurse looks at her for a moment and then goes back to the letter she is writing.

"Please," Corinne says, "thank you."

She is unconscious, she supposes; she is imagining the lights. Or perhaps the lights are indeed bright and she sees them as they really are *because* she is unconscious. Or perhaps her sight has come back as strong as it used to be. Whatever the case, she doesn't want to think about it right now. Besides, for some reason or other, even though the lights are blinding, they are not blinding her. They do not even bother her. It is as if light is her natural element.

"Thank you," she says. To someone.

The singing is wonderful, a cappella things Corinne recognizes as Brahms, Mozart, Bach. The baby's voice can assume any dimension it wants now, swelling from a single thin note to choir volume; it can take on the tone and resonance of musical instruments, violin, viola, flute; it can become all sounds; it enchants.

The contractions are more frequent; even unconscious, Corinne can tell that. Good. Soon the waiting will be over and she will have her wonderful baby, her perfect baby. But at once she realizes hers will not be a perfect baby; it will be deformed. "Please," she says, "please," as if prayer can keep Russ from being told—as he will be soon after the birth—that his baby has been born dumb. Russ, who has never understood comedians.

But now the singing has begun to swell in volume. It is as if the baby has become a full choir, with many voices, with great strength.

The baby will be fine, however it is, she thinks. She thinks of Russ, worried half to death. She is no longer worried. She accepts what will be.

The contractions are very frequent now and the light is much brighter. She knows the doctor has come into the room, because she hears his voice. There is another nurse too. And soon there will be the baby.

The light is so bright that she can see none of them. She can see into the light, it is true; she can see the soft fleecy nimbus glowing beyond the light, but she can see nothing in the room.

The singing. The singing and the light. It is Palestrina she hears, in polyphony, each voice lambent. The light envelops her, catches her up from this table where the doctor bends over her and where already can be seen the shimmering yellow hair of the baby. The light lifts her, and the singing lifts her, and she says, "Yes," she says, "Thank you."

She accepts what will be. She accepts what is.

The room is filled with singing and with light, and the singing is transformed into light, more light, more lucency, and still she says, "Yes," until she cannot bear it, and she reaches up and tears the light aside. And sees.

Jess Mowry

One Way

ROBBY PUSHED OPEN the station door, carrying his board by the front truck, downside in. At least it was cool inside. He smelled burgers from the restaurant and his stomach growled, but five and change wouldn't go far. Maybe he could live off his fat awhile like those bears on TV? He saw a whole cigarette under a chair and snagged it fast. Matches were always a prob, but Jeffers had given him his Bic and it was still half full.

He walked across to a black plastic TV-chair, just like the one in Fresno. He slid behind the little screen and pulled out his lighter, wondering if they had the Thunder Cats or Ninja Turtles here. It wasn't worth risking a quarter to find out. The cigarette was one of those pussy kind, so he broke off the filter before firing. The smoke eased his hunger a little, but that cleaning shit they used on the floor was giving him a headache.

A rattler in a baggy uniform came over. He was white and bored. He glanced at the cigarette, but seemed to figure out there were better things to hassle about, "You got a ticket, kid?"

Robby dug it out. The rattler gave it a look, then flipped it back, jerking a thumb at the big clock over the doors. "Next one leaves at five-twenty, kid. Be on it." He smiled with his mouth. "And put a fucking quarter in or get outta the chair."

"Dipshit," came to Robby's mind. He took a big cool hit off the cigarette and blew smoke, watching the rattler's eyes narrow.

194

Then he slid out of the chair and walked *the* walk toward the bathroom, feeling the rattler watching. "Lame-o," he whispered.

A tall skinny black boy stood by the door. They'd call him dribble-lips in Fresno. He looked about sixteen and also like he knew everything about Robby. "Crackers," he murmured. "A dollar."

Robby knew crackers, though they were called nukes in Fresno, and a dollar was way too much. He almost smiled. Like the TV said, "Just say no," asshole. He ignored the dude: scoring the right local word was worth the shove he got. He did smile then, hearing the rattler's squeaky cop-shoes cross the floor and the one word, *"Out!"*

"Yeah, right," the skinny dude yawned. Robby knew he'd be back.

The bathroom was all shiny tile under flickering fluorescents. It smelled like piss and Pine-Sol. There was a white dude, old, twenty-something, leaning on the line of sinks. He smiled at Robby.

Homo, Robby thought. Perv. Anybody who hung out where it smelled like piss had to be weird. Things weren't so different here. He saw the long trough and the dude watching him. He hated those things—out in the open, always too fucking high. How could anybody piss trying to stand on their toes? Everything else was a goddamn pay toilet except one and there was somebody in it. A fucking dime to piss! At least he could shut the door. He paid the box a dime and went in, sighing, yanking his zipper, and making as much water-noise as he could. He should've used the one right there on the bus; had to start figuring stuff like that.

He jerked up his zipper, flipped the cigarette in the toilet, and flushed. Then he laid the skateboard across the seat and sat, swinging his legs. Should he go for San Francisco? Trouble was, he didn't know how long that would take. It would probably be dark when he got there, too late for the ocean, and they'd run him off without a ticket. He'd slept on the street before, a few times when his folks were fighting, a couple more with Jeffers and Tad when they'd scored some beer and gotten too wasted to skate or even walk. It'd be a lot easier to find some place behind a dumpster....

Somebody tapped on the door. Robby saw the perv's Adidas underneath. "Hey, kid, want to play a game?"

Robby grinned. Games were shit old people thought up for kids. He'd never let a perv touch him before but Jamie had, in Rotting Park, and got $20. He'd said it was weird, but not bad. Jeffers said you could score a sixer that way, sometimes, but to get it first. Robby sat and kicked his legs. The door was locked, even if the perv put in another dime. What was he going to do, crawl under?

"How much?" Robby asked. That's what Jeffers would say.

The perv sounded like he had hurt feelings or something. "Hey, little guy, I just want to be your friend."

"Yeah right, duuude!" Suddenly Robby laughed and almost couldn't stop. It was *too* funny. A dime bought you a piss and a perv in Oakland. "Fuck-off, AIDSball," he said.

The perv said nothing, but the Adidas didn't move.

"I'll scream," Robby added. "Loud."

The Adidas went away.

Sunlight slanted yellow in hot evening air as Robby pushed open the station door. He'd figured he might as well check the place out. There must be an ocean around somewhere. A black kid went by on a board, a thrasher old VariFlex. They ignored each other but checked boards; Robby's was better and they both knew it. The kid wore ragged jeans and had his shirt tied around his waist, hanging down in back. Robby pulled his off and did the same. The cracker dude was standing by a streetlamp, looking like he wanted to kick the shit out of somebody. Robby decked and rolled. It didn't matter which way, but he thought of the ocean again. Jeffers said you could sleep on the beach.

Wheels clicked cracks and the blocks passed. Robby stayed on a straight line to somewhere. These sidewalks were crowded, and he was too busy dodging people to pay much attention to anything else. The concrete was old and rough. The curbs were different too, but there was a lot of scraped skateboard paint on them.

The sun lowered and grew orange in distant fog. The air cooled and he stopped sweating. He passed another boy on a board, a little black dude on a Punk-Size. The kid didn't seem to figure there was anything special about Robby and that felt good and bad at the same time.

The food smells from the restaurants bothered him: there were so many. He tailed in front of a Doggie Diner and thought about a hot dog, but there was another cigarette under a bus bench and he snagged that instead, firing as he rolled. It didn't seem to help his hunger much and it buzzed his head a little. He pinched it halfway, dropping it in the bag for later.

The streets were quiet now, and he heard a car come around the far corner. He tensed a moment, glancing up the street—van, Dodge, dark blue, maybe black, it was getting hard to see as the daylight faded. He looked around but there was no place to hide. Was there any reason to? Heavy-metal music echoed between the buildings. Robby flipped up his board and pretended to be checking the trucks while watching the van from the corner of his eye as it neared. It didn't have its lights on but the driver must have seen him because it eased toward the curb. Robby almost decked, but the music faded low and a kid-voice called, "Yo, shredder!"

The van pulled over and stopped. The voice was friendly, breaking in the middle the way Jeffers' did sometimes. "Want some beer, brother?"

Robby came slowly to the open passenger window, ready to book fast. The kid inside was white, thin, with super-long bleached metaler hair. He wore black Levis, black Iron Maiden T-shirt, big studded collar, and a heavy spiked wrist-cuff. He also had on those expensive studded riot-gloves. Total showtime, Robby thought, no good for skating. But his blue eyes were friendly.

Robby leaned on the door, looking in. If the kid was old enough for a license, it was just. The dude grinned at Robby. Both his front teeth were those stainless-steel kind they sometimes put in kids until they were old enough for real fake ones.

Total metaler or what, flashed through Robby's mind. But at the same time he felt a little sorry for the dude—other kids probably called him tin-grin, or something. The dude held out an open can of Bud. Robby took it, sipped, then chugged a decent hit. It was kid-beer, kind of flat and warm, but he was thirsty and warm beer kept you from being hungry.

"What's up, bro?" the dude asked.

Robby considered. "Um, just skatin' home, man."

Robby handed back the can and the dude nodded, chugging, not even wiping the top first. Robby stood on tiptoes, pressing closer to the door. The metal was still sun-warm and felt good.

"Yeah?" said the dude. "Figured you must live around here 'cause you've got a board. Um, what kind?"

Robby held it up. "Just a thrasher old Steadham. Nuthin' rad. You ride, man?"

The dude grinned again and passed back the Bud. "Not since I got my wheels!" He patted the dash. "Used to have a Roskopp."

"Yeah?" said Robby. "They're totally bad!"

"Where do you live? I could give you a ride if you want."

Robby's eyes flicked to the back of the van. Carpeted, paneled, but totally empty, nowhere anybody else could be hiding. "Um, by the beach."

Robby left a couple swallows in the can and passed it back. It wasn't cool to kill it. The dude gave Robby another metal grin and finished it. *"Beach?* Oh yeah. I guess it would be for you. Well, guess that means you're almost home anyway, don't it?" He studied Robby a minute. "Um, how old are you, man?"

"Thirteen."

"Naw. Hey, open the door a second, let me see ya."

Robby did, stepping back. The dude checked him and grinned. "No way, man! You're way too big for thirteen."

Robby smiled a little. At least he hadn't said fat.

"Hey!" said the dude. "I got one more Bud left. You wanna slide in an' we'll just sit here an' split it? You like Slayer?"

Robby considered. It was getting darker by the minute and the street was empty and dead. The van smelled good inside—like leather and kids, beer and smoke. The dome light had come on when the door opened. It was painted red and made the interior look warm. Maybe with a half-Bud in his stomach he wouldn't be hungry tonight. Robby climbed in.

The dude pulled another Bud from between the seats and popped it, checking Robby again. "Hey, bro, no shit, you are big an' bad. I guess all you dudes are like that, huh?" He gave Robby firsts.

Robby frowned a little. "Um, what do you mean?"

"Aw, nothing." The kid smiled again. "Hey, I know how lame this's gonna sound, but my best friend is a black dude. I known him since third-grade. All you dudes are just naturally cool."

Robby sipped beer and smiled. "Or what."

The kid gave Robby another long look. For just a second, Robby wanted to cross his arms over his chest. "My little brother's thirteen too, only he's a total marshmallow compared to you. I guess all you bros have to be super bad to live here, huh? I mean, you know how to fight, an' carry guns an' everything?"

Robby thought a second. "Yeah."

"Full-autos, huh?"

"Sometimes." Robby passed back the Bud. The dude studied him a few moments. "Um, could I touch you, bro? I mean, I ain't no homo or nothing! I just can't believe you're only thirteen."

Robby tensed and slid close to the door. "Um, no, man. I know you're not a homo. I just don't wanna be touched, okay? I, um, gotta get home anyways. Thanks for the beer, bro." Robby slid out, watching the dude watching him. The kid started to reach for something between the seats, then gave Robby another grin.

"Hey. It's cool, bro! I don't blame you. We had those pervert movies in school too."

Robby stood on the sidewalk for a moment then closed the van's door. "It's okay, bro. I just gotta get home, that's all. My dad'll get pissed. Um, thanks again for the Bud...an' I think your van is totally bad."

He rolled a couple blocks more, then stopped and looked around. The buildings were old and dirty brick, faded like rust in the evening light. No more stores, only a little corner market. The rest were garages and body shops, all closed. The sidewalk was totally thrashed, broken and littered with bottles and trash. There was a wino in a doorway. It was so ugly and familiar and stupid that it made him homesick. But the salt smell was strong and he rolled on.

Parked trucks and abandoned cars lined the curbs. Windows at street level were barred or covered with plywood. He looked at the spray-painted words and pictures, some familiar—the Anarchy sign, Hip-Hop, good old FUCK YOU. But there weren't any squared-off Chicano letters and there was lots of heavy-metal and punker stuff and rap.

Robby jumped the gutter, cut the street, and slapped the opposite curb. A spray-paint design in red and black, like a Tiger Dog snarling from a letter A, faced him from a corner wall—a gang-mark for sure. It was old, but nobody'd painted "sucks" or something underneath or an "anti" sign over it. Whatever the Tiger-Dog stood for, it got respect. It wasn't very high on the wall, he noticed, just about where he'd have painted it. For sure, there were kid-gangs in Fresno, but the big dudes always painted out their marks fast.

He rounded another corner and there it was. He tailed and stared and fought back tears. It sucked!

There was no surf. The water stretched away, silent and sullen. There was no beach. The water lapped at rotten pilings, broken rock, and rusty junk. No sand, only stinking black mud. Further up the shore, dim in a fog as gray and ugly as a tule fog in Fresno, was a short wharf alongside a crumbling warehouse.

Snagging his board, Robby walked over to a rusted chain-link gate. The wire on one corner was peeled back and he squeezed through. The wharf planking was rotten and gone in places. He walked to the end and sat, dangling his legs, looking down at dirty black water where garbage floated. He pulled out the half-cigarette and fired. Tears burned his eyes again, and this time he let them fall.

He should've figured it would be like this. The ocean was just as worn-out and thrashed as everything else in the whole fucking world! Things were no different anywhere; and, if there really were white sandy beaches and surf-kids, it would be a kind of mall-place with rattlers to keep him out. This was all the ocean he was ever going to get.

The last light faded and Robby sat alone in foggy darkness. He smoked until the cigarette burned his fingers. The fog was wet and cold and he put his shirt back on. He wished he had enough beer so he could drink until he couldn't see or feel anything anymore. Then he pulled his knees, put his head between his legs, and cried.

Something creaked behind him, but he didn't look. He didn't care. Let the Tiger-Dogs come and beat the shit out of him; maybe they'd kill him. Maybe that was better.

There was breathing, the deep kind, like you make when you're drunk. Then, a kid-voice: "Whitey?"

That was funny. Even now. Robby turned, looking up at the fattest kid he'd ever seen.

For sure, a lot of Mexican kids were fat, but this dude was black. He looked about Robby's age, though it was hard to tell in the dark. He wore jeans that sagged under his belly, thrasher Nikes that used to be white, and a ragged black T-shirt with what looked like RATT on the front and couldn't cover his middle. The fat kid stopped a few feet away and checked Robby. "You ain't Whitey."

Robby shrugged. He couldn't see anybody else around and sure wasn't scared of this fat tub. "Duh."

That didn't seem to bother the fat kid. He smiled a little, funny, like he knew a secret or something and Robby wondered if he was a retard.

"Yeah? You ain't from here," the dude said.

"No shit."

"Yeah? So, where?"

"So nuthin'! I'm Panthro from Third-Earth, duuude!"

The fat kid only smiled wider and that bothered Robby.

"Yeah? I'm into the Thundercats too, man. You look more like one of Mum-ra's dipshits. Wanna get your ass wiped?"

"By *you?* I doubt!"

The fat kid grinned, teeth big and white. "Yeah? You in Animal-Land now, dude. Lion-o ain't gonna save your ass here."

Robby considered that and the fat kid moved a lot faster than it looked like he could, snagging Robby's board with a grunt. Robby jumped up, but the dude was checking his board like an expert, though he couldn't have ridden one for his life. Robby wanted to snatch it back and punch that huge belly, hard, but the dude handled the board with respect.

"Steadham," the fat kid said. He grinned even wider. "That's what Whitey rides too. Um, synchronicity, man!" He checked the downside, and pointed to a sticker. "Skully Brothers. I heard of them. They gots an ad in *Thrasher*. They in, um…"

"Fresno."

"Yeah." The fat kid handed the board back, and Robby couldn't help it, he asked, "You, um, *ride,* man?"

The dude smiled, shy. "Naw. But the other Animals all shred to the max, 'specially Randers an' Kevin." He studied Robby a minute. "Whitey's pretty intense too. You sure look a lot like him."

Robby was used to white kids saying stupid stuff like that, but a black dude should know better. Anyway, "How the fuck could I look like a whitey, man?"

"Whitey's black, an' kinda fat too."

"I ain't fat! Not like you!"

The fat kid giggled. "Yeah? Now you even *sound* like Whitey!"

"Fuckin' A!"

"Nobody says *that* anymore."

"Then, why's he called Whitey?"

"'Cause."

Robby thought a minute. There was an open doorway on the side of the warehouse and the other…Animals…were probably in there laughing. For sure, he was going to get beat up. He shrugged again. "What the fuck, man. I'm Robby. You got a smoke or you just gonna kick my ass? Go ahead. I don't give a shit."

The fat kid gave him that funny smile again, then dug a squashed Marlboro hardpack from a pocket and straightened two cigarettes. They fired off Robby's Bic.

"I'm Donny," the fat kid said. "Randers might kick it." He considered. "Or maybe just do you best-moves-for-keeps an' score himself another board."

Robby didn't say anything. He'd lost his last board that way. He took a big hit off the Marlboro and it buzzed his head. He didn't care about that either. The other dudes would probably show in a minute anyway.

Donny sank down and dangled his legs. Robby checked the doorway again, then slowly sat alongside. They smoked and spat in the water. Donny smelled a little like burger grease and Robby's belly rumbled.

"So, where's Fresno?" Donny asked.

"A long ways."

"Yeah? How'd you get here? You don't got to say."

"On a lame-o bus."

"Yeah? How come? You don't got to say."

"I ran away, man."

Donny blew smoke. "Yeah? Kevin don't hardly go home no more either. He didn't run as far as you. Just used to get wasted all the time an' sleep in dumpsters."

"I done that."

"Yeah? Only now he stays at the Center a lot with Nathaniel."

"Who's Nathaniel? Some kinda social-worker lady?"

Donny spat. "Nathaniel is a *boy,* man! Kinda."

Robby told himself to be cool. He could blow it easy with stupid questions and these dudes would figure him a squid and kick his ass. "That, um, Tiger-Dog your mark? It's pretty hot."

"Yeah. I do 'em." Donny looked back at the water. "I figure that's why they let me be a Animal."

Mascot, Robby thought. That figured. But some gang mascots were pretty important. He knew better than to ask how many Animals there were...or *where* they were. "Must be some bad dudes?"

"Or what! Even the dealers leave us alone. Most of the time." Donny sat a little straighter. "We kicked the shit outta some old perv that beat up Kevin a few weeks ago! Sent him bawlin' back to Silicone-land, man!" He looked at Robby. "So, where you sleepin'? You don't got to say."

Robby shrugged and looked back at the doorway. He really didn't feel like getting beat up.

Donny smiled. "Like King Kong?"

"Huh?"

"Any fuckin' place he wants to?"

Robby looked down at the water and nodded.

Donny glanced over his shoulder at the doorway, then back at Robby. "I'm alone, man." He flipped his cigarette away and stretched. "You hungry?"

Robby nodded again.

"Yeah? Me too. C'mon. My mom don't get home till around ten an' we got lots of stuff. You stay out here, for sure you get your ass wiped. Randers is cool, but he got no time for strange dudes, an' Kevin, shit, man, you wouldn't want to meet Kevin in the dark!" Donny struggled to his feet. "Um, why was you cryin', man? You don't got to say."

Robby thought a minute, then shrugged and pointed. "Your ocean sucks."

Donny looked out over the Bay. The fog was too thick to see San Francisco or even the Bridge going across. He gave Robby another funny smile. "Yeah."

Donny led through the doorway into blackness. They came out the front, walked a couple of blocks back up from the water, and turned into a door, then up a narrow box-stairs that smelled like old piss. The steps ended at a hall. A dim bulb burned halfway down and more light filtered through a window from a streetlamp. It looked to Robby like the floor tilted. The boards squeaked and popped and there was a lot of stuff spray-painted on the walls. Donny went to the far end, dug two keys from a pocket, and undid the locks on a door that looked like somebody'd tried to kick down a couple of times. The hinges were loose as Donny shoved it open. He flipped a switch and Robby got that homesick feeling again. Not much was different anywhere.

There was one room, half of it kitchen. The other half had some thrashed furniture and pictures of Martin Luther King and JFK on top of an old TV. There was a messy bed under the window, Donny's for sure. A half-open door showed a bathroom, and another door, closed, was probably his mom's room.

Donny pushed the hall door closed and snapped the locks. "Okay, huh?"

Robby nodded.

Donny pulled off his shirt and kicked out of his Nikes. "You like burgers, man?"

"Or what! Um, can I use your bathroom?"

"For sure. Um, pick up the seat or my mom has a cow." Donny snapped on the TV, then went to the fridge and started knocking stuff around inside. He held up a can of Budweiser as Robby came back. "Wanna beer, man?"

"For sure! Um, your mom *let* you drink beer?"

"Naw...leastways not at home. She seen me drunk on my ass a couple of times an' had a cow. I got this sixer from Weasel today an' gotta do somethin' with it before she gets back. We can drink it if you wanna."

"Um, don't Weasel get pissed?"

"Naw. The Animals always got beer."

Robby took the can and popped it, taking a small hit. He knew better than to chug on an empty stomach. "Um, you dudes do anything but beer, man?"

Donny squashed some globs of hamburger on the counter and plopped them in a big black pan. "Beer mostly. For sure everybody's checked out all the other shit, but it's hard to ride on most of that stuff. Kevin still does some rock once in a while an' Rix an' Randers both did some dust a couple weeks ago." He dropped the pan on the stove. "They both blew it an' Nathaniel had to chill 'em out. Nathaniel don't like that kinda shit. He's cool an' don't say nuthin', but you can tell. What you do in Fresno, man?"

"Me an' my friend Jeffers did some nuke a couple of weeks ago."

"What?"

"Um, cracker?"

"Yeah? Intense, huh?"

"Aw, only for a little while. You got to keep doin' more. Shit's cheap but it still runs into bucks. I don't like to mega-think anyways. Scary sometimes." He looked at the Bud can. "Figure most of the shredders only do this stuff...maybe some doob once in a while."

"Yeah. That's about like it is here. What's Fresno like, man? You got mountains an' stuff?"

"Naw, Fresno got total zip, man! It sucks!"

Donny turned. "Yeah? Didn't you see nuthin' nice comin' on the bus?"

"It was at night, mostly. Then today I was sleepin'. Ain't nuthin' nice nowhere, man."

"Yeah."

Robby looked at the TV. It was an old *Silver Spoons* rerun. Ricky was all bummed-out and crying because his dad wouldn't get him a new video game. Robby sipped beer. Behind him, Donny said, *"That* dude's got some nice shit."

"Yeah. But he's still got probs, man. He's got all that stuff an' still gots probs. I never seen him just hangin' with his friends, y'know? Just hangin' out somewhere an' doin' nuthin'? Like he don't really got no friends. Sometimes I feel sorry for him, man. Me an' Jeffers fuckin' get off more in a hour just curb-grindin' than I ever seen him do."

Donny nodded.

Robby walked to the bed and checked the posters—Iron Maiden, Mega-Deth. There were some drawings too, good ones, with the Tiger-Dog in color. "You do some hot shit, man. The Tiger-Dog should be a sticker!"

Donny pushed the burgers around with a fork, dodging grease spatters. "Um, thanks, dude." He looked up. "Um, you could probably stay here tonight if you wanna...The bed ain't very big, but I ain't no homo or nuthin'."

Robby sat on the rumpled bed. It smelled like sweaty-kid and burger grease. "Your mom get pissed?"

Donny flipped the meat. "Naw. But she ask you all kinds of stupid stuff, like where you live an' that sorta shit." He shrugged. "She's really pretty cool, but it might make you feel weird. You could make somethin' up."

Back against the wall by the bed was a good old Santa Cruz Slasher, ridden hard, but dusty now. "Um, that your board, man?"

Donny glanced up. "Naw. That was Duncan's. You can check it if you want."

Robby leaned down to snag it, then stopped. There was dried stuff all over, like old crumbly mud. Robby studied it a long time, but didn't touch it. "Um…Duncan get a new one or somethin'?"

Donny didn't look up. Robby hardly heard him above the burger sizzle. "Duncan's dead, man."

Donny mashed the meat hard with the fork. "He jumped off that warehouse by the wharf, man, a few months ago. I found his board in the mud between the rocks next day after the cops leave…like he tried to take it with him or somethin'! His mom was a bitch an' I wasn't gonna give it to her! None of the dudes wanted it either. Nobody's rode it again…figure the bearings all rusted now anyways. My mom don't like it. She won't even touch it, man!" He opened a cupboard and pulled out a pack of buns. "Duncan was my friend, kinda."

Robby took a big hit of beer. "Sorry, man. I just figured it was yours…before you got fat or somethin'."

Donny shrugged. "I always been fat."

Robby drank some more beer and turned to the pictures. Donny could draw to the max! There was one, five dudes on boards, sort of half-cartoon and half-serious. All were black except two, and none looked much over fourteen. One white kid was small and skinny but looked badder than hell. The other was like a total maller, blond and friendly. The black dude in the middle had muscles and it was easy to see he knew what is, is, and what ain't, wasn't worth nothing. That had to be Randers. Another was chubby and did look a little like Robby: Whitey. The last was like the cracker dude at the station, only younger.

Donny came over with two plates and four steaming burgers maxed with stuff and a beer under one arm. He sat beside Robby. "Scarf time."

"Or what!" Robby grabbed a burger and took a huge bite. He turned a little and pointed to the mean-looking white kid. "Weasel, right?"

Donny shook his head. "Naw. That's Kevin. Weasel's the other whitey."

"Don't look like no weasel."

Donny sucked beer and burped. "He put a rat in his mom's microwave once."

"Huh? Oh…yeah, right. I think I figured Randers—in the middle and, for sure, he could kick-ass. Who's the skinny dude with the teeth?"

"Rix."

"Ricks?"

"Naw. R-I-X, man. Wait…" Donny slid to the floor and pulled a cardboard box from under the bed. It was full of magazines and had the Tiger-Dog on it. He dug out a Thundercats comic, flipped it open, and pointed to a Moleman. "Rix is the leader of the Molemen. Like, at first they hate the Thundercats an' keep tryin' to kill 'em, but then they get to be friends. There was this big monster-thing tryin' to kill the Molemen an' steal all their stuff an' it kept on blamin' the Thundercats, so Rix starts this big war. Then they finally figure out that they shouldn't be fightin' each other when it's this big monster-thing that's their real enemy."

Robby looked at the picture. The Molemen had huge front teeth. "Shit, they sure don't look friendly!"

"Yeah. Maybe that's why the Thundercats was ascared of 'em at first. Really, they was pretty good dudes behind them teeth."

Robby nodded. "You read a lot, man?"

Donny shrugged and stuck the book back. "Nuthin' else to do 'cept watch TV. The Animals all come up here a lot…probably 'cause my mom's not home. She don't mind, really, 'cept I figure she thinks they might not be good dudes, man."

"How come you ain't in the picture?"

"Aw, I drew it. Didn't seem right, y'know? 'Sides, I know what I look like."

"Shit, man. Killer dudes like you Animals could be makin' megabucks runnin' rock! There's one board-pack doin' that in Fresno. Even the little kids score a hundred a day just bein' watchers! Fuck. You dudes could have all new boards an' stuff!"

Donny shrugged. "Yeah. There's this bigger kid, fifteen or somethin', keeps comin' 'round tellin' Randers all that shit. He ain't even old enough for a license an' he drivin' a new Corvette, man! Randers think about it a lot, you can tell. Nathaniel don't like that dealer dude, kicked the shit outta him once. Dude say he gonna kill Nathaniel, only Nathaniel just laughs at him. 'Course, right then, the Animals would've killed the dude anyways, no prob."

Donny went to the fridge and snagged two more Buds. He brought them back, along with a box of Ding-Dongs, and sat. He looked at the old board and then out the window. "Duncan was a Animal then. This dealer dude finally talked him into bein' a runner. No prob an' he was makin' mega-money...scored everybody new wheels an' Swiss bearin's an' found some store'd sell him cases of Heinie at three times the price...'cause he was only fourteen still." Donny shrugged. "He got sorta like that Ricky on *Silver Spoons*—all kinds of shit but nobody liked him much. Then he started into doin' rock himself. Max. Stayed wasted all the time an' didn't even ride no more. Spent all his money an' didn't have no friends....Then he goes an' fuckin' jumps off the buildin' one night, man! Shit! I still wanted to be his friend only he wouldn't let me!"

Robby chugged the rest of his Bud, picked up a second. "Jeez, you gonna cry?"

"Naw!"

Robby ate a Ding-Dong and washed it down with beer. "They got this place in Fresno, man. The dudes call it the Rock House. It's for kids. You go there an' they kinda lock you inside, sellin' you rock an' give you food from Burger King." He shrugged. "One dude from school even sold his board so's he could keep goin' there a little more. I don't know, man. Maybe Randers is right? Sometimes I figure I don't know enough about shit, but ain't nobody tells you nuthin'! All that dogshit on TV looks like it's for squid-kids, man!"

"Yeah."

"So, how come this Nathaniel ain't in the picture?"

"Nathaniel ain't a Animal. He could be if he wanted, but maybe the other kids at the Center'd be ascared of him then?" Donny pointed to another drawing. "That's Nathaniel."

Robby looked. The dude was white, with really light blond hair like a surfer, down over his shoulders like a metaler. He was thin but not skinny and his face was hard but not mean. Robby studied the picture a long time. It was only a drawing but the dude was old. He looked about nineteen or something. "I thought you said Nathaniel was a boy?"

Donny ate a Ding-Dong and drank some more beer. "Naw. I said, *kinda.*" He thought a while, "Ain't nobody knows what Nathaniel is. Sometimes he's a boy, but he can be a man when he gots to."

"Kinda like one of them homos that dresses like a kid?"

"Nathaniel ain't no homo, dude!"

"Aw, that ain't what I meant anyways."

Donny nodded and looked back at the picture. Then he whispered, "I figure he's some kinda werewolf."

"Naw! There ain't no such thing!" Robby turned back to the drawing. "Maybe in Germany or somethin'?"

Donny shrugged. "Yeah? Well, it's like he never gets no older…like he's gonna be what he is forever. He rides this ancient Hosoi Street board an' shreds to the max!" He chugged the last swallow and got up. "Anyways, if he is a werewolf or somethin', he's the coolest one you'll ever see! He *likes* kids, man! An' not the way all them pervs always tellin' you! He fuckin' *cried* about Duncan, man! Like it was his fault or somethin'! He talks real talk too…not like old people with all that dogshit stuff don't mean nuthin'. He ain't no pussy neither! Dude gots a prob, he can tell it to Nathaniel an' he *help!*"

Robby nodded and drank some more. "Wish we had a dude like that in Fresno."

Donny smiled. "I don't figure there's anybody else like Nathaniel anywheres! All the Animals would die for him, man! He don't tell us what to do neither. One time, Randers called slavers on him an' he didn't even hassle about it."

Robby finished the second Bud. He was a little buzzed and his belly was tight and full. It felt good. "Um, can I score another smoke off you, man? I'll pay you back."

"For sure." Donny held out the pack and they both fired from the Bic again.

"So, what's slavers?"

Donny got up and went to the fridge for the last two Buds. "You don't got that in Fresno?"

"I don't know. Maybe we call it somethin' else?"

"Yeah. Um, say you fuck-up on one of your friends? He gets to call slavers on you an' you got to do anything he wants till he calls it off again. Shit. Randers would call it on you right now just for bein' here!"

"Naw. We got nuthin' like that. If you fuck-over one of your friends or do something hurts all the dudes, you just get beat up."

Donny smiled and handed him a Bud. "Yeah? Slavers is better. The other dudes get to make you do stuff, *any* stuff, or they can just save it back till there's somethin' really gross or scary to get done." He shrugged. "You get your ass wiped an' it's over. Maybe it hurts awhile but no prob. Slavers makes you think about the shit you done longer an' you don't do it again."

"What if you don't wanna do it?"

"*Then* you get your ass wiped! You wouldn't be a Animal no more either!"

"Sounds like some little-kid shit. You ever get it called?"

"Yeah. Once."

"What'd you have to do, lick dog-piss or somethin'?"

"Naw. *That* would be little-kid shit!" Donny slid to the floor again and pulled out the box. He dug under all the skate magazines and comics and held up a black .45 automatic, then tossed it to Robby. "I had to roust it outta this dealer's car! Right in the street in the daytime!" He giggled. "Weasel helped a little. He threw a big handful of dogshit at the dealer-dude's bodyguard who's 'sposed to be watchin' the car. Right in the fuckin' *face,* man! Weasel booked on his board an' I score the gun while the guard was chasin' him! Dude had a Uzi, I think, but was ascared to use it on the street 'cause it was daytime."

Robby checked the big gun. "This's hot, man! It's like an army one! Jeffers gots this old thrasher .38 but I only seen this kind in movies. Eddie Murphy gots one." Robby held it in both hands and aimed at Donny's chest. He made a gun-sound and Donny grinned and fell back on the floor. Robby checked the gun again—heavy, black, and important as hell. "Ain't nobody gonna kick your ass when you got somethin' like this, man! Um, it loaded?"

Donny sat up and held out his hand. Robby gave him the gun and Donny pulled the clip and held it up. "Only seven. 'Sposed to have eight an' then you can keep one in the chamber too, but I shot it once at the old Navy yard to see what it'd feel like." He grinned. "Slams your wrist, man, max!" He shoved the clip back in and threw it to Robby again.

"Awesome! How do you cock it?"

Donny sat on the bed. "Like this." He worked the slide. "Take off the safety…" He did. "An' you ready to waste somebody."

Robby held it in both hands, arms out, finger on the trigger, and looked down the sight. "Wanted to waste this dude at school one time. Kept on beatin' me up…for *nuthin',* man! Every fuckin' day!"

Donny nodded. "Yeah. I figure everybody gots somebody they wanna kill."

Robby lowered the gun and looked at it a while longer. Then he handed it back. Donny pulled the clip, worked the slide, and the bullet popped out. He pushed it back in the clip. "Randers said I could keep it. He already gots this huge .44 mag. Duncan give it to him when he was makin' all the money an' still tryin' to stay friends. Randers shot it a couple times. He say it kicks like hell."

"I like yours, man," Robby said. "Maybe I can score one too?"

Donny shrugged and put the gun back in the box, covering it with comics. "No prob if you gots the bucks. Kevin wants a Uzi like the dealers got, but he had to use some of his money to buy a new deck." He glanced at the dusty old board again. "Figure pretty soon he gonna try rock-runnin' too."

There was a clock on a box beside the bed and Donny glanced at it. "Nine-thirty, man. My mom'll be home in a little while." He handed Robby the last Ding-Dong. "She works at this bakery thrift-store; that's how come we always got lots of this stuff." He thought a minute. "Maybe I gots somethin' figured tonight. Chug the beer so's we can dump the empties."

Robby grinned and did. He stood up and fell against Donny, who laughed and caught him. "Hey, dude, three wimpy Buds an' you wasted?"

"Jeez, I ain't had nuthin' to eat in two days, man! What'd you expect?"

Donny held his shoulders. "Yeah? You ain't gonna puke or nuthin'?"

"Naw."

Donny kept hold of Robby's shoulders. "Um, I was gonna ask if you wanted to take the cans down to the garbage—climbin' them stairs sucks—but you out-of-it!"

"No I ain't! Shit, I could handle another sixer!"

"Yeah, right, dude. Get in bed against the wall. I'm so big mom'll never figure there's two kids in there. She might come over an' kiss me or somethin' but you just keep your head covered. Okay?"

"Or what." Robby pulled off his shirt and Donny had to catch him again.

"You totally ripped, man."

Robby laughed and fell back on the bed. He kicked off his Pumas. "Yeah? I wish I was like this all the time! No probs *forever!*"

Donny grinned. "Yeah. Be right back."

"I'm cool."

The window was open a little and that strange/familiar sea-smell drifted in on the breeze and played over Robby's body. He slid off his jeans and it felt good. Once in a while things didn't seem so bad, but it helped to be a little wasted. He was almost asleep when Donny came back and nudged him.

"Get under the blanket, dude."

"Huh? Oh, yeah, right."

Donny turned off the TV and the light, slid off his jeans, and climbed in the bed. Robby snuggled his head on the pillow. Donny's big body gave off heat like a radiator and the kid-smell was good. Except for the burger grease. Donny smelled a lot like Jeffers.

"Um, Robby?"

"Yeah?"

"Um, *you* ain't no homo, are you?"

"No way, man!"

"Sorry."

"It's cool. Um, Donny?"

"Yeah?"

"Why was you down there by the ocean tonight?"

"I don't know. I go there sometimes when there's nuthin' else to do. I think about Duncan, I guess. Nobody liked him anymore, but he used to be a pretty cool dude."

"Ain't your fault he's dead."

"Yeah. But I still think about him a lot. Nobody gives a shit, man."

"Or what. Um, I'm sorry I called you fat."

"That's cool. Night, man."

"Night."

Howard Norman

The Chauffeur

MY ONLY CLIENT WAS Mrs. Moro. With what she paid me, I didn't need to drive anyone else. She lived at 1960 Jones Street, on Russian Hill, here in San Francisco. I live at 488 Columbus, Apt. 6-B, a few blocks up from North Beach. Every Tuesday, I picked her up at 6 a.m. In the almost two years she employed me, she was never ill or out of town.

The tableau soon became familiar. Mrs. Moro would be sitting on the dark red, wooden bench on the left side of her porch. I must say she looked childlike against the two-story brown house, with its tall door and slate shingles. It never varied, she'd be wearing cotton blue pants, a blouse, a sweater, and a black all-weather parka on top. This was her year-round attire. She'd either be sipping tea from a thermos or holding the closed thermos on her lap. The few times she was asleep I didn't tap the horn. I simply kept the car idling until she opened her eyes, stood, smoothed both sleeves of the parka with her hands, took up her walking stick, and navigated down two levels of cobbled stairs to the curb. Naturally, I'd hold open the door. She was about five feet tall; she didn't have to bend much to get in. Then, I'd drive her across the Golden Gate Bridge, up Highway 1 past Mill Valley, out to Sir Francis Drake Highway, on through Inverness, and up to Point Reyes National Seashore, where she'd walk and bird-watch, rain or no rain.

Mrs. Moro was my patron, my driving companion, and, truth be told, one of the few people I had any sort of regular conversation with. And that was fine. Friendlier chauffeurs got extra work, word-of-mouth. I had Mrs. Moro, stuck with her, she stuck with me, and she paid me better than I could've ever imagined. Two people in a car for so many hours rely in equal measure on each other for things said and things unsaid.

Not that I hadn't had previous clients. I'd worked for Airport Limousine for five years before Mrs. Moro hired me. I was on call with a beeper. Mostly, I drove businessmen, airport to hotel, hotel to restaurant, to a nightclub. Waiting for a client on summer nights, I'd lean against my Lincoln Town Car, just looking at whatever street activity. Or sit in the car, reading one of my Joseph Conrad novels. Or Graham Greene. I did my book shopping at A Clean Well-Lighted Place for Books. I had a small portable library in the front seat. It included some Italian authors, too; there was Elsa Morante, Dino Buzzati, Tommaso Landolfi, Natalia Ginzburg, my favorite. Whereas many of the chauffeurs I met at hotels, bar mitzvahs, concerts, weddings, and so on preferred music tapes to reading. I didn't have a single music tape. When my clients wanted music, I found something on the FM.

In this employment, I wasn't happy or unhappy, and it paid my rent. On occasion, I drove a stretch limousine, TV, wet bar, stereo system in the back, but I preferred the Town Car. In terms of human behaviors, life seemed less complicated with the Town Car. With the limousine, not often, but once in a while, there was love-making in the backseat, and then the awkward moment with the clients' mussed-up shirt or blouse, their extravagantly oversized tips out of embarrassment. Usually these were people who'd started out the evening all neatly tucked and tied, but ended up like a boozy scene in a film noir, or aspired to. From the get-go with my boss David Tallen, I refused prom nights or rich kids just out for a lark—you could tell by what my boss called their "on-phone demeanor." In a Town Car, there's no privacy from the driver, no privacy window, whereas in the limousine, there was, so in Town Cars the clients predictably acted in a more civilized manner. Only once did I ever say "Get another driver," and that guy was an out-and-out jerk, bully-the-chauffeur, obviously a show-off-for-his-girlfriend celebrity type, I think a weather channel host. I wasn't much bothered by it, really. I take things personally only from people I know personally. In that instance, I didn't even adjust the rearview in order to see his face after I'd dumped him back at his hotel. In fact, his girlfriend stayed in the car and I dropped her off at a party. Shame and embarrassment, just wanting to get away from the chauffeur, quite often resulted in hurried, oversized tips. I'm just describing human nature in such situations. Let's see, oh yes, and one time I had Dustin Hoffman and his wife in the car. They were very polite and friendly and kept driver-client exchanges very cut-and-dry, which a driver appreciates. They went out for dinner, then to someone's apartment, then back to their hotel at 3 a.m. Generous tip that time, too. I worked for a pair of Buddhist monk dignitaries, the cellist Janos Starker, and, a year before he died, the famous deejay Wolfman Jack, and they are the extent of my name-dropping. Whereas some chauffeurs go on and on, like they became personal confidants in a few hours. "Yeah, Harold Robbins—the author? His wife always requests me." And like that.

Mrs. Moro, born in Tokyo, a bird-watcher and nice person, was anonymous, as far as I knew, to the world at large. She struck me as a very private soul, so I appreciated our conversations, some of which were only a few minutes long. On our fifth or sixth drive together, she said, "Tuttle Albers"—she always used my complete name—"Tuttle Albers, I have a present for you. A little gift. It's a book." She set a book called *Rashomon,* by the Japanese writer Akutagawa Ryunosuke, on the front seat next to me, then pronounced his name on my behalf. "Give it a try maybe." I read it while she was walking at Point Reyes, a murder story told from different points of view. When we started back to San Francisco, I said, "I read the book," and she said, "I'm pleased you read it so quickly. I know you did so because it was a gift, but I'm pleased just the same," and wanted to hear my opinion. In her questions, she was a bit like a schoolteacher, but I could tell she was enjoying herself. As usual, she fell asleep just as we got to the Golden Gate Bridge. I always had to wake her up when we got to her house.

To put it simply, working for Mrs. Moro got me out into nature. I mean that in two old-fashioned ways.

First, at Point Reyes, there was never an absence of hawks, and there were the smaller flitting kinds of birds, the usual crows. All sorts of ducks, Mrs. Moro told me, "abounded"—she used that word—in the lowland estuaries. There are maybe ten hiking trails at the National Seashore, names like five Brooks, Chimney Rock, Mount Vision, Muddy Hollow. Some of the trails meander back before reaching the sea, but Mrs. Moro walked the same trail every time, the Estero Trail, which went all the way to Sunset Beach. "I take a quick nap leaning against a fallen tree," she once told me. "I believe it was struck by lightning."

Parked next to the Estero trailhead entrance gate, I'd do pretty much what I did when I used to wait for clients in the city. I'd sit in the car, or, weather permitting, lie on the ground and read. Or listen to KPXP Country. I had my Joseph Conrads, my Italians, and, as the weeks went by, the Japanese novels generously given to me by Mrs. Moro: Tanizaki, Kawabata, more Akutagawa, and a number of others. "No reason to expect you'd ever read in Japanese," she said. "Still, I feel sorry for you, that you cannot." In short, Mrs. Moro had provided me with my entire Japanese library. Remarkable as it first seemed, that a woman her age could make the three-hour trek to the ocean and back, after a few trips her stamina didn't at all surprise me. And she had her nap on the way to Point Reyes, at the beach, on the way home. Some days, after I watched her disappear over the hill, I'd drive into Point Reyes for lunch, even catch a noon matinee at the art house in Mill Valley, but I'd always get back in plenty of time. I made sure to tell Mrs. Moro my exact plans and wrote out telephone numbers, the car phone, the police, the movie theater, even the general store in Point Reyes Station. She kept these numbers in a small notebook. A separate notebook from her bird lists. "Birds are my greatest pleasure," she once said.

Turn left off Sir Francis Drake Road, go down a quarter mile of blacktop, continue along the hard-packed dirt road for another mile and a half, and you get to the parking area at the Estero trailhead. It's situated between dry grassy hills. In summer, there are dust devils, even an occasional brush fire; the National Seashore has its own volunteer fire department, men and women from Inverness, Point Reyes Station, and other nearby towns. Volunteers had VFD decals on windshields, lower left-hand corner. To either side of the trailhead, cattle grazed up close behind fences. I'd hear cattle lowing all day. And as I mentioned, hawks were always in abundance. Hawks were a constant. They'd be circling overhead, buffeted by the wind, they'd drift and rise on the thermals and swoop down into the crag gullies, and hawks were always patrolling the fields as far as the eye could see. I'd watch them but not study them, really, although I knew that Mrs. Moro studied them and even wanted hawks to be a common thing between us, because she gave me a field guide. "Hawks may be the easiest to tell apart. They're observable for long periods," she said. "However, the true test is shorebirds. To distinguish one sandpiper from the other has, for the twenty years I've walked the same path, been my nemesis. I have almost given up."

"Why do you keep walking to the same beach?" I said.

"Oh, that is simple. I hope to see white pelicans. I hope to see them. But why should they be in any hurry to let me see them?"

"Maybe if you'd come up here more than one day a week," I said. "I'll bring you up here for free, an extra time per week, if you want."

"That holds out the possibility of my not seeing white pelicans twice a week, instead of once. I don't think that would be a good thing."

Second, there was human nature. Because during Mrs. Moro's walks to the sea, I would visit Grey Zamarkis, who was a resident research zoologist at the Tule Elk Reserve, out on foggy Tomales Bay, at the northern edge of the Inverness Ridge.

I looked this up in my appointment book, which I kept in my glove compartment: I met Grey the twenty-third time I brought Mrs. Moro to the National Seashore. I'd waited until Mrs. Moro drifted over the hill—the day was hazy and she looked a little like a mirage—and then I drove into Inverness to gas up the Town Car. I was standing next to the gas pump in front of the Inverness

General Store when I saw this woman—I'm speaking of Grey, of course—putting air into the tires of her Land Rover. Not a candlelight dinner in sight, as the country-western song defined a romantic moment in a non-romantic setting. Not to leap ahead too far, but we ended up having country-western music in common; we made love to it and argued about it. For instance, one time I claimed that, although I enjoyed it, C and W basically promoted a drastically simple take on people. To support this, I cited a popular joke: What do you get when you play a country-western song backward? Well, you get your wife back, your kids back, your car back. "No, sir, uh-uh, nope," Grey said, shaking her head back and forth. "They may be drastic little soap operas, but they tell some basic truths about love and life. Just like great novels do. In less time, of course." Anyway, for the approximately six months Grey and I were together, we kept the radio on KPXP, and never changed stations, not in her Land Rover, the Town Car, or in her one-room "fisherman's hovel," as she called her rented clapboard structure at the end of a dock stretched out into Tomales Bay. Next to the Golden Hinde Boatel on Sir Francis Drake Highway. The dock slats were so unevenly rotted it was like walking on a long wooden xylophone; it made that many different hollow tones. Grey's rent was fifty dollars a month. She lived a twenty-five-minute drive from the herd of elk.

I met Grey on August 17, and later, as I mentioned, I entered our meeting in my work diary. I already had strong feelings for her, yet all I wrote was "Grey Zamarkis."

Standing at the gas pump, I'd noticed Grey's bumper sticker: I BRAKE FOR SASQUATCH. Now, normally, I'd have been repelled. Because driving as much as I did, I'd evolved an ever-narrowing tolerance for bumper sticker philosophies. I made it my obligation to disagree with each and every one of them, on principle. The principle being that any joke, platitude, Bible quote, political harangue, or ethical judgment that ends up on a bumper sticker asks you to be like-minded. But somehow, Grey's sticker didn't put me off. I felt generous toward it, willing to be persuaded that it declared that she was open to surprises in the natural world: should

Sasquatch step out onto the road, she'd give it the right-of-way. I immediately thought of Grey as someone who'd defer to the mysterious. It's quite likely that all of this quick interpretation was based on the fact that Grey, at first glance and from that time forward, was so striking. The word "smitten" accurately applies to me, and I remember everything about that morning, including that her red hair was shaped into a tight configuration of braids, but was frizzed out anyway. When she stood up, I saw that she was taller than me by at least an inch; I am five foot eight. Though she was not a park ranger, a Smokey the Bear-type hat hung by a woven cord down her back. When she leaned over again to test the air pressure, the hat fell to one side. She got annoyed and flipped it back, and then must've felt me staring, because she turned and glared at me. She had a sprinkle of freckles along her nose. Since I thought she looked pretty elegant while just putting air in her tires, naturally I needed to watch her walk to the cash register, chat up the clerk, buy a pack of Neccos, go in and out of the ladies. And then I was both stupefied and pleased when she walked directly up to me and said, "Hate your car."

"Well, I'm a chauffeur."

She had a nice laugh. We had coffee while standing up in the store. Coffee and bagels to go. Conversation. Betraying no excitement. And two hours later, this was about 11:30 a.m., we were standing up in her open-top Land Rover, looking at a dozen or so tule elk. "I'm the only researcher in residence right now," Grey said. She handed me her binoculars and I looked through them at the elk. I could see that their noses were wet. I could see them scuffing up ground cover. I could see them nodding, shivering up along their thick necks, gazing in our direction, sniffing the air, nervously shuffling. "We're in the elk's house—the Indians who used to live around here said—and some days, it feels like heaven to me," Grey said. "But I'll tell you what, elk can be nasty. They've gone for my vehicle. The reserve gets socked in by fog, midsummer or not. And the forest—all these trees—can get like one enormous ventriloquist."

"How do you mean that?"

"Well, depending on the fog, how thick, how not thick, it's like an elk throws its voice. You hear one bellowing or coughing—it's more a chuffing bark—coming, say, from over to your left. But then suddenly the animal crashes right past you not ten yards away on your right."

"Could it be there's really two elk?"

"You don't get what I mean. Because you haven't experienced it yet. No offense."

"That's okay. We just met. I'm out here in my chauffeur's suit. These shoes. And these are the first elk I've ever seen, except for on Marty Stouffer's *Wild America* program."

"I hate that show."

"So do I—now."

"Yippee, our first thing in common."

Grey and I first started sleeping together two visits later. She had just turned twenty-eight that July 11, and my thirtieth birthday had been on March 14. She'd been married at nineteen in Fresno, moved to Castroville, and gotten divorced at twenty-three. "He—that being Eddie—wanted me to be an artichoke wife," Grey told me, our first noontime in bed. "His family business was artichokes. All the women he was raised around and by became artichoke wives. They took care of the house, kids, did the books, et cetera. And I was that for four years of my life, Tuttle, right out of high school. Except that I had no children. I was derided for taking night courses at the community college. In biology. They were tough courses. And I mean derided. Sitting with family or friends, in a bar? My own husband, Eddie—he'd say, 'And what does our local intellectual say about that?' Whatever the topic. I think he was jealous because he read comic books and the occasional farm report, and there was TV. I'd married him, though; nobody put a gun to my head. Going from artichoke wife to zoology major was twice around the planet Earth, considering where I started out."

Grey was working on what she called her "late doctorate" in zoology, at the University of California, Davis campus. She knew a dictionary's worth of zoological terms, and had a nonplussed way of simplifying for me all the important theories in her field. She expected me to be interested, but didn't ask me to read any of the Ph.D. thesis she was writing. She was up-front about her need to budget her study time. I admired her constancy. Whenever I drove up to spend a weekend, I admired that she took her time in bed, too. And admired when she'd then get up, go to her desk, open her notebooks, and work until 3 a.m. If I was there on a weekday night, she'd get maybe two, three hours of sleep, off goes the alarm, she'd drink half a pot of coffee, and leave for the Tule Elk Reserve.

The working title of her thesis was "Predator-Prey Relationship Between Saber-toothed Cats and Tule Elk." At Davis, she'd studied with one of the world's foremost experts on sabertooth—the large, extinct cat that used to roam California—behavior. His name was Dr. Peter Volk. He was British, and had supervised excavations at the La Brea Tar Pits. Grey said he was demanding. He gave every single one of his graduate students *The Autobiography of Charles Darwin* for inspiration. He'd made sure that Grey steeped herself in all the paleontological writings about sabertooths, and she had to cross-reference that with predator-prey studies about other large cats of the world. "Partake of hours and hours of imaginative thinking and daydreaming," Volk said, "and spend as much time with tule elk as possible." One of Volk's theories—the one that excited Grey the most, actually—was that present-day elk might have a genetic memory of being hunted, say a thousand years ago, by sabertoothed tigers. She once let me read her notebook: "Passing the exams will be child's play, for you, Grey," he'd told her during an office appointment. "But if you want to make real discoveries, stretch your brain, get obsessed by far-reaching possibilities."

"At first," Grey said, "with all his talk about a poetic approach, I felt lost, and thought that Dr. Volk was patronizing me. That he didn't really think I had the scientific smarts. I mustered up the courage to confront him on this, and he said, 'I don't take just anybody into this program, Miss Zamarkis,' and that ended that discussion."

I admit I didn't grasp all of the ambitions of Grey's fieldwork, and very little of her thesis topic, but she made it sound exciting; I cared because she cared so much, and I told her that. She was dedicated. "I told Dr. Volk I was working long hours because I wanted to make up for lost time," Grey said. "He downplayed that. He said that, with a living animal—the elk, he meant, and then add this sabertooth deal to boot—you have to take your sweet time."

The first week in September I'd driven up on a Saturday afternoon to be with Grey. I got to her place at 4:15, and we were in bed by 4:30. That evening, we had dinner at The Station, in Point Reyes Station, a lively joint that specialized in Mexican. Grey was in a chatty mood. She'd gotten dressed up in a pleated, black Western skirt, a belt with a steer-horn buckle, a white cotton sweater, no bra, and a necklace of black pearls. And cowboy boots. She had her hair up in one braid, and otherwise it tumbled down, frizzy as it was. "Tuttle," she said, the moment we sat down, "I'm going to play the jukebox. I actually went to the bank yesterday to get quarters, hoping we'd be here tonight."

"We can go three doors down to Max's afterward to dance, if you'd like."

"I'd just as soon go home."

"That's fine, too."

"Or there's a movie, *The Lacemaker,* with that beautiful Isabelle Huppert. Down in Mill Valley. My mother, I mentioned it to her on the telephone last night. She said she saw it when it first came out, *The Lacemaker,* and that it had the saddest ending of any movie she'd ever seen. The camera just holds on a brokenhearted Isabelle Huppert's face for at least three minutes. I said, Mom, you always thought that was me in the school playground, you know, sitting off by myself alone, and that's how I'd end up, too. But that was a movie star sitting alone, jilted and forlorn, at the end of a movie, not your own daughter, Mom."

"You just gave the ending away."

"It doesn't matter, does it? I mean, you only really experience the end by going through the whole story start to finish. A story's not ruined just by knowing the ending ahead of time. Only a limited person would think that. And that's not you, Tuttle. You're not in the least bit limited."

"Well, to a movie or back to your place. Either one's fine. I know you like to work up your notes on Saturday nights. Miss Lonely-hearts, huh?"

"I enjoy being alone sometimes, but not tonight. Tonight I'm sticking with you. And I'm extra happy. Want to know why? Because I felt like a sabertooth yesterday, all afternoon yesterday. Usually, I try to imagine—like Dr. Volk suggested—imagine myself as a tule elk, a female. Nibbling grass in the fog. Picking my way down to a rocky beach. You know, get inside an elk's head. But two nights ago, coffee, coffee, coffee, and the term 'predator-prey' came into my brain, and I thought, *hmmmmm*, that I'd been one-sided in my concentration all of these months. So, yesterday, I was out at the range at 4 a.m., and I had a pretty normal morning. But in the afternoon—pow! I really got into being a sabertooth. It made a big difference, emotionally at least. Now, if I could only somehow get that experience down on paper."

The waiter brought our salads first, then enchiladas and Dos Equis beers. Grey ordered a pitcher of ice water, too; she was planning ahead for the spiciness. She'd ordered two chicken-and-cheese enchiladas, I got one beef and one chicken. When our food was all set out, I lifted my bottle and said, "May a saber-toothed tiger materialize right out of the fog, so you can see that."

We clinked bottles and each took a swig. "Talk about getting into someone else's head," Grey said. "You got into mine with that toast, Tuttle." She leaned over and kissed me. "It was a thoughtful toast. I mean that. Totally unselfish."

"Well, there's not too many people I'd be truly happy for, if something fantastic happened to them."

"I'm happening to you, Tuttle."

"Yes you are."

We ate and talked about this and that, and Grey played five songs in a row on the jukebox, which we could barely hear over the surrounding conversations. Finally, Grey slid her chair close up to mine. "How'd you actually choose your profession, Tuttle?" she said. "I should have asked sooner, I know." She turned beet red. "God, half a beer and I'm slurring. What a cheap date, huh?"

We both laughed, and I could tell by the directness of her smile that we wouldn't be going to a movie. In fact, my heart actually felt like it fluttered in my throat, and I wanted to leave the restaurant right then. But Grey was relishing her meal, she wanted to talk, as did I, really. All of which composed the happiness I'd have been loath to ruin.

"I didn't go into the family business, if that's what you mean?"

"I suppose I meant, what keeps you being a chauffeur?"

"Mrs. Moro—I told you about her. She keeps me in it."

"On the practical side, sure, Mrs. Moro pays you well."

"Not just the practical."

"You like talking with her about the novels and so forth."

"Plus, I admire her overall character, I guess is the way to put it."

"Obviously, though, she's a wealthy lady."

"I don't know for sure. I've never set foot in her house. It's an old house, old for San Francisco, at least. She told me it's the only one on Russian Hill that was designed by the architect Maybeck, very famous. One morning, I saw a man, much younger than Mrs. Moro, standing in the front window, and when she got in the car, she said it was her son, visiting from Tokyo. Maybe I'm wrong, but just the way she said it, she sounded disgusted. Yeah, probably she's very rich. I don't think my being her chauffeur's her only extravagance."

"You really really like her a lot, don't you?"

"In a funny way—and I'm not asking for violins. And present company excepted, she's turned out to be my one friend. Sounds unlikely, I suppose. I mean, she's sixty-seven. But, she trusts me to drive her. She trusts me to share books. In the car, we either talk or don't. It's nice for me. One time, it was raining cats and dogs, I said, 'Now, Mrs. Moro, you're not really going to walk down to Sunset Beach in this monsoon, are you?'"

"What'd she say to that?"

"'Tuttle Albers—'"

"Sorry to interrupt, but your Japanese accent is atrocious."

"'—Tuttle Albers, my hope is to one day see a white pelican.' Then she got out of the car, put up the hood of her parka, and just started walking. She travels pretty light, the backpack, thermos of tea, maybe an extra sweater. Her walking stick, notebook, binoculars. That's about it."

"That's nice, Tuttle. I like hearing about her. I like hearing about you and her together."

"I didn't realize how much I liked her, though, till you asked."

"You probably just never said so out loud."

"I bet that's it."

We went to Baskin Robbins for an ice cream, sat on the enclosed porch. It wasn't crowded at all. We each got double scoops of vanilla in a cup. "Truth be told," I said, "I've lost my taste for driving. Not my knack for it. Just my affection. I don't have another profession in mind yet. I used to work for this guy, David Tallen, at Airport Limousine, and he was a good employer. I don't like working for anybody, really, but I didn't mind working for him."

"You must've run into some doozies. Clients, I mean."

"I'll tell you a story sometime."

"Tell me now, Tuttle. We're just eating ice cream."

"Yeah? Well, okay—this one time. David Tallen calls me up, he says, 'A Miss Banaktian—' this was about five years ago. David says, '—her mother and father are from Armenia. And they're flying in via New York for her wedding. She's a student at UC-Berkeley, and she's marrying a guy she met in school.' Okay—so these parents have never been to the U.S. I'm supposed to pick them up at the San Francisco airport, right? Then drive them to the Mark Hopkins. The wedding's that night at the hotel. Then the next morning, I'm supposed to drive them—a group—to Carmel, where they've got a house rented for a week. I'm supposed to wait a week, then pick them up, the airport, and they go back to Armenia.

"It's pretty cut-and-dry. And it's a nice job, because, one, since everybody's staying at the Mark Hopkins, I don't have to stick around for the wedding in order to drive them anywhere else that night. And, two, I get to see Carmel. And, three, I could take on other clients during the week. I did some addition ahead of time, and figured I'd come out with around six hundred dollars, plus a tip, but do you know what I ended up with? Three thousand dollars."

"How'd that miracle happen, pray tell?"

"I pick them up at the airport, and the future bride is in the backseat, and, Grey, she is very beautiful, very exotic-looking in a way. I couldn't understand a word they said in the car, but it was a teary reunion. The whole way to the city they spoke Armenian and laughed and looked at photographs from the old country and so forth.

"So. The wedding takes place. The next morning, 10 a.m. sharp, I'm at the hotel, standing by the stretch. A very sunny day. And out comes Mr. Banaktian, and he is looking highly agitated. He is not happy. I thought, hangover mixed with jet lag. I saw the rest of the family, aunt, uncle, mother, and the bride's brother, I think—and then I see the bride and groom. He's holding the bride's hand. But nobody—none of them—is looking in the least bit happy. I say to myself, 'You're going to Carmel. The seals. The sea otters. The beautiful scenery. Just roll the privacy window up, forget it, no problem. Down and back, it's the beautiful coast highway.'

"When all of a sudden, the father, Mr. Banaktian—he's about sixty—he comes up to me. His accent, mind you, is very thick. I say, 'Congratulations, sir. The bellhops will put your luggage in the trunk. I'm ready to go whenever you are.' I've already got the trunk popped open.

"'Wait a minute—driver,' he says. 'Wait a minute.' I can't do the accent. He says, 'Tuttle—' because I've got my name tag on. 'Tuttle, look. Look. Look, there, there's my new son-in-law, and what a piece of shit he is. My friend, my driver. I'm a *disappointed* man. This piece of shit she's married. Dirty. Dirty hair. And no job. He's what we call—' and he said something in Armenian. The words twisted up his face. 'He doesn't eat. At his own wedding banquet, he drank Coca-Cola—he's a fucking *string bean.*'" Grey was laughing. "'You call it here, a *string bean.*'

"'Tuttle'—and now he places my hand directly over his heart. He had a silk suit on, I think '—you can't feel anything, can you, because I'm dead.'

"'I'll get the bellhops,' I said.

"But now he grabs my arm tightly. 'Tuttle, look at my daughter,' he says. 'Look at her face. In her face is not a happy future.' Now he steps up close to me and whispers, 'Tuttle, my friend. In my country, I have position. I come from an important family. My mother, she's ninety-three. Ninety-three years old. She's seen a lot. She's been through a lot. She deserves peacefulness. A peaceful death. She controls the family money—you mention this to anyone Tuttle, my driver, and I will run you over with this big limousine, eh? I'm smiling. I'm smiling. It's my big joke. Relax. But, Tuttle, my American friend, my goodwill ambassador.' He takes out a wad of American hundred-dollar bills. He peels off two thousand dollars' worth, stuffs it into my suit pocket, and says, 'In *addition* to your driving fee, Tuttle.'

"'I don't understand,' I say.

"'My mother,' he says, 'was too weak to come to America California for the wedding, her only granddaughter. I promised I would bring back photographs. We had hundreds taken. But no matter, no matter, because I promised her a special one, the bride, the groom, together—a photograph for enlargement—the groom stands next to the bride, eh? Tuttle, I look at you. I appraise you. You're a handsome man. I beg you—please.' He's actually got tears in his eyes. 'See that man across the lobby—our photographer. He's my cousin. He's going to take a picture of you next to my daughter. Just standing next to the impressive limousine. To my daughter, it will seem nothing, just a natural proud thing for her father, to show off the car, the driver. But I will personally see to it it is the only photograph of the bride and groom my mother ever sets eyes on, and she'll die in peace. Because you, Tuttle, are not a drug-head hippie string bean. Who somehow hypnotized my daughter.' He peels off ten more bills and stuffs them in. And he puts his face an inch from mine and says, 'To make my mother happy.'"

"And so," Grey said, "tossing chauffeuring ethics to the wind, Tuttle Albers accepts a whopping bribe."

"Weeks after it happened, you know what? I had very detailed, weird dreams."

"Such as?"

"It got pretty paranoid. See, this actual real event did happen, I *did* stand next to the Armenian bride in front of the limo. The cousin snaps maybe ten pictures. I drive them to Carmel and all the rest, no problems, no glitches, and I didn't hear another word from Mr. Banaktian. All that was real life. But then came these dreams.

"In dream number one, the ninety-three-year-old mother—"

"Oh, oh," Grey said.

"The old mother sees the photograph of me and her grand-daughter together, and she completely recovers from her illness. She's all perky now. She's got the photograph on the mantel, and Mr. Banaktian's put in a fix, and the bride's not going back to Armenia so she can't say, 'That's not my husband!' One day—this is my dream, now—the old mother calls Mr. Banaktian to her side and says, 'I want to see my granddaughter and her new husband. If you don't bring them to me, I'll leave all the family money to a flock of crows.'"

"Crows?" Grey said, laughing.

"Grey—I'm just telling what I dreamed."

"Sorry—it's just that it's a Grimm's fairy tale, Tuttle."

"Anyway, that's dream number one. Dream number two. I'm sitting home in my apartment. I've got my chauffeur's suit on. I'm drinking coffee. It's late at night. The downstairs buzzer rings. I say into the intercom, 'Who is it?' It's a sultry voice with an accent 'It's me.' I press the buzzer. I hear the elevator bell. There's a knock on my door. I open it."

"Of course, it's the Armenian bride," Grey said. "The bitch."

"She's got her wedding dress on. Oh, my God. Oh, my God. She pulls the dress right off and gives me the deepest warmest kiss, then she says, 'The airplane is waiting.' 'Where's your husband?' I ask. 'Oh, it was so tragic,' she says." I took some bites of ice cream.

"So naturally there's a dream number three," Grey said.

"Dream three. We're living in Armenia, I've fallen madly in love with her. There's no turning back. We have children."

"Bad ending for me," Grey said.

"You asked me to tell this story."

Grey and I finished our ice cream. She ordered a cup of coffee. She looked at me, shaking her head back and forth. "God, Tuttle, you mean you and this bride—actually, *real life* now, might be in a photograph, in an actual house in actual Armenia?"

"I'm certain of it. This *actual* Mr. Banaktian wasn't kidding."

"If I see any Armenian license plates around Inverness, Tuttle, I'm going to get upset."

Grey went to the ladies' room. When she came back, I was sipping her coffee. She sat down and I slid the mug over to her. "I'm shifting subjects here," she said. "But, Tuttle, how much do you like your apartment? Because you really only have to be in San Francisco Tuesday morning and Tuesday night, Mrs. Moro up and back, correct?"

"Are you asking me to be up here with you more?"

"Not live with me. Not yet. My grant's only good for another year. I'm under a bit of pressure there. I was thinking, we could see each other maybe at least one, two other days a week. Or at least steadily weekends guaranteed. The Holly Tree Inn has excellent off-season rates. You could start out there—it's ten minutes from my place."

"She likes me. She likes me."

"You drive home, okay? I'm still a little tipsy."

I drove the Land Rover back to Inverness. Beautiful starry night. I parked as usual in the lot of the Golden Hinde Boatel. I kept the engine idling, the heat turned low. We were looking at a few scattered house lights in the hills across the bay. Grey started to use a fake Armenian accent, much more on purpose exaggerated than mine, "Tuttle, Tuttle," she vamped, "we make love on the dock. We make love like mermaids under the dock. My handsome American love ambassador-driver chauffeur Tuttle." She draped herself over me and we kissed for a long time, a real drive-in-movie make-out session, replete with steaming up the windshield. When we took a breather, Grey said, "How many children did you have with her." She wasn't using the accent. "I'm just wondering."

In Grey's room, we put on KPXP, "all night country, country all night," as the deejay said. We had a good time.

Over the next month, I noticed that the books Mrs. Moro gave me to read were either about suicide or edited, incomplete novels by writers who had committed suicide, according to the "About the author" in back of the books. There was Akutagawa Ryunosuke's *Hell Screen, Cogwheels, A Fool's Life,* which I found beautiful, but difficult reading. It was made up of three stories. The third was called "A Fool's Life," and it was like a diary. Each entry had a title such as "Laughter of the Gods." Though Mrs. Moro more and more chose to sleep and not talk, we still had animated conversations about the books, if noticeably briefer ones. She'd given me the Akutagawa book on a particularly glum overcast and cold day, which didn't help, or it might be argued was the perfect accompaniment to reading it. Mrs. Moro and I agreed—we said this in quite different ways—that the writing was powerful and disturbing (her two words), mainly about feeling puny and useless. "It's none of my concern, Tuttle Albers," she said, without a hint of sarcasm or even humor that I could detect, "but I wouldn't suggest reading it out loud to Grey Zamarkis in the bedroom." I glanced at her in the rearview mirror; she shut her eyes and fell asleep, and did not wake up until we were on Russian Hill.

Still, that day, Mrs. Moro had intrepidly set out along the Estero Trail in the rain. I walked over to the telephone booth and called Grey. The way I'd seen rainstorms lash the Tule Elk Reserve, I thought she may not have gone into the field. Besides, the night before, when I'd phoned, she said she'd come down with an achy cold, possibly the flu. It turned out she was at home. When she picked up the phone, I heard her teakettle whistling in the background. "Oh, Tuttle, it's you," she said. "One sec, okay?" I heard her turn off the kettle. "I'm back."

"You sound pretty awful," I said.

"It's full-blown flu. I was really looking forward to seeing you."

"What're you talking about? I'm coming right over. The deli section of the Inverness store's got chicken soup, remember?"

"I already bought some. But I still feel lousy. I've got all this work, and it's slow-motion when you're sick, right? Energy's real low. But call me tonight, okay? Plus, I might be contagious."

"Did you call a doctor?"

"It's the flu. I don't have to call a doctor."

"Did you at least take your temperature?"

"It's 102.5. Temperature's only alarming data if it's 105. In between that and 98.6, I figure it's just the flu."

"I could just sit in the kitchen with you for an hour or two."

"Not worth it, really. Because if it's going to stay the flu a while, it means precious time away from the elk, too. So, you *know* I'm not doing too well, huh?"

"Poor girl. I'll miss you, Grey."

"Me, too."

"Okay, I'm hanging up then."

"Tuttle?"

"Yeah?"

"Why'd you call from a booth? Usually, you'd just drive right over."

"I was going to sit in the car and read a little. I figured in this rain you'd be working on your notes. But since last night you said you were sick, I wanted to check up on you."

"Sweet, and thoughtful."

"And. I'm worried about Mrs. Moro."

"Why's that?"

"It's hard to explain. She gives me Japanese novels, right? Well, lately, the ones she's given me—I don't know. I mean, there's this author, Akutagawa."

"That's like a knock-knock joke. Akutagawa *who?*"

"The guy's a genius, he wrote a novel called *Kappa,* which is about spirit-amphibians, or something like that, but he makes them seem human—more real than people you see on the street. Anyway, Akutagawa killed himself. Mrs. Moro gave me what amounts to his fifty-page suicide note. Besides which, for the last two weeks, she's been sleeping most of the way up and back from the city. Whereas before, she might take a nap, but mostly we'd talk, too."

"She's allowed to be a little depressed."

"I'm not explaining it right."

"You sound upset, though. You just haven't thought it through. How much of her personal life does she tell you?"

"Not much. Two weeks ago, she mentioned that her son canceled another visit."

"Mother-son. That's always a possible culprit. Maybe it's the son."

"Butt out, is what you're saying."

"Sort of, yeah."

"She gave me this author Mishima—he's a suicide. Kawabata killed himself. After he won the Nobel Prize, too. Five out of five books she's given me in a row, the writer—each and every one."

"Is she out walking as we speak?"

"I said, Why not have a cup of tea at Point Reyes Station, wait and see if the rain lets up? But off she went."

"She's got sixty-some years' experience making up her mind."

"You don't think, just this once, I should follow her."

"Breach of trust. Or something like that."

"Okay. You're right. I'll phone you tonight then."

"Kisses to you, Tuttle. I feel like shit."

"Hope that doesn't last too long."

Mrs. Moro was coughing the entire drive back to San Francisco that evening. Every ten or fifteen minutes, she'd doze off, but coughing would wake her up. She wrapped herself in the blue thermal blanket I kept in a wooden box on the floor of the backseat. The box also contained a first-aid kit. I had a flashlight stashed in the glove compartment. I had a leather satchel for road maps. I had a state-of-the-art coffee thermos. In the trunk I kept flares. Anyway, the only thing Mrs. Moro uttered was so personal, I actually checked the rearview mirror to see if she was talking in her sleep. She was tented deep in the blanket, so all I could see was the top of her head, white hair. I heard her cough. But I could barely understand her hoarse whisper above the windshield wipers and rain on the roof. "Tuttle Albers," she said, "I've had the same dream for many nights in a row. I walk to Sunset Beach. It is raining. I've run out of tea. A beautiful flock of white pelicans is on the beach.

One of them speaks in the exact voice of my mother, in Japanese. 'People at home want to see you—here, have some tea.' Then, like a magician, she makes a porcelain teapot appear. I taste the tea, but it is too hot and I singe my tongue, and it makes me wake from the dream." Mrs. Moro didn't ask what I thought of the dream. Telling it to me seemed to exhaust her and she fell asleep. She sank entirely down into the blanket.

The following Tuesday Mrs. Moro was not on her porch. This was so strange that I checked the date in my appointment book, then checked the front-page date of the *San Francisco Chronicle*: Tuesday, December 14. I idled the car and waited, heat turned on, until 6:45. Morning traffic had picked up along Jones Street, fog was thinning, and around Alcatraz tourist ferries were already out, and an oil tanker moved slowly across San Francisco Bay. There was a cluster of seagulls on Mrs. Moro's roof. I'd always wanted to see the view from her window. Russian Hill was the section of the city I'd live in if I could afford it. I turned off the ignition and waited exactly another fifteen minutes. Finally, I drove to a magazine stand on Jones, parked, jumped out, and telephoned Mrs. Moro from a street booth. No answer.

I drove back to 1960 Jones Street. It was 7:30 a.m.

I stood on her porch, knocking. I rang the buzzer. Nobody came to the door. I drove to my apartment. I telephoned Mrs. Moro, letting it ring at least thirty times. I had a coughing fit out of anxiousness, I guess, because I knew, then and there, that if she could Mrs. Moro would've answered the phone. I telephoned her every ten or so minutes throughout the morning. I sat at my kitchen table and tried to read *Thousand Cranes* by Kawabata, tried to stay as calm and focused as his writing, and not obsess that Mrs. Moro had been mugged, murdered, or whatever other ambushes of city life. At noon I went to the Mission Diner, ordered the meat loaf, mashed potatoes, and coffee special, and called Mrs. Moro twice during the meal. Back at my apartment by 12:50, I watched daytime TV. The movie channel. *The 39 Steps,* directed by Alfred Hitchcock was on. I kept telephoning Mrs. Moro. Around five o'clock, I telephoned Grey and explained the situation, why I hadn't had lunch with her as promised, or shown up at all. I related Mrs. Moro's dream to Grey.

"So, Tuttle, you think somehow she's, what—been called home, so to speak? By her mother. I'm honestly trying to understand."

"Grey, I don't think *anything*. All I know is she wasn't on her porch. And she's not answering her telephone. None of this is familiar. None of it makes sense. My question is, shouldn't I call the police?"

"I'd leave a note on her door."

"What about hospitals? Last week she was coughing like mad. Like she might've caught pneumonia."

"Then call hospitals. You should call hospitals, Tuttle. Otherwise it'll drive you nuts."

"I'll drive up to see you as soon as I can."

"Okay. Keep me posted."

And in fact, I did telephone the five hospitals, public and private, closest to Russian Hill, plus a private clinic; none had an inpatient Mrs. Moro.

I got in the Town Car and drove to 1960 Jones Street. In my apartment, I'd written a brief note and found a thumbtack, and was going to tack up the note, then keep trying to call until I got through. But I decided to knock once more. This time, an elderly Japanese man opened the door. He was dressed in an elegant black suit, light blue shirt, black tie with a silver tiepin. "How can I help you?" he said. He had a tight-lipped smile, almost a grimace, and a serious, kind voice.

"I'm Mrs. Moro's driver," I said. "Tuttle Albers. She wasn't on the porch this morning so I could take her to Point Reyes, and I was worried."

"I won't invite you in. I'm Mrs. Moro's brother. Mrs. Moro died last night. Peacefully or not, how can we know? I flew in from Los Angeles."

I sat down on the wooden bench.

"I'm sorry," I said. "My condolences."

"You may sit as long as you wish."

"Thank you."

"Tuttle Albers. Yes, my sister spoke fondly of you."

"I'm very pleased to know that."

"You may sit as long as you wish."

"Thank you."

"Well, then. Please. I'll go into the house. There's arrangements. I'll be taking my sister back to Japan."

"I see. Of course."

"Goodbye then."

"Mrs. Moro loaned me a number of books."

"Books."

"Yes. Japanese novels."

"You read Japanese?"

"No, they were in English. In translation, I mean."

"I see."

"I'll return them."

"No need. Please. I must go inside."

"My card. My telephone number is somewhere in the house, I'm sure."

"My sister was very organized. I'll locate it."

"Goodbye, then. I'm very sorry. If you need to be driven anywhere—."

"No need."

I drove directly from Mrs. Moro's house and got to Inverness at 6:50. Grey was dumbstruck by my news. She made me spaghetti, but mostly we polished off a bottle of French wine. At about eleven at night, we were lying in bed. Grey had all sorts of new strength after her weeklong bout of flu. Across the room, her desk lamp was on, and on the table two candles were flickering low. Looking at the ceiling, she lay diagonally to me on the bed, her legs stretched over my stomach in such a way that I could massage her feet. "Maybe try and find another steady client," she said. "You can't replace her. I don't mean that. But the steadiness part, as soon as possible, might help."

"We spoke about you once," I said.

"You never told me that, Tuttle."

"The first time we——."

"Did what we just did, you mean?"

"Yeah—that morning, she'd given me a novel. By Kawabata, called *Snow Country*. Of course, I didn't do much reading that day. When Mrs. Moro got in the car, she noticed the bookmark. I had this fancy bookmark. It was only on page ten or so."

"Observant woman."

"'You didn't stay interested in the story,' she said. So, I told her about you, partly to not hurt her feelings about the book. But mostly because I wanted to. Besides, she had an employer's right to know where I spent my afternoons. In case of an emergency."

"In case, sure."

"Another time, she said, 'How is Grey Zamarkis?'"

"You're pretty heartbroken about her, huh?"

"Heartbroken. I'm going to borrow that word."

"That's fine."

The next morning at 5 a.m. we sat at the breakfast nook table. We had orange juice, coffee, and toast. Grey was already dressed for the Tule Elk Reserve. I was wearing her oversized striped bathrobe. "I bought you a sweater," I said. "And I'm going to tell you something that's normally impolite. It cost one hundred fifty dollars, at Le Sweater. It's so rarefied an atmosphere in that store, when I bought your sweater, the clerk rang it up and said, 'Anything else?' One hundred fifty dollars plus tax, and she asks that."

"I like knowing the price. Maybe that's vice-versa impolite. Where is this mysterious sweater?"

I took the gift-wrapped box out of my overnight bag and handed it to Grey. She carefully undid the wrapping paper and put it on the table. She opened the box and lifted out the handmade sweater, black with a subtly pleated black pattern. "It's really beautiful, Tuttle," she said. "And it's very feminine. You must be sick of my field duds, huh? Thank you, thank you, thank you. I was thinking just now: can we go to your apartment? Tonight, I mean. Can we drive down to San Francisco after I'm done working? I haven't been to the city in a year. I'd like to eat at Kuleto's. It's the best Italian. I'd like to see your apartment, too."

"Fine with me."

"Of course, I'll wear this," she said, pressing the sweater flush against her chest, then fitting the sleeves against her outstretched arms. "This is *so* nice."

"It's a good color on you."

"I've got to get going, though," Grey said. She kissed me, a better kiss than the Armenian bride—that actual thought came into my head. She put the sweater on her bureau. "What're your plans for the day?"

"I brought one of Mrs. Moro's novels. I might not get out of this robe till lunchtime. Maybe I'll buy some new slacks and a shirt, Route 1 Cal-Mart. It's just a twenty-minute drive. I can't go out with you tonight looking like a chauffeur. We won't want to stop at my apartment first. I might even splurge on a new sport coat."

"You okay, Tuttle?"

"When her brother came to the door, I peeked around behind him, and I saw this hallway full of family photographs. It was a long hallway, with a wooden floor. There were five or six Japanese people sitting in the kitchen at the end of the hallway, too."

I made a quick sobbing sound, but it wasn't actually crying; events had just suddenly caught up with me.

"I don't have to go right now," Grey said. "Want some company?"

"You go to work. If I get lonely, I'll drive to the reserve."

Grey took up her day pack, kissed me on top of my head, and went out the door. I watched her until she got to the other end of the dock.

By 5:30 there was a light drizzle. The wind had picked up, too. I could hear ducks muttering under the dock. After she took a shower and put her hair up in mismatched braids, Grey put on the new sweater along with a black skirt, high, lace-up felt boots. She looked tremendously pretty. I had on gray slacks, white shirt, and a dark, herringbone sport coat, sleeves a touch long. In the car, Grey said that I looked nice, and I told her I'd spent $250.

"Between that and what my sweater put you back, you might qualify for the Living-Beyond-Your-Means Award," she said. "Or are you holding out on me, Tuttle?"

"I'm spending the rest of my meager savings at Kuleto's, too."

"Oh, boy."

"My apartment's not as bad as I might've hinted."

"Is there a bed?"

"Of course there's a bed."

"Is there coffee? Is there bread for toast?"

"We can pick up some bread."

"Money in our pockets. We're all set, then."

We were trying hard, in a mind-reading kind of way, not to mention Mrs. Moro. Grey knew I was pretty torn up over her. We drove along Sir Francis Drake Highway, south toward Route 1. It was about six o'clock, dusky light over Tomales Bay, and the rain had stopped.

"Let's start talking about Italian food," Grey said. "Naming different dishes. That'll guarantee we'll be starved for it."

"You know anything about Kuleto's menu?"

"I've been there twice."

"Oh."

"Don't ask."

"I won't. I'm just glad we're going, you and me."

"You could be a tiny bit jealous, if you want."

"You didn't go with Eddie. Not from how you described him."

"Not with Eddie, no. No, I went with girlfriends, actually. The first time. The second time, I went by myself. Anyway, I'll start: Penne with a perfect tomato and chopped mushroom sauce, accompanied by an Italian Chianti."

"That's what I'm ordering."

Just past Willow Point, at the southern tip of Tomales Bay, Grey hugged herself and shivered. "Tuttle," she said, "maybe pull the car over, okay? You left the back window open."

"Must've been out of habit, to clear the air. Sorry."

"People don't think California gets cold—"

What interrupted Grey mid-sentence was a loud blur of white off the bay to our immediate left. Then the backseat was completely filled with noise. It was a squalling half cry, half-guttural moan, the combination of which was so bizarre and startling, I almost swerved the car. Grey somehow kept quite composed, though, and she swiveled around and said, "Tuttle, we've got a pelican in the car." As if to verify the fact, the pelican let loose a rusty pump-handle squawk, and I quickly pulled off to the side of the road. Grey and I both turned toward the backseat. The pelican was now hunched to the left-side corner. Its leathery-pouch beak was actually vibrating, clicking. "Jesus, *weird*," Grey said. "Interesting noises come out of that bird, huh?" The pelican feebly caped open its left wing, which drooped. "It might have a broken wing," Grey said. But then—the pelican lunged forward and I shouted, "Watch it!" Grey threw her hands up in front of her face.

Grey tumbled out her door, and I heard the splash of her boots in water. "Shit on a shingle—my boots, Tuttle, and I'm bleeding!"

Grey stepped from the shallow ditch and walked over to my side of the car. I was standing near the front bumper. She peered in through the front window, and her sympathies shifted. "Guess what?" she said. "That's a white pelican. Rare to get them bay-side. They like the wide-open sea."

"Let me see your forehead a second," I said. I examined Grey's face, touched the cut and slight bruise on her forehead above her left eye. "I doubt you'll need stitches. I've got a first-aid kit in the backseat."

"Some uninvited houseguest, huh?" Grey said, and started to laugh. "I didn't see it coming off the bay, did you?"

"We got blindsided."

"Well, I'm basically okay, so we have to figure things out now."

"Let's go to the Point Reyes Walk-in Clinic. We should find out if pelicans carry diseases to worry about."

"I don't think it was the beak. I think it was the wing. It has hard, sharp wings."

"Just a precaution, Grey."

The pelican lifted and squawked, then beat its good wing hard against the closed window. It produced a mournful baritone gurgle, then rasping barks. "It's in pain, Tuttle," Grey said. "I think its wing is broken. I feel terrible for it."

I crouched along the car and opened the back door. Grey and I stood across the road. "Come out, come out, come out!" Grey said, but the pelican kept to the car. Every so often it fluttered its wing, half toppling, but its movements and distress calls had become half-hearted.

"This is pitiful," Grey said.

"How about the police?"

"They might shoot it."

"I doubt it, Grey. They might have a net or something. You must know somebody in Fish & Game, or somebody else."

"Donnie Rush, the veterinarian's assistant! I've had coffee with her. Her boss is a large-animal vet, though."

"Come on, Grey, he's not going to turn down a pelican."

"Donnie'd be home, I bet. She has three young kids."

"And she'd contact the vet, right?"

"That's the idea."

"Okay. The Holly Tree Inn's a hundred yards from here. I'll go call this Donnie Rush. Is she listed under that name?"

"Rush, yeah."

"You stay with the car. I'll be right back."

A hundred or so feet up the road I turned and saw Grey toss her dress-up English raincoat over the pelican, then back away from the car and start to sing to the bird.

The Holly Tree Inn had a pay phone on the porch. A phone book was dangling by a chain. I decided to call the veterinarian directly. I looked it up, and found a Dr. James Glass. I dialed and Dr. Glass picked up, which surprised me because it was after usual office hours, though maybe not for a veterinarian. I explained about the pelican. He said to try and put a sweater or blanket over the pelican to calm it down. "What about singing to it?" I said. "See what

works," he said. "I'm only a few minutes' drive from where you are."
He gave me exact directions and I ran back to the car.

We drove to the veterinarian's. He lived just outside of
Inverness, off Sir Francis Drake, up a winding road, in a house overlooking Tomales Bay. Grey's having put her raincoat over the pelican had in fact calmed it. On the way to the veterinary clinic, Grey
looked into the backseat. "It's not talking," she said, giving a worried, nervous laugh.

The clinic was adjacent to the house. I ran up the stairs and
knocked on the door. Dr. Glass answered right away. He was a tall
man, about fifty years old, with the strongest-looking hands I've
ever seen—wide, thick-fingered hands, not freakish by any means,
no doubt hands comforting to an injured horse or cow, or a deer
struck by a pickup truck. He walked down to the Town Car. Grey
had opened the back door. Dr. Glass gently lifted the pelican, which
was inside Grey's raincoat, and carried it up the wooden steps to his
clinic. Inside, he set the pelican on an examination table. Grey and
I stood against the wall across from the table. When Dr. Glass
removed the raincoat, the pelican remained perfectly still. With
slow, deliberate movements, he held the pelican firmly against his
chest and administered a hypodermic. He'd had it filled and ready
when we arrived. The needle made the pelican squawk open its
mouth once, its only reaction. The air now smelled of fish. In a few
moments, the pelican slumped like someone had cut the strings of
a big marionette.

Dr. Glass began his examination. The pelican was anesthetized
and Dr. Glass laid it down without its protesting. He lifted and
examined each wing and leg, under its tail feathers, where he found
a splotch of blood, and a little dripped onto the table. "Looks like a
broken wing and some internal bleeding," Dr. Glass said. "We can
x-ray right here. Fish & Game will rush an animal to Mill Valley
Animal Hospital, if necessary."

He carried the pelican into the x-ray room, set it on the
table below the machine, lowered the machine, calibrated it, turning two knobs. He then stepped into a small side room. Through

the window, Grey and I watched the pelican get x-rayed. Dr. Glass then slid a thick metal plate out of the camera, if that's what you call it. We sat in the waiting room. Magazines were on the table. There was an aquarium with tropical fish in it. In about ten minutes, Dr. Glass stood in the doorway. "It's pretty well broken up inside," he said. "Internal bleeding, just as I suspected. A fractured left wing as well. It may be concussed. That's hard to determine. To be honest, this is my first pelican, and I'm not familiar with the literature. I had a heron in here two years ago. An owl sometime later. I think it's best to call Fish & Game, have it brought down to Mill Valley. That's my advice."

"How long will that take?" Grey said.

"Depends who's available. I'll make the call."

Dr. Glass went into his office. I saw four framed diplomas on his wall. Grey bent over, tilted her head, and looked into the aquarium. When Dr. Glass came out, he said, "Damn answering machine at Fish & Game. But I did reach Mill Valley Animal Hospital. There's a round-the-clock staff."

"We'll drive it there," Grey said.

"A good forty-five minutes, at least," Dr. Glass said. "I'll carry the pelican to your car. Keep the heat on. But don't suffocate it." He wrapped the pelican in a blanket. Then he helped Grey on with her raincoat; considering that the pelican had been inside the coat, and might well have bled on it, this was still so absentmindedly polite a gesture it made Grey blush and slightly stammer, "Thank you."

In the car, winding our way out onto Sir Francis Drake again, Grey said, "What we really need is a siren."

For at least ten minutes I was going well over the speed limit. But then, I'd guess four or five minutes south of Tomales Bay, the pelican died. We knew it had died, because it produced a classic kind of death rattle, which rolled up from deep inside its chest, unnerving kind of acoustics, really. It was the saddest sound I'd ever heard; Grey burst into tears, and that got to me, as well. We couldn't look at each other. I adjusted the rearview, and saw that the pelican looked like it was still alive, its eyes wide open. I noticed that Dr. Glass had fastened the seat belt around it.

Of course, San Francisco was long ago out of the question. I turned the car around in the parking lot of a seafood restaurant, and we drove directly back to the clinic. I carried the pelican up the stairs, Grey a few steps ahead. Dr. Glass was doing paperwork. He only had the small desk lamp on. He answered Grey's knock. "It died," she said.

"Bring it in," Dr. Glass said. "Just put it on the table, if you would."

I laid the pelican on the examination table, then joined Grey in the waiting room. "It doesn't surprise me," Dr. Glass said. "It took a hard blow. Pelicans fly pretty low and can build up good speed, as you know. Fish & Game will want an autopsy, even though it's clear *how* it died. The accident, I mean. There might be other information we can gain. Then there's taxidermy. For a community museum, or to bring around to elementary schools. Something along those lines."

"I understand," Grey said, as if comforting Dr. Glass. She was still sniffling and had swollen eyes. "I work at the Tule Reserve. Last spring, an elk slid off a muddy cliff. Fish & Game knew how it'd died but wanted it checked for all sorts of things, naturally."

"Yes, that particular elk was in my clinic, here. Small world," Dr. Glass said. "Look, you both seem upset. Can I get you a cup of tea? Or something a bit stronger?"

We both said no thanks.

"By the way, I'm Jim Glass." Grey and I each shook hands with him.

"There's nothing more to do, really," he said. "I'll take it from here. A little paperwork. That's about it."

"Thanks for your time," Grey said.

"Well, that's what I'm here for."

Grey and I didn't say a word driving back to her place. She sat at the kitchen table staring at her notes, or staring at the moonlight spread out on the bay, or putting her face in her hands, trying not to get upset all over again. We didn't have the radio on. I fell asleep on the sofa. When I woke up at 6 a.m., Grey wasn't there. I had slept in my new shirt, slacks, and sport coat. Grey's sweater and skirt were on the bed. Coffee was in the coffeemaker, and there was a note on the table:

Tuttle, darling. Needed to work. I just know you think the pelican has some connection to Mrs. Moro, but it doesn't.
It was a sad freak accident. Don't be superstitious, okay?
Hope you want to stay over tonight.

Pals with you,
Grey

But I didn't stay. I drove back to San Francisco, and I don't know all the reasons why. I suppose I fled something. And I didn't visit Grey for three straight weeks, though we spoke on the telephone every night. We were very loyal to this nightly appointment. I'd call at 10 p.m. Grey would answer, "Hi." But, then, so much went unspoken, in fact most everything of real importance. What we should've said to each other was very, very close by, like the silences between tappings of Morse code. But we didn't speak it. Instead, it was, "How's the thesis going?" Or, "I drove a client today—yeah, I'm working, nothing taxing, though. My heart's not in it, really." The barest hints of our day. And after we spoke I'd drive around. And on Jones Street one night, I noticed a FOR SALE sign in front of Mrs. Moro's house.

One day, into the fourth week of not seeing Grey, I drove past a fairgrounds. They were dismantling the Ferris wheel. Across the field, two men were standing in front of an enormous helium-filled balloon, like a zeppelin. The men were holding the anchor ropes, but at the same time, the balloon, with its gondola and bright lettering, was being deflated. I stopped the car to watch. I thought that the zeppelin might thrash about, act like a desperate, panicked huge animal when losing air like that. I'm not sure that seeing one thing caused the other, but I said "Grey" out loud, and then felt like my very breath had been knocked out of me.

Two days later, February 11, to be exact, I telephoned Grey, and instead of saying, "Hi," she said, "You thought the pelican was Mrs.

Moro's ghost, didn't you? I've been thinking hard about this, Tuttle. I know we're not going to see each other anymore. Real Sherlock Holmes, huh?"

"Grey—."

"I'm going to a conference this weekend in New York. I'm not going to call you, and don't call me, either."

"What ghost?"

"That dream she told you. With the pelican, the teapot, the whole thing, Tuttle."

"Okay. Maybe it's been haunting me in some way. Maybe you've just articulated it."

"Good for me."

"Let's start this conversation over."

"No, no, you listen, Tuttle. You've been so distant. I mean, weeks of phone calls. We could've been—. You could've been at the Holly Tree Inn at least two nights a week. We were doing fine. We were moving ahead.

"You know what's scariest? What's scariest is when somebody you love makes a private decision, but he doesn't tell you what it is. And the result of that decision—the privately held conclusion—becomes like a ghost. It affects you deeply. It acts on you. But you don't get to fight back. It's very very very unfair, Tuttle."

"I haven't made any such decision, Grey."

"You haven't been here in a month. That's a decision. What we should address here, Tuttle—can you stop being such a fucking coward and own up to this? It's the pelican. After the pelican, something went wrong. It was bad luck is what it was, Tuttle. But you've purposely let us get estranged over it. You took it as some kind of omen. Look, I'm no shrink, Tuttle. I'm no psychiatrist. I've never been to one. But what I think—and I've been thinking a *lot* about us. I mean, I know you a little by now, right? You know what? Remember you told me Mrs. Moro was always hoping to see a white pelican?"

"That's what she said, yes."

"Well, she *didn't* ever see one, did she?"

"No."

"You liked her so much, didn't you? And you felt close to her. You wanted her walks to the ocean to go safely. You worried. When it rained, you worried. I mean, do you know how often her name came up in conversation? Very often. And I enjoyed hearing about her, don't get me wrong."

"What're you saying here, Grey?"

"I'm *saying*, Tuttle. What I'm saying. Is Mrs. Moro's dying got to you. You felt she gave you things in life, Tuttle. I'm not trying to be sappy or philosophical, but she did give you things. Those novels. All that conversation. The sweet opportunities to worry over her. I don't know what all.

"So maybe—this is just a guess. Maybe, in your mind, you've turned Mrs. Moro into the one thing she most deeply wanted to see. Because that way she'd become her own good luck, the kind of luck she didn't have when she was alive.

"See? See, Tuttle? Her suicide was bad enough. Now you have to go and make it twice as bad."

"Her brother never used that word."

"Come on, Tuttle. It's me you're talking to."

"Since you've come up with such a complicated psychological theory, maybe you're the one who believes the pelican was a ghost."

"I'd be willing to have that in common with you, Tuttle."

There was a silence on the line then. "Look," she finally said, "I'm sorry. Probably my thinking's way off. At the time—you know, when the pelican flew into the car? Between the two of us, I was the one most visibly upset. But since then, you've taken the incident and hoarded it from me, and you won't let me back in. Half the time, on the phone, it's been like we've just met."

We both didn't speak for another moment. I heard KPXP in the background, then heard Grey turn the volume down. "I hate this kind of talk," I said.

"Well, thinking about Mrs. Moro wandering some rainy beach was probably a torment."

"No, I meant us breaking up."

Grey gave a short sigh, then said, "This conference, Tuttle. It's all the bigwigs in my field. It's to interview for jobs. Research, teaching, you know, all the grant applications I've been typing. I bet you'll miss the sound of typing in the middle of the night, huh? Look up and see this naked girl typing. Anyway, I was going to grasp at one last hopeful straw, and ask do you want to come to New York with me, but I don't think it's a good idea anymore, truth be told."

"You'll be gone how long?"

"Probably a week. I have an open return flight."

"Which hotel?"

"I'm not saying."

"Well, it sounds mostly like a professional trip, a work thing, huh?"

"I might catch a Broadway play."

"Don't mind me asking. But do you want a lift to the airport?"

"The airport's got long-term parking. I'll drive myself, thanks."

"Just offering."

"I'm tapping my forehead, Tuttle. Tap, tap, tap. I'm tapping my forehead but pretend I'm tapping yours. Because I'm thinking, here I'm going three thousand miles away from Tuttle, but he's already— in his head—farther away than that."

Then the phone clicked down.

I kept on with my freelance chauffeuring, making ends meet, but not much more. As I said, my heart wasn't in it, but I didn't yet have the gumption to invent a new life. Then, eight months since I'd seen or spoken with Grey Zamarkis, she sent the newspaper announcement of her marriage to Dr. Glass. The envelope had the veterinary clinic as her return address. A month after that, a package arrived at my apartment. It was plastered with Japanese postage stamps. There was a customs receipt taped to the top. I opened the package on my kitchen table, it contained Mrs. Moro's bird lists. There were eighty-eight lists, in eight separate notebooks, all written in English, but with Japanese writing in the margins, too. Each entry was dated, along with the name of each bird, and time of observation, and brief description of where along the Estero Trail she had seen it. The official-looking letter that came with the lists was from the family's attorney. It was typed in Japanese, with the translation below it. Part of which said, "You are bequeathed..." I knew that Mrs. Moro had employed drivers previous to me, to take her to Point Reyes. I hoped that I was the only one who'd been willed her bird lists.

I put the lists in my desk drawer. Another week passed, and I decided to drive up to Point Reyes. It wasn't anywhere near the anniversary of Mrs. Moro's death; it wasn't a morbid kind of sentimentality or anything. That is, I didn't want to try and please her ghost. I just wanted to see if I could remember the names of hawks. It was a crisp, sunny day, no traffic to speak of when I set out at 10 a.m., and I made good time. I got a coffee at the Inverness store, then drove up Sir Francis Drake, past Grey's cottage—well, it was no longer hers, of course, and she never called it a cottage. I turned left and drove the few miles to the Estero trailhead sign. The glassed-in display held a few stuffed birds and mammals, paintings of local flora, a list of proper trail etiquette, a warning about deer ticks, with an enlargement of a microscopic tick, and a dotted-line map of the Estero Trail.

I had on jeans, tennis shoes, a flannel shirt, a sweater, a parka. In my backpack, I carried a thermos of water. I had binoculars around my neck. I had the field guide in my pocket. In two hours, I was able to identify two kinds of hawks with certainty, but I didn't really care about anything, except to look at them. I got to Sunset Beach. It was a pebbly, wide curve of sand, zigzagged with shore, birds, dozens of them scurrying along the edge of the froth, like they were stitching each wave to the beach with their beaks. Though I knew that they were trying to find something to eat. I sat on the fallen tree. I took up the binoculars and scanned the horizon. Brown pelicans—I knew that bird. And seagulls diving just out past the whitecaps.

I stayed for an hour or two, I guess. I ate the tuna sandwich I'd packed. I drank some water. I may have dozed off for half an hour or so. When I woke, the sun was a sharp glare. Chill wind, sun, a clear view of the sea. I thought a moment about Grey. I missed her. I didn't forgive myself about her, didn't forgive myself in the slightest. Every worst maudlin C and W song would've wholly captured my stupidity and regret, then multiply by ten. "Sadness in severe disproportion to the opposite," as Akutagawa wrote. Other than about Grey, I don't remember what I thought. But I know this: what fixed me in that present time and place was my deep happiness at not seeing white pelicans. I was hoping that I wouldn't. This was my first time. They might've been indignant, knowing I hadn't earned such good fortune.

Roy Parvin

A Dream She Had

THESE WOODS ARE full of strange music. Maybe that's why Carmella doesn't realize it's a bear that's crashed into their lives. But most likely it's because she doesn't want to hear what's out there.

What she hears sounds like the roll of timpani in the third movement of Verdi's *Requiem*. Or perhaps a far-off storm. But not the wildness. It's a clear day, only a ghosted splinter of moon hanging in an eggshell sky.

It's nothing, Carmella tells herself, remembering the thousands of sounds she used to hear in the city, traffic and dogs and neighbors, all the hum and noise that ran through her as silently as her own blood. It's only the country, she thinks, and starts the motor, pumping water into the thousand-gallon tank that supplies their cabin. And the sound of that tears a hole in the afternoon.

When the tank is full, water spitting out from the pipe at the top, Carmella switches off the engine. All she hears is the wash of China Creek coming through the glade of sugar pines and oaks, cedars and Douglas firs; wind like a distant locomotive chug-chugging up the small runnel on the other side of the creek; screeches and hoots and woodnotes.

Then she hears it again, follows it back, walking beyond the pump house, through the stand of slash, up the small berm, and finally to the mouth of the old well. The tin lid isn't covering the opening anymore and the sound, now like big kettles knocking together, is coming from inside. Looking over the rim, she sees the lid hung up on a thin ledge fifteen feet down, and below that, five feet lower in total darkness, is something big and black and moving.

Carmella runs for the phone. Harry isn't in the office. They're wiring their corner of the county for service, she's told; he could be anywhere.

She has some question about whom to call next. Back in San Francisco the Yellow Pages were the stuff of circus-strongman-ripping legend—two fat volumes to cover the whole alphabet, the answer always somewhere inside. But up here, Salyer, the entire Trinity County phone book, yellow and white pages combined, is so thin, sixty pages at most, Carmella could easily tear it in half herself.

Ultimately she decides on fish and game. "There's something in our well," she says to the man who answers, realizing at once how silly this sounds. "I don't mean water, of course. An animal. A deer, I think. I'm not sure. I couldn't look."

All she hears on the other end is the dispatcher radio crackling like fire. People up here always pause before they talk, as if constantly having to catch their breath. "How about us starting at the beginning?" he says. "Why don't you tell me who you are first, your name."

Carmella flaps her hand, tells him. About their little cabin that sits like a tilty hat above the copse of secondary growth. About how far they've come from the city to get where they are—north of the Central Valley, west across the shoulders of the Trinities, north and west to the ridge in Salyer that snugs up close to the Humboldt County line. "My husband Harry inherited the place from some uncle," she says. "Calvin, I think it was. Maybe Chester. It was one of those kind of names."

"Okay," he says. "Now tell me about the well."

She looks out the window toward the berm. "The well? I don't know what I can tell you. It's not in use anymore."

"Any water in it?"

Carmella shakes her head. "I never thought of that. Can deer swim?" she says. The picture of deer treading water suddenly seems entirely improbable. "I can check," she says. "About the water."

Again the pause. "No," he answers finally. "Why don't you sit tight until we get there. It doesn't sound like you're in any danger. Don't worry, I'm sending my men right away to your place."

His voice is smooth, thick as velour. Carmella can see why he has this job, answering the phones. "What a lifesaver," she says. "You are——?"

"Oren," he says. "One of those names."

The sun is barely making it to the top of the giant ponderosa these days. When the wind comes down off Sawtooth now it's cold, from somewhere else, from out of the north. Harry says he remembers the snows from when he was a kid. Bigger than the cabin, he says.

But the season isn't what Carmella thinks about walking down the quarter-mile dirt drive to unlock the gate for fish and game. She knows all too well where the animal down there has come from. It's the same place everything else has: her curse.

Six months ago, in March, when they were still living in San Francisco, God tried to punish Carmella but missed. It can happen. The rainy season was only starting to lift its foggy skirt.

On that evening in particular, in the witchy hours of night, the sky was wearing an extra layer of muslin. Carmella remembers. She got up to go to the bathroom, had the taste of Edward DeLuca, the Laurel Heights Ensemble's violinist, still in her mouth from that afternoon. After she returned to bed and back to sleep in the gray night was when it happened. Two feet to the right and it would have been Carmella, the rightful target, and not Harry.

On the very same bed thirteen hours earlier Edward had plucked her as delicately as he did his antique Guarneri. Those fingers: watching them move up and down the neck of his violin in rehearsals reminded her of the finches at the feeder outside her living room window, a fluttering of wings. His other hand held the bow so gently it almost wasn't holding it at all, his long, tapering, nearly feminine fingers curling into a cave around the bow, each pink nail having the even symmetry of a sidewalk square.

His fingers were as far as it went. It wasn't love, this thing with Edward. Even lying in his arms she knew Harry was love, knew he was true and giving, sweet and for keeps. Any man could buy flowers like the spray of dahlias and baby tears Edward had brought her. But Harry, he was the kind of man who not only brought flowers but built window boxes to plant them in.

That afternoon had nothing to do with Harry and everything with her. It was about being married for six years and seeing their coffee mugs in the same place in the kitchen sink every weekday morning, about hearing the magic Edward's fingers could produce and wanting, just this once, to follow.

She had dreamed those hours together would be the way Mozart skipped off Edward's bow, perfect as math, magical, a precise passion that would run to the very center of her, fill her up. In her head it was a witty, metropolitan picture she'd painted, a trifling romance that, like the neighborhood's number 3 Jackson bus, would only go so far but no farther.

What she found afterward was only a fat violinist sleeping like a mutt, tip of his tongue sticking out of his teeth. And across the bedroom in the mirror Carmella saw herself—long, heather hair direct from the Italian Alps, gently arching aquiline nose, bosom that at thirty-five was still glorious, still as full and rich and round as a whole note. And at that moment she knew it was that, her reflection, a curse of vanity, that had actually cast the spell, not the beauty Edward's fingers could produce.

It was just the once with Edward but that was enough. What Carmella woke to the next day was an ugly mass of pulp and skin on Harry's pillow. "My God, Harry," she said. "Your head's inflated like a basketball." And it was. Gone were the cheekbones sheer as steeples, jaw square as the state lines of Wyoming, smile sweeter than manna. "Baby, what on earth has happened?" she said but already knew the answer to the question.

"I don't know, Carly," Harry said, testing himself gently with fingertips, then getting up to look at himself in the mirror. "Jesus, I look like the nephew of the Elephant Man."

It got worse. "Do you have any pets?" the doctor asked. His office smelled exactly like the kind of soap Carmella used to wash her face with when she was a teenager.

"Fish," she said. "We have neon tetras. Two catfish that clean the algae from the tank. Some of those, I don't know what they're called. Angel fish, I think."

"No dogs or cats?"

"No," she said.

"I don't like saying this," he said, "but you're going to have to get rid of the fish."

"But they're underwater."

Harry laughed, face fleshy, sallow as an onion, eyes goggly, the sound of it like clucking, not laughter. It was a painful thing for her to watch. "Carly, honey, where else would fish be?" he said.

"I mean we don't come in contact with them," she said, looking to him, then the doctor.

"You don't need to." The doctor cleaned his glasses, put them back on, frowned, breathed on them, cleaned them again. "The virus can become airborne from the surface of the water, if that's what indeed is causing Harry's acute dermatitis. In any case, the fish go." In the reflection in his lenses, her face was as misshapen as Harry's.

"So what do we do about Harry?" Carmella asked.

"We'll put him on a regimen of medication. There will be a lot of pills and injections at first. Until we know what works, what takes."

Carmella said, "What about side effects? What about babies?" She pictured flushing them down the toilet, too.

"Are you planning on a family?" he ran his thumb down Harry's chart, sneaked a glance at the wall clock.

"No, we aren't. Not yet."

"Well, there might be a problem with the medication," he said and mentioned a catalog of words as if ticking off a shopping list: depressed sperm count and lack of motility, temporary sterility, potential for impotency. "The first year it's a crapshoot," he said. "After that the situation usually stabilizes. Then the medication can be reduced to a maintenance level and your chances should increase back to near normal."

"Is that one of your new medical terms," Carmella said, "crap-shoot?" Harry tapped her hand, rubbed her forearm. The doctor didn't say anything.

She knew better about the fish but kept the dark truth to herself, and later that night, hoping on the skinny possibility that the doctor was correct, she scooped them up in a plastic bag and placed them in the freezer, on top of the frozen orange juice. This was a far more humane way of disposing of them, she was told, freezing them. An hour later their color was practically gone, the fish hard as stones, a pocketful of cloudy, washed-out agates and jades.

Harry didn't get better. Carmella added the fish to the darkness steeping inside her. His head became puffed as a dinner roll. "Just pop me in the oven," he said, "and I'll be ready to eat in no time." But Carmella couldn't laugh, had taken to wearing black as if mourning.

At the home where Carmella played her flute for the terminally ill, Eunice Schwartz noticed the black. "Did you lose someone, dear?" she asked.

Thinking of the fish, of Harry, her eyes flitting like sixteenth notes, Carmella couldn't talk at first. "Oh yes," she said eventually. "It was...A whole school was wiped out."

The old woman huffed, went rheumy around the eyes, passed her hand over the clumps of hair that hadn't yet been knocked out by chemo. "Good Lord. Were they little?"

"Very," Carmella said, spreading her thumb and index finger an inch to show her.

"You'll be in my prayers."

"Thank you."

And when Eunice reached over, ran her chapped hand along Carmella's face, Carmella felt the truth in her growing crazy, deadly, ugly like a tumor, felt it climbing right out of her. "I'm sorry, Eunice, I have to go now," she said and left the room, ran down the hall to the bathroom, dropped her flute on the floor of the stall, threw up. But it didn't eliminate the blackness spreading inside her.

That evening as Carmella marinated salmon for dinner she didn't notice her blue-sapphire world outside the kitchen window: the bay and the sky, Angel Island winking in the surface haze, the finger of Point Reyes reaching out into the Pacific way off in the distance, a foghorn near the Marin footing of the Golden Gate Bridge sounding, a lonely tuba.

Inside the room was dark as ink. She still reeled from how dreadful she'd been with Eunice. With the wet, pliant salmon in her hands, suddenly everything was too much for Carmella and she opened the freezer, removed the foil-wrapped packets of halibut and swordfish and mahi-mahi, and tried to flush the whole mess down the toilet but they wouldn't go, just circled the bowl.

The animal in the well isn't the first thing that's fallen into Carmella's life today. That morning there had been something else. Harry had already left for work and the sun was only starting to define the ragged edge of treetops behind the cabin. It was cold these mornings; the madrone in the woodstove that Harry relit before leaving was just then taking. In the bathroom Carmella shifted from one foot to the other on the cold linoleum. She read the box. Pink was for positive. Hers was the color of healthy flesh.

She couldn't think of it then, seven hours ago, can't now. After all she's done—Harry, the fish, Eunice, having to move up here to Salyer—the thought of her being a mother, that something could still be unspotted from the thing inside her that's grown like a pitchy fungus, seems as improbable as deer swimming.

Now the three men from fish and game shine a light down the well. The little one with the fat face, eyes green as the trees up on Hyampom, enough hair for only a top-knot, whistles, hikes up trousers, turns back to Carmella. Brady his name is. "I've got a little surprise for you," he says.

She nods.

"That's not a deer. It's a bear."

The one next to Oren, Fess, spits some juice, cheeks working like an agitator on an old washing machine, brown bushy sideburns rising, falling. He turns back to look down the well, says, "Holy shit.

It's a real monster. Look at that head. Biggest one I've ever seen. Must be a four-hundred-pounder, a male I'd say."

Oren says, "He must have ridden that tin lid down like it was a sled or something." He smiles at Carmella, his dark eyes kind and wise. "It's okay to look," he says to her. "That bear's not going anywhere."

And she does. The bear is standing in three feet of water looking up, breathing heavy, head as wide as the top of a garbage can, eyes that seem to hold a world of sorrow, fur blacker than coal. When it sighs, Carmella almost mistakes it for human. "He looks so beautiful," she says.

"It's a dump bear probably," Brady says. "Most probably tastes exactly like what it's been eating. Garbage."

Fess rubs the string of chewing dottle off his lips. "At this angle we couldn't even manage a heart shot."

"What's that?" Carmella asks. "A heart shot."

He taps just above the pocket on her denim shirt, the feel of it going right through her. Over in their truck she sees their rifle on the mount and something inside her sinks. She knows now how this will end.

"Don't worry," Oren says. "It's not going to come to that. We couldn't possibly kill something this grand. Do you have a ladder?" he says.

Carmella leads Brady past the cabin to the generator shack, the two of them returning with the ladder. The men extend it on the ground next to the well, locking the stops in place, then feed the ladder down inside. It hits the bear on the shoulder, bounces against the side, makes a dull, bass tuning-fork sound and he grumbles, tries to swat at it. Eventually he seems to understand what the ladder's for, rests back on the corrugated well wall, and the men inch the ladder down to the bottom.

Oren pulls on the rungs sticking out the top, trying to lessen the angle. "If this works," he says, "be prepared to run." Then to Carmella, "You might want to go for the house now."

But it's already clear there's too much bear at the bottom, the ladder leaning only a few clicks south of ninety degrees. Inside the well the bear rests an arm on a lower rung.

"That's not going to work," Brady says. "What next?"

Carmella says, "I bet you'd like some coffee," and the three of them agree and she heads back to the cabin. Mid-afternoon is coming on; the sun is poking up over the enormous Douglas fir down by the creek like the top of an orange-yellow big toe.

Walking back to the cabin, she hears a growl from the well, one of the men saying something she can't hear, Fess laughing. The wind picks up, knocking down pink and red dogwood leaves.

On the kitchen counter the coffee machine breathes hard, steam coming out the drip, the last of the water already in the filter. Carmella tries to imagine what's inside her, listens, feels nothing. She watches the men out the window. They lean against a tree talking, Brady smoking.

Carmella is playing the flute when Harry drives up, Handel's Sonata in A Minor. When she comes outside he's already talking to the men. He smiles at her, turns away from them, walks over to her.

"You're home early," she says.

Harry is better, the lines of his face already redrawn to the easy handsomeness that can still cross Carmella's wires. It was sick building syndrome, what he had in the city. "Microbes," he said when they finally found out in April.

"Microbes?" she asked.

"Little microscopic organisms in the building at work." Harry exploded with coughs as he explained it. "They don't know if it's the air-circulation system, the heating, the air conditioning, what have you. It could be any number of things—agents, they call them."

"Cooties, you mean," she said, pushing her hair behind her ears.

The next week Harry told her about his idea of moving up to Salyer to flee the microbes. Inside her she felt the real truth of the situation, her curse, eating away at her stomach like a solvent. But all she said was, "How's leaving the city going to cure anything? Cooties are everywhere. It's an established fact of nature."

But they drove so far from the city they eventually outran the radio. Dizzy Gillespie's "Tin Tin Deo" called out from the speakers like an old friend, Carmella transposing the notes in her head, practicing the fingering of the jabby horn lines on her leg.

Three hours on I-5 and Harry's face was still cranberry, his breath coming in wheezes, rattles, not unlike the wonky vacuum cleaner they sold at the moving sale. The July day was hot enough to bake pottery, the freeway running straight as a gun shot, the spine of the Central Valley exactly how she pictured hell, except with grass.

At Redding, Carmella and Harry left the freeway. There were smaller blue routes and country western. Later, surface roads and farm reports. Eventually the only road to Salyer and no radio at all.

With Brady smoking by the well opening, Fess and Oren talking off by the truck, Harry puts his arm around her shoulders.

He smells the way he always does now: of trees and wind and earth.

"You think I'd miss this?" he says. "I have to admit when I got the field call, I was afraid you might have been picking mushrooms or something. It's a bear, you know, not a deer."

"I know," she says.

He squeezes her arm. "It's perfect. Absolutely perfect," he says and turns, walking back to the men. "Hey, fellas, I have an idea." Harry is the kind of man who still uses the word *fellas*. Seeing him describing what he's thinking, arms moving up and down, touching Fess's shoulder, Oren studying him intently, little Brady nodding as if his head was spring-loaded—seeing all this, Carmella knows why the phone company in Cedar Flat offered him a job the first day he walked into the office.

"That could work," Oren says. Harry leads Brady to the phone and the two other men discuss the logistics of his plan. In half an hour a truck from P&H Towing drives up and fifteen minutes later the vet.

"All right," Harry says and waves his arms, directing the driver back toward the mouth of the well. "It has to be a slipknot," he tells Oren after the truck's in place and starts rigging it. When he's done Oren drops it down the well, the sling falling over the bear's head.

"The knot isn't slipping," Fess says.

"Pull harder," Harry says. When the knot finally does release, the sling isn't pulling tight enough around the bear. "Okay," Harry says. "That's not going to work. Let's pull it off. I'll redo it."

The string comes back up the well, Harry reloops the rope, and this time when Oren throws it back down the well, it catches around the bear's head and front leg.

"You see that?" Brady says. "That bear didn't even try to avoid it. Like it knows what's going on." The bear bites at the rope a little, looks back up the shaft at the men and Carmella.

"Pull," Harry says. The ropes break away, the sling pulls tight. Next the vet climbs down the ladder, ten-foot jab pole with tranquilizer tip in his hand, hits the bear twice with the syringe, the bear complaining.

They stand around for fifteen minutes waiting for the tranquilizer to take. "Honey, why don't you go inside," Harry says. When she sees them from the front window of the cabin, the men look blotty, the edges of them getting lost in the shadow and dark of early evening.

The truck starts up, the cable starts spooling in. When the bear lifts up out of the top the driver guns the engine, the truck popping forward, and the bear flies three feet from the well, landing, stepping out of the sling, standing up, looking at the crowd of men. They scatter like duckpins. The bear lumbers off.

It's seven forty-five that same night and from the window of the cabin Carmella can see none of the trees, only her reflection on the glass.

"That was something," Harry says. He's elated. "What a perfect ending." Right after the bear left, the men crowded around him, slapped him on the back. Brady even hugged him. Harry came back in for the bottle of tequila and shot glasses. "You want one?" he'd said to Carmella. "You want to come outside with us?"

"It's a guy thing, I'm sure," Carmella had said. "I'm happy to watch all of you standing around and scratching yourselves from here."

Now just the two of them there, Harry goes over to the refrigerator. "Do you smell propane?" he says.

Carmella sniffs, recognizes the inky Magic Marker smell. "Now that you mention it, I do."

He opens the bottom of the rickety old Servel, pulls out the metal tube, relights the pilot, blows into the tube to create the sideways draft. The Freon heating element is cold and it takes a while. He blows for ten minutes. Finally the flame is coherent, a thumb of blue that points horizontally.

When Carmella sees him, red as a bing cherry from blowing, she's stopped short. "I don't deserve you," she says. "You are too good." And she picks up her flute, still on the table from this afternoon, and walks outside.

Once away from the cabin, she finds that it's not so dark, the stars leaking tiny, spurry light in the navy bowl of the night sky. Off behind her the generator gargles gently in its shack. Carmella takes the little winding path to China Creek, sits on the redwood bench under the giant, old-growth Douglas fir, tries Handel's Sonata in A Minor again.

After they moved to Salyer, Harry cemented the bench into the ground, the posthole digger sparking whenever it struck rock, he cursing "Fucking bench, fucking bench" every kiss of metal on stone. Two days after, the cement set like granite, he said, "Let's go down to the fucking bench." Flat on her back on top of it, her hands made a beard of knuckles and nails on his cheeks. Harry pumped away, his face moving above her from extreme close-up to mid-range. The branches waved like palsied arms. A gibbous moon hung in the early night like a blasted plate of china.

Now the notes of the sonata become shapes she can't draw with her flute, the notes running away from her. Carmella gets up, walks along the bank. She trips over the flexible tubing that leads from the creek to the pump house, follows the path of the tubing, then turns toward the berm.

The ladder is still in the well. With flute wedged under her arm, she climbs down and rests her feet on a rung above the water, her back leaning on the corrugated sides that are too dark to bounce a reflection back, her body curved like a clef. The nutty smell of bear scat hovers over the water, thick and almost sweet.

She plays her flute. It is not the sonata this time but something else, what Carmella hears inside her—the strange music that is there. The notes pour out, climbing all the way up to Ursa in the sky.

From above a voice: "That's beautiful," Harry says. "What is it?"

"It's nothing. I mean I'm making it up as I go."

"It's beautiful," he says. Then, "I knew about it, Carmella. It doesn't matter."

She says nothing, looks up at the featureless head, the sky behind it.

"Keep playing," he says. "I'll be here when you're ready to come up."

When he retreats from the opening of the well, she puts the flute to her mouth again. Down here, the notes spinning up the shaft from the black bottom, the city seems only like a dream she had. This is real: the bear funk in the water, Harry up there waiting, probably straightening the slat of siding that's come loose from the back of the pump house; the wind blowing off Sawtooth cold and clear; living up here in Salyer; this pinkish thing that came into her life this morning.

It is not sweet harmony coming from her flute but it is music, a heart shot. "Harry," she calls up to him.

His head reappears. "Yes, Carly?"

Climbing up the ladder, she says, "Can I tell you something you don't know?" And what she tells him as she steps out of the well, what she finally tells him is what is inside her, and that is the most beautiful music she's ever heard.

Greg Sarris

The Magic Pony

MY NAME IS JASMINE, but I'm no sweet-smelling flower. Names are just parents' dreams, after all. I'm thirty pounds too big and even more dull-faced than my mother, since I make no effort to camouflage it with powder and lipstick. My cousin Ruby is pretty, but it's not the kind of pretty boys see. She's thin and clothes hang on her just so, like her mom, my Auntie Faye.

Us Indians are full of evil, Auntie Faye said. She told lots of stories about curses and poison. We call it poison. Not that we're bad people. Not like regular thieves and murderers. We inherit it. Something our ancestors did, maybe, or something we did to bring it on ourselves. Something we didn't realize—like having talked about somebody in a way they didn't like, so they got mad and poisoned you.

She knew a lot about poison. She said she had an instinct for it. She'd nod with her chin to a grove of trees. "Don't walk there," she'd say. Her eyes looked dark and motionless, like she was seeing something she didn't want to see and couldn't look away from. She traced poison in a family. Take the receptionist at Indian Health, who has a black birthmark the size of a quarter on her cheek. Faye said the woman's mother stole something from someone, so the woman was marked from birth. It happens like that. It can circle around and get someone in your family. It's everywhere, Faye said.

Which is why she painted a forest on the front room wall and painted crosses over it with pink fingernail polish, to keep poison away. She wanted us to touch one of the crosses every day. "You'll be safe," she said.

I knew she was half cracked. I never believed any of her nonsense. I knew what Mom and my other aunts said was true: Faye had lost it. She was plumb nuts. And Ruby, who was fourteen, my age, wasn't far behind her. Ruby talked to extraterrestrials who landed on the street outside. She'd read books in the library and come out acting like some character in the book: Helen Keller or Joan of Arc or some proper English girl. She made no sense. Nothing about Ruby or Faye made sense, but I lived with them anyway.

I wasn't normal either.

I wanted to hear Auntie Faye's weird stories. I wanted to know what the extraterrestrials told Ruby. I wanted to sit at the kitchen table that Faye set each day with place mats and clean silverware and fresh flowers and hear nothing but their voices in the cool, quiet air of the room. I begged my mother. "Auntie Faye said I could live there," I told her. She looked at me as if I told her I had an extra eye on the back of my head. She knew me and Ruby were friendly, but she didn't think I'd go as far as wanting to live there. Seeing how shocked she was, I begged that much harder. I cried, threatened to run away. What could she say? She didn't have a place for us, not really. We lived with Grandma Zelda. Like all of my aunts and their kids when they get bounced out of their apartments for not paying the rent or something. Only Mom seemed permanent at Grandma Zelda's. She could never keep a place of her own for long.

Grandma Zelda's apartment is like the others, a no-color brown refurbished army barracks at the end of Grand Avenue. Grandma Zelda, Faye, my other aunts—all of us lived there. It was like our own reservation in Santa Rosa, just for our clan. Each apartment was full of the same stuff: dirty-diaper-smelling kids, hollering, and fighting. But Grandma's place was the worst. It stunk twenty-four hours a day, and you never knew where you were going to sleep: on the floor, on the couch, in a chair. Babies slept in drawers. And then all the sounds in the dark. The crap with Mom and her men. And my aunts, too. All their moaning and stuff. All the time hoping none of it got close to you.

So you can see how Faye and Ruby's BS sounded to me like water trickling from a cool mountain stream, pleasure to the ears. It wasn't water that could drown you. Sometimes it was even amusing. I'd guess how their stories would turn out because they got predictable. Of course Grandma Zelda and my other aunts were shocked when I carried my things to Faye's. I knew they wouldn't stop me, and they wouldn't come looking for me either. Faye's place was just two down from Grandma's, but it might as well have been in San Francisco, fifty miles away. No one hung around Faye's. If they came over, they'd stay half a second, then leave, like if they didn't get out fast enough they'd catch a disease. I was safe.

Then Auntie Faye found a man, and one day me and Ruby came home from school and found Mom and all our aunts at Faye's like it was an everyday thing.

Billyrene. Pauline. Rita. Stella. Mom. Even Grandma Zelda. All of them were there putting on a show. Big dull-faced Indian women with assorted hair colors. They fooled with their hair and tugged at their blouses, each one hoping Faye's man would take notice. Each one had her own plan to get the man for herself. I know Mom and my aunts. Nothing stops them when they get ideas, and nothing gives them ideas like a man does. First the lollipop-sweet smiles and phony shyness, then the cattiness, the sharp words. By the time Ruby and me got there they had their claws out.

"Did you come from the mission?" Grandma Zelda asked the man, who sat next to Faye on the couch.

He didn't seem to hear her. Maybe he was overwhelmed by the line of beauties that surrounded him. Me and Ruby stood pushed up against the wall. No one saw us, not even Faye, who was looking in our direction. Her eyes weren't strange. They weren't still. She looked back and forth as people talked. I felt funny all of a sudden. I'd seen the man before. There was nothing to him, I saw that right off. He was white, ugly, orange-colored, with thick hairy arms and eyes that were little blue stones, plastic jewelry in a junk shop. It wasn't him that bothered me, really. It was Faye, the way she followed the conversation, and Mom and all them in the room. My stomach slid like a tire on an icy road.

"Did you come from the mission?" Grandma asked again. She was the only one in a dress, an old lady print, with her stained yellow slip hung to her ankles.

"What kind of question is that?" Mom snapped. She smiled at Faye's man, as if telling him not to pay any attention to the idiot old woman.

"Frances," Grandma said, "all I meant was is he Christian?"

Faye laughed, trying to make light of all the talk. She gently elbowed her man to let him know to laugh too.

I turned to Ruby. With all that was going on in front of her, her eyes were a million miles away. It aggravated me that she stood there in never-never land. I grabbed her arm and whispered, "That man's going to be your new father."

She didn't focus, so I said it again, this time loud and clear.

"That man's going to be your new father."

Grandma Zelda looked in our direction. "Hush up," she snapped. She didn't really see me and Ruby. We could've been Rita's three-year-old twins for all she knew. She didn't hear what I said either. No one did.

Then Billyrene piped up, Billyrene in her aqua stretch pants and a white blouse that didn't cover her protruding belly. "Lord knows Faye don't meet men in the mission. Not like some people here." She was looking straight at Mom and Pauline and Rita, giving them an evil gap-toothed smile.

On and on it went. Then out came the beer. They drank awhile, then left. Faye and her man went with them.

I hadn't cooked a meal since I left Grandma Zelda's eight months before. Even with this guy in Faye's life, she hadn't missed cooking for me and Ruby until that night. Tuna casserole, that's what I ended up making, just like I used to for everybody at Grandma's. Ruby set the table. We ate and didn't say anything to each other. Not until we were doing the dishes. I was washing, she was drying. I was thinking about Faye and Mom and my aunts, all their catty talk. Faye would laugh but she had to know how bad it can get, especially if they're drinking. If they don't beat on one another, they'll go after somebody else. Like the time Pauline and

Mom got into it over who used all the gas in Pauline's pickup. They were hollering at each other in Cherri's Chinese Kitchen. Cherri, the owner, tried to settle them down, and Mom hit her over the head with a Coke bottle. The cops came and took Mom, the whole thing. I was picturing all that when I looked at Ruby, who was drying dishes calm as you please. She might as well have been standing next to a sink on the moon. "Your mother's crazy," I blurted out. "She's a freak and so are you."

She finished wiping a plate and placed it in the cupboard. Then she reached for another plate from the dish rack.

"Did you hear me?" I yelled. My aggravation had turned into pure pissed-off. She paid no attention to me. "Damn you, you freak!" I cupped my hand into the sink and splashed her with the hot, dirty dishwater. She was stunned. The dishwater hit her in the face, all over the front of her. But she did just what you'd expect. She got a hold on herself. She dried the plate, even soaking wet as she was, and set it in the cupboard. Then she put down the towel and walked away.

She got out the Monopoly board. I knew what she was up to. She wanted me to sit down and play with her. Whenever I got upset, like with my flunking-out grades at school, she opened the Monopoly board. She cheated so I could win. She wanted me to feel better. I knew what she was up to, but I didn't say anything. I looked at her, sitting on the couch, waiting, soaking wet. I turned, picked up the towel, and finished the dishes she was drying.

The man's name was Jerry. Where Auntie Faye found him I'm not sure. The grocery store, I think. When I first saw him come into the house with her, he was carrying a bag of groceries. He was nothing special, like I said. White, ugly. He'd come each afternoon and visit with Faye. He'd come around three, about the time me and Ruby got home from school, and leave at five, when Faye started cooking supper. He always brought something: flowers, a can of coffee, a pair of candles. It went on like that for a couple weeks, until the day Mom and my aunts came into the house and him and Faye left with them.

I knew Faye was lonely. She had bad luck with men. Ruby's father died in a car crash on his way to the hospital the night Ruby was born. He had been over in Graton drinking. But Faye didn't see it that way. She said she was cursed for loving his brother first. The brother's name was Joaquin. He got killed in the Vietnam war. Six months later Faye married Ruby's father. From the way she talked, I don't think she ever stopped loving Joaquin. She never dated after Ruby's father died. I know because I used to hear Mom and my aunts go on in that dirty woman-talk way about Faye not having a man, and until Jerry came I never saw a guy near the place. It wasn't that Faye couldn't get a man. Just the opposite. She didn't look like Mom and my aunts. She wasn't heavy, plain-looking. She was slender and wore clothes like a lady in a magazine. Everything just so, even the dark pants and white blouse she wore around the house.

But Faye's loneliness was about more than not having a man. It was bigger, more than about Joaquin and what happened to Ruby's father. I saw it in her eyes when me and Ruby left each morning for school. Her eyes got wide, not really focusing on me and Ruby but just staring. She'd be sitting at the table, plates of toast and half-empty bowls of cereal all around, and from the door, where me and Ruby said good-bye, she looked so small, sitting there dressed just so.

When she told stories about poison she looked lonely, scared. She'd sit me and Ruby at the table and tell us what certain pink crosses on her painting meant. She had painted the big green forest first, the dark trunks and thick green leaves, then kept adding crosses here and there with fingernail polish, a pink color she never used on herself. Each cross had a story of its own. When she talked her eyes narrowed. They seemed to squeeze like two hands trying to hold on to something. It was always about what happened to somebody, like the one about our Cousin Jeanne's Old Uncle. It's why Jeanne and them don't live in the barracks with us, why they split off from the family a long time ago, when everybody was still on the reservation. Her Old Uncle—I guess he's our Old Uncle too— liked this woman from Clear Lake, but she was married. He liked her so much he put a spell on her husband. Old Uncle could do things like that, poison people. But the poison turned on him. Something happened. It got his sister. One night she was playing blackjack; the next morning she was as cold and still as a rock in winter. That's how our great-aunt died, Faye said. She held a pointing stick, the kind teachers use with a rubber tip, and aimed near the center of the painting. "And it's why your Cousin Jeanne has cancer," she told us. "She inherited it. His misuse of power, it's living yet."

When she talked about Ruby's father or Joaquin, she pointed to a cross near the bottom of the forest, on the right-hand side. "Man sickness," she said. "Man poison."

Somehow because of that cross and the way she talked about it I figured she'd never have a boyfriend. Maybe she thought she was poisoned when it came to men, so she'd never have one. After Jerry started coming, she stood by the painting with her fingers on that cross and whispered, "Oh, Father, help against this poison. Keep me safe from it. Don't let it turn on me." I couldn't hear her, but I knew what she said. If me and Ruby got the urge to steal something, we had to say these words and touch the cross with the stealing story. If someone wanted to hurt us, beat us up for something, we had a cross for that too.

I never thought much about Faye praying on the mansickness cross until after Jerry and Faye left with Mom and them that day. Jerry started coming around more, not just in the afternoons but late at night, after supper, and Mom and my aunts visited more and more. I thought about my own words, what I said to Ruby that day about the ugly man becoming her new father. Faye told me more than once I had a mean mouth sometimes and I should watch what I say. Never mind that her daughter made up the tallest tales on earth. She never said nothing about that. I don't remember if there was a cross for me to touch regarding my mean teasing mouth; what I said turned out true. The man moved in.

Me and Ruby moved out of the bedroom where we used to sleep on the bed with Faye. Now we slept on the couch, with our heads at opposite ends. "You can camp out on the couch," Faye said one night, as if it were something we had asked to do and she was letting us. Our legs met in the middle, and every time one of us moved or turned we got kicked. I thought of Faye in the bed with Jerry. The door was closed. I couldn't hear anything. Still, I couldn't sleep. I tried squeezing my eyes shut, but I kept seeing Faye with Jerry, disgusting things. Either way, with my eyes opened or closed, everything was dark, a perfect empty backdrop for all I was seeing in my mind. I looked to the painting above us, over the couch. The crosses glowed faintly in the light coming through the front window. "Ruby," I whispered, "maybe your dumb mother can find a cross that'll get us a bed."

Of course she didn't answer me. I sat up and looked at her. She was awake, staring, the window light in her eyes. I knew she heard me.

"Damn you," I said and yanked the blankets off her. She didn't move. She was probably in deep communication with a Martian that was signaling her from the back side of the barracks. Hours later I was still awake. Ruby was asleep. I sat up and covered her with the blankets. I woke up that way in the morning, sitting up.

Faye didn't pray at her painting anymore. She dusted it with her feather duster the way she dusted the top of the TV. She'd remind us to think of the crosses when we left for school each morning, but that's about all. No more stories about poison and what can happen to people. No more holding hands after one of the stories, which is what we always did. She'd finish the story, put down her pointing stick, and then we'd hold hands over the table while she said the prayer about Father God helping us against the poison.

Now she talked about ordinary stuff. The ladies she knew at the cannery. Specials at the grocery store. What was in the window at the secondhand shop on Fifth Street. She talked about getting a new place, a house someplace where me and Ruby could have our own bedroom, maybe even out of Santa Rosa. She had it planned. She wasn't going to work at the cannery anymore, where she was laid off half the year. She was going to be a nurse's aide in a convalescent hospital. Jerry knew someone who could get her a job. Once she talked about tenderness, its merits; it makes people smile, she said. It makes them have faith in others. It makes people feel connected. Then she threw her head back and dropped her shoulders, like she'd got goose bumps all of a sudden. "It's like a light's inside you." Jerry was there, and I felt embarrassed, like I was hearing what I didn't want to imagine seeing behind the bedroom door at night.

Jerry was always there, since he was out of work. Temporarily, Faye said. He helped Faye with the shopping and stuff and he still brought her things, flowers and once a coffee mug with red hearts on it. Lots about him bugged me. Like the way he chewed his food. He mashed it, curling his lips out so you could see the food in his mouth. He asked if me and Ruby were cheerleaders. That was funny. I wanted to ask him if he thought we looked like cheerleaders.

But I didn't.

Faye was happy these days. She used to get moody sometimes, just stare into space, and she'd snap at you if you talked to her. Now she was always up, and just by the way she acted you knew she wanted everybody else up too. She'd look at you and there was something in her eyes, something behind the brightness, that was scary. You wouldn't want to cross her. Seemed like Mom and my aunts saw this in Faye's eyes too. They came to the house almost every day now; there was none of their bitchy talk. Everybody was nice, the way Faye wanted. Her and Mom and Grandma went on and on about how they could help Pauline get her two younger kids out of Juvenile Hall. Stuff like that. It made me nervous. I know my aunts. There was something behind their niceness, something like what I saw in Faye's eyes.

Me and Ruby spent more and more time doing things. It was toward the end of the school year. The days were longer. We took walks. We'd go to the fairgrounds, up to the slaughterhouse on Santa Rosa Avenue, and even to the mall. Anywhere except the library, which I couldn't stand. I'd put up with anything, her stories about extraterrestrials, anything to keep her head out of a book. That's why I got caught up in the horse thing, the magic pony.

It was a regular horse, a small pinto gelding, not much bigger than a pony. She called it a pony. It was at the slaughterhouse with the other horses. One of the things me and Ruby did those days was sit in the rusted-out boxcar by the slaughterhouse and watch the horses. She had them all named: King Tut, Cleopatra, Romeo and Juliet, the Duke of Earl. We didn't talk about what happened to them when the owner took them from the front corral, where we watched them, to the back corral: a loud buzzer, then the gun blast. Sometimes the horses got lucky. If they were gentle and sound, rich people bought them for their kids.

One day this pony darted out from a group of bigger horses by the trough. He was munching a mouthful of hay, and he kept running here and there, snatching hay from the troughs. He moved so fast the others didn't see him. After a while he walked to the cement tub by the fence for a drink. That's when Ruby flew off the boxcar to pet him. True, he lifted his head and whinnied at her. He probably would have done that for me if I had gotten there first. But Ruby didn't see it that way. He communicated with her.

That night in bed I heard everything. Far as she was concerned, the pony wasn't black and white but pure silver and gold. A horse who never drank water. He lived off the morning dew and the pollen of spring flowers. A magic pony that carried princesses into fields of poppies and purple lupine. He soared on wind currents over this town with wings stretched wide as an eagle's. He told Ruby he needed a home.

Faye and Jerry were gone, out with Mom and them. I was trying to sleep. I didn't want to be awake when they got home. Ruby wouldn't quit this horse business. "Shut up," I finally said.

Strange thing, though, the horse could do tricks. We went to the slaughterhouse every day. Before long Ruby was in the corral with it, riding it and everything. Smoke, the owner, a tall black man, gave her a bridle. Even he was surprised to see the pony back up and kneel down on command. He let Ruby take the pony into the open field across the street, where the last flowers of spring were blooming, poppies and lupine. He said the pony might've been in the circus. He didn't know much, except the man who dropped the pony off said it had foundered. "Too bad," he said. When he told me this, we were leaning on the fence watching Ruby and the pony in the field. His words fell like dust and piled on my shoulders. I didn't know what foundered was, but I looked back to Ruby just then, and in the early evening light, she seemed to be floating, nothing holding her as she glided above the dried oat grass and flowers.

I told her to forget the pony. I opened her dictionary and pointed to the word "founder." "Nobody's going to want that pony," I said. "You know what's going to happen." I expected her to argue with me, to point out that the stiffness in the pony's front legs was barely noticeable. But she didn't. She took the dictionary from me, set it on the table, and said matter-of-factly, "That's why he told me he needed a home. I have to find him one."

She couldn't think of anything else. Day and night she figured and planned. For two weeks she approached everybody who came to the slaughterhouse, telling them how the pony was magic. She'd jump on its back, without a bridle, and show folks how well trained he was. The pony would back up and kneel with just a little tug on its mane. By this time Ruby could get the pony to do anything. People watched, young pretty-looking girls and white shirt-and-tie fathers. They'd clap, cheer Ruby on, but they always ended up looking at other horses. Finally it occurred to Ruby what I had been telling her all along. Smoke told people about the pony's legs.

Then she went to Jerry, which was the dumbest idea ever. "If he's my father now, he can help me get the pony," she said. Jerry didn't have a pot to piss in, for as things turned out he was living off Auntie Faye's unemployment from the cannery, just like me and Ruby. The flowers he brought Faye he picked out of people's gardens, and the other things, like the coffee mug, he found in trash bins or stole from garage sales. One morning I saw him pocket me and Ruby's lunch money. I didn't tell Faye. I feared that person I had seen behind her happy eyes. But I told Ruby. I reminded her of that and of Jerry's money problems. She didn't listen.

"I want the pony," she told him one night.

He was sitting at the kitchen table, having a beer with Faye and Mom. It was late, after supper. I watched from the couch that I had just covered with a sheet and blankets for bed. Ruby stood only a couple feet from Jerry, determined. Jerry didn't answer her. He seemed surprised, as if he had looked up and just seen Ruby for the first time.

"Ruby," Faye said. "You know we're moving soon. That takes extra money. Jerry and me are saving. Wait until after we move." Her voice was muffled, far away, like a seagull calling over crashing waves. I noticed she sounded like this when she drank.

Ruby looked straight at Jerry. "I want the pony."

Mom took a swallow of beer and set down her bottle. "Ruby," she said, "you should talk it over with Grandma. She could help maybe from her social security check." Mom acted as if she were really interested. She thought she was important these days since she'd found a job at a convalescent hospital.

Jerry, who was still looking at Ruby as if he didn't know her, turned suddenly to Mom. "Your mother's old," he said. "She needs her money." He looked at Ruby. "Go to one of the farmers around here."

Ruby was up against a wall. Finally she quit. She came back and sat on the cot next to the couch. Later, after Mom left and Faye and Jerry went in the bedroom, she said, "See, Jerry did help me. He told me what to do." She was lying on top of the cot, still dressed. She stared at the ceiling, already seeing a thin Indian girl with long straight hair standing before a farmer's open front door.

We walked five miles down Petaluma Hill Road to the dairies. We went to front doors and into noisy milk barns and smelly calf pens, looking for farmers who might want the pony. Ruby never said hello. She didn't introduce herself. "There's this pony," she'd say and go on and on. Most people let her finish before they asked us to leave. One farmer was interested. He was a fat, whiskered man in dirty pants that hung halfway down his white ass. He signaled us to follow him so he could hear us over the loud milking machines in that barn where he and two Mexican men milked enormous black-and-white cows. We went into a dark, windowless room. Metal pipes fed a huge shiny tank, where they kept the milk. The farmer leaned against the wall and folded his hands over his belly. His fingers were thick and hairy.

"You can see him at the slaughterhouse," Ruby said.

"What's wrong with him? Gotta be something wrong with him," the man said. I didn't like the way he took time between his words, and I felt his eyes on Ruby, though I didn't look. I took her hand and gauged my distance from the door.

Ruby took her time answering him. "He needs a home," she finally said. "He gets around good, and he can get up and down with me on him."

The man told us his daughter wanted a horse. Then he said, "I'll go look at him. Meet me back here next week, same time."

I yanked Ruby out the door.

On the way to the main road, we passed a farmhouse where a girl about ten years old stood watering a vegetable garden.

"See, Jerry was right," Ruby said.

"At least he has a daughter," I said. "I still think he's a pervert."

I knew Ruby wouldn't listen to me, but I didn't like the idea of us going back to that dairy. I didn't like that dark room. I felt trapped.

It's not that I hate men. I just know them too well. I've been around Mom and my aunts and seen what they bring home. I've seen it all. The stuff that goes on in the dark, the stuff you're not supposed to see but end up seeing anyway. Like when I saw Auntie Pauline's man pulling off my Cousin Angela's pants in Pauline's pickup, Pauline's daughter who's my age, the one in juvee. Or when that guy Armando hit Auntie Rita in the chest. Or Tito, Mom's last man: the way he tried to get at me at night when Mom was asleep. You develop a sixth sense for it. You see things you don't want to see. You run right into it. It isn't always something heavy like with Pauline's man and Angela. It can be something simple, innocent-looking.

Like the way Mom and Jerry were sitting in Pauline's pickup outside the supermarket. You could say there were a lot of groceries on the seat, or maybe a dog or a child that caused them to have to sit so close together. You knew, though, that they could have put a dog or a child between them. But it's more than their sitting that way; it's something about them that is still, something about the way they quietly turn their faces to each other, Mom looking up so that her eyes meet his, that tells you the whole story, not just in this moment but in all of those in the dark, where Faye hadn't seen them. And you can hear the excuse: "Jerry and me are picking up some things at the store."

I watched them from behind a car in the parking lot. First, I saw Pauline's pickup, the red Toyota, then the back of Mom's head, her teased orange-red hair that was supposed to be blond. I knew the whole story even before I had time to think about it. My stomach turned. I wanted to heave. I started up Milton toward Grand. I yanked my hair just so the pain would take my mind off things. It wasn't that I was shocked by Mom and Jerry or the things people do, sex and all that. I was worried about what was going to happen at home.

Already things were nuts. Faye's place was no different now from Grandma Zelda's or Pauline's. Me and Ruby ate canned soup on the couch for dinner. In the mornings we made our own toast and poured our own cornflakes, since Faye didn't get up with us anymore. The door stayed closed, locked. Ruby did nothing but obsess over the pony. She didn't even do her schoolwork now. I couldn't talk to her. Her eyes were like a pair of headlights on the highway, staring straight ahead, zooming past me. She spent all her time at the slaughterhouse, waiting to see if the farmer or anyone else came to see the pony and making sure Smoke didn't move him to the back, behind the white barn. "The farmer could come while we're in school," I said. But she wouldn't budge. She wouldn't leave the pony's side. The afternoon I saw Mom and Jerry in Pauline's pickup I had left her braiding the pony's scraggly mane.

When I got a hold of my senses, I thought of telling Ruby. I was sitting on Grandma Zelda's porch step. I had come to Faye's first, but when I got to the open screen door and heard all the folks yapping inside, I continued along the row of barracks to Grandma's and plunked myself down. I could hear the loud laughter at Faye's two doors away.

It was a couple of hours before Ruby came up the path at twilight. I jumped up and ran to meet her, feeling desperate to let out everything in my swelled brain. But I ended up saying nothing. I stopped, seeing her face as she turned to go inside, and knew that if I told her what I had seen, her eyes would only look harder and move away from me.

In the days ahead I wanted to talk to Ruby, not just about Mom and Jerry. The weather would have been enough to carry on about, far as I was concerned. But nothing. No way. I'm one to shout, shake her up with what I say, but I could've screamed at the top of my lungs and it would've done as much good as trying to stop a hundred-mile-an-hour train with a whisper. I couldn't stand being in the house. I wanted to kill Mom while she sat nice as could be talking to Auntie Faye. I wanted to pour gasoline on Jerry and watch him burn to black ashes. I stuck by Ruby. I lived at the slaughter-house with her. But it seemed to make no difference. I was alone.

We went back to the dairy after a week, just like the farmer said, same time. "We're not going in that back room," I said. But there was no need to worry. The farmer must've seen us coming up the road. He met us in front of the milk barn. He pulled up his sagging pants, then adjusted his stained green cap to cover his eyes.

"That little Indian pony," he said, "I went and seen him. I don't know what you girls was thinking. He's useless."

Of course Faye would find out about Mom and Jerry. For me waiting was like standing on a tightrope, not knowing when I'd fall or where I'd land when I did. I didn't have to wait long. On the last day of school, after me and Ruby got home at noon, Faye explained everything.

Suddenly things were back to the old routine. Faye was sitting at the kitchen table with her pointing stick. She motioned with her chin for me and Ruby to sit down. She was plain-looking again, pale like she was before she'd met Jerry. Her eyes were distant, pre-occupied. The table was set, with flowers in a mayonnaise jar. When she lifted her pointing stick to gesture at the painting on the wall, I saw she had drawn circles around many of the crosses and connected them with lines from one to another. She had used what looked like a black crayon.

She pointed to the cross circled near the bottom of the painting. "Man sickness," she reminded us and got up and went to the painting. "Man poison." She looked to Ruby. "Your father and also Joaquin, his brother. I loved Joaquin first."

She followed a line that connected this cross to one that was circled near the center of the painting. She was straightforward, a history teacher giving a lecture for the hundredth time.

"This one here," she said, now looking at both of us, "is Old Uncle's poison. Misuse of power. Do you see how they connect here?"

I sat motionless.

"I'll tell you," she said. She let her pointer hang by her side. "This is what happened. You know I loved Joaquin first. Isn't that right?"

We nodded in agreement.

"You know I loved him. Yes, but I never should have." She paused and swallowed hard, color coming to her pale cheeks. "I stole him from your Cousin Jeanne's mother, Anna. I stole him from Anna. I stole him in the worst way. I plotted with my sisters, your aunts, Billyrene and Pauline. We embarrassed her. We told Joaquin that Anna was poison because she and her mother lived with Old Uncle, who poisoned our aunt. It worked. It split them up. Anna and her mother disappeared. We didn't see them for many years, until we moved here. But that's not the point. What really happened is that Old Uncle's poison found me. Misuse of power. I opened a hole in my heart and it found a place to live."

She took a deep breath and pushed back her hair with her free hand. "I killed two men." She pointed to the two circled crosses and traced the line between them, back and forth. "Each man I love I kill. Each man I touch because the poison in me does that. Now my own sisters are full of the poison. It's growing in them and they're using it against me. They plotted and took Jerry."

Faye walked over and set the pointing stick on the table. "Now drink your orange juice," she said.

I heard her push the toaster down behind us and I smelled the toast. But it wasn't until I saw the buttered toast on the table that I realized how far Faye had gone with her story. Things weren't back to normal. Faye had gone off the edge. "Now hurry or you'll be late for school," she said.

Later that day I followed Ruby to the slaughterhouse to try and talk to her. "Look," I said, "this is serious. Your mother's nuts." Ruby had hardly said a word to me the whole week. "Listen to me," I said. We were standing just outside the corral. "Damn you, you stupid fool, wake up."

She slipped through the board fence to where the pony was waiting for her. Its white ears were perked up and it whinnied, just as it did every time it saw Ruby. She stroked its neck and led it to the front of the corral, by the main road where passersby could see them. The buzzer went off in the white barn; then I heard it, a gunshot. I climbed over the fence and made my way past the bigger horses to Ruby and the pony. She had her arms around its neck, tightly, and its head was over her shoulder facing my direction.

"OK," I said. "I'm sorry. Anyway, it's my stupid mother's fault. I'm sorry." I don't know how many times I said it. But she never turned around. Even the pony ignored me, never perked up its ears. I felt like a fifth wheel. Like I had no business there in the little world that was all their own.

Faye got her time straight, a good sign. When me and Ruby got home, after dark, she scolded us for staying out so late. "Dinner's cold," she said. She was truly angry. She shoved the food she had prepared into the oven and slammed the stove door shut. Ten minutes later me and Ruby were sitting at a table set with flowers, eating pork chops, fresh green beans, and a baked potato with sour cream, my favorite. Ruby talked on and on about the pony, crazy stuff about how it could fly and disappear, and Faye forgot about us being late.

When we finished eating, Faye went to the painting and so did Ruby. Faye wiped her mouth with her folded paper napkin and then got up, and Ruby followed her, as if Faye wiping her mouth was a signal. How else did Ruby know what Faye was doing? Usually Faye went and stood by her painting before dinner or in the morning or early afternoon. Then I saw Ruby's eyes. Walking to the painting, she looked back at me. She looked at me so I knew she was looking, and I felt like I did earlier with her hugging the pony. Only I felt worse now; I saw more, even after she looked away and joined Faye, starting in on Father God for help. I saw that Ruby wasn't in never-never land. She was always here. She was always aware of me next to her. Faye was OK too. How could she not know how hard her life had been and that my mother, her sister, had just stolen her man? Ruby knew and Faye knew, just like me. But they believed in something—Faye her crosses, Ruby the pony—and I didn't. I clung to them, and they let me.

We slept together that night. Faye told stories about when she was a girl living on the reservation. She told us the Indian names of flowers. She told us about wild birds. "*Cita*," she said. "Bird. *Cita, cita.*" I fell asleep and must've slept hard because I woke up late, without Faye or Ruby.

I went to the front room, and just as if it had jumped out at me, I saw Faye's painting—or what was left of it—before I even saw Faye. It was black, totally black, the color she had circled the crosses with the day before. Black, except for the edges here and there where you could see a bit of green from the trees underneath. It was as if I were waking up just then, as if in the bedroom I hadn't been awake at all. The fragile peace I had felt shattered like thin glass into a million pieces.

I turned to Faye, who was sitting at the table. Nothing was set, no breakfast dishes, nothing, and the flowers from the mayonnaise jar were laid out around a butcher knife, a halo of green and yellow and purple around the silver blade.

"Faye," I said. "Auntie Faye."

She didn't look at me but kept staring at the painting. It took a minute, and then she started talking. "I must kill Frances—"

"My mother?" I asked.

"I must kill Frances. Otherwise she'll kill Jerry. She's full of poison. She'll kill Jerry. Tonight I will kill her. She is hate. The poison is hate."

"Auntie Faye," I called, but she didn't see me.

I realized talking about it was useless when I saw her eyes. The fearful person I had seen behind her bright eyes the past few weeks had come out now; she was that person. She had told stories to save herself—now she was telling them to excuse herself. Hatred. Jealousy. Anger. Evil. All I had seen in my mother's and my aunt's eyes at different times was here in Faye's. I looked back at the black wall, where Faye was looking, then ran out of the house.

I went to the slaughterhouse. Ruby wasn't there so I ran through the corral and shouted up into the hay barn, where the horses were eating. I hollered and hollered. Nothing. Only the yellow bales of hay stared at me. I went around the back, behind the big white barn across from the front corral, and that's when I spotted the pony. He was there along with a crippled bay mare standing on three legs, a few unshorn sheep, and an emaciated whiteface cow. A large eucalyptus tree shaded the cramped pen. "Ruby!" I hollered. "Ruby!"

Smoke appeared in the door above the chute. "She ain't been around today," he said. "Ain't seen her. Now get, you shouldn't be back here."

First I thought Ruby had run away. But that wasn't like her. I figured she had seen how the pony was in the back. Any day could be its last. Ruby wouldn't give up. She wouldn't run. She'd work harder. She'd go back to the dairies. She'd go farther down Petaluma Hill Road, all the way to Petaluma.

So that's what I did—went back to every dairy we had stopped at, asking everybody along the way if they had seen her. I made up stories, like she needed medicine. I described her, but no one had seen such a girl. I walked clear back to town. One last place, the library—but no luck. The only place left was Faye's.

Faye hadn't moved. All afternoon while I'd been running back and forth to the slaughterhouse looking for Ruby and checking to see if the pony was alive, Faye never looked away from her painting to see me coming and going. I slammed the door. Once I even shook the table. I thought of reaching for the knife, but it was too close to Faye. She might snap, and I'd be within her reach.

I plunked myself down on the couch, and as the afternoon wore on I began hating Ruby. She had abandoned me. Faye was worse than useless. She was worse than gone. I thought of running over to Grandma Zelda's and telling her or Mom. But then what? Have them come down and get stabbed? I thought of calling the police, but why start trouble when it hadn't started? I guess, too, that I didn't want anyone to see Faye like this. They would take her away. I waited and waited. I wanted Ruby to come home, for things to be fine. Maybe Faye would flip back to her old self, I thought, if I just waited.

Faye must have gotten up so quietly I didn't notice. She was standing at the kitchen table looking toward the screen door. Slowly, deliberately, she walked to the door and stopped. "Jasmine," she said, "come here." Her voice was cool, even.

I went to the door.

"A miracle," she said.

And then I saw the sky, where Faye was looking. It was lit by a huge ball of fire, yellow, purple, golden, and red. I was stunned by the sight of it. Then I heard the sirens, and before I could think, I knew. Ruby had set the barn on fire.

I tore past Faye, around the crowds gathered outside the barracks. I ran up Santa Rosa Avenue, past the flashing lights. Horses were everywhere, all over the street, stopping traffic, halting police cars and fire trucks. I was stopped by police and yellow tape, but in the thick of lights and uniforms, through the haze of smoke, I saw a plain-looking girl being escorted to a police van.

There was nothing to do but go back and tell what had happened. There was nothing to hide now. I felt heavy, tired. The first people I saw were Auntie Pauline and my cousins. They were standing on Grand. Then I went in and told Faye. "I know," she said. "I know." She was sitting on the couch.

Funny thing, no one asked me how I knew it was Ruby. Everybody collected in Faye's. They waited for the police car. Something my family always does when there's trouble—wait together. Wait for the details. Auntie Pauline. Auntie Billyrene. Grandma Zelda. Auntie Rita. Mom and Jerry. Auntie Stella.

As it turned out, there wasn't a lot to the story. Ruby had opened the gates and then set the hay barn on fire. She let the horses go. Of course I was the only one who understood the details. I don't mean about how she hid out and poured gasoline on the hay and all that, which we found out later, after she was released from juvee and came back to Faye's. I mean about why she did it. What led up to it. I understood it plain as day even while I was sitting there next to Faye, waiting with everybody else for the police to come with Ruby.

There was nothing I could do. Faye was a crying mess on the couch, and the cops had Ruby. Face it. Face reality, which I always did, which I told myself I should never have stopped doing. I had been hiding at Faye's. With her and Ruby I had been fooling myself. See the road ahead, I kept saying inside my brain. But when I saw Ruby come through the door, a uniformed policeman on each side of her, I stopped. My heart turned and never righted back.

"Jasmine," she blurted out, seeing me. "He's free. He flew away."

I said what made no sense. I said it like a prayer. "Everything's going to be all right, Ruby."

Mari Sunaida

Heat

THE TEMPERATURE IN THE Sacramento River Delta had been over a hundred degrees for 12 days in a row, and the nights hadn't been much cooler. Brown fruit, decaying fish and black earth filled the hot, still August air with rancid odors. It was as if each day was rolled up into a soggy woolen blanket and hung for a few hours in the night sky, to be let down the next morning heavier and smellier than before. There was no escaping the fierce heat, and in the afternoons when it was hottest, Tora Hayashi could actually see the atmosphere of it, the waves of phantom flames dancing across the roof of the cramped, four-room, half-log, half-frame house.

The house was old, the color of dried bones. The paint had worn off long before 1910, the year Tora and her husband had moved in. The secondhand furniture inside was shabby and faded. Peat dust spewed through the well-worn slabs at times, clumping on the baseboards and settling into cupboards and closets. Tora had been feeling sluggish all day and had dozed off in the broken-down rocking chair while nursing the baby. A man's voice at the back door startled her awake. A sharp pain streaked through her right breast. Such a greedy drinker, she thought, pulling the baby's head out of her blouse as she beat her shoulder with the heel of her palm to loosen the stiffness. Squinting up at the dark outline of a man in a straw hat who hunched in the doorway with one hand raised above his head and the other framed around his eyes, she sensed him catch sight of her. In the crisscross of mesh she couldn't make

286

out the expression on his face, but all at once she had the suspicion that he was peering at her open bodice. Instinctively, she lowered the gauze over the baby's face and covered her exposed breast.

"Who is it?" she called out, surprised by the edge in her voice. The angle of the man's rounded body in the half-open kitchen door, with the blazing light streaming out around him, reminded her of the plum sapling, bent from the scorching rays of the sun, just outside the bedroom window. She had brought the seed from Japan and had planted it when she was first married. Its once tender leaves were now shriveled into brown balls along the lower branches, and near the stunted top, one spindly limb stretched out. To Tora, it looked to be shaking its fist at the sun. Shifting low in the rocker, she ignored the sharp jabs from the broken spindles and moved the baby into a sitting position on her lap. How she disliked that chair. If only she could lie on soft tatami again! She waved the thought away, knowing it would only take root in her mind and fester if she let it, knowing it was useless to call up anything that reminded her of Japan.

"Is this the Hayashi place?" the man repeated, pausing between each word as if the moisture-charged heat of his new surroundings somehow intoxicated him.

"Yes, just a moment, please." Swiftly buttoning her blouse, Tora ducked into the small bedroom off the kitchen and lowered the baby into his crib. She had a clear view of the man through a chink in the log portion of the wall that divided the two rooms. He waited on the top step, a slender, boyish-looking man about her age, no more than 27 or 28. She watched him take off his hat and nod stoically, fanning himself around the face.

"My name is Hara. Mr. Kami asked me to come and see you." The mention of Kami immediately put Tora on guard. She waited a moment, expecting him to continue, and when he fell silent she wondered what to do. As a rule she didn't invite people inside when she was alone with the baby, and although this man Hara looked harmless enough, he was still a stranger. If her husband had been home, chances are he would have asked the man to come in, a small courtesy he often extended to fellow countrymen passing through their area.

"I'm sorry to have to disturb you like this, but it will only take a moment." Reassured by the tone of obeisance in his voice, she probed tentatively, "What did Mr. Kami have to say?"

Hara did not answer. He rubbed a handkerchief across his forehead, folded it and wiped the back of his neck. His silence made Tora even more fearful about the reason for his visit. Tying on a bib apron, she squatted beside the crib, made faces and crooned. She turned the baby over on his stomach and patted him gently, letting her mind drift to the events of the summer before.

Kami had been older than most of the young bachelors following the transient life of picking and packing crops up and down the Central Valley. Everyone who came into contact with him immediately sensed that he was living far below his original station in life. There were rumors he had started up a newspaper in Vancouver but lost the business when his partner gambled it away. He didn't socialize with the other men mostly because he was something of an outsider to the others, who had been hired as a group, and on his day off he kept to himself. On several afternoons she spied him through the foliage of the trees, sitting cross-legged under a eucalyptus, deep in reverie or writing furiously into what she assumed was a diary.

A series of brief incidents stuck in her mind. One evening in July around the Tanabata, the air was thick and sweet with the aroma of drying fish and ripe pear. She was hard at work pumping water from the well for the next morning when Kami appeared out of the darkness and offered to carry several buckets of water back to the kitchen for her. He seemed unconcerned that the other men might think less of him for doing women's work, and as he spoke, she sensed his eyes sweeping over her. Tora was not pretty in the classic definition of the word. But in the delta islands, mostly populated by single young men, her round Japanese face and short, firm body attracted much attention. She had grown accustomed to the sidelong stares from the men, but the quality of Kami's glance was different. It was a look full of tender yearning. No man had ever looked at her that way, not even her husband, and she felt the blood rush to her face. He would reappear every few days to offer his assistance, and each time his eyes moved over her, it felt as if he was seeing her for the first time. One night he turned to her and said matter-of-factly, "If you weren't married and I was 10 years younger, I'd be tempted to ask you to run away with me."

There was nothing vulgar or suggestive in his manner.

"I'd say to you, 'Meet me at the river, we'll head down to Antioch and catch the 5:40 to Los Angeles and once there, we'd start to live.'"

Overwhelmed by an unexpected feeling of delight, she looked away.

Some three or four weeks later, the two chanced to meet in the packing shed. Kami poked his head in the doorway as she was collecting empty asparagus crates and offered to help stack them against the wall. Tora worried about appearances. She had been thinking about Kami ever since their last meeting and was concerned. The encounters at the well had not gone unnoticed. She had endured a bit of teasing from three of the men, who had followed her around, sighing loudly, wringing their hands over their hearts and moaning in unison.

"Hold still. There's a spider on you."

She stood silent, afraid to move as he flicked at the back of her head with a rag. After a few moments, she felt something the size of a centipede skitter across her shoulder and down her arm. She swung her arm up and down and started to jump and hop about.

"Get it off of me! Get that thing off of me!"

In a blur, she saw a flash of white and heard the loud snap of the rag. She began spinning faster and faster and as she made a sharp turn she was caught up and lifted from the ground. Kami grasped her arms tightly.

"It's all right. It's all right. It's gone now."

He set her down slowly and seated her on an upright crate. After a time, he pulled out a handkerchief from his back pocket and wiped her face. Then reaching behind her, he softly brushed the back of her head and patted her neck and arm. Tora did not resist him. She simply yielded to the comfort of his touch and waited for her body to stop trembling.

"What was it?"

"A black widow."

She nodded. "I had a feeling."

They stared at each other. When he spread his arms, she moved into them. She lay her head against his chest and felt his breath on her neck. As he lifted the hem of her blue calico dress, she raised her hips to receive him.

A short time later they heard voices coming from the direction of the pear orchard, so they hurriedly dressed and finished stacking the crates together in silence. When he left the packing shed he promised to come back and check for nests. She thanked him with a bow.

To her deep distress some of the older men seemed to sense what had happened between them and decided to drive a wedge between Tora and Kami. Suddenly there were eyes watching her every move and she began to feel like a prisoner in her own home. There were rumors, talk that Kami was slow. Lazy. Too old. A leftist. Then one day, he was gone. He left without saying goodby. The men, emboldened by their victory, loudly speculated in front of her on Kami's lineage and claims of political exile. Tora was angry at the men for shunning and driving Kami away and sorry she had not had the courage to defend him. Her husband seemed not to have noticed anything. She knew that he must have suspected, but he never spoke directly to her about Kami and she was grateful that he never brought it up.

Now crossing back into the kitchen she could hear the sound of her slippers slapping the back of her heels and glimpsed her dark complexion and thick lips reflected on the steel rim of the soap dish. Disgusted, she looked quickly away. The mention of Kami and the unexpected presence of the man standing at the back door strangely disoriented her. Tora gathered herself and stepped to the screen door.

"Sorry to have kept you waiting."

Hara tapped the hat against his leg and his rail-thin body slumped slightly, betraying an air of sadness.

"I apologize for not writing you before coming to call, but I happened to be in the vicinity, so I took the chance of stopping by."

He shifted his weight from one foot to the other foot and brushed the hair out of his face with his hand.

"Mr. Kami died six months ago from a swelling in the brain," he said quietly. "He spoke of you often and wanted you to have this."

Hara tugged at a bundle under his arm and ceremoniously pulled an envelope from under the cloth wrapping. Tora opened the screen door, took the envelope and thanked him. Avoiding her eyes, he coughed nervously and looked down at his feet. She sensed he had another request but wasn't sure if it was his place to ask. Tora thought it best that she take the initiative and turn him down nicely but firmly. It was probably best not to have anyone associated with Kami working at the farm.

"I appreciate you coming all this way but I'm afraid harvest season is almost over. Perhaps you can try again next year."

He nodded emphatically.

"Thank you, but I already have a position with the Mission."

"Oh, are you a minister?"

"Someday I hope to be."

He smiled sheepishly.

"I see."

"Is it all right with you if I clean up a bit?"

He rubbed his hands together and mimed washing his face. There was something gentle, almost shy, about his manner and it disarmed her.

"Of course, of course. Please help yourself. Use the water in the barrel next to the well." Tora pointed a few yards away east of the house. "If you need a washbasin, it's on top of the cover and extra facecloths are on the clothesline. They should be dry by now. Can I offer you something to drink?"

Hara blinked.

"Thank you, but there's a boat waiting for me at the landing."

"Then please help yourself to some fruit. We have pears, lemons, peaches."

Tora smiled firmly.

"That's very kind of you. Thank you very much."

Tora couldn't help feeling that there was something else on his mind. She waited until he clicked down the steps before turning the envelope over in her hand. It was addressed to her. Inside, there were two sheets of heavy white paper folded in thirds, and neatly folded in the first was a sheet of seaweed with some money inside. Tora counted six $50 bills. Bewildered, she examined the front and back of each bill, carefully noting the engraving of the man with a bow tie on the front and the man, woman and train on the back. How did Kami acquire such a large sum of money? Why was he giving it to her? How was she going to explain this to her husband? She unfolded the letter. It was written in ink with a fountain pen. The handwriting was shaky and veered to the left, making the columns of kanji look like the leaning towers of Pisa she had once seen in a postcard. Despite the sloppy appearance, it was apparent that a great deal of thought and care had gone into the letter.

December 29th

Dear Tora,

The new year is just a few days away and I imagine at this moment that you are very busy with all of the preparations. I often think of the eucalyptus grove near your house and of the sounds of the bark peeling and dropping. I spent many quiet hours there and it gave me great comfort. I will make this as brief as possible. I am deeply sorry that I was the cause of so much trouble for you last summer. I am most grateful to you for your good humor and indulgence in my moment of weakness. My life has had its ups and downs, and for some time now it has been on a downhill slide. You brightened it with your kindness. In appreciation I want to leave you a little token of my thanks. I suppose an explanation is necessary. After many years an old debt I had given up on was finally repaid to me. I thought perhaps you might be able to put some of it to good use.

I hope you will not be offended that I've chosen to leave it in your care and not your husband's. To be honest, I was afraid of what he might think and that worried me. I think you understand. Please do with it what you wish. Take care of yourselves. Mr. Hara has agreed to personally deliver this letter to you after I've gone.

Sincerely,
Kami Yukio

Tora reread the letter, reflected a few moments and decided that sentiment would be the ruin of her. The letter would be the only keepsake she would have of Kami, but she knew if her husband found it there would be consequences. Before she had time to change her mind, she opened up the firebox of the cast iron stove and wedged the letter into the coals. She waited for the paper to catch fire and watched it curl and burn until it was reduced to ash. Stuffing the money back into the envelope, she pulled out the tea chest stored under the baby's crib, opened the lid, and shoved the packet deep into the sleeves of a silk kimono decorated with plum blossoms. The money would be safest there.

The baby stirred and suckled the air noisily. As if on cue Tora felt the milk begin flowing. She gazed at her son, the small chest rising and falling, and thought that he resembled an ancient balding monk. His hair had fallen out and grown back in uneven patches, forming a wispy halo from ear to ear. The baby opened his arms and smiled up at her. She recognized the shape of the arms and she knew the smile. In that instant she understood what she would do with the money. She picked the baby up and cradled him in her arms and paced from room to room, talking to him softly about his future. He watched her face as if he understood the meaning of her words. Just then she heard a tapping on the glass, and thinking it might be Mr. Hara, she lifted the curtain. A branch from the young plum tree was hooked on the window frame. There was no sign of Mr. Hara.

She leaned against the window, closed her eyes and let out a long sigh. Then she began to cry. The baby nuzzled his head on her shoulder as if to comfort her. Much later, she wiped her eyes with the hem of her apron and noticed for the first time a row of hard green buds beginning to form on the lowest branch of the plum tree.

Katherine Vaz

Original Sin

ONE DAY WITHOUT provocation my brother hit me with a shovel. That it came as a dark flash from nowhere stunned me as much as the blow, and after the doctor stitched up my head, he peered into my eyes to make certain I had not gone too far into another world. When my parents asked my brother why he had struck me, he looked without expression at them. "Because I've never seen Miranda cry," he finally said, as bewildered as anybody. From that day I have never doubted the existence of original sin. Nothing has since grown on my head where the shovel landed.

The artichoke was king in Castroville. We sold them, ate them, and under the guidance of Father Armando Ortigão stuck their thorns into our fingers for penance. Actually, until we died we could chew raw onions and traipse the perimeters of our farms on our knees, and it would still not wash clean the stain of what man was. Father Ortigão drew a heart on the chalkboard to explain: At first glance it looks blank and pure, until we realize that it must take its shape against a black background if it is to exist.

In fifth grade I discovered sorrow and longing. Merely touching the new hair around my labia set off a grotesque aching. I developed a fever for riding horses, I did unspeakable things to dolls. I figured, this being a finite world, that after coming a certain number of times I could be done forever with depravity, but when this did not appear to be happening I had terrible visions of myself as an unsated old woman, still sliding down banisters, still burning. Perhaps original sin was another name for desire.

Because we could not build snowmen in Castroville, we made men and babies out of mud. We gave them dry straw hair and invited them to our tea parties, where we served sugar water infused with mint leaves that were white from crop dusting. When the men dried and cracked in the sun, we mixed up new ones. All over the inner valley in our part of north central California, we could uncover the dust of the broken. Ants swarmed over shattered arms and coal eyes.

The Portuguese women left *figuras de cera* for God where the sun could anoint the glints of melting wax with prism rainbows that would catch His eye. During a flu epidemic, we tripped over puddles of wax stomachs in the fields. Behind the church was the favorite spot for wax hearts. If the heart melted and the patient lived, God had accepted the offering and spared the man. If the heart melted and the patient died, it was a personal sign that God was calling him home to the great pool of souls.

The Church always won.

When Almir Cruz got drunk and shot off one of his testicles, the girls searched high and low, past the softening eyes, legs, and livestock *de cera* of petitioners, hoping to discover his wax balls. I stayed out late with a flashlight, desperately wanting to find Almir.

This desire to make a treasure hunt out of the sad prayers and wants of others ended when my father and brother died in a car wreck, in the stretch where we converged with outsiders. The road, like most of the ones in California, always smelled like blood. Tourists pulled on and off the highway so fast, stopping to buy cheap artichokes, that our lives were always hemmed in by fearsome machines. Witnesses called the accident a blinding flash, too fast to anticipate. Within a year my mother took to her bed with lung cancer. She breathed clean air and did not smoke, so I knew she was dying for love.

My aunt helped me make wax lungs, complete with realistic veins. They looked like butterfly wings when we put them in the sun.

Father Ortigão would come to the house, urging my mother to make her peace with the world.

Tia Ofélia would come to the house, urging me to melt on her lap in the slump of the grieving child.

My father once explained to me the solitude of the Portuguese: We would rather go out to sea alone in a small boat than fish together on a big one. The Mexicans and Italians in Castroville had a much better grasp on the strength behind the collective haul. We clamored instead after distance, *put your back to me and let us pace apart.* We bought land for power but mostly for isolation.

Solitude breeds two things: lust and a need to scour. One of my neighbors was sleeping with both the wife and daughter of a nearby farm, except on Sundays, when he undertook the impossible job of trying to clean a stable so thoroughly that it would never need cleaning again.

Father Armando Ortigão patted my mother's hand and assured her that it was completely within her power to care for me, if she would simply help him provide. "Even the dying can perform good works," he said.

Portuguese boasts succinct words for every nuance of ardor and purification.

Ansiar: to burn for, and to be a source of anxiety to. No one word in English so clearly states that love can be such a pestering, unattainable, unquenchable blind side as to instill fear in another's heart.

Esfregar, limpiar, arear: to scrub, to clean, to scour with sand. How many ways can solitary people restate the wish to tidy their lives? Eyes evolved in isolation see disorder in the smallest corners and tucks.

Despite so many dark and light words, there were none that covered how I longed for a restorative for my mother as I watched her skin sink. Nor could I think how to blot away my silence and the poison that swarmed in the room when Father Ortigão held up, as if in consecration, the deed to my dead father's land.

Before she died, my mother agreed that she should make her life a clean slate. While I stood by, Father Ortigão helped her sign the deed over to the Church. He promised it would slash her Purgatory time down to only the laundering away of original sin, a spate in the fire from which only martyrs were exempt. He wished he could do more, but some things, he told her with a smile, were beyond his grasp.

An oily feast marked my official ushering into the care of Tia Ofélia. She was an aging woman who would never dream of accepting money from a priest, even if the land on which he planned to build a winery had once belonged to my family, even if he had offered.

She was grateful that Father Ortigão had relieved her and me of trying to enter heaven with the weight of earthly property putting us down near the rich man who had denied his table leavings to Lazarus the beggar. The rich man had ended up in hell, screaming for a drop of water. That story always rang false in my ears. If the afterlife was all forgiveness and peace, why did Moses allow Lazarus, when safely in heaven, to deny the burning creature's request?

Father Ortigão had promised my mother that I would have food and a roof over my head, but he did not mention that Tia Ofélia and not the land would be my delivering angel.

Crabs and artichokes were served at my adoption banquet. Men cracked the briny shells and legs with mallets to get to the soft ocean taste. They pulled leaves off the artichokes, and cleared aside the choke to unearth the roots. Knives sliced through the vibrissae and the purple tissues that fluttered out from the hearts like butterflies. The table was heaped with discards. Father Ortigão would occasionally lift his head from his feasting, his face shining with grease.

I remembered a night when I stumbled across Almir Cruz in a field with Angela Figueira before his accident. He had peeled away the layers of clothing protecting her, snapped open her legs, and was about to dive for her tender flesh.

I ran away then from fear, and I ran from the table now because this time the violation was against me.

My dear Tia Ofélia died the same day as the groundbreaking for the new Transfiguration School gym. For a long time I slept ten hours a night, my arms around a pillow, but when the Castroville Christian Winery increased its admission to one dollar a person and charged the tour buses five to park, I donned a spotless white uniform and headed over to the rectory. Father Ortigão had grown silver-haired and much beloved by the parishioners. It was widely noted that even the money he had so generously given me after the sale of my parents' house, razed to clear a spot for wine cellar expansion, had failed to attract a man to me. Naturally I smiled at this kind of talk.

I persuaded him that with the turmoil surrounding the new buildings, he needed a housekeeper. With Tia Ofélia gone, I had no one left in the world. Didn't he remember how my mother had trusted him to take care of me?

To teach Father Ortigão to dive, I would toss a gold hoop into the shallows of the lake. In water I had license to put my arms around him, to hoist him up for air. I pressed my breasts against his back, my nose against his neck, and pulled. I could touch his shoulders and run my bare foot against his knees to relax him for the plunge.

Soon after the summer heat drove me from a one-piece to a two-piece suit, he declared our swimming lessons over. I scolded him for giving up before the deed was done. Now that he was getting set to build a Transfiguration pool, how would it look when everyone found out that he sank like a stone? What was he afraid of? Like every good priest, he was supposed to think of water as baptism, renewal, the beginning of a new life.

"You win, Miranda," he said.

When I forgot to bring a towel or change of clothes, I would undress back at the rectory while dripping into some of his long white shirts. I would stretch my bikini out to dry on the veranda.

Swimming gave him an appetite for charred meat, potatoes, mayonnaise, strawberry pies, rum, cabernet sauvignon. I poured him different wines with each meal, insisting that as driving force behind the Castroville Christian Winery he must sample what he had all along been giving to others.

I kept the rectory immaculate. One would not think a man alone could do so much damage, but I managed to find plenty to clean. I sponged spiders' nests out of corners, dusted light bulbs in their sockets, refilled the brandy decanter. When I aired out comforters and broke into a sweat, my blouse turned translucent in patches.

"Miranda," he said to me one day. "O my God, I can't get rid of you. Can I?"

I weakened for a moment, when I saw him as a man alone, grown thick around the middle, with liver spots on his scalp, when, with eschatological bent, I thought a brutish build should not condemn him as a brute. He blinked at dust in a light mote, and I considered that every single one of us is defenseless unto death. But not all of us dabble so freely with others defenseless *in* death, and I reminded myself that the so-called forgiving God had answered Adam's plea for mercy by forbidding automatic sanctifying grace to eons of generations after him.

When I discovered Father Ortigão working over the Castroville Christian Winery's annual tally, my nerves steeled. I pulled off my shirt and melted onto his lap in the slump of the aggrieved child.

During my affair with Father Armando Ortigão, he satisfied himself again and again, but my feelings were obviously not his concern. I preferred the arrogance of him imagining that what was making him burst was doing the same for me. I could not bend over with my scrub brush without him unleashing a torrent of frenzy from behind. He pushed my face into the couch or against a table so I could not gaze at his pent-up years coming undone. Whenever he pressed full length on me I wrapped my legs around him but even with the dig of my heels I did not exist in this embrace.

How Father Ortigão could toy with life without thinking of consequences will always astound me. *If* the entangled vines on my father's land are allowed to grow, *then* don't they yield wine? *If* all he can see is his own desire, *then* doesn't it take a baby to make him see me?

He accused me of being Eve with the apple.

I said that all I did was provide the black background against which he could shape his heart.

I had no intention of being bundled up under cover of night, the way the plagued are borne away, to wait for the Good Shepherd nuns to seize my child the second the crown split my legs and deliver it to a nice deserving couple. The home was hidden away in Napa, a place of too-visible secrets, where gospel readings and the rain drilled the bad girls clean. We would be handed buckets of pine water to keep our scandalous home pure.

Desperation made Father Ortigão shameless in his arguments about why I should commend myself to the nuns.

I told him I had commended myself to him instead. I also told half of Castroville, although one parishioner would have been sufficient for everyone, down to the workmen in the damp, musty Christian cellar, to know within moments that acts of love and grace can be actual, if not always sanctifying.

Some nights now I look around my house, at my husband slumbering in his chair after a hard day at the dairy, and it is hard to muster quarrel with life. Old-fashioned Christmas ornaments, an avocado seed sprouting near a window, silk from the valley's corn stuck like cat hair on the furniture—merely seeing these things can trigger contentment. What I do not have is the love of my daughter, who is traveling through America with a man I have warned her is nothing but trouble. When we do speak, it is because she gets me on the phone instead of Darryl, who feels that her demands for money and her cries from the bottom of a glass are the burden of being a priest's child.

Darryl is a good and forgiving man, or he most certainly would not have taken up my cause when shame drove Father Ortigão from Castroville and my plan to reclaim my father's land backfired. The Bishop laughed at my demand, in fact, but agreed that I was entitled to a small, one-time amount to make certain that the innocent child was not punished for the sins of its parents and its Church. I told myself that although I had not won back my legacy, I had rid myself of the perpetrator of the original sin against it.

Whenever I see my daughter's photo on the mantel I know that I am a fool. I have won nothing—aside from the man who became my rescuer from hateful stares—other than the warning that answering evil with evil ensures that it stays in the blood.

In my aloneness when Darryl falls asleep, I wonder why the only person I have brought to life is so far from my reach. The burning in me will not wash clean. I slip ice onto my tongue and into my clothes to fight the valley heat, but even many drops of water bring me no relief.

Helena Maria Viramontes

The Jumping Bean

1

HE COCKED HIS fisherman's face, seared and rumpled and buoyant in the sea of glass, combed the Tres Roses pomade onto his hair jamming three fingers to make a slick, shimmering wave. From where she stood, the gold-plated crucifix which anchored his neck sparkled in the mirror until he buried it beneath his shirt buttons. The young girl thought her papa pretty in his oversized salt-and-pepper suit jacket, the triangular lapels so wide they peaked to his padded shoulders.

He had no reason to see her. She was just one of the many children he labored for, carrying wet cement and grit on the bridge of his back. The others, the gringo plasterers, called him the jumping bean, he thought, not for his pencil-thin mustache or Spanish surname, but because of his ability to scale a ladder towing more than his weight in cement with the speed of a man half his age, as circles of salty sweat rung like the age of a tree on his work shirt. Even as the wooden poke of the hod stabbed against his belly like the spiked heat of midday, he had never thought to quit this work. Even when the thorny whiskey could no longer drown the sound of his own bones aching, he would never abandon his children. He reminded her mother constantly of his contributions and all of them were made to feel indebted to his relentless back and the two hands he rinsed with vinegar daily to relieve the burn of the abrasive, gray grit powder. He was a finch of a man, a sparrow of nerves, his fingers like swollen live wires too dangerous to touch.

He spotted her reflection and his smile made her feel as though it were permissible to approach him. He turned to her, and fished his hand into the deep pit pocket of his ironed trousers, jiggled loose change, reeled out a white coin. His head came forward to hers, his nose wide and flat from a boxer's punch, his eyes black as burnt stone, against an unfamiliar face. He handed her the coin, and she stared at the disc, licked off the cement dust to discern that it was a buffalo nickel. She brushed his cheek with her lips, then disappeared into the kitchen voices of her family while he disappeared, the flask of Wild Turkey clinking against his house key.

2

She was the only one with patience to do it, lull her mother back to sleep with long brush strokes. So when her oldest sister, Maria de la luz, woke her with "Mama's not sleeping again," the young girl dragged her heavy feet to where mama sat. The young girl's heart bucked wildly when she saw the prayer cards filed in a parade of saints on the kitchen table, as if readied by her mama for the pot banging miracles that never came.

"Don't be afraid," Maria de la luz whispered and handed her an Avon brush. But the young girl was still. Mama had the look of cold sin in her eyes. Maria gently rubbed the heated olive oil with concentrated effort on Mama's temples to ease and loosen the tumor of disappointment, and motioned for her to come. After a while, Maria bent to thaw Mama's feet in warm, clear water while her own knees itched from the cool floor.

"It's okay," Maria said. She cupped water over Mama's left foot gently, the trickling pebbles of water drops the only sound in the room. "Go on now. Brush her hair."

The young girl approached them. The fall of Mama's long hair reassured her, and she began unraveling the hemplike braid. The white dandruff flakes drifted silently to the bones of Mama's shoulders as she brushed. Brushed. She leaned on one foot then the other to keep herself awake, brushed, but dreamed anyway; dreamed of snowcap mountains, brown saintly faces that tumbled away like dead leaves in a rising wind.

A grayish phosphorescent stream flowing from the window was enough for the young girl to decipher a slithering form. She brushed faster. She waited for Maria to say something about the long, white snake which S'ed its way under the table, its forked tongue savoring the cool autumn air, but Maria talked to her mama instead.

"You do what you have to do to live," said Maria when Mama broke like the morning light, broke into sobs because she'd kept her daughters up half the night. "That's what you taught us." Mama cried passionately, never realizing there was so much grief inside her.

"You're tired, Mama, is all." Maria replied, too tired herself to speculate on the demons Mama was battling. She caught water in a pot, turned the faucet off, put it on the flames to boil.

The snake slipped under the murky gray morning like wet soap until the young girl felt the slithering tube slide over her bare feet, and the chilling sensation prompted her to drum her toes on the worn floor. She wanted to speak, but was silenced by the snake which spiraled itself around her ankles and tightened its grasp. She held her breath, felt her body swell with terror. She tried in vain to interrupt the exchange between the two women, but they had no reason to see her.

"You're not going crazy." Maria warned her mama, while she stirred the last of the Quaker Oats into the boiling water. The snake had disappeared. It was the first day of school, and the children would be hungry.

3

The foreman, the junior of the company, liked Papa. He felt this Spanish man had heart. But the plasterers, welders, bulldozer drivers resented his centaur ability to endure the work, creating a standard they would inevitably be compared to. In turn, they created their own standards and exiled him to exist only in their peripheral vision.

He worked in their oblivion. They denied the sweat that bled like torrents over his eyes when he claimed the scaffolds with one hundred and sixty pounds of cement on his back, balancing himself on the thin planks, two stories, three stories high. They never imagined his rebelling bones collapsing like noisy spoons at the end of the day, where he lay on their living room floor, his arms and legs spread wide, the children tiptoeing around him; or the midnight whiskey that made him resentful and violent to those who tiptoed too loudly. They never imagined that his was a body too, made of flesh and bone and bleeding blood and had hit the canvas hard years ago. It was only from the monumental fear of going hungry that he rallied his strength, raised and buckled his knees, cast himself into the swelling heat, to draw or pull up what was necessary to yield another meal. He feared many things, but work was not one of them.

Papa sat on his haunches, outside the lopsided circle of workers, and chewed on a sandwich he insisted be made with Wonder Bread, sipped lukewarm coffee from his plastic thermos cup. He watched the men laugh, offer cigarettes, crumble wax paper into a ball, and discard it without a care. One of the plasterers, a decent man who always said God willing, stood away from the circle while he chewed a toothpick. Theodore, the bulldozer driver he knew by name, poked his ear.

"Hey Zorro! You don't like us or what?" Papa knew that some people hated more easily than others for reasons which were as thin as balloons and just as empty. He knew because he was one of these. He was beginning to hate Theodore.

"Do we smell or what?" One man chuckled at Theodore's comments. "Come on. I gotta question to ask you." Papa straightened up, carried his lunch box and coffee cup, joined the circle. Theodore smiled. He lifted one toe steel boot on the step of the bulldozer, looked down at Papa.

"I gotta question for you." Theodore leaned on his raised knee and pointed a finger at Papa. "What's the difference between a spic and a drunk?"

The man with the toothpick removed it from between his teeth to speak: "You're a real asshole, Theo."

"Can't take a joke, Ray?"

"You're gonna get your ass kicked some day. God willing." Like a line traced on the dirt, Papa understood the words to mean a challenge of some sort between the two men though spoken too quickly for him to understand them all. The decent man bit on his toothpick again, kicked gravel with his mustard colored construction boots. The gravel twisted beneath his boots when he walked away.

Someone sneezed loudly, another pinched pebbles in the center of the circle.

"Got any clues, Zorro?"

Papa shook his head No.

"The difference is a drunk will sober up, but a spic will always be a spic, ain't that right Zorro?" A few plasterers laughed. Papa watched the men with their mouths open in big round O's. Theodore slapped Papa on his back causing him to spill his coffee. Others sat silently, smoking cigarettes, downcast eyes inspecting their cement caked boots.

Papa missed the solitude of the sea and he felt no shame being insignificant against its immensity. There, without the pounding of jackhammers, pieces of sun glittered on the water. There, adrift, he would cast the net, feel the challenge of resistance in his hands whenever he pulled in the reigns of his livelihood. He did not understand what Theodore was saying. He would memorize the question, repeat it to Maria de la luz, have her explain it to him. And yet, the urge to quash Theodore was overwhelming.

Papa turned to view the men clustered on the corner of Sixth and Central in downtown L.A., men like himself, scanning the oncoming traffic in hopes of some signal that would promise a day's work, a chance to prove their worth, to carry tools, work with iron, shovel cement, any chance, any work. The urge was overwhelming, but he forced a smile anyway. The foreman stepped out of his trailer to see what the commotion was about.

Papa screwed the cup of his thermos in place, put his thermos in his lunch box, and forced himself up from his haunches.

"A real company man," a plasterer said, no longer laughing, watching Papa who began work before the others. Not waiting for the cement truck, Papa scooped three shovels full of gravel into a wheelbarrow, scooped three shovels full of sand, one shovel of cement, the powder bathing him and he held his breath, shut his eyes until the dust settled. He pushed the barrow to a metal trough and poured the dusty mixture in. He ran the water hose to the trough, turned it on, took a handful and splashed it on his neck, his face, to remove the residue before it began burning his skin. Once filled with enough water, Papa began kneading the cement with a long poked hoe and his resistant muscles pulled forth the hoe, scraping the bottom of the trough, folding and sloshing the mix then pushing, again scraping, pulled pushed, fold, pull push fold the cement into thickening grit.

"Don't he know he's cutting in on our lunch hour?" asked the truck driver.

"Who the hell does Zorro think he is?"

"His spic," Theodore replied, gesturing to the foreman, who stood on the trailer steps and exaggeratedly pointed to his watch. The plasterers watched the foreman put his arms akimbo in mock impatience. Theodore spit to one side as the foreman approached them angrily when no one moved from the circle.

4

Maria de la luz knew nine was an unlucky number. It was the number of pills prescribed to her mama and it was the number of cigarettes her mama smoked a day. It was the number of mouths which had to be fed, the number of towels, calzones, socks, shirts, shorts, blouses that were washed on Thursday hung out to dry on Friday, ironed on Saturday, worn on Sunday. And it was the number of nights that Maria didn't sleep because she waited up for her brothers or the children caught colds and ran fevers and coughed and had nightmares.

On the ninth week of Mama's illness, the truant officer arrived. His appearance edged the neighborhood dogs into junk yard madness, yapping and growling and throwing themselves against the chain-link fences. From behind the curtains, peeking between the laths of venetian blinds, the neighbors stared at the officer who stumbled his way into a maze of clean laundry hung on slack wire lines, asked themselves about this official looking gringo with a clipboard whose shirt buttons strained to dam back a flooding belly. The officer loosened his red tie, looked behind him suspiciously, knocked again on the screen door, and the young girl with a runny nose hid behind Maria de la luz. The officer addressed her as "Mrs." and asked why her daughter, "Mar ee a Loose" (he said the name so that it sounded real crooked to the young girl's ears), had been truant nine weeks from school.

"My mother's real sick," she told the officer. She held a broom and he wrote something on his clipboard. The young girl didn't like all this writing he was doing and she put her fingers in her mouth.

"Stop biting your nails," Maria reprimanded, turning around to see the young girl behind her.

The truant officer signed. "Is this the kinda life you wanna have, huh? Washing clothes, shoveling dog turd? You need to be learning," and he tore off a sheet and handed it to her.

Maria returned the incredulous stare. Didn't he understand what she said? Her mama was sick. The young girl wiped her nose with the sleeve of her sweater.

"You'll end up like some old lady in the shoe."

"Fuck off," she told the officer (which also sounded crooked to the young girl's ears) and Maria slammed the door edging in another wave of crazy dog frenzy. The sheet of paper with writing fell to the floor. A few moments passed, and the girl looked up at Maria who stared at the closed door. Finally, Maria palmed her loose hair back, placed the broom behind the door and went to another room. The dogs settled down to their mid-noon nap. The girl found Maria in the only room in the house with a lock. The girl touched the knob and with a certain warmth in the palm of her hand, was able to unlock the door. She poked her head in to see Maria with an open book, sitting on the lid of the toilet. Maria looked up, marked a page with her finger, then closed the book.

"Let me be. I need to figure this out," she told the young girl. Maria was sure she had locked the door, but knew too the young girl had a knack for doing things like this. Since her sister didn't move, Maria tried to ignore her, opened the book and began underlining a sentence with her finger until she noticed the girl approaching. "Let me be, goddamnit!" And with that, the young girl fled.

The young girl went into the kitchen, her fingers in her mouth, passed her mama who sat silently at the table, flipping a stack of playing cards in a game of solitaire, cigarette smoke in a corkscrew above her head. The smoke made the young girl sneeze, and she went outside and sat on the porch, watched the hanging sheets snapping senselessly like sails on a shipwreck.

5

It was her papa's words addressing Maria. The words came into the bedroom in the form of a white moth, wingspan of her hands and landed on the wall, its wings spreading and rising in slow medita-tion. The young girl watched. She lay between two sisters; one sis-ter threw her arm over her chest, the other a hefty leg, and she felt smothered like a fly caught in a cobweb of limbs.

Maria drudged through the fragile thin ice of morning, stum-bled over beds and blankets, settled her bones on a roll-away cot next to their bed. Her arm fell to the side, limp, like a dead animal. Outside, the lamppost shone a foggy yellow glow. The white moth fluttered to the window and banged itself against the glass endless-ly with dull and scratchy thuds.

The young girl had heard the words from the other side of the door. Mama wasn't well enough to come home from the hospital for Christmas.

The girl tried to levitate her body to open the window but was firmly vised between her sisters. She whispered Maria's name, saw the name mist linger in front of her, then slowly evaporate. She began to see small streamers like molten silver, streak gently down-ward on the window glass. The moth stood silent, its wings rising and spreading, waiting for her.

Icicles fell like Christmas tinsel from the ceiling. No one would believe that the window and the ceiling bled tears. Her sis-ters slept soundly and every once in a while one of them would grind her teeth or pass gas. But the girl was the daughter of her mother, and she rose to the occasion until her body banged against the glass, felt the chill against her cheek. She strained to break the window, but felt her arm pulled away, felt weak against the gravita-tional force, filled her lungs to release.

Maria opened the window to a blast of cold wind. The moth fluttered out. She slammed the window down.

The young girl cried. If only she had the capacity to walk barefoot on broken and jagged words like Maria, then she wouldn't have to release the words, and she could smash them into a thou-sand pieces of glass, just like she wanted to smash the window. But Maria pulled her close to her, sealed her mouth, hushed her for nothing was worth this much unbroken silence.

6

One of the trucks sped by loaded with the last of the scaffolds, leaving dust behind, grinding gravel beneath its tires. The welders worked above him, sparks raining to the sides of them, reinforcing the window sealants. Papa looked up at the building while standing on the top step of the foreman's trailer, admired the erect and shiny structure in all its newness, felt a certain pride, then felt ashamed of that pride. He wiped his boots before entering the trailer. It was unusually hot for a spring day. The foreman swung his chair back, and without standing up handed him a check, talked in a tight stitched sentence over the buzzing of the air conditioner.

"I do weekend jobs, nothing big, a little extra cash on the side, maybe you can work for me then."

Papa nodded, stared at the check. He studied his name in block typed print, felt the texture of official paper, stared at the amount engraved above his name. He studied the amount as the foreman talked, translated the amount to a down payment on the pickup he had set his eyes on a few months before. The used truck was in good working condition. The fact that it had a new shiny spare chained to the back made him content. He folded the check neatly so as not to smudge the name or amount, placed it in his billfold, asked in crooked English if he should leave now or hang around until his shift was over; wondered what to do next. He offered his hand to the foreman who shook it with a hardy grip.

Outside the sun blazed, making the smoky air stick to his lungs. Spring was here too soon. If he couldn't find work by summer, they would have to move to where the migrant work was guaranteed: tomatoes in Indiana, asparagus in Illinois, strawberries in Michigan. But until then, he planned to hammer and chisel the cemented walkway near the laundry lines, make room to plant nopal, verdulagas, chayotes. Of course, things would get better. He was a good worker, one of the best, not afraid to use his back. His lemon tree did not yield this year, but the pomegranates cracked with beet red juice. Things would get better.

He lifted his lunch box, but when he opened it, he discovered a crinkled bag stuffed to the side of the thermos. On the palm of his hand he shook out the contents, held a handful of jumping beans, watched the half-moon beans itch and shake in the heat of the sun.

He remembered repeating the question to Maria about the spic and the drunk, asked that she explain it to him. She said that he worked with a bunch of assholes, and he slapped her for saying a bad word, and she pushed him aside to get out of the house, holding her hand on her mouth. The children cried, judged him with accusatory eyes and he began yelling at them all, calling them beggars and leeches and told them to hide or he would kill them all and they scattered, the young girl hiding under the bed where he found her hours later, fast asleep.

It made him wonder about his wife who believed demons possessed her, about his sons who stayed out half the night, the children who scattered in fear, and his beautiful daughter Maria whom he had slapped with all his might, made him wonder if he was the one being possessed by the questions he did not understand.

He decided against throwing the beans out, returned the contents to the bag. The beans would be a reconciliatory offer to his children and the thought made him content. He walked home to save the bus fare, the beans quiet in his lunch box.

By midafternoon he entered their small walkway which led to their backyard. He called the children and the neighbor's children over. They rushed and circled around him, craning their necks to see what Papa held in the brown paper sack. He poured the contents on the porch where a strong beam of sun spotlighted the tranquil beans. The children watched, unimpressed by the beans which stood as still as stones. Suddenly, like popcorn bursting, the beans began to twist, tremble, finally jump, and the children laughed in utter astonishment. "Is it magic?" one of the children asked, and the young girl turned to Papa for an answer.

Maria de la luz opened the screen door to look down at the heads watching the beans jumping. "How do the beans jump?" another asked Maria, for Papa never gave answers. Curious, Maria picked one up and bit it open against Papa's protest. Inside the cracked opening, a small white caterpillar unfolded its larva body.

"Leave it alone," Papa ordered, but Maria immediately bit open another and another.

"They're trapped. They wanna get out." The children grimaced, contorted their faces from nausea as they watched Maria crack the hard bean between her teeth with delicate force.

"Leave it alone," Papa said in a voice the children were afraid of.

"They're gonna die." First the children looked at Maria cracking the beans, then turned to look at Papa whose voice was turning louder. The young girl panicked, put her fingers to her mouth.

Papa's temper rose like his nostrils. As of today, he was unemployed, had a sick wife, now couldn't even win over his children's forgiveness without being accused of something. He raised his hand at her insubordination, but before he could strike her, before the children began their screaming and crying again, she caught his raised hand in mid-motion, and it stunned him, this betrayal of her nature. Maria had managed to let free all but one caterpillar. She grasped Papa's hand, the one with the blue thumbnail, laid his hand open. Her eyes melted with red anger. She pressed the single bean in the palm of his hand, steadied her trembling voice.

"Go ahead," she said, a tear streaming down her cheek, "if it means that much to you."

Go ahead and what? he thought. What was he supposed to do? He had to make her an example for the rest of the children. If he let the caterpillar go, she would certainly feel she had won, which would be only the beginning of her rebellion. If he killed the caterpillar, let it bang itself inside the brown bean, something else would die as well. He just couldn't figure out what. The children stared at his every move and he stared at the single bean.

The young girl shoved her way closer to her papa. She looked up at Maria de la luz, her nose running, looked at Papa, small and twitching and frightened, looked up at the blank door frame where her mama should be standing right now and putting a stop to all of this madness. Without thinking, the young girl removed the fingers from her mouth, swept the bean from the palm of her papa's hand.

For once, everyone's attention shifted to the young girl. Her brown eyes wide, a dimple forming. She put the bean in her mouth and swallowed it.

7

The day her mother returned from the hospital, was the day the young girl tasted the sweetest, reddest, juiciest watermelon she had ever had. Mama looked pale, her cheeks fallen and waxen, her nose red as if she suffered a cold. She looked nervously about at her brood of children, but smiled just the same. The children, the smaller ones like the young girl, stiffened up, shoulders back, mouths quiet except for a whispering question, here or there. For them it was such an unnatural position that even Maria de la luz and Papa felt their bones contort. Mama decided it was best that she sleep first, then get up and make some arroz con pollo, fresh tortillas. The children clapped and laughed and were relieved, for they were tired of Maria's Hamburger Heaven, Beto even calling it Hamburger Hell. They felt the rigid air ease when Mama left the room, felt the lazy heat make their eyes drowsy.

They had packed the clothes and belongings in boxes and piled them like a pyramid in the walkway, ready to load them up in the pickup come tomorrow. Today, Maria plugged an extension cord and dragged her prized GE radio outside and tuned it to her favorite oldies station, sat cross-legged on the little patch of grass, her dress over her knees. Papa changed from his salt-and-pepper suit to a paper-thin speckled shirt which he didn't button, and which flapped open from a slight summer breeze.

Spreading some newspapers on the porch, he placed the green watermelon, green as the brine of the Belvedere Park lake, on top and then he plunged the knife in, the watermelon cracking like thunderbolts into two halves, the juice bleeding droplets on the newspaper. He carefully removed the seedless center of the melon and put it on a plate for Mama who always got the heart. After that,

Papa sliced and gave, sliced and gave, and the young girl took two boat pieces, handed one to Maria and sat, cross-legged next to her.

The young girl bit into the red flesh of the watermelon slice and the flavor burst like confetti on her tongue. The juice dripping from the sides of her mouth tickled, and she wiped her face clean with Maria's dress. Maria stopped spitting out the black seeds using her ducking brother as a target, stopped spitting to scold her. She scolded the young girl with such a funny face, calling her a silly goose, you silly little goose, the young girl laughed so hard, felt something inside of her growing so red, she couldn't help but feel like something as sweet and full of confetti was in the making.

Sherley Anne Williams

Tell Martha Not to Moan

MY MAMMA A BIG woman, tall and stout and men like her cause she soft and fluffy looking. When she round them it all smiles and dimples and her mouth be looking like it couldn't never be fixed to say nothing but darling and honey.

They see her now, they sho see something different. I should not even come today. Since I had Larry things ain't been too good between us. But—that's my mamma and I know she gon be there when I need her. And sometime when I come, it okay. But this ain't gon be one a them times. Her eyes looking all ove me and I know it coming. She snort cause she want to say god damn but she don't cuss. "When it due, Martha?"

First I start to say, what. But I know it ain't no use. You can't fool old folks bout something like that, so I tell her.

"Last part of November."

"Who the daddy?"

"Time."

"That man what play piano at the Legion?"

"Yeah."

"What he gon do bout it?"

"Mamma, it ain't too much he can do, now is it? The baby on its way."

She don't say nothing for a long time. She sit looking at her hands. They all wet from where she been washing dishes and they

317

all wrinkled like yo hand be when they been in water too long. She get up and get a dish cloth and dry em, then sit down at the table. "Where he at now?"

"Gone."

"Gone? Gone where?" I don't say nothing and she start cussing then. I get kinda scared cause mamma got to be real mad foe she cuss and I don't know who she cussing—me or Time. Then she start talking to me. "Martha, you just a fool. I told you that man wan't no good first time I seed him. A musician the worst kind of man you can get mixed up with. Look at you. You ain't even eighteen years old yet, Larry just barely two and here you is pregnant again." She go on like that for a while and I don't say nothing. Couldn't no way. By the time I get my mouth fixed to say something, she done raced on so far ahead that what I got to say don't have nothing to do with what she saying right then. Finally she stop and ask, "What you gon do now? You want to come back here?" She ain't never liked me living with Orine and when I say no, she ask, "Why not? It be easier for you."

I shake my head again. "If I here, Time won't know where to find me, and Time coming; he be back. He gon to make a place for us, you a see."

"Hump, you just played the fool again, Martha."

"No mamma, that not it at all; Time want me."

"Is that what he say when he left?"

"No, but...."

Well, like the first night we met, he come over to me like he knowed me for a long time and like I been his for awmost that long. Yeah, I think that how it was. Cause I didn' even see him when we come in the Legion that first night.

Me and Orine, we just got our checks that day. We went downtown and Orine bought her some new dresses. But the dress she want to wear that night don't look right so we go racing back to town and change it. Then we had to hurry home and get dressed. It Friday night and the Legion crowded. You got to get there early on the weekend if you want a seat. And Orine don't want just any seat; she want one right up front. "Who gon see you way back there? Nobody. They can't see you, who gon ask you to dance? Nobody. You don't dance, how you gon meet people? You don't meet people, what you doing out?" So we sit up front. Whole lots a people there that night. You can't even see the bandstand cross the dance floor. We sharing the table with some more people and Orine keep jabbing me, telling me to sit cool. And I try cause Orine say it a good thing to be cool.

The set end and people start leaving the dance floor. That when I see Time. He just getting up from the piano. I like him right off cause I like men what look like him. He kind of tall and slim. First time I ever seed a man wear his hair so long and it nappy—he tell me once it an African Bush—but he look good anyway and he know it. He look round all cool. He step down from the bandstand and start walking toward me. He come over to the table and just look. "You," he say, "you my Black queen." And he bow down most to the floor.

Ah shit! I mad cause I think he just trying to run a game. "What you trying to prove, fool?" I ask him.

"Ah man," he say and it like I cut him. That the way he say it. "Ah man. I call this woman my Black queen—tell her she can rule my life and she call me a fool."

"And sides what, nigga," I tell him then, "I ain't black." And I ain't, I don't care what Time say. I just a dark woman.

"What's the matter, you shamed of being Black? Ain't nobody told you Black is pretty?" He talk all loud and people start gathering round. Somebody say, "Yeah, you tell her bout it, soul." I embarrassed and I look over at Orine. But she just grinning, not saying nothing. I guess she waiting to see what I gon do so I stand up.

"Well if I is black, I is a fine black." And I walk over to the bar. I walk just like I don't know they watching my ass, an I hold my head up. Time follow me right on over to the bar and put his arm round my shoulder.

"You want a drink?" I start to say no cause I scared. Man not supposed to make you feel like he make me feel. Not just like doing it—but, oh, like it right for him to be there with me, touching me. So I say yes. "What's your name?" he ask then.

I smile and say, "They call me the player." Orine told a man that once in Berkeley and he didn't know what to say. Orine a smart woman.

"Well they call me Time and I know yo mamma done told you Time ain't nothing to play with." His smile cooler than mine. We don't say nothing for a long while. He just stand there with his arm round my shoulder looking at us in the mirror behind the bar. Finally he say, "Yeah, you gon be my Black queen." And he look down at me and laugh. I don't know what to do, don't know what to say neither, so I just smile.

"You gon tell me your name or not?"

"Martha."

He laugh. "That a good name for you."

"My mamma name me that so I be good. She name all us kids from the Bible," I tell him laughing.

"And is you good?"

I nod yes and no all at the same time and kind of mumble cause I don't know what to say. Mamma really did name all us kids from the Bible. She always saying, "My mamma name me Veronica after the woman in the Bible and I a better woman for it. That why I name all my kids from the Bible. They got something to look up to." But mamma don't think I'm good, specially since I got Larry. Maybe Time ain't gon think I good neither. So I don't answer, just smile and move on back to the table. I hear him singing soft-like, "Oh Mary don't you weep, tell yo sister Martha not to moan." And I kind of glad cause most people don't even think bout that when I tell em my name. That make me know he really smart.

We went out for breakfast after the Legion close. Him and me and Orine and German, the drummer. Only places open is on the other side of town and at first Time don't want to go. But we finally swade him.

Time got funny eyes, you can't hardly see into em. You look and you look and you can't tell nothing from em. It make me feel funny when he look at me. I finally get used to it, but that night he just sit there looking and don't say nothing for a long time after we order.

"So you don't like Black?" he finally say.

"Do you?" I ask. I think I just ask him questions, then I don't have to talk so much. But I don't want him to talk bout that right then, so I smile and say, "Let's talk bout you."

"I am not what I am." He smiling and I smile back, but I feel funny cause I think I supposed to know what he mean.

"What kind of game you trying to run?" Orine ask. Then she laugh. "Just cause we from the country don't mean we ain't hip to niggas trying to be big-time. Ain't that right, Martha?"

I don't know what to say, but I know Time don't like that. I think he was going to cuss Orine out, but German put his arm round Orine and he laugh. "He just mean he ain't what he want to be. Don't pay no mind to that cat. He always trying to blow some shit." And he start talking that talk, rapping to Orine.

I look at Time. "That what you mean?"

He all lounged back in the seat, his legs stretched way out under the table. He pour salt in a napkin and mix it up with his finger.

"Yeah, that's what I mean. That's all about me. Black is pretty, Martha." He touch my face with one finger. "You let white people make you believe you ugly. I bet you don't even dream."

"I do too."

"What you dream?"

"Huh?" I don't know what he talking bout. I kind of smile and look at him out the corner of my eye. "I dreams bout a man like you. Why, just last night, I dream—"

He start laughing. "That's all right. That's all right."

The food come then and we all start eating. Time act like he forgot all bout dreams. I never figure out how he think I can just sit there and tell him the dreams I have at night, just like that. It don't seem like what I dream bout at night mean as much as what I think bout during the day.

We leaving when Time trip over this white man's feet. That man's feet all out in the aisle but Time don't never be watching where he going no way. "Excuse me," he say kind of mean.

"Say, watch it buddy." That white man talk most as nasty as Time. He kind of old and maybe he drunk or an Okie.

"Man, I said excuse me. You the one got your feet in the aisle."

"You," that man say, starting to get up, "you better watch yourself, boy."

And what he want to say that for? Time step back and say real quiet, "No, motherfucker. You the one. You better watch yourself and your daughter too. See how many babies she gon have by boys like me." That man get all red in the face, but the woman in the booth with him finally start pulling at him, telling him to sit down, shut up. Cause Time set to kill that man.

I touch Time's arm first, then put my arm round his waist. "Ain't no use getting messed behind somebody like that."

Time and that man just looking at each other, not wanting to back down. People was gon start wondering what going on in a few minutes. I tell him, "'Got something for you, baby,'" and he look down at me and grin. Orine pick it up. We go out that place singing, "'Good loving, good, good loving, make you feel so clean.'"

"You like to hear me play?" he ask when we in the car.

"This the first time they ever have anybody here that sound that good."

"Yeah," Orine say. "How come you all staying round in a little jive-ass town like Ashley?"

"We going to New York pretty soon," Time say kind of snappy.

"Well, shit, baby, you—"

"When you going to New York?" I ask real quick. When Orine in a bad mood, can't nobody say nothing right.

"Couple of months." He lean back and put his arm round me. "They doing so many things with music back there. Up in the City, they doing one maybe two things. In L.A. they doing another one, two things. But, man, in New York, they doing everything. Person couldn't never get stuck in one groove there. So many things going on, you got to be hip, real hip to keep up. You always growing there. Shit, if you 'live and playing, you can't help but grow. Say, man," he reach and tap German on the shoulder, "let's leave right now."

We all crack up. Then I say, "I sorry but I can't go, got to take care of my baby."

He laugh, "Sugar, you got yo baby right here."

"Well, I must got two babies then."

We pull up in front of the partment house then but don't no one move. Finally Time reach over and touch my hair. "You gon be my Black queen?"

I look straight ahead at the night. "Yeah," I say. "Yeah."

We go in and I check first on Larry cause sometimes that girl don't watch him good. When I come in some nights, he be all out the cover and shivering but too sleepy to get back under em. Time come in when I'm pulling the cover up on Orine two kids.

"Which one yours," he ask.

I go over to Larry bed. "This my baby," I tell him.

"What's his name?"

"Larry."

"Oh, I suppose you name him after his daddy?"

I don't like the way he say that, like I was wrong to name him after his daddy. "Who else I gon name him after?" He don't say nothing and I leave him standing there. I mad now and I go in the bedroom and start pullin off my clothes. I think, that nigga can stand up in the living room all night, for all I care; let Orine talk to German and him, too. But Time come in the bedroom and put his arms round me. He touch his hair and my face and my tittie, and it scare me. I try to pull away but he hold me too close. "Martha," he say, "Black Martha." Then he just stand there holding me, not saying nothing, with his hand covering one side of my face. I stand there trembling but he don't notice. I know a woman not supposed to feel the way I feel bout Time, not right away. But I do.

He tell me things nobody ever say to me before. And I want to tell him that I ain't never liked no man much as I like him. But sometime you tell a man that and he go cause he think you liking him a whole lot gon hang him up.

"You and me," he say after we in bed, "we can make it together real good." He laugh. "I used to think all I needed was that music, but it take a woman to make that music sing, I think. So now stead of the music and me, it be the music and me and you."

"You left out Larry," I tell I him. I don't think he want to hear that. But Larry my baby.

"How come you couldn't be free," he say real low. Then, "How you going when I go if you got a baby?"

"When you going?"

He turn his back to me. "Oh. I don't know. You know what the song say, 'When a woman take the blues, She tuck her head and cry. But when a man catch the blues, He grab his shoes and slide.' Next time I get the blues," he laugh a little, "next time the man get too much for me, I leave here and go someplace else. He always chasing me. The god damn white man." He turn over and reach for me. "You feel good. He chasing me and I chasing dreams. You think I'm crazy, huh? But I'm not. I just got so many, many things going on inside me I don't know which one to let out first. They all want out so bad. When I play—I got to be better, Martha. You gon help me?"

"Yes, Time, I help you."

"You see," and he reach over and turn on the light and look down at me, "I'm not what I am. I up tight on the inside but I can't get it to show on the outside. I don't know how to make it come out. You ever hear Coltrane blow? That man is together. He showing on the outside what he got on the inside. When I can do that, then I be somewhere. But I can't go by myself. I need a woman. A Black woman. Them other women steal your soul and don't leave nothing. But a Black woman—" He laugh and pull me close. He want me and that all I care about.

Mamma come over that next morning and come right on in the bedroom, just like she always do. I kind of shamed for her to see me like that, with a man and all, but she don't say nothing cept scuse me, then turn away. "I come to get Larry."

"He in the other bedroom," I say starting to get up.

"That's okay; I get him." And she go out and close the door. I start to get out the bed anyway. Time reach for his cigarettes and light one. "Your mamma don't believe in knocking, do she?"

I start to tell him not to talk so loud cause mamma a hear him, but that might make him mad. "Well, it ain't usually nobody in here with me for her to walk in on." I standing by the bed buttoning my house coat and Time reach out and pull my arm, smiling.

"I know you ain't no tramp, Martha. Come on, get back in bed."

I pull my arm way and start out the door. "I got to get Larry's clothes together," I tell him. I do got to get them clothes together cause when mamma come for Larry like that on Sadday morning, she want to keep him for the rest of the weekend. But—I don't know. It just don't seem right for me to be in the bed with a man and my mamma in the next room.

I think Orine and German still in the other bedroom. But I don't know; Orine don't too much like for her mens to stay all night. She say it make a bad impression on her kids. I glad the door close anyway. If mamma gon start talking that "why don't you come home" talk the way she usually do, it best for Orine not to hear it.

Orine's two kids still sleep but mamma got Larry on his bed tickling him and playing with him. He like that. "Boy, you sho happy for it to be so early in the morning," I tell him.

Mamma stop tickling him and he lay there breathing hard for a minute. "Big mamma," he say laughing and pointing at her. I just laugh at him and go get his clothes.

"You gon marry this one?" Every man I been with since I had Larry, she ask that about.

"You think marrying gon save my soul, Mamma?" I sorry right away cause mamma don't like me to make fun of God. But I swear I gets tired of all that. What I want to marry for anyway? Get somebody like daddy always coming and going and every time he go leave a baby behind. Or get a man what stay round and beat me all the time and have my kids thinking they big shit just cause they got a daddy what stay with them, like them saddity kids at school. Shit, married or single they still doing the same thing when they goes to bed.

Mamma don't say nothing else bout it. She ask where he work. I tell her and then take Larry in the bathroom and wash him up.

"The older you get, the more foolish you get, Martha. Them musicians ain't got nothing for a woman. Lots sweet talk and babies, that's all. Welfare don't even want to give you nothing for the one you got now, how you gon—" I sorry but I just stop listening. Mamma run her mouth like a clatterbone on a goose ass sometime. I just go on and give her the baby and get the rest of his things ready.

"So your mamma don't like musicians, huh?" Time say when I get back in the bedroom. "Square-ass people. Everything they don't know about, they hate. Lord deliver me from a square-ass town with square-ass people." He turn over.

"You wasn't calling me square last night."

"I'm not calling you square now, Martha."

I get back in the bed then and he put his arm round me. "But they say what they want to say. Long as they don't mess with me things be okay. But that's impossible. Somebody always got to have their little say about your life. They want to tell you where to go. how to play, what to play, where to play it—shit, even who to fuck and how to fuck em. But when I get to New York—"

"Time. Let's don't talk now."

He laugh then, "Martha, you so Black." I don't know what I should say so I don't say nothing, just get closer and we don't talk.

That how it is lots a time with me and him. It seem like all I got is lots little pitchers in my mind and can't tell nobody what they look like. Once I try to tell him bout that, bout the pitchers, and he just laugh. "Least your head ain't empty. Maybe now you got some pictures, you get some thoughts." That make me mad and I start cussing, but he laugh and kiss me and hold me. And that time, when we doing it, it all—all angry and like he want to hurt me. And I think bout that song he sing that first night bout having the blues. But that the only time he mean like that.

Time and German brung the piano a couple days after that. The piano small and all shiny black wood. Time cussed German when German knocked it against the front door getting it in the house. Time want to put it in the bedroom but I want him to be thinking bout me, not some damn piano when he in there. I tell him he put it in the living room or it don't come in the house. Orine don't want it in the house period, say it too damn noisy— that's what she tell me. She don't say nothing to Time. I think she half-way scared of him. He pretty good bout playing it though. He don't never play it when the babies is sleep or at least he don't play loud as he can. But all he thinking bout when he playing is that piano. You talk to him, he don't answer; you touch him, he don't look up. One time I say to him, "pay me some tention," but he don't even hear. I hit his hand, not hard, just playing. He look at me but he don't stop playing. "Get out of here, Martha." First I start to tell him he can't tell me what to do in my own self's house, but he just looking at me. Looking at me and playing and not saying nothing. I leave.

His friends come over most evenings when he home, not playing. It like Time is the leader. Whatever he say go. They always telling him how good he is. "Out of sight, man, the way you play." "You ought to get out of this little town so somebody can hear you play." Most times, he just smile and don't say nothing, or he just say thanks. But I wonder if he really believe em. I tell him, sometime, that he sound better than lots a them men on records. He give me his little cool smile. But I feel he glad I tell him that.

When his friends come over, we sit round laughing and talking and drinking. Orine like that cause she be playing up to em all and they be telling her what a fine ass she got. They don't tell me nothing like that cause Time be sitting right there, but long as Time telling me, I don't care. It like when we go to the Legion, after Time and German started being with us. We all the time get in free then and get to sit at one a the big front tables. And Orine like that cause it make her think she big time. But she still her same old picky self; all the time telling me to "sit cool, Martha," and "be cool, girl." Acting like cool the most important thing in the world. I finally just tell her, "Time like me just the way I am, cool or not." And it true; Time always saying that I be myself and I be fine.

Time and his friends, they talk mostly bout music, music and New York City and white people. Sometime I get so sick a listening to em. Always talking bout how they gon put something over on the white man, gon take something way from him, gon do this, gon do that. Ah shit! I tell em. But they don't pay me no mind.

German say, one night, "Man, this white man come asking if I want to play at his house for—"

"What you tell him, man, 'Put money in my purse?'" Time ask. They all crack up. Me and Orine sit there quiet. Orine all swole up cause Time and them running some kind of game and she don't know what going down.

"Hey man, yo all member that time up in Frisco when we got fired from that gig and wan't none of our old ladies working?" That Brown, he play bass with em.

"Man," Time say, "all I remember is that I stayed high most of the time. But how'd I stay high if ain't nobody had no bread? Somebody was putting something in somebody's purse." He lean back laughing a little. "Verna's mamma must have been sending her some money till she got a job. Yeah, yeah man, that was it. You remember the first time her mamma sent that money and she gave it all to me to hold?"

"And what she wanna do that for? You went out and gambled half a it away and bought pot with most of the rest." German not laughing much as Time and Brown.

"Man, I was scared to tell her, cause you remember how easy it was for her to get her jaws tight. But she was cool, didn't say nothing. I told her I was going to get food with the rest of the money and asked her what she wanted, and—"

"And she say cigarettes," Brown break in laughing, "and this cat, man, this cat tell her, 'Woman, we ain't wasting this bread on no non-essentials!'" He doubled over laughing. They all laughing. But I don't think it that funny. Any woman can give a man money.

"I thought the babe was gon kill me, her jaws was so tight. But even with her jaws tight, Verna was still cool. She just say, 'Baby, you done fucked up fifty dollars on non-essentials; let me try thirty cents.'"

That really funny to em. They all cracking up but me. Time sit there smiling just a little and shaking his head. Then, he reach out and squeeze my knee and smile at me. And I know it like I say; any woman can give a man money.

German been twitching round in his chair and finally he say, "Yeah, man, this fay dude want me to play at his house for fifty cent." That German always got to hear hisself talk. "I tell him take his fifty cent and shove it up his ass—oh scuse me. I forgot that baby was here—but I told him what to do with it. When I play for honkies, I tell him, I don't play for less than two hundred dollars and he so foolish he gon pay it." They all laugh, but I know German lying. Anybody offer him ten cent let lone fifty, he gon play.

"It ain't the money, man," Time say. "They just don't know what the fuck going on." I tell him Larry sitting right there. I know he ain't gon pay me no mind, but I feel if German can respect my baby, Time can too. "Man they go out to some little school, learn a few chords, and they think they know it all. Then they come round to the clubs wanting to sit in with you. Then, if you working for a white man, he fire you and hire him. No, man, I can't tie shit from no white man."

"That where you wrong," I tell him. "Somebody you don't like, you supposed to take em for everything they got. Take em and tell em to kiss yo butt."

"That another one of your pictures, I guess," Time say. And they all laugh cause he told em bout that, too, one time when he was mad with me.

"No, no," I say. "Listen, one day I walking downtown and this white man offer me a ride. I say okay and get in the car. He start talking and hinting round and finally he come on out and say it. I give you twenty dollars, he say. I say okay. We in Chinatown by then and at the next stoplight he get out his wallet and give me a twenty dollar bill. 'That what I like bout you colored women,' he say easing all back in his seat just like he already done got some and waiting to get some more. 'Yeah,' he say, 'you all so easy to get.' I put that money in my purse, open the door and tell him, 'Motherfucker, you ain't got shit here,' and slam the door."

"Watch your mouth," Time say, "Larry sitting here." We all crack up.

"What he do then?" Orine ask.

"What could he do? We in Chinatown and all them colored folks walking round. You know they ain't gon' let no white man do nothing to me."

Time tell me after we go to bed that night that he kill me if he ever see me with a white man.

I laugh and kiss him. "What I want with a white man when I got you?" We both laugh and get in the bed. I lay stretched out waiting for him to reach for me. It funny, I think, how colored men don't never want the colored women messing with no white mens but the first chance he get, that colored man gon be right there in that white woman's bed. Yeah, colored men sho give colored womens a hard way to go. But I know if Time got to give a hard way to go, it ain't gon be for no scaggy fay babe, and I kinda smile to myself.

"Martha—"

"Yeah, Time," I say turning to him.

"How old you—eighteen?—what you want to do in life? What you want to be?"

What he mean? "I want to be with you," I tell him.

"No, I mean really. What you want?" Why he want to know I wonder. Everytime he start talking serious-like, I think he must be hearing his sliding song.

"I don't want to have to ask nobody for nothing. I want to be able to take care of my own self." I won't be no weight on you, Time, I want to tell him. I won't be no trouble to you.

"Then what you doing on the Welfare?"

"What else I gon do? Go out and scrub somebody else's toilets like my mamma did so Larry can run wild like I did? No. I stay on Welfare a while, thank you."

"You see what the white man have done to us, is doing to us?"

"White man my ass," I tell him. "That was my no good daddy. If he'd got out and worked, we woulda been better off."

"How he gon work if the man won't let him?"

"You just let the man turn you out. Yeah, that man got yo mind."

"What you mean?" he ask real quiet. But I don't pay no tention to him.

"You always talking bout music and New York City, New York City and the white man. Why don't you forget all that shit and get a job like other men? I hate that damn piano."

He grab my shoulder real tight. "What you mean, 'got my mind?' What you mean?" And he start shaking me. But I crying and thinking bout he gon leave.

"You laugh cause I say all I got in my mind is pitchers but least they better than some old music. That all you ever think bout, Time."

"What you mean? What you mean?"

Finally I scream. "You ain't going no damn New York City and it ain't the white man what gon keep you. You just using him for a scuse cause you scared. Maybe you can't play." That the only time he ever hit me. And I cry cause I know he gon leave for sho. He hold me and say don't cry, say he sorry, but I can't stop. Orine bamming on the door and Time yelling at her to leave us lone and the babies crying and finally he start to pull away. I say, "Time…" He still for a long time, then he say, "Okay. Okay, Martha."

No, it not like he don't want me no more, he—

"Martha. Martha. You ain't been listening to a word I say."

"Mamma." I say it soft cause I don't want to hurt her. "Please leave me lone. You and Orine—and Time too, sometime—yo all treat me like I don't know nothing. But just cause it don't seem like to you that I know what I'm doing, that don't mean nothing. You can't see into my life."

"I see enough to know you just get into one mess after nother." She shake her head and her voice come kinda slow. "Martha, I named you after that woman in the Bible cause I want you to be like her. Be good in the same way she is. Martha, that woman ain't never stopped believing. She humble and patient and the Lord make a place for her." She lean her hands on the table. Been in them dishes again, hands all wrinkled and shiny wet. "But that was the Bible. You ain't got the time to be patient, to be waiting for Time or no one else to make no place for you. That man ain't no good. I told you—"

Words coming faster and faster. She got the cow by the tail and gon on down shit creek. It don't matter though. She talk and I sit here thinking bout Time. "You feel good…You gon be my Black queen?…We can make it together…You feel good…" He be back.

Author Biographies

Alice Adams moved to California in the 1950s, and since then, the state and its residents have figured prominently in her stories and novels. She is the recipient of a rare O. Henry Special Award for Continuing Achievement, and her short stories have appeared in twenty O. Henry Awards collections and several volumes of *Best American Short Stories.* Her latest collection of stories is *The Last Lovely City* (1999). She currently lives in San Francisco.

Gina Berriault is a native Californian. She has been writing short stories, novels, and screenplays for more than forty years, and she taught creative writing at San Francisco State from 1977 to 1983. Her critically acclaimed work has been published in such magazines as *The Paris Review* and *Esquire.* Her 1996 short story collection, *Women in Their Beds,* won the National Book Critics Circle Award and the PEN/Faulkner Award.

T. Coraghessan Boyle has lived in California for over twenty years. His novels include *World's End* (1987, winner of the PEN/Faulkner Award for fiction), *Tortilla Curtain* (1995), and *Riven Rock* (1998). In 1998, his short stories were collected in *T.C. Boyle Stories.* He currently lives in Santa Barbara, California, and teaches creative writing at the University of Southern California.

Michelle Cliff is the Allan K. Smith Professor of English Language and Literature at Trinity College in Hartford, Connecticut. The Jamaican-born writer is the author of three novels, including *Free Enterprise* (1993), as well as two story collections, *Bodies of Water* (1990) and *The Store of a Million Items* (1998). She makes her home in Santa Cruz, California.

Chitra Divakaruni was born in India, then lived in the San Francisco Bay Area, where she taught creative writing at Foothill College. She has published four books of poetry; two novels, *The Mistress of Spices* (1997) and *Sisters of My Heart* (1999); and a collection of short stories, *Arranged Marriage* (1995), which won the PEN Oakland/Josephine Miles Award for fiction. She currently lives in Houston.

Judith Freeman is the author of a short-story compilation, *Family Attractions* (1988), and three novels, *The Chinchilla Farm* (1989), *Set for Life* (1991), and *A Desert of Pure Feeling* (1996). She lives in Fairfield, Idaho, and Los Angeles.

Dagoberto Gilb won a Whiting Writers' Award and also received a National Endowment for the Arts creative writing fellowship. *The Magic of Blood* (1993), a collection of his short stories, won the Hemingway Award and was a finalist for the PEN/Faulkner prize. He is also the author of a novel, *The Last Known Residence of Mickey Acuña* (1994).

Gerald Haslam was born and raised in the San Joaquin Valley. His short fiction includes *Condor Dreams & Other Fictions* (1994) and *The Great Tejon Gang Jubilee* (1996). He has edited *Many Californias: Literature from the Golden State* (1992), *The Other California: Great Central Valley Life and Letters* (1990), *Jack London's Golden State* (1999), and co-edited, with James D. Houston, *California Heartland: Writing from the Great Central Valley* (1978). He currently lives in Sonoma County.

Mark Helprin began publishing short stories in *The New Yorker* shortly after graduating from Harvard in the late sixties. He came to love California while attending graduate school at Stanford in 1969. His stories were first anthologized in *A Dove of the East and Other Stories* (1975). His second collection, *Ellis Island and Other Stories* (1981), won the PEN/Faulkner Award and was nominated for the National Book Award. The author of several novels, he is a contributing editor to *The Wall Street Journal*.

James D. Houston was born in San Francisco and now resides in Santa Cruz. He taught at U.C. Santa Cruz for many years, and has published six novels, including *Continental Drift* (1978), as well as several works of non-fiction on the West. With his wife, Jeanne Wakatsuki Houston, he co-authored the classic memoir, *Farewell to Manzanar* (1973), and co-edited, with Gerald Haslam, *California Heartland: Writing from the Great Central Valley* (1978).

Catherine Ryan Hyde lives on the Central Coast, where she has taught at Cuesta College in San Luis Obispo. Her first collection of short stories, *Earthquake Weather,* was published in 1998. Her novels include *Funerals for Horses* (1997) and *Pay It Forward* (1999).

Laura Kalpakian, a native of Long Beach, was educated at U.C. Riverside and U.C. San Diego. She has written two collections of short stories, *Fair Augusto* (1986) and *Dark Continent* (1989), and seven novels, including *These Latter Days* (1985), *Graced Land* (1985), and *Caveat* (1998), all set in the fictional desert town of St. Elmo, somewhere "east of L.A. and west of everywhere else." Her most recent novel is *Steps and Ex's* (1999). She lives on Washington's Puget Sound.

Steve Lattimore is a former Stegner Fellow at Stanford University. His first published collection of short stories, *Circumnavigation* (1997), was a finalist for the PEN/Hemingway Award and received a California Book Award for first fiction. He currently teaches at John Carroll University in Cleveland, Ohio.

John L'Heureux was a Jesuit priest before he began teaching creative writing at Stanford University in 1973. He is the author of fifteen books, including *The Shrine at Altamira* (1992) and *The Handmaid of Desire* (1996), both novels, and *Comedians* (1990), a short story collection.

Jess Mowry grew up in Oakland, where he attended school until eighth grade. In 1988 he bought a used typewriter and started writing. His first book of stories, *Rats in the Trees* (1990), won the PEN Oakland/Josephine Miles Award for fiction. He has also published two novels, *Way Past Cool* (1992) and *Six Out Seven* (1993).

Howard Norman is the author of three novels, *The Northern Lights* (1987), *The Bird Artist* (1994), and *The Museum Guard* (1998), as well as a collection of short stories, film scripts, and articles on ethnography and natural history. "The Chauffeur" was inspired by his travels around Northern California. He makes his home in Vermont.

Roy Parvin alternates between living in a cabin in the Trinity Alps and a house in San Francisco. His first book of stories, the critically acclaimed *The Loneliest Road in America*, was published in 1997.

Greg Sarris grew up in Northern California. His mother was white, and his father was Native American, a member of the Coast Miwok and Pomo tribes. His multicultural background drives his 1994 short story collection, *Grand Avenue*, as well as his novel about a fictional Pomo group, *Watermelon Nights* (1998). The chairman of the Federated Coast Miwok Tribe, he teaches literature and creative writing at UCLA.

Mari Sunaida was born in Santa Monica and raised in California, Japan, and the Phillipines. She is both a performer, having trained in acting, and a writer. Since 1987, she has lived in Los Angeles, where she is managing artist of Pacific Asian American Women Writers West. She is currently working on a novel.

Katherine Vaz grew up in Castro Valley, California. Her Portuguese-American heritage figures prominently in her work, which includes two novels, *Saudade* (1994) and *Mariana* (1997), and a short story collection, *Fado and Other Stories* (1997), winner of the Drue Heinz Literature Prize. She earned her M.F.A. at U.C. Irvine and is now an Associate Professor of English at U.C. Davis.

Helena Maria Viramontes was born and raised in East Los Angeles. She is the author of a short-story collection, *The Moths and Other Stories* (1985), and a novel, *Under the Feet of Jesus* (1995). The recipient of numerous awards, she received the John Dos Passos Prize for Literature in 1995. She is currently working on her second novel and teaches writing at Cornell University.

Sherley Anne Williams was born in Bakersfield and grew up in Fresno. In the early 1970s, she joined the faculty of U.C. San Diego, where she is the M. A. Brown Professor of American and African American Literature. She is the author of various works, including a novel, *Dessa Rose* (1986); a collection of poetry, *The Peacock Poems* (1975); and a children's book, *Working Cotton* (1992).

Permissions

Adams, Alice. From *After You've Gone* (Alfred A. Knopf). Copyright ©
1989 by Alice Adams. Reprinted by permission of Alfred A. Knopf, Inc.

Berriault, Gina. From *The Infinite Passion of Expectation* (North Point
Press). Copyright © 1982 by Gina Berriault. Reprinted by permission of
the author.

Boyle, T. Coraghessan. From *Without a Hero* (Viking). Copyright © 1994
by T. Coraghessan Boyle. Reprinted by permission of Viking Penguin, a
division of Penguin Putnam Inc.

Cliff, Michelle. From *The Store of a Million Items* (Houghton Mifflin
Company). Copyright © 1998 by Michelle Cliff. Reprinted by permission of the author.

Divakaruni, Chitra. From *Arranged Marriage* (Anchor Books). Copyright
© 1995 by Chitra Divakaruni. Reprinted by permission of Doubleday, a
division of Random House, Inc.

Freeman, Judith. From *Family Attractions* (Viking). Copyright © 1989 by
Judith Freeman. Reprinted by permission of Viking Penguin.

Gilb, Dagoberto. From *The Magic of Blood* (University of New Mexico
Press). First appeared in *Puerto del Sol*. Copyright © 1993 by Dagoberto
Gilb. Reprinted by permission of the author.

Haslam, Gerald. From *Condor Dreams & Other Fictions* (University of
Nevada Press). Copyright © 1994 by Gerald Haslam. Reprinted by permission of the author.

Helprin, Mark. From *The Bread Loaf Anthology of Contemporary American
Short Stories.* (The University Press of New England). First published in
The Atlantic Monthly. Copyright © 1987 by Mark Helprin. Reprinted by
permission of The Wendy Weil Agency, Inc.

About the Editor

STEVEN GILBAR is the editor of several anthologies about California, including *Natural State: A Literary Anthology of California Nature Writing* (University of California Press) and *Santa Barbara Stories* (John Daniel and Company), as well as books about reading, including *Reading in Bed: Personal Essays on the Glories of Reading* (David R. Godine) and *The Reader's Quotation Book: A Literary Companion* (Pushcart Press). He currently lives in Santa Barbara with his wife, Inge Gatz, a social work consultant.